MANZAKAR

THE SLAVE-SOLDIER SERIES

R. LAHAM

OLIVER HEBER BOOKS

Manzakar Copyright 2025 © R. Laham

Cover art by Dar Albert at Wicked Smart Designs

Published by Oliver-Heber Books

0 9 8 7 6 5 4 3 2 1

Anzor's Class Structure

THE KING

ANZORI NOBILITY

DURAIS

CLERGY (MAGES, PRIESTS)

ASLAN MANZAKARS

MANZAKARS

MERCHANT CLASS

ANZORI COMMONERS

GOHARI WOMEN (MANZAKAR WIVES, COURTESANS)

GOHARI SERVANTS, EUNUCHS, SOLDIERS

CHAPTER 1

Gohar
Year 206 of the Dark Age

The sun was bright that day, but a black cloud of fear hung over Tikran's head, blotting out the light. His left hand clutched Wig, his tattered stuffed rabbit, while his right gripped his father's tightly. They left their horses tied to a hitching post and approached the center of the town more quickly than Tikran wanted. He tried to hang back, but Da tugged his arm gently, coaxing him along.

Tikran had never been in a town. He peered about in amazement at the structures—with thatched roofs and mud walls that were clearly not meant to be packed up and carried around—lining the well-worn road that wound between them. A wood fort loomed in the center of the garrison settlement, bearing the bright blue flag of Anzor. Soldiers watched from the tower, their lances and pointed helmets gleaming. There were children as well, laughing and tossing balls, who stopped to stare as Tikran and his father walked by. The smell of roasting meat and rising bread filled his nostrils, making his stomach growl loudly.

He willed his legs to move forward, even as his heart thumped anxiously in his chest. He clutched Wig tighter against him, leaning down to sniff its matted fur for comfort. Wig smelled safe. Wig smelled like Mama.

Da glanced down at him, his brow furrowed. "Tikran, when will you stop carrying that old rag around? You're too old to be attached to such a thing."

Tikran didn't loosen his grip on Wig and remained silent. He was too concerned with where they were going to take offense.

At the end of the road sat a green covered wagon and before it stood a short, stout, dark-skinned man with a thick henna-dyed beard. He wore a tunic from the west—it was brightly colored and delicately embroidered with leaf patterns along the hem. The man's face, in stark contrast with his clothes, was weathered and creased all over, particularly around the eyes. He watched Tikran with interest as they approached and smiled, revealing a gap-toothed grin that terrified Tikran enough to make him stop dead in his tracks.

"Tikran," Da said firmly, tiredly. "Come now. He won't bite. He will take care of you."

The boy wanted to believe his father, but his legs wouldn't move.

"What have we here?" The red-bearded man smiled widely and squatted down to greet Tikran. At first, the boy wanted to turn and run, but his father's tight grip kept him in place. He looked away, gasping, trying his hardest not to cry. The red-haired man heaved a big sigh, his smile dissipating, and said, "Boy, I am not your father or mother. I cannot pretend to be. But I can be a good friend. Will you let me be a good friend?"

Tikran refused to meet the man's eyes. He held Wig to his face, hiding behind its fur.

"I'm sorry about the rabbit," Da said with an uneasy smile. "He refused to leave it."

The old man raised a palm at Da and shook his head. "No reason to apologize. He is a child still." Then his expression softened as he looked at Tikran. "My name is Mago." He raised a bushy eyebrow. "And I have date cookies."

This made Tikran look. He didn't know what a date was but he knew very well what a cookie was, and it had been several days since he'd had anything substantial to eat. His animal instincts took hold. Before he even saw the cookies, his mind could smell them and his mouth watered. Mago smiled, pulling a brown biscuit covered in powdered sugar from the folds of his tunic and offering it to Tikran. The boy hesitated despite his hunger and looked up at his father.

"Go on," Da encouraged. "Take it."

He didn't need to be told twice. Being careful not to drop any crumbs, he snatched the cookie and began devouring it. He needed those crumbs. And the cookie was delicious. For a moment, Tikran was whisked away to a place of happiness while the men talked over his head. He was brought back to reality when he heard the clinking of coins and Mago say, "A healthy seven-year-old Gohari boy who can ride and use a bow. I will give you one hundred and fifty aspers."

"A deal," Da said quietly, a bit hoarsely.

A purse was exchanged over Tikran's head. "All one hundred and fifty are there, but feel free to count them."

Da took the purse and replied, "You have a reputation for trustworthiness. I believe you."

Panic surged in Tikran's chest and he clung to his father's sheepskin vest. "Please don't leave me," he begged, tears springing to his eyes.

Da knelt before him, gripped him by the shoulders, and commanded, "Stop crying. You are to become a Manzakar, Tikran! A Manzakar doesn't cry. This is a great honor, and you should be forever grateful."

Tikran willed the tears to stop but could not keep his lip from trembling. "Will I ever see you again?"

"Yes," Da said. "When you are a powerful Manzakar, you will send for us and we will come to you."

Tikran felt a tiny fraction better. His father stood and nodded to Mago, who set a large, callused hand on Tikran's head. Mago said, "He is in good hands, my friend."

Tikran watched Da walk away without looking back. *A Manzakar doesn't cry. A Manzakar doesn't cry.* His nose burned with the desire to sob until another cookie appeared before him.

Mago smiled. "Your father did what he had to do. You and your family would have starved to death otherwise." He placed the cookie in Tikran's hand. "You saved your family, boy. Stand tall and proud."

GOHAR WAS, in Mago's humble opinion, beautiful at night—and not just because the desolate landscape was finally hidden in the dark. The stars were crisp and bright in the black sky, the air was dry and cool, and the burrowing owls hooted as they hunted, diving into the long grass and emerging with field mice in their claws.

The old slave trader crouched by a small campfire he'd made to prepare food for the nine children who now slept soundly in the back of his wagon. He spooned the leftover rabbit stew into his mouth, staring pensively into the flames. He'd been buying Gohari children and selling them in Anzor for forty years, and while it was a lucrative profession, it never got easier. Certainly, Mago ensured the children were sold to wealthy, kind masters, if not to the king himself. And when they were sold to the king, their lives as slaves seemed far from slavery. What broke his heart was *this* part—exchanging coins for children from destitute, stoic nomads with no other choice.

Mago himself had grown up in Gohar, and he knew the hardships of being Gohari. Gohar was a steppe—much too dry for a forest, but not quite dry enough to be a desert. It had once been different, before the Dark Ages, or so it was said. Now, however, it rained very rarely, was blazing hot in the summer, and bitterly cold in the winter. Horses had once been native to Gohar, and the Gohari had been the first to domesticate them. Nothing could be compared to a Gohari horseman, which was why Anzor took such interest in their children: Gohar provided a steady supply of young military recruits who had sturdy constitutions and a fundamental grasp of horse and bow. Moreover, they were not innately territorial and, as slaves with no kin, their loyalty was easily acquired. By harnessing the Gohari nomads' skills in horsemanship, archery, and their general ability to survive the harshness of the steppe, Anzor had built a powerful military class of slave-soldiers that was above and beyond any other kingdom's army on the Continent.

They were called Manzakars.

Standing and turning toward the wagon, Mago peeked in at the children he would take to Anzor. The Anzori did not become soldiers—that's what the Gohari slaves were for. The boys would certainly be bought by the military, but whether they went on to become Manzakars depended on their individual characters and abilities. The training, he knew, was not for the weak, and the few who were inducted into the knightly class would become the king's men. The other boys would become soldiers in the standing army or servants to the king and the aristocrats.

The girls would learn to be wives and mothers of Manzakars, and some of the prettier girls would also be trained as courtesans for Anzori noblemen. There was also a chance—albeit a very slim one—that they could produce offspring with the Essence, since magical abilities were found only among those with Gohari blood.

Finally, in the very rare case that one of the children had the Essence themselves, they would be taken straight to the king's clerics and trained to become a royal mage.

Tikran mumbled in his sleep, rolling over to face Mago, his tear-stained face peaceful in slumber, the rabbit tucked tightly under his arm. Mago studied the child for a few moments, contemplating the boy's future. It was hard to imagine the youngster becoming a fierce warrior, but he'd seen it happen plenty of times before. There was no mistaking him for anything but a Gohari nomad—the dark olive skin and curly black hair gave him away. And even skinny as he was, he clearly had the robust physique of his people.

Mago retreated, letting the canopy of the covered wagon flap close over the children. He grunted to himself. He was growing too soft. *This is business. Business is business.* He was satisfied with his human merchandise. They would bring him a small fortune, and he, in return, would ensure that they never went hungry again.

THERE WERE other children in the green wagon, and the wagon was among a caravan of ten. Six boys, all older than Tikran, and two girls sat huddled in the wagon. One girl was nearly an adult, as far as he could tell, and the other girl was younger than he was.

The younger one cried a lot, and Tikran felt the need to comfort her. He had younger sisters, after all, and had been tasked with watching over them while Da and Mama went hunting. Tikran often let the little girl hold Wig at night, and Wig inevitably soothed her to sleep. He knew it would. Tikran missed Wig, but also felt a strange sense of satisfaction, knowing that he was doing something to help.

Her name was Coxani. She was four years old, according to her estimation, and from the Davlat tribe. She had enormous green eyes and a cloud of curly brown hair around a heart-shaped face. Her brow was often furrowed and she had the most ear-shattering scream he had ever heard. Even so, she made him laugh with her antics and seemed to tolerate him much better than she tolerated the other children.

The older children didn't bother speaking to Tikran or Coxani, the "babies" of the group. So the pair would sleep and eat in their own corner, entertain each other with stories and silly games, warily watch the bigger boys shove and punch each other over the last bit of dinner, and gape enviously as the winner devoured it. Mago, however, was tender with the two youngest slaves, often letting them sit with him while he steered the wagon and sneaking them cookies when the older children weren't looking. At night, he would cover them with a thick blanket, tuck them in, and occasionally tell them a brief story about the wonders of Anzor.

They crossed over from Gohar into Anzor after weeks of slow but steady travel. Very quickly, the landscape changed from arid grasslands to balmy, lush woodlands. The border between Anzor and Gohar was heavily fortified with an immense stone wall, and guards lined the parapet walk high above, pacing back and forth, spears in hand. An Anzori guard stopped the wagon and demanded to see Mago's official travel documents. Mago sighed and pulled a folded parchment from his pocket.

"I am a merchant and I cross these borders often, my boy," Mago said gruffly. "Ask your superiors, several of them know me by name." The guards peeked into the wagon, saw the Gohari children, and nodded, letting them pass with no further harassment.

The day they reached Anzor City, Mago whooped. "Come children! See your new home, how magnificent it is!"

They shoved each other to get a look, peering out from underneath the dirty hemp canopy. Coxani wailed from behind the bigger children until the older girl lifted her up so she could see as well. Silence befell them as Anzor City emerged from behind the trees, shimmering white. Tikran gasped. He and the others were children of nomads, and any settlements they'd seen had been nothing more than a garrison town. This was a *city*. Beyond the high city walls, a massive Citadel sat atop a hill, formidable with its thick battlements, bastions and towers. Within the Citadel, a palace with golden turrets glittered in the sun. All around the hill, stone temple spires rose past the city walls, some with balconies, and all intricately carved with designs resembling flames and droplets of water.

"What are those?" one of the boys asked, pointing to a spire.

"That's where the Anzori worship their god, Cenk."

Even Tikran, young as he was, had heard the stories about Cenk, the wrathful Anzori god who only favored the king and his bloodline, his greatest apostles. Tikran didn't understand why anyone would believe in a god they'd never seen, and who was always angry to boot. He'd been told Cenk's wrath was on account of his magic—or Essence—being stolen by the mage,

Archil the Gohari, 206 years ago, bringing on the Dark Age to punish humans, particularly the Gohari people, for their heresy. His parents had spoken of Archil in hushed tones, reverently, but discouraged Tikran from speaking about the mage out loud. None of it made any sense to him, but he knew that the Manzakars were fierce disciples of Cenk. Tikran wasn't sure he wanted to become one of them.

Mago's wagon bumped through one of the great gates into the city, alongside other wagons and horses and people on foot. Two soldiers stood at the guardhouses on either side of the gate, looking down on them as they passed through. They stood holding their lances, their lamellar cuirasses blinking in sun, their watchful eyes moving with the crowd from behind their leather helmets. "Are those Manzakars?" Tikran blurted, shielding his eyes from the sun and craning his neck.

"Oh, no," Mago said, chuckling. "Those are regular soldiers. The Manzakars don't deal with the rabble, boy. They are the king's elite, the bravest, strongest soldiers of them all. You'd be so lucky as to see one out in the town. They live and train in the Citadel."

Tikran gaped slack-jawed as the wagon jostled along a winding, narrow road that was crowded with both human and beast—horses, donkeys, and the occasional camel. The road was a thoroughfare between the gate and the marketplace, and suddenly it opened up. Beneath a bright morning sky, Mago's wagon rolled between shops and stalls selling everything from fish to honey-drizzled sweetmeats beneath their awnings. The air was thick with the scent of spices that mingled with the occasional waft of sweat and manure. People—so many people —flowed restlessly through the marketplace like a wave of color, on foot, on horses, in carts, on donkeys. The merchants they passed hawked cotton garments, maize, millet, water-melon, apples... The draft horse pulling Mago's wagon trudged on, through shady residential quarters with lovely little squares, and beyond the public bathhouses, schools, and temples.

The crowd thinned as they began their ascent to the Citadel, crossing an enormous stone bridge over the moat that surrounded it. A hushed awe fell over the children as they approached the vaulted entrance, guarded by several soldiers (still not Manzakars, Mago confirmed). The Commander of the Guards approached the wagon, saw Mago, and nodded once. The guards opened the gate, and they entered the Citadel—an even more beautiful city within a city. Cobblestone streets ran between gilded buildings, all white and gold. Everyone within seemed to be a soldier or a prince or a princess, and none seemed fazed by the dilapidated wagon that meandered past them. At this point, the children had pulled back behind the canopy, fighting to peek, one-eyed, at the opulence outside.

The wagon finally stopped with a loud creak, and Tikran could hear Mago speak gently to the horse, then to someone else. Their voices echoed as though they were surrounded by stone. Tikran held his breath, feeling a complicated mixture of fear and anticipation. Then the canopy was pulled aside and Mago peered in at them, smiling widely. "Come now, children! Come out one at a time. Your new home awaits."

The oldest girl descended first and was immediately bought by a portly man in a red turban. Even though she stood tall and betrayed no emotion, Tikran wondered if she was afraid to go with the man, because he would have been terrified. The boys followed and they too were spoken for within minutes by a man in a soldier's uniform. Coxani clutched Tikran's hand in terror, Wig pressed against her face. Tikran swallowed his fear and whispered, "Don't worry, I'm here. I won't let go." His heart hurt at the words, as they were not the words Da had spoken to him when he was most scared. In spite of it, he squeezed her hand in silent promise. Her small hand relaxed in his.

When he and Coxani emerged, Mago smiled widely and swept them both up in each arm. Tikran was acutely aware of how good Mago smelled. Like pepper and clean sweat and melted sugar. Mago said to several men who had gathered around the wagon, "These two. These two are my prizes. Two Gohari children, beautiful as the sun, both of hearty nomad stock, able to ride a horse, and already skilled with a bow."

One of the men, the most remarkable of those standing before them, approached. He wore a gorgeous blue silk jacket that was embroidered with gold and red thread and tied at the waist. Underneath the jacket were white silk breeches that were tucked into riding boots. His hair was long and loose to his shoulders underneath a white turbaned cap, and his short beard was neatly manicured. He motioned for Mago to set the two children down. He kneeled before them, smiling slightly, his dark eyes passing over each of them with precision. Tikran resisted the urge to shrink away. To his astonishment, Coxani did too. For the first time since arriving in Anzor City, he didn't feel the need to ask Mago if this man was a Manzakar. He knew.

The man looked pointedly at Mago, who said, "Tikran and Coxani."

The elite soldier then smiled the whitest smile Tikran had ever seen and said, "Welcome, Tikran. Welcome, Coxani," and bowed his head to each of them. He spoke Perchuhi—the language of both Anzor and Gohar— but it sounded different to Tikran's ears. "I am Gohari, like yourselves. My name is Haydar. I hail from the Sachin tribe."

Tikran jumped. "I am... me too..."

Haydar's smile widened. "A kinsman. You are blessed by Cenk, Tikran. You as well, Coxani. Anzor is the greatest kingdom in the world, and you have been chosen to become Anzori." He paused, his brow furrowing. "No, not just Anzori." He looked at Tikran. "With some hard work, you could become a *Manzakar*."

"And me?" Coxani demanded. "What about me?"

Haydar tilted his head back and laughed heartily. "You are spirited, Coxani. Yes, perhaps you, too. It will take doubly hard work for you, but it's not unheard of, a female Manzakar." Coxani smiled, satisfied.

Haydar stood. "The king will take them, Mago, for five times what you paid for them."

Mago bowed. "Of course, Lord Haydar." He hesitated, looking kindly at the children.

"Yes?" Haydar asked. "What is it?"

"My lord, if I may... I would like to visit them on occasion..."

"Of course." Haydar sighed deeply. "You grow too easily attached to these little ones, Mago."

Mago shrugged, grinning his gap-toothed grin. Then he gathered Tikran and Coxani in his arms. "I will come and see you. I will bring date cookies." Both children relaxed, smiles on their faces. "Go now, with Haydar," Mago said. "He will keep you safe."

Haydar took the children down a street that led into a gated area adjacent to the palace. They walked through the gates into a garden, resplendent with flowering bushes and trees. They paused at a bench, where Haydar sat and pulled sweetmeats from his pocket. To Tikran, it seemed that every time a trial was coming on, the adults would throw sugar at them.

Not that he protested.

A woman appeared from behind the trellis of grapevines, her glittering skirts billowing behind her, her sun-kissed hair escaping the scarf around her head. She nodded at Haydar, who lifted Coxani into his arms before either she or Tikran could protest. "Coxani, this is Ola, the headmistress of the girls' school. She is happy to—"

Coxani began to wail, squirming from Haydar's arms. "I want to stay with Tikran," she said, sobbing and looking down at him with watery green eyes. In her despair, she dropped Wig.

Tikran swept Wig up and raised the doll to the little girl. "Coxani, you must take care of Wig. He will be very scared if you're scared. You must make sure he's okay, for me."

Haydar smiled down his approval. Coxani stopped crying and accepted the tattered rabbit back in her arms. She gazed down at Tikran solemnly. "Okay," she said, sniffling. "But you have to check on him once in a while. He needs to know his Da loves him too."

Once again, Haydar tossed back his head and laughed, his white teeth flashing. He passed Coxani to Ola, then turned his attention to Tikran. "Come now, boy."

Tikran held back, watching Coxani get carried off. She gazed back at him as well, not crying, and gave him a small wave from over Ola's shoulder while holding up Wig, as if to say, *He will be okay.*

He turned, facing Haydar, willing himself not to cry. *If Coxani can do it, so can I.* He raised his chin. Haydar's expression softened. "Tikran. I promise you Coxani will be safe. More than that, she will be happy. As will you."

He stood and began walking toward the garden gates. "Follow me. I will take you to the barracks. It's where the boys learn to become Manzakars."

CHAPTER 2

Anzor

Three Years Later

Year 209 of the Dark Age

The sound of pounding hooves and clashing weapons never failed to make Tikran's heart race with excitement. He watched, rapt, as the graduating cadets, in their final weeks of training, rode into the hippodrome in two parallel lines. They held their spears in their right hands and smoothly formed two concentric circles to engage in the "game of lances." At the lance-master's call, the cadets commenced single combat with a cadet in the opposite circle. The cracks of lances echoed throughout the arena as the cadets parried and thrust their weapons like swords. After several minutes the lance-master called again, and the cadets stopped skirmishing, zigzagging back into their original lines. Tikran sighed longingly. These men would be Manzakars by the end of the week, but he couldn't even begin his military training for another five years.

"It's not fair," Tikran lamented to his best friend, Naran. The boys were hiding in one of the hippodrome's galleries, peering down at the Manzakar cadets on the training grounds from between the wooden slats of the railing. They had snuck out of religion class—something they did as often as they could—to watch the older boys and, sometimes, the Manzakars themselves practice their martial skills. At ten, Tikran had learned all the formations in the lancing exercises and was intimately familiar with them. While the neophyte cadets were given manuals on warfare, it was only when they turned fifteen—no younger—that they were allowed to commence their formal combat training. He'd devoured those manuals, re-reading them before bedtime several nights a week, memorizing all the specialized weapons, mounts, and strategic maneuvers.

"What do you want to be best at, Tik?" Naran asked. "I want to dominate with a sword. The Dilovari warriors will fear me!" He pretended to hold a saber and swiped left and right, as if cutting down the enemy. Naran was two years older, which meant he was two years closer to beginning his training. To say Tikran was envious would be an understatement.

"I'm sure you'll be an amazing swordsman," Tikran said. The truth was, he thought Naran would likely be good at everything—his friend was tall for twelve and had the build of a boy who would become a powerful man. Naran was also funny, kind, and mischievous, leading Tikran to trouble far too often.

Naran squinted an eye at Tikran. "I bet you'll be good with a bow."

Scowling, Tikran said, "We're all good with bows already. We're Gohari." Tikran had been given his first bow at age four and had hunted his first partridge at age five. All Gohari children, as far as he was concerned, were good with bows.

"No, I mean *really* good." He grinned, his amber-colored eyes gleaming excitedly, then pressed his face to the slats. "Look at how they shoot on horseback. See that one cadet riding the roan horse on the far right? I've seen him shoot backwards while in full gallop and hit a perfect bullseye!"

Tikran gaped down in wonder. "I promise I'll be able to do that too one day. I—"

The sting of a hundred angry hornets suddenly burned the back of his neck. *We've been caught.* He heard Naran yelp as he covered his head with his arms. The eunuch's switch came down on both of them from every direction with a repeated *thwap!* The boys were hauled up by their ears to face Magister Gor, who was red from the base of his neck to the top of his bald head. "That's *it*," he hissed through his teeth. "I've had it with you two. That's five demerits for each of you. You will beg Cenk's forgiveness for your insubordination then head straight to kitchen duty for the rest of the day."

Magister Gor dragged the boys by their collars to the temple that adjoined the barracks and dumped them into the hands of Cenk's clerics. Of all the clerics, the mages were by far the most intimidating, but after them, the priests reigned with an iron fist—or rod, as it were. The priests dressed in long white hooded robes, similar in style to the ones the mages wore. But that's where the similarities ended. Rather than a veil over their noses and mouths, they wore yellow skullcaps over their shaved pates and rope belts of the same color. They were all Anzori men and were filled with Cenk's rage—which made their punishments brutal.

The boys stripped and washed with holy water, which cleaned them in preparation for their floggings. The water had been blessed by Cenk's priests, infused with lemon and peppermint, and left in an ewer at Cenk's altar for three nights. The boys had been taught that, as Gohari, they were naturally unclean and intrinsically wild, and only Cenk's guiding light would help transform them into civilized Anzori slaves. Naked, they entered the sanctum, where two elaborately carved and painted posts stood before an altar. Both cadets were familiar with the ritual, and obediently wrapped their arms around their respective posts, where their wrists were bound with silk cords. The priests chosen to conduct the punishment stepped forward, rods with five gilded branches each in hand.

With practiced efficiency, the rods came down in unison on each boy's shoulders, back, and buttocks. Tikran squeezed his eyes shut as the stinging became burning—then flaming—pain. After what felt like an eternity, the birching stopped, and sheets soaked in cold water were draped over the boys' beaten backs. Tikran gasped at the feel of the sheet on his blazing skin. He glanced at Naran, who was panting, trying to blink away the pain. The boys then stepped toward the altar and kneeled, bowing their heads. For an entire hour, they prayed for Cenk's forgiveness on their knees. *We suffer for Archil's heresy... Aspire to cleanse ourselves of his sin... In Cenk's name... Grateful to Anzor for its protection from Gohar's savagery...*

Finally done, they dressed, teeth grit tightly as the clothes touched their raw skin. As they headed back to the barracks, their strides short and stiff, Naran said, "You didn't cry this time."

"I haven't cried in years!" Tikran said, indignant.

"I'm pretty sure you cried last time."

"I did *not*."

"Yeah, you did."

"Naran, take it back."

Naran chuckled then winced. "I'm playing with you. I wouldn't really know if you cried, since I was too busy trying not to cry myself. Holy Cenk, has Believer Armazi gotten stronger or am I imagining it?"

"I think I'd rather not know," Tikran said, trying to keep his shirt from sticking to his back.

In the kitchen, the cook quickly put them to work scrubbing pots. Sullen and in pain, they worked quietly for most of the afternoon. Tikran couldn't help but think mutinous thoughts. *I don't regret sneaking away. I never will.*

"What have we here?" The boys looked up to see Lord Haydar leaning against the doorway, shaking his head. "What have you boys done now?"

The boys immediately stood and bowed. "Same as always, my lord," Naran grumbled. "We just got tired of listening to Magister Gor drone on and on about Cenk's wrath and wanted to watch the Level Three cadets practice."

Haydar smiled. He looked around to make sure the cook had made himself scarce then said, "I, for one, don't see anything wrong with that." He pointed to the pile of glistening pots. "Are you done here?" When the boys nodded, he asked, "Do you feel up for some fowling?"

Their eyes widened and, despite their pain, both jumped. "Yes!"

The Manzakar gestured to them to follow him, placing a finger on his lips. They hurried to the royal stables, where Haydar had readied two hounds, three horses, and three bows for the occasion. The day had brightened, and Tikran barely thought of his sore backside as he leaped into the saddle and ran his hands over the Manzakar recurve bow, admiring the shine of the laminated maple wood and horn. *I'll have my own someday.*

They didn't wander far from the city—there were plenty of partridges and pheasants in the woods surrounding the metropolis. They strung their bows and, with full quivers at their hips, followed Lord Haydar into the brushy meadows.

"When will we be old enough to hunt boars?" Naran asked, pretending to shoot his bow into the bushes.

"It's not a matter of age, Naran," Haydar said. "It's a matter of skill."

"I guess that means we'll have to be at least fifteen," Tikran said glumly.

"Boys," Haydar said, "please remember that you must pass your religious studies to begin your martial training. I understand why you dread them but think of them as a means to an end."

"Yes, my lord," Tikran and Naran said in unison—with zero enthusiasm.

The hounds began to bark and dove headlong into the brush ahead, flushing several fat pheasants out from hiding. The boys shot their arrows as they'd been taught by family left behind in Gohar, relying on raw instinct more than skill. In quick succession, the birds dropped from the sky.

Haydar grinned. "Well done, lads."

They shot several more birds before Haydar informed them that it was time to return to the barracks. The boys obeyed, clearly dreading their return to books, eunuchs, and switches. As they rode back to the city, Tikran said, "Lord Haydar, why do the priests make us wash so often? They know the color won't come out, right?"

At this, Haydar appeared to choke on his own spit. Once recovered from his coughing fit, he laughed quietly and said, "I'll be honest, Tikran, I'm not sure they know it." He cleared his throat and his tone changed. "Regardless, their intentions are good—they wish to cleanse your souls of Archil's sins."

"Blast that Archil," Naran muttered. "I still don't understand why he stole the Essence from Cenk."

"He wanted to do the work of the people, not the king,"

Haydar answered. "And as we know, the king is Cenk's most devout apostle. To defy the king is to defy Cenk himself."

Tikran frowned. "What work did the people want?"

Haydar turned to look at him curiously. "What do you mean, Tikran?"

Tikran shifted his bottom in the saddle, aware that he was likely going to have a great big blister on one butt cheek, where the priest's rod had bitten especially hard. "I just mean that. . I don't know. What did the people want Archil to do that the king didn't like?"

"It doesn't matter, lad," Haydar said firmly. "You must understand and accept the order of things. The king's wishes come first. Anyone who doesn't accept that is a heretic."

That ended the conversation, and when Haydar dropped the boys off at the barracks, he winked. "Magister Gor will not punish you for hunting with me, I can promise that. And tomorrow I will make sure you have some pheasant for dinner."

The boys beamed, dazzled by the good fortune that Haydar, of all the lords, was their protector as proxy for the king. As he walked away, Tikran turned and saw the Manzakar ride into the distance and swore to himself that he would grow up to be just like Haydar. *No matter what.*

"Coxani, stand up straight. And for goodness sake, close your mouth. You look like a fish," the headmistress snapped, slapping the table before Coxani with her palm.

Seven-year-old Coxani went rigid, following the instructions even as she wondered why she had to do those particular things. Headmistress Ola folded her hands. "Now. Recite the poem again, and remember, it's like a song. The harmonies of the words matter as much as the meaning. No Anzori nobleman wants a mistress who sounds like a Gohari sheepherder. Watch your vowels!"

Coxani's brow furrowed. She still didn't completely understand why the headmistress often insulted the Gohari when she herself was clearly from Gohar. She'd even admitted as much.

"Stop frowning and *stand up straight*," the headmistress commanded.

She obeyed, pulling her shoulders as far back as they would go. Her lower lip trembled as she began to recite words that made little sense to her. "Love, thou hast taken possession of me, and I burn, how I burn, in my quest—" *Does love burn? That sounds awful. I think I'll avoid it.*

"Stop," Ola interrupted, pinching the bridge of her nose. "Start over. I told you to watch your vowels. You sound like a warbling nomad."

The older girls snickered. Coxani's face grew hot. She could feel the tears welling in her eyes and threatening to spill. Her voice cracked as she began again, which didn't bode well for this next round either. "Love, thou—"

"Good afternoon, ladies. I hope I'm not interrupting." The entire class turned to see Lord Haydar standing at the door.

"Lord Haydar, what an honor." Ola smiled and fluttered her lashes, her face becoming a pretty pink. "Girls, stand up! Goodness! Where are your manners?"

Chairs scraped loudly against the stone floor as twenty-five Gohari girls between the ages of four and thirteen stood abruptly. Haydar laughed uneasily. "Oh, there's no need... I'm only here to request a bit of time with Coxani."

Coxani's eyes widened and she peered up at him. "Me?"

"Of course, my lord," Ola said, turning a firm gaze at her. "Coxani, his lordship has beckoned you. Don't just stand there!" Frantic, Coxani rushed to Haydar's side, hearing the restrained laughter of the other girls as he led her away. She felt Haydar's warm palm on the top of her head and her desire to cry vanished.

"Where are we going, my lord?" she asked, peering up at him.

He smiled down at her. "Just for a quick adventure to the hippodrome."

Coxani knew well that the hippodrome was where the Manzakars trained. "Oh! Will I see Tikran? But I can't! I don't have Wig. He hasn't seen Wig since we came to Anzor."

Haydar chuckled. "It's all right, Coxani. You probably won't see Tikran. But I have a surprise for you."

"What is it?"

"You'll see."

The hippodrome was immense, and she found herself inching closer to Haydar, intimidated by the sheer expanse of it. The grounds of it stretched as far as her eyes could see, stopped only by the walls of stone benches that curved upward and all around. He took her hand and led her to a small corner of it, where some stable boys hovered about, no doubt waiting for commands from Lord Haydar. A gourd hung from a pole several yards away from where they stood, swinging slightly. Something about the hanging fruit triggered a sense of familiarity in her mind that wasn't formed enough to qualify as a memory. It was, however, enough to make her pause and stare in wonder.

"I have a gift for you." Haydar crouched down beside her, holding a beautiful small bow. She knew what a bow was, of course—it was the Manzakars' weapon of choice. As she looked at it, her memory stirred once again. She wanted to hold it. She *knew* how to hold it. As if reading her mind, Haydar said, "Go on. Take it."

Her small hands wrapped around the smooth wood. *It feels… right.* She had no idea why the bow felt so comforting. She looked at Haydar in puzzlement. He responded by handing her a small arrow and pointing to the gourd—which suddenly seemed very far away. "Can you shoot the bow and hit that gourd?" he asked.

Her chest tightened. Why would she be able to do that? She couldn't do anything right—not even speak correctly, according to Ola.

"Coxani," Haydar said gently. "This isn't a test. It's a game. Do you like games?"

"Of course, my lord."

Haydar rubbed his bearded chin. "Imagine you're playing a game with friends. Just for fun, see if you can hit the gourd with the arrow. You can't lose in this game, Coxani. You get to keep the bow regardless."

I get to keep it! Suddenly, she wasn't so scared. She took the arrow and examined it. Well, she'd seen enough to know that the end of the arrow went on the string… The arrow and bow fell from her hand several times as she played with them, trying to get a sense of how they worked. Haydar sat patiently, watching in amusement. "Would you like me to show you how to hold it?" he asked.

She nodded. As he placed her hands in the right positions and showed her how to nock her arrow, draw, and anchor her hand at her cheek, she abruptly realized she knew how to do it. "I can do it myself," she said, pulling away from Haydar, aiming, and releasing. The arrow soared past the gourd, but not by much. "Can I try again?"

"Of course." Haydar handed her another arrow, a smile on his lips.

This time, the arrow flew directly into the gourd, hitting it with a *pop!*

Haydar laughed. "Very good, Coxani. By Cenk, you caught on quick!"

She turned to Haydar. "Can I do it again?"

"Of course." He held out a quiver of arrows. "Help yourself. This time, however, we're moving the target further away." He gestured to one of the stable boys to bring another gourd and tie it to a pole several paces further than the first one.

Coxani remembered Haydar's instructions without having to try to remember them. *Nock, draw, anchor, release.* It was like breathing. She struck that gourd as well, and the next one, and the next one.

"You know," Haydar said, leaning in conspiratorially and lowering his voice, "You have a knack for this. You're better than many little boys who are older than you."

She beamed proudly and would have asked to do it again, except Haydar said he had yet another surprise for her. *Another surprise!* She waited with bated breath as Haydar disappeared into the portico for a few minutes.

He returned with a beautiful gray gelding. "Do you remember how to ride?" he asked her. She nodded vigorously. Of the few things she remembered of her life in Gohar, this was definitely one of them. "Let's go for a ride, then," Haydar said, lifting her in his arms and setting her in the saddle.

The afternoon flew by far too quickly for Coxani. Riding a horse, shooting a bow... Those were things she could do, things she *wanted* to do. "Lord Haydar, why can't girls become Manzakars?"

He rode alongside her. "They can and they have," he said. "But it's much more challenging for them than for the boys, not just because women tend to be smaller, but because our society doesn't approve of women doing the things men do. And the ones who do become Manzakars usually have short careers, since all Gohari women must marry and have children eventually."

She thought about this for a moment. "I could do it."

Haydar raised his eyebrows. "Could you, now?"

"I think I'm better at shooting bows than reciting poems," she said, wrinkling her nose.

Smiling, he said, "It certainly seems that way, doesn't it?"

Later on, as Haydar walked her back to the girls' school, she asked, "Can we do this again tomorrow, my lord?"

"Perhaps not tomorrow, Coxani," he said, "but maybe the next day. I have to get permission from Headmistress Ola first."

Disappointed, she said, "Okay. I hope she says yes."

He winked at her. "I will make sure she does. Don't worry."

CHAPTER 3

Anzor
Eight Years Later
Year 217 of the Dark Age

Gritting her teeth, Coxani deliberately avoided eye contact with the Anzori noblemen. They perused the selection of Gohari slave girls, including herself, who sat together in one of the palace's secondary halls. It was Coxani's first choosing party. Dressed in white and roseate gowns of silk and brocade over loose cotton breeches, the girls were no older than eighteen and no younger than fifteen. They had been adorned in luxurious clothes and gold earrings, bangles, and necklaces that rivaled those of any Anzori aristocrat. This, after all, was what their entire lives had led up to; it was the aspiration of almost every slave girl there.

As a courtesan, a Gohari woman would have more freedom than married Anzori women: Her protector would buy her a home in the Citadel, give her a household of slave servants, a horse, and a monthly salary. Other than continuing to cultivate her artistic and social skills, she would have no duties—except for certain "intimate obligations" (as Ola called them) to her protector. Of course, this freedom was short-lived—usually less than two years—since all Gohari women had to marry and bear children with Gohari men. Her property would revert to her protector or pass on to her husband if her protector so wished. A married Gohari woman could continue to be an Anzori nobleman's courtesan, if the nobleman wished it. An Anzori man's wishes always superseded those of a Gohari's—no matter how "elite" that Gohari man was. A Gohari, after all, was still a slave.

Another choosing party would be held for all the young women, both those chosen as courtesans and those not, this time with Manzakars. Finally, the girls who were not chosen by either noblemen or Manzakars became household slaves to the residents of the Citadel and married to Gohari men of the same standing.

Coxani shifted slightly in her chair, suppressing a wince as her gown brushed against the backs of her legs. She'd tried sneaking out of the girls' school this morning to avoid having to be here. That, of course, had earned her a good birching across her legs and bare behind—good enough that sitting was quite painful. The only thing keeping her from making a scene at that very moment was Haydar's agreement to let her test to qualify as a Manzakar cadet—*if* she went along with Ola's request that she attend the choosing and be civil to any potential suitors. She'd been training with the bow since Haydar had gifted one to her at age seven, often at the expense of her other lessons and much to Ola's chagrin. Archery and riding her horse (also a gift from Haydar) were all she wanted to do, the only things that brought her joy. And she knew in her bones that she was good at them. Haydar must have taken notice because he'd promised her that, in the case she was chosen, he would negotiate for her to continue her training.

Coxani knew she was an outlier, wanting to become a Manzakar. None of her girlfriends had similar aspirations, and with good reason—it marked a girl as "masculine" and "difficult," and all the time spent training and in the company of men sullied her in society's eyes. This significantly reduced her chances of finding a Manzakar husband and Anzori protector, without which she was fated to become just a lowly house slave. Coxani knew of only one other girl, Zarina, who'd become a Manzakar four years ago. She'd never met Zarina and suspected they were kept apart on purpose. Two years into her time as a Manzakar, Zarina was forced to marry a fellow soldier, and she tried to run away. After that, Zarina disappeared, and rumors abounded regarding her fate, the most popular being that she languished in a dark prison somewhere, begging for Cenk's forgiveness. Zarina became a cautionary tale that Coxani heard all too often these days. Still, she would not be swayed. *I'm not afraid of Cenk or the prisons.* To her, life as a Gohari woman was itself punishment.

She stole a look at the other girls as they sat straight, their hands folded in their laps, serene, hopeful smiles on their faces. *We're like an assortment of sweetmeats, waiting to be plucked up and devoured.* She desperately prayed the men would find her ugly. Ola had reassured her that it was rare to be chosen so young and during one's first choosing, but it wasn't enough consolation for Coxani. Her stomach began to churn. Out of the corner of her eye, she saw one of the noblemen speak softly to Ola. He was looking at Coxani. *Oh, no.* Ola smiled, nodded, and approached her.

"Coxani, Lord Revaz wishes to have tea with you in the garden." A wide smile was on Ola's face, but the look in her eyes was threatening. *Do not make a fool of me*, it said.

"Yes, Mistress," Coxani said, plastering a smile on her own face. She stood and followed Ola to greet her potential suitor. He looked to be in his twenties and was handsome in the Anzori way—ivory skin, flaxen hair, bright blue eyes. He wore a jacquard tunic in a deep maroon, indicating his status as an Anzori aristocrat, and a matching turban. She lowered her gaze and bowed. Revaz offered her his arm and they walked together from the hall with a eunuch trailing behind them. *I'm going to be sick.* It helped that he smelled good, like ginger and bergamot. They reached the garden, where a table had been prepared for the occasion beneath a fig tree. They sat and the eunuch poured fragrant mint tea from a long-spouted pot into small, gilded cups.

Revaz took a sip of tea and finally spoke, offering her an uneasy smile. "I've never done this before. I'm not entirely sure how it works. I suppose I'll start by saying that you are quite beautiful."

"Thank you, my lord." She didn't care if he was nice or handsome. She wasn't going to make conversation. She didn't want him to like her. She also took a sip of tea, hoping it would soothe her roiling stomach. The nausea began to ease a bit.

He hesitated. "I guess I'll tell you a bit about me, then you can tell me about yourself. I am one of King Delger's newest advisors. I advise him on domestic issues, specifically law enforcement in Anzor." He paused, looking uncomfortable. "What else? I enjoy playing polo and reading. I am a bachelor and intend to stay that way."

She raised her eyebrows at the last bit. "You don't want a wife, but you're looking for someone to keep your bed warm, I assume?"

Startled, Revaz began to laugh, his face going red. "Ah... I prefer to say that I seek companionship."

In the bedroom, she thought insolently. "Do you know Lord Haydar?"

"Yes, but not well. What I do know of him, I like. Also a confirmed bachelor, in case you were wondering."

Coxani blinked. As one of the king's former Aslan Manzakars, Haydar had the option not to marry, so for some reason it had never occurred to her that he was, after all, a man with needs, just like the rest of them. The thought made her nausea threaten to flood back. She changed the subject. "Don't you think I'm a bit young for you?" She was pushing it, she knew. She had to walk the line between being forward without being insulting.

He narrowed his eyes at her. "How interesting. You don't want a protector, do you? You're trying to turn me off."

He was perceptive, if nothing else. She said, "No, my lord. I don't want a protector."

He leaned forward, his face lit with curiosity. "That's a new one. Why not?"

Where to begin? "Will you tell on me?"

"No. Gentleman's honor."

For some reason, she believed him. She took a deep breath. "I don't want someone to choose me because of my appearance or because I can sing and play the lute—both of which I am atrocious at, in case you were curious. You'd absolutely hate listening to me and beg me to stop, I promise. I, like you, never want to get married. I don't want to be anyone's mistress, wife, or mother."

He listened intently, resting his head in his hand. "But— What do you want, then?"

She lifted her chin. "I want to become a Manzakar."

He stared quietly, his mouth ajar. Coxani was familiar with that reaction. Finally, he smiled, looking genuinely entertained. "I would ask how you plan to go about that, but I have a feeling I already know."

"Do you?"

"Yes. Haydar." He shook his head, chuckling. "From what I've heard, the fiend loves transforming Gohari slaves into elite soldiers. I think he's even done it once or twice with girls, too." He searched her face for a moment. "But even so, you know, you'll have to marry and have children eventually. It's the law."

She shrugged. "I'll worry about that when the time comes."

His smile broadened. "You've got spirit, I'll give you that." He leaned back and crossed his arms on his chest. "I have very basic military training, but it's mostly so that I can do my job—which is administrative—more effectively. Actual fighting doesn't interest me at all. I can hardly kill an insect without feeling remorse. I don't think I could bear to kill human beings."

She kept her gaze steady. "You have the luxury not to. You're not a slave."

His smile faded. But instead of the indignation she expected, he looked pensive. "Beautiful, courageous, and smart. I'll be honest, I'm disappointed you won't have me."

At this, Coxani flushed. "Lord Revaz, any of the girls would die for someone like you to choose them. You're handsome and kind, which is so much more than many of them can hope for. I've heard horror stories from some of the girls... stories about being chosen by very old, very ugly, very fat noblemen..."

Revaz laughed out loud. "By Cenk! Coxani, I could sit here all day and listen to you."

She grinned, realizing that she was, ultimately, enjoying her conversation with this blue-blood Anzori. *I guess they're not all bad.*

"The eunuch is signaling that our time is up," he said quietly. "Before we return, I'd like to wish you the best of luck in your endeavor to become a Manzakar. And if you should change your mind..." He smiled coyly.

She averted her eyes, suddenly unsettled by her own feelings. "I promise you will be the first to know, my lord."

He then offered her his arm and they walked back to the hall, pretending to talk about the weather.

NARAN GRINNED FIENDISHLY at Tikran as he reined his horse around in a cloud of dirt, his blunted and padded saber drawn. Tikran didn't smile back—he was entirely too focused on winning this round. At twenty, Naran had been a Manzakar for nearly two years. He towered at a height of six-foot-four and had a body that was mostly dense muscle. He'd grown out his naturally course, saffron-colored hair and twisted it into thick ropes that fell past his shoulders. He had also been true to his word and become a fearsome swordsman, one of the best among the Manzakars. Tikran was not yet a Manzakar, and he considered himself just as good as Naran.

At Naran's signal, they galloped toward each other across the arena, each holding their blades in guard position. As he approached, Naran swung his saber horizontally and to the side, but Tikran broke the cut and followed with a back cut as he rode past, striking Naran in the back of the neck. Naran cursed aloud and turned, his smile gone. Tikran didn't have time to grin tauntingly at his friend before Naran raised his saber overhead and sliced diagonally. Tikran managed to parry the blow but wasn't fast enough to stop Naran's immediate thrust. The weapon struck his chainmail hauberk over his solar plexus, hard.

It was Tikran's turn to curse. "Try that again," he said. Naran obliged, this time thrusting immediately, and Tikran successfully parried. As they passed each other, Tikran kept his saber horizontal from the parry and stopped short of striking Naran at the base of the throat. "I just cut your head off," Tikran declared triumphantly.

Naran's nostrils flared. "Absolutely not."

"What! Are you implying I didn't see what I saw? My saber would have hit you right in the gullet."

"Not a chance."

"Naran, I swear to Cenk—"

Naran rode by and smacked Tikran upside the head with the flat of his sword, laughing. "Looks like you have company. I'll finish you off later."

Tikran glanced behind him to see Mago standing at the edge of the training grounds, smiling from ear to ear. Tikran rode over and dismounted, tossing his hauberk aside.

"What a Manzakar you'll make, lad!" Mago wrapped his arms around the cadet in a rough embrace, rumbling with good humor. These days, Tikran had to lean down to hug the old man. Mago had visited Tikran as often as he could for eleven years, always bringing date cookies. *Still* bringing date cookies. He'd become the second closest thing to a parent Tikran had besides Haydar, and he suspected Mago knew it. Throughout their visits, up until he was nine or ten, Tikran would often slip up and call Mago "Da." At first he'd been embarrassed, but Mago had passed over it expertly. No doubt he was used to it.

Tikran smiled affectionately at Mago, still catching his breath. "I wish they would let me graduate already," he grumbled.

During the first eight years of his life as a cadet, he'd been indoctrinated into Cenkism. When he and Naran weren't sneaking out of religion class or being punished for sneaking out of religion class, they'd spent most of their time numbly memorizing, reciting, and copying verses from the Book of Cenk. Much time was spent learning about Archil's heresy and the punishment he brought on his people. Gohar, now under Anzor's control, had once been a fertile land, but Archil's actions ushered in the Dark Ages, and Gohar became a bleak, desolate place. The belief that the Gohari needed Anzor's guidance to ensure they did not spiral into chaos was beaten into the cadets' brains. The boys also learned the "gentlemanly" disciplines of governance, literature, and grammar. They had lessons in elocution and articulation to teach them the nuances of the Anzori dialect of Perchuhi and eliminate their Gohari accents.

Now, at eighteen, Tikran was nearing the end of his term as a Level Three cadet. He'd easily mastered archery, lance-casting, and swordplay—all while on a galloping horse. He was the top cadet in his cohort of ten, as well as one of the top two cadets in the entire class of a hundred. All that was left was to graduate and go on his first campaign.

"Always chomping at the bit, eh? It will happen all in good time." Mago cleared his throat before saying, "Tikran, I've come bearing news, and to ask a favor."

Tikran immediately raised an eyebrow. "Yes?"

Mago hesitated a moment, then said, "I assume you remember Coxani? The little urchin who arrived in Anzor City with you, those many years ago?"

"Well, yes, of course I remember."

"I wasn't sure," Mago chuckled. "For a couple years you asked about her, then stopped. I thought you might have forgotten."

"Not forgotten," Tikran reassured him. "It's just that she and I live in different worlds." He shrugged. Since Ola had carried her away that fateful morning in the palace gardens, he had seen Coxani a few times and from a distance, but not since he was eleven or twelve. She was a girl, and therefore lived in the women's quarters. Boys lived in the barracks. They didn't mingle unless there was official reason, and then it was in a formal setting under the watchful eyes of the eunuchs.

Mago smiled. "No need to explain, lad. It's just that you might be sharing a world again. Coxani has been training with the bow since she was seven and she's fought hard to become a cadet. She had to thoroughly prove herself against boy cadets her own age before Haydar decided to allow it."

Tikran's eyes widened. "What? You mean to say..."

"She will train to become a Manzakar," Mago said, completing his thought. "She is fifteen, and of the age. She will begin in just a few weeks."

Tikran was at a loss for words. His mind was awhirl with questions he couldn't and probably shouldn't articulate at that very moment. In eleven years, he'd only witnessed two women become cadets, and only one of them had been initiated into the Manzakar ranks. And she had tried to avoid marriage and landed herself in prison—at least as far as he knew. He had a hard time imagining the small girl with the enormous eyes, who cried often—about bloody everything—becoming a warrior. But then, that was ages ago. She'd been barely more than a toddler. He said, "But isn't she the right age for a choosing party?"

"Yes, she recently had her first choosing." He shook his head in amusement. "A nobleman took a fancy to her, but she somehow managed to scare him off, I'm told. She has been a... ah... somewhat *difficult* student at the girls' school. As soon as she was old enough to understand what 'courtesan' meant, she set her mind to becoming a cadet. And lucky for her, Haydar indulged her. He seems to think she has enough skill and determination to accomplish it."

"Good for her." Based on what he remembered about her,

Tikran had no difficulty imagining the trouble she must have been at the girls' school. It sounded like she was still very much the little girl with the ear-shattering scream. If he was being perfectly honest with himself, she sounded like a nightmare. And regardless of what Haydar thought of her skills, there was no way she would survive the rigorous training. *I give her two weeks at most*, Tikran thought smugly.

Mago cleared his throat again. "And here comes the request."

Tikran mentally steeled himself. "Go on."

"Watch over her, lad," Mago pleaded. "She plays tough, but she's entering the world of men after being completely secluded from them. She's at a disadvantage."

Oh, no. Tikran was singularly focused on graduating at the top of his class as soon as possible. He didn't have time to watch over a girl he barely knew, who was likely going to be the only female in a sea of adolescent boys with... certain urges...

But Mago had been there for him all these years, and he could hardly say no to the only request the old slave merchant had ever made of him. He replied stiffly, "Okay. I'll try."

Mago's eyes twinkled. "I knew you'd become a man of honor, my boy."

Feelings of guilt and envy washed over Tikran. Guilt, because his thoughts were anything but honorable. Envy, because it was clear that Mago loved the girl like a daughter. "You've been visiting her all this time as well, then?"

"Of course."

Tikran looked at his hands. "What's she like?" What he really wanted to ask was, *How much trouble is this girl going to cause me?* He had a sinking feeling he already knew the answer.

Mago grinned, as if reading his thoughts. "You'll see."

FROM HIS SPOT in a shaded gallery, Haydar watched the Manzakar cadets engage in swordplay with their sabers below in the hippodrome. The young men battled on horseback and on foot, the steel of their sabers blinking with each cut, thrust, and parry. Haydar had bought many of the boys himself, in the name of the king. He'd chosen them based on age, constitution, family history (if known), and whether there was a glimmer of intelligence in their eyes. He expected them to be afraid—they were children, sometimes very young. But signs of curiosity, of courage, even defiance, often shined through the fear.

As if on cue, Tikran walked out from the portico and onto the training grounds, holding a saber in each hand. Haydar smiled to himself, leaning on the balustrade to watch. Eleven years ago, he'd chosen the boy before knowing anything about him. Everything he'd needed to know he saw in an instant. The child had been afraid when he'd climbed out of the wagon that day, and yet he'd held a little girl's hand steadfastly, whispering reassurances to her, his expression resolute.

Haydar immediately sensed that the boy had courage, intelligence, and something he rarely saw these days... empathy. Why else would he comfort another child he hardly knew when he himself was terrified? As it turned out, he got something of a package deal that day—the little girl likewise had those attributes in abundance. It wasn't until later that Mago told him the boy's story... and while undeniably tragic, it worked very much in Haydar's favor.

"Haydar of the Lightning Arrow, what a proud father you resemble," King Delger said with a laugh as he walked out to join Haydar at the balustrade, his royal purple tunic and turban in striking contrast to his sharp blue eyes and russet-colored beard.

"Your Highness." Haydar bowed. "I do feel like one, I will admit."

Delger looked out into the hippodrome. "Who among them would you bring to my attention?"

"The one dual-wielding and clearly winning," Haydar said.

Delger watched Tikran with interest, placing his palms on the stone and leaning forward. When the bout was over, he stroked his chin thoughtfully. "He is very talented."

"You should see him on horseback and with a bow in his hands."

Delger smiled. "I will most definitely keep an eye on him."

Haydar looked at the king. "Have you had any luck with the new physician?"

The pleasure dissipated from Delger's eyes. "No. Vazha is slowly getting worse, I'm afraid."

At twenty-three, Prince Vazha was the heir to the crown but was not expected to live long enough to see the day. He was a leper, and while the disease was slow in its progression and still in its early stage, the kingdom had begun to lose hope that Vazha would succeed his father. With no other sons, Delger's most likely successor, in that case, would be the man chosen to be the eldest princess's husband.

Haydar said, "During my last diplomatic visit to Dilovar, King Bilguun bragged quite a bit about the medical university in Ogedei. He selects his personal physician from their ranks and claims they have found ways to protect against the red plague through insufflation."

Delger let out a humorless laugh. "You would have me allow the enemy to treat my son? Why don't I just kill him myself?"

"Your Highness, we are not at war with Dilovar."

"Not now, we aren't," Delger grumbled. "But Bilguun seems set on changing that."

"At some point, they will run out of the Essence and want access to Gohar, my king," Haydar confirmed. "But that was to be expected." In 112 of the Dark Age, Anzor defeated Dilovar, the second largest kingdom on the Continent, in the Akmaral War, taking all of Gohar. While a truce was called granting Dilovar limited ingress to Gohar, the peace had become increasingly tenuous. "Another bargain will need to be struck with them to renew the truce, and that will include allowing them into Gohar."

"And what if I don't want another truce?" Delger said petulantly. "We are powerful enough that we don't need to grant Dilovar anything. If they want war, we will give them a war."

Haydar said carefully, "I trust you to do the right thing for your kingdom, Your Highness. Don't forget, however, that we might be able to use Dilovar's help in keeping the nomads in line—the attacks on Anzori outposts have increased recently, and Bilguun's troops could help crush the insurgents."

The king grunted, then smiled at the former Manzakar and his most trusted advisor. "Haydar, you will always be my voice of reason and moral compass. You should have been a cleric."

"I didn't realize that was an option," Haydar replied with a grin. "But in any case, I much prefer to serve you than Cenk, my king."

Delger nodded, looking pleased with Haydar's ability to always say the right thing, and gazed back out over the training grounds. "What's the lad's name?"

Haydar bowed. "Tikran, Your Highness."

CHAPTER 4

The curved blade of Tikran's saber flashed in the sunlight, a blur of whirling steel. His gelding raced at full speed toward two rows of tall, thin reeds, one row on his right and the other on his left, alternating and spaced several yards apart. He twisted in his saddle and swung at each one as he flew past them, slicing off a perfect one-inch piece from each reed. When he reached the end of the rows, he turned around and continued, wielding his saber to cut in two directions. As the reeds got shorter, Tikran had to twist faster and lean further and further down in his saddle, rapidly blinking the clouds of dust from his eyes. When the reeds were knee-high, he slowed to a trot, panting, sweat running down his face.

"Bravo!"

Tikran turned toward the voice to see Haydar across the training grounds, approaching. A young woman walked beside him, dressed in breeches and riding boots. He dismounted, his breathing slowed, and gave Haydar a short bow. "Good morning, Lord Haydar," he said, his eyes flicking briefly to the girl.

Her long, dark hair was braided away from a startlingly beautiful face, golden-toned with large green eyes. She regarded him suspiciously.

"That was quite impressive, Tikran," Haydar said with a grin, crossing his arms on his chest. "You are ready to graduate, there is no question."

"Thank you, my lord. I'm looking forward to it."

Haydar cleared his throat and looked at the girl. "Does he look anything like the boy you remember?"

She smiled slightly. "Somewhat. He's just much bigger now."

Haydar laughed. "Indeed. And you, Tikran? Surely you remember your little travel companion?"

Tikran swiped the sweat from his eyes with the back of his hand. He made sure to keep his expression bland, betraying no emotion. "Yes, of course I remember." He met her gaze and smiled stiffly. "It's been a while." Coxani put her hands behind her back and said nothing.

"Well," Haydar said, "I imagine Mago has spoken to each of you about the situation?"

Coxani nodded but Tikran frowned. "Situation? What situation? I was only told... well, asked to make sure she..."

"To make sure I what?" she snapped. "Stay out of trouble?"

That sounds more like the toddler I remember. Tikran rubbed the back of his neck. "Yes, more or less."

Haydar tilted his head. "Is that all he told you? He is a sneaky one, that Mago, isn't he?" He chuckled, rubbing his bearded chin. "It's a bit more than that, lad. We've decided to have you train her."

Tikran's heart dropped. *Oh, shit.* "My lord, with all due respect, I don't think I have time to—"

"Coxani," Haydar interrupted, "could you busy yourself in

the armory for a moment? I need to have a quick man-to-man with Tikran."

"Yes, my lord." She scowled at Tikran before walking away.

When she was well out of earshot, Haydar said, "She is an incredibly skilled archer, lad. More skilled than many Level Two cadets. You wouldn't guess by looking at her, but she's significantly stronger than she looks. She's been training consistently with a bow since she was seven, and she can compete in clout archery with the best."

"That's great," Tikran replied, trying—but failing—to keep the testiness from his voice.

Haydar sighed. "I wouldn't have approved of her training if I didn't think she'd be a valuable asset to us, surely you realize that. Not to mention, she was bloody determined to find a way out of the girls' school, and I'm not sure what we would have done with her otherwise."

"I understand," Tikran said. "But why doesn't she just begin with the other Level One cadets? Why must *I* train her?"

"Come now, boy," Haydar said, lowering his voice. "You got a good look at her. Can you imagine her training alongside a hundred fifteen-year-old boys who've had next to no exposure to women? Not only would it be unsafe for her, but she'd be an immense distraction. Every female cadet has had a trainer and trained separately from the boys to avoid any unsavory situations."

"But why me? Surely there are other cadets more qualified to train her."

"I have several reasons. Firstly, you are the only cadet who is advanced enough that you can spare six months of practice and still graduate on time."

"That's not—"

"Secondly, training others is an important skill for a Manzakar to have. This is not wasted time for you."

"Yes, but—"

"Thirdly, when Mago brought you to me eleven years ago, the two of you had formed a touching bond, like brother and sister. I imagine after a bit of time that relationship can be rekindled. And to show you how implicitly I trust you, I will allow you to train her without those prudish eunuchs observing your every move."

Tikran exhaled slowly, feeling defeated.

Haydar smiled and placed a firm hand on his shoulder. "Finally, even a Manzakar needs to learn how to keep the company of women. Perhaps you will even be one of those who marries, when you become a durai with your own property and household."

"I highly doubt it," Tikran muttered.

"You can't possibly know that now, boy, when you've spent more than half your life living only amongst men." He paused, squinting back at the armory. "So it is decided, then. You will spend the mornings training the girl, then after midday supper, you can continue your own training. We'll begin tomorrow."

The following morning, Tikran gulped down a cup of strongly brewed coffee before heading to the stables. Naran called out, "Have fun babysitting!" Tikran grumbled in response, slammed the empty cup down, and left the barracks in a huff. Instead of joining the other Level Three cadets in their sunrise exercises with the sword and lance, he was going to spend his morning teaching a pouty girl how to ride a horse properly, and it put him in a foul mood. He had no doubt she knew how to ride to some degree— she was Gohari, after all, and they'd been practically raised on horses. Even at the age of four, a Gohari child would have known how to ride a pony or donkey on their own. But riding a horse and riding a horse in combat were two very different things.

He walked under the arches of the vast royal stables, through the cool vaulted halls and past the horse market where noblemen haggled over a beautiful chestnut mare. He ventured beyond the saddlery that displayed luxuriously decorated harnesses, and the menagerie of falcons and other birds of prey. He finally reached the stalls of the Level One cadets, where the boys seemed to be more interested in something in the last stall than they were in tending to their horses. Tikran didn't doubt that something was Coxani. He said gruffly, "There's nothing to see over there, cadets. Back to your duties!"

She stopped brushing the bay gelding and looked at him when he entered her horse's stall. She wrinkled her nose and said, "They smell."

"The horses? Of course they smell."

"Not the horses. The boys."

Tikran rolled his eyes. "You can't possibly be able to smell the boys over the horses."

She set a hand on her hip. "I have smelled horses my whole life. I know how horses smell. Boys smell worse. Do they even bathe?"

He had no desire to continue the conversation. He said, "Mount up. We're going to a small training area outside the city."

"What about my bow?"

Tikran smirked. "You won't be needing that for a while."

"I *know* how to ride a horse."

Tikran blew out his breath. His student was turning out to be just as big of a pain in the ass as he'd anticipated, and they'd been together all of thirty seconds. "Coxani, for the love of Cenk, trust that I know what I'm saying. Now mount up. We're wasting time."

He heard her grumbling under her breath as she obeyed, placing her hands on her horse's back and lithely vaulting on.

As they rode side by side through the Citadel's pristine streets, past the terraced homes, shops, orchards, and gardens, Tikran could feel her gaze on him. He knew she had something to say. Finally she said, "You've changed."

"Oh, you mean since I was seven years old?" He snorted. "I should hope so."

"I don't just mean you've stretched out and can grow a lot of facial hair. You've become something of an asshole."

Tikran laughed in spite of himself. "You've known me for five minutes."

She sniffed. "That's apparently long enough."

Tikran pressed his lips together in annoyance. She had a lot of nerve, making assumptions about him. Besides, what did her opinion matter? It didn't matter at all. Not a single bit.

COXANI PEERED SIDELONG AT TIKRAN. Other than Mago, Lord Haydar, and briefly Lord Revaz, she hadn't had any prolonged interactions with boys or men since she was very small. Not that she'd wanted any—they seemed, for all intents and purposes, mostly unrefined, immature, hairy, and, well, smelly. She'd always resented that they had the opportunity to become an elite class of soldiers while she and the cultured, educated, artistic, absolutely amazing Gohari girls had to wait around for men to decide whether they were worthy of becoming wives or concubines.

"Resented" was likely too gentle a word, in fact. It enraged her.

Now, as she faced a minimum of six months in the company of this ill-tempered cadet, the only male from her past that she'd thought of on occasion in a remotely fond manner, she had to admit he was extremely good-looking. He had a straight nose, a masculine but shapely mouth, and deep-set brown eyes. His wavy black hair reached his shoulders and was tied back in a tail, revealing a defined jawline that was peppered with stubble. Growing up in the women's quarters, she'd thought Haydar was the epitome of handsome (as men went). Despite the silver hairs in his beard these days, he was still exceedingly handsome—and not just to her, of that she was certain. He was a "fine specimen of a Gohari male," as Cia had put it.

But Coxani saw Haydar as a father figure, whereas Tikran, well, he was closer to her age and... *he might be even more hand-some.* Unrefined, hairy, and probably smelly, but definitely handsome.

They rode across the moat and Coxani breathed in deeply. She had not been outside the Citadel since she had arrived that fateful day eleven years ago, with the surly man-child who rode beside her now. Granted, the views from the palace of Anzor City and beyond were breathtaking, but she'd longed to be outside the walls. The city outside the Citadel was dirtier, messier, and filled with humans who were neither nobles nor Manzakars. Barefoot children chased one another down the street as a woman in a threadbare skirt shouted at them. A hunched old man led a donkey laden with trinkets and wares while two young women balanced baskets of bread on their heads and turned down a shady alley, chatting together.

Coxani watched the people—the Anzori commoners—in awe as they went about their morning routines but was also acutely aware that they watched her too, in even greater amazement. She realized that they weren't even really gazing at her as much as they were gaping at Tikran, in his long navy blue jacket with a standing collar over loose breeches; white sash and leather belt; yellow boots with slightly curved soles at the toe; and a brown felt cap that was wrapped in a white turban, the end of the cotton cloth folded loosely under his chin and over his shoulder. It was the uniform of a Manzakar —a Level Three Manzakar cadet, but a Manzakar nonetheless. A small crowd had formed behind them, and people lined the street to gawk at him. Coxani asked softly, "Do they always stare at you like this?"

Tikran kept his eyes forward and his back straight. "We're rarely allowed to leave the Citadel and forbidden from engaging with the locals."

She considered this for a moment, then asked, "What if a fight broke out? Or if a thief swiped something in front of you?"

"That would be the city soldiers' problem."

Coxani thought of Lord Revaz briefly. She peered back at the crowd as they whispered amongst themselves. "What would happen if you engaged them?"

"I believe that would depend on context. If a fight broke out that didn't involve me directly and I got involved, I'd probably be suspended from my training for a long while and have a mark on my transcript. On the other hand, if I were to, say, secretly have a relationship with an Anzori woman, regardless of her rank, I would be flogged and demoted, and she would likely be sent away or forced into the service of Cenk."

Her eyes widened. "That's... harsh."

He nodded. "Unfortunately, it happens. When I was a Level Two, one of the Level Threes impregnated an Anzori girl, a merchant's daughter, and we had to witness his flogging. It was brutal. He never graduated. I think he's now an infantryman at one of the outposts."

She swallowed. "Dare I ask what happened to the girl and baby?" She already knew the answer, since the mixing of Gohari and Anzori bloodlines was forbidden by law.

Tikran's jaw flexed. "I'm not sure. The girl was probably quickly married off or banished to one of Cenk's temples. As for the baby, I can't imagine it was allowed to live."

Coxani pursed her lips and went silent. Growing up in the Citadel, it was hard to miss the differences in appearance between the Gohari and the Anzori. The people of Gohar were a spectrum of swarthy, whereas the Anzori were fair and fairer still. Although the Gohari people who lived in Anzor had what Ola called "charmed" lives, Coxani had always known deep down that the Anzori looked down on them. Nomads versus city dwellers. Pagans versus believers. *They don't want our brownness to pollute their whiteness.*

She wondered if Tikran had been brainwashed like most Gohari slaves and believed the stories they had been fed by the Anzori. Over the years, Haydar had often taken her into the palace's vast libraries, and unbeknownst to him, she'd found texts about Gohar tucked between tomes about Cenk. She'd read as much as she could in those stolen moments. Something in her core being would not let her believe that the Gohari were lawless savages, or that they deserved to suffer. She secretly resented the notion that Anzor had saved them from their barbarous ways. And she certainly wasn't the only Gohari slave to feel that way—defiance bubbled in every slave girl "not pretty enough" and hidden away in the kitchens to do menial work, in every slave boy "not manly enough" and made a eunuch so that he would not pass his effeminate traits to the next generation of Gohari boys.

Tikran broke the silence. "I must have said the right thing."

She looked at him. "What? Why do you think that?"

His lips twitched. "Because you stopped talking."

THEY ARRIVED at the training grounds just on the outskirts of Anzor City to find it virtually empty, save for a couple Level Threes fencing under the sun. Tikran shaded his eyes. "Good. We practically have the place to ourselves." As he led them further out onto the grounds, he said, "Before you can even think about using weapons, you must have full mastery of equitation." He glanced at her quickly before adding, "In other words, your horse."

"I know what equitation means," she said hotly.

Tikran stifled a smile and continued. "Since you seem to know the basics of bareback mounting, the next step is to learn how to fall off a horse."

Coxani sighed. "I've *never* fallen off a horse."

"Oh, you will. And often." He flashed her a look. "After learning how to ride, this is what we teach every single cadet. I'm not deliberately coming up with ways to embarrass or discourage you. And if you think this is hard, wait until I teach you how to put on and take off armor while on a moving horse... at night."

She narrowed her eyes suspiciously. "Fine. Go on."

With a brisk nod, he continued. "Since you will be falling often, it needs to become a routine response, and you need to be able to fall from either the right or left side with complete ease, at a walk, trot, canter, and gallop." He reined his horse around to face her. "The trick is to tuck your chin and roll like a ball, while bringing up your arms to protect your head. I'll demonstrate."

He removed his turban and jacket and set them aside. Coxani watched as Tikran deliberately fell off his horse at a trot, canter, and gallop, switching sides with each. When he was done, his tunic stamped with dirt and twigs in his hair, he said, "Now it's your turn, cadet."

Determined, she coaxed her horse into a walk. Falling

correctly on both sides proved to be easy for her. The trot and canter were a bit more difficult, and the gallop had her yelling curses each time she didn't quite manage to curl quickly enough and, with legs and arms flailing, slammed into the earth. After about an hour of falling, Tikran made her stop. "I think that's enough falling for one morning, no? Let's practice vaulting onto a moving horse."

She nodded, gasping for breath and hobbling, trying to push strands of sweaty, dusty hair from her eyes. "Yes," she panted. "Good idea."

Tikran hid a smile but had to admit to himself: he was impressed with the girl so far. He'd half expected her to beg to stop after one particularly bad fall during a gallop, but after yelling several exceedingly colorful swear words, she limped back to her horse and mounted once again, kicking back into a gallop without so much as looking at him. It wasn't until he stopped her that she wilted a bit and admitted she was ready to be done.

He'd seen many a Level One cadet quit the exercise sooner than she, unable to go on.

To say that he looked forward to their training sessions was a stretch—he could think of a million other things he'd rather be doing. But her determination and stamina made it almost gratifying to train her. Whatever she was able to accomplish would, ultimately, reflect well on him.

A week into her training, he said, "Now that you've mastered falling, we'll move on to something a bit more challenging." He chewed the inside of his cheek, wondering if he should skip the lesson altogether on account of its... impropriety. He decided to move forward with it since it was an essential skill for a warrior, which was what he was training her to become.

"Thank Cenk! My body has been aching all over for days," she said, a flush to her cheeks from her exercises.

"Hold off on your thanks for the moment." He set his hands on his hips. "I'm going to ride after you and try to knock you off your horse."

Her eyes widened. "With what?"

"My hands. No weapons for now."

"But you're stronger than me."

"Yes?" He raised an eyebrow at her. "And when you're on the battlefield, the enemy won't be?"

"Can I try to knock you off as well?"

"Of course."

A mischievous glint came into her eyes. "Let's go, then." She began to trot away and he followed. She sped up to a canter and he came up alongside her. Before she could get to a gallop, he leaned over, grabbed her ankle, lifted, and pushed, toppling her over. She let out a curse but curled into a ball in the nick of time, rolling to the ground in a cloud of dust. He stopped and turned. "Nicely done, Coxani," he said, referring to her fall.

Her eyes blazed. "Let's try that again."

Back on their horses, she picked up speed as he followed, but this time as he pulled up next to her, she leaped up onto her horse's back and flung herself at him. Tikran tried to keep his balance but to no avail. They both went crashing to the ground in an explosion of dirt, rolling until they hit a thicket of bushes. She was lying half on top of him, her hair in his mouth and her elbow in his gut. Finally stationary, Tikran groaned. "What the *fuck*—"

"I knocked you off," she said with a gasp, rolling off of him.

He sat up, rubbing his ribs. Coxani was no wisp of a girl, that was for certain. She was more muscle than he cared to think about. "I think you missed the point of the exercise," he said acerbically.

She looked at him for a long moment, her face bruised and dirty, and his stomach tightened. *Please don't start crying,* he thought nervously. Unexpectedly, she burst out laughing. "I'm sorry," she said through her laughter. "Did I hurt you?"

Relieved, Tikran stood, then pulled Coxani up by the hand. "Yes. And you probably hurt yourself as well. We could have both been trampled or broken bones from the fall. The horses could have been injured. That was a seriously stupid move."

She sobered. "I'm sorry, truly. It's just... for a whole week I feel like you've been beating up on me. I think I had some pent up... frustrations."

"Coxani, I'm trying to *train* you!"

"Yes, yes," she answered gruffly. "But I know you'd rather be doing anything else, and sometimes it feels like you enjoy making me suffer."

Tikran paused, considering. The corner of his mouth quirked up in a lopsided smile. "I wouldn't call it enjoyment. But you aren't completely off the mark."

She let out a laugh. "That's the most open you've been with me since we were re-introduced. It almost makes me happy." She rolled her shoulders, wincing. "I will say, it's certainly glorious not having those eunuchs giving me the evil eye. They would be utterly horrified at what just happened."

He looked away, suddenly uncomfortable. Perhaps there had been a bit *too* much bodily contact. "Let's practice jumping and snaking between reeds for a bit."

When they finally headed back to the Citadel, they rode in pleasant silence for a while. Tikran had a sneaking suspicion it wouldn't last. He was correct. She smirked at him and said, "You look like shit."

"Hmm, I wonder why?" He shot her a look. "You don't look so great yourself, by the way." He was lying. She was covered in dirt from head to toe, had a tangled mess of hair, abrasions and smudges on her face, and she was nothing short of radiant. He didn't like it at all.

She grinned. "It's a wonderful feeling. All women should be able to feel this... alive. I was truly lucky that Haydar gifted me a bow when I was seven and that he convinced Ola to allow me to train with it. Haydar has done it before with Gohari girls he buys for the king—he gifts them a bow and watches to see if they take to it. Most don't. Some do. From the ones that do, he considers their abilities at the age of fifteen after several years of training and only occasionally has one become a cadet. I was a lucky one. One of the other girls, Tashi, was also pretty good at it. But I was far better."

Tikran rubbed his face. "Holy Cenk, do *all* women talk this much?"

"What's wrong with talking? It's how we learn about people, how we form relationships," she fired back, her expression darkening. "Are *all* men this emotionally constipated?"

He chose not to answer. To his mind, silence was the only suitable response.

She was quiet for several minutes, then said, "He was sad you never visited, you know."

What now? Tikran looked over at her, frowning. "Who?"

"Wig."

He paused for a moment, thinking. "Oh." He let out a short laugh. "The rabbit."

She didn't look at him. "I never forgot what you did."

"What did I do?"

"At a time when you needed him most, your last and only thread to your family in Gohar, you gave him to a little girl you barely knew to make her less afraid." She looked down at her hands.

He couldn't have said why, but Tikran wanted this particular conversation to end quickly. He said, "Oh, it was just a toy." He cleared his throat. "But I'm glad it gave you comfort."

"He did." She paused, her brow furrowed. "I don't remember my parents. They died of the red plague when I was a baby. My father's sister took me in, but she wasn't happy about it. She had five children and I was another mouth to feed. As soon as she heard a slave merchant from Anzor was at a nearby outpost, she took me and sold me." She looked at him, her eyes like twin moons. "Do you remember your parents?"

He took a long, deep breath. As much as he hated remembering his life in Gohar, the girl was confiding in him, allowing him to peek inside her heart and mind. He couldn't just change the subject. "I do. After my mother died, my father couldn't feed me and my sisters. I was the oldest, healthy and strong, so he knew he'd get several years' worth of income from me. I can't imagine he had much of a choice. Plus, he knew I'd be taken care of."

Coxani contemplated this, then asked, "How did your mother die?"

"I can't remember. I remember her acting strangely before she died, telling me she loved me often and to be strong. I can remember nothing between that and when my father was scattering her ashes in the wind." He paused. "She must have known she would die."

Coxani bit her lip. "Do you really believe that Gohar is paying for the sins of Archil?"

Are we really going to talk about this now? Tikran hesitated. "It's what we've been taught. I have to admit it's odd that only the Gohari have the Essence. And it certainly seems that Gohar is being punished." The story they'd been taught was that the armies of Anzor and Dilovar were closing in on Archil and he knew he would die. So he killed himself with Cenk's magic and shattered into shards of light that scattered across Gohar, spreading the Essence amongst his people so that Cenk could not take it back.

He scratched the stubble on his chin, desperate for a different topic. After a beat, he settled on, "I think you're ready to saddle up. Maybe practice with a weapon. What do you think?"

She sat up straight, smiling brightly at him. "Truly? Yes! Yes, I'm ready."

"Good. We begin tomorrow morning."

Relief washed over him when she didn't return to the subject of theology, their past lives, or that silly rag of a rabbit.

***

Tikran held his saber and shield and rode his horse in a circle around Coxani slowly, his body tensed and his eyes narrowed. His gaze was fixed on her as he said, "When you're face to face with the enemy, keep your sword drawn and at your right side, hilt down. Never attempt to hold more than one weapon at a time. If your sword is still in its scabbard and it's hanging from your saddle, you're likely done for. That said, you should unsheathe it as soon as possible." He continued to circle her, clearly enjoying the theatrics. "So now, tell me, cadet. What do you do with your shield?"

Coxani rolled her eyes at him. "You keep it on your left arm at all times."

"And if you set it down?"

"You always set it down with the grip facing up so you can grab it quickly." A month into her training, she and Tikran had developed something she might have called a friendship—on the good days. "What do you do if, say, you're sleeping when there's an attack?" she asked.

Tikran frowned. "You don't sleep. A Manzakar never sleeps."

She sighed, rubbing her temples. "Right. But seriously, what do you do?"

He pulled on the reins and came to a stop. "You sleep with your breeches on."

"Thanks," Coxani snapped. "As if I have the option of sleeping with my breeches *off*."

Tikran closed his eyes briefly, as if clearing his mind, before saying, "In addition to your breeches, sleep with your jacket, boots, and sword on, and make sure your horse is always saddled."

"Well, that's practical," she muttered, sarcasm dripping from her voice.

"It's practical when you might have Dilovaris shooting and hacking at you at any moment," Tikran said, dismounting. "Now, cadet. You'll learn to put your armor on while at a gallop." He held out a heavy cavalryman's lamellar cuirass. It mainly consisted of a mail hauberk, made of large, flat metal rings and horizontal plates of gilded steel. The neck of the cuirass was woven with rawhide to create a stiff mail collar. It hung down to the knees—or, in her case, halfway down her calves.

Coxani raised an eyebrow. "I'm going to be a flight archer. My armor will be way lighter than that."

Tikran knitted his eyebrows in disdain. "Are you training to be a flight archer or a Manzakar?"

Curse you, Tikran. There was no question he was enjoying this. Coxani forced an indifferent look onto her face. "Fine. I will remind you, however, that I'm a fraction your size."

He grinned fiendishly. "I'm not the one who suggested you become a cadet, I'm fairly certain of that."

Puffing out her chest, Coxani decided that her only course of action was to show him she could handle anything he threw at her—including shooting her bow while wearing armor that weighed as much as she did. She grabbed the cuirass and was immediately distraught by how heavy it was. *Are you kidding me?* Her breath hissed out through her teeth. He was getting her back for pouncing on him from her horse those weeks ago. He'd been subtly and not-so-subtly punishing her for it fairly continuously, she was certain of it.

Tikran approached her, a serene look on his face. "Here." He took the armor from her. "I'll hand it to you once you're on your horse."

"Oh, what a bloody gentleman." She spun away from him and mounted her horse with a huff. "Now what?"

"Set it in front of you face down. Once at a gallop, put one of your hands in its sleeve while holding the edge of it, then with that same hand, grab the chest portion and the hem and lift them up and over your head." He demonstrated. "Then grab the reins with the same hand and slide your other hand into its sleeve."

"Fine." She took the heavy cuirass from him and immediately kicked her horse into a gallop. She managed to get the first arm sleeved, then attempted to pull the garment over her head. It was heavy enough that she got lost in a blanket of metal and had to rein her horse to a stop, blindly seeking the neck hole and cursing violently. She could see Tikran snickering at her in her mind's eye.

Her second attempt was likewise a failure, but she was determined to wipe the shit-eating grin off Tikran's face. On her third try, she managed to get the cuirass over her head. Once that was accomplished, she easily slipped her other arm through its sleeve. Dripping sweat, she returned to Tikran, who stood with his arms crossed and legs apart, a twitch of amusement on his lips. "Well done. Now you learn to shoot while riding at a trot, then a gallop."

She dismounted and began removing the cuirass when he stopped her. "I meant while wearing the armor as well."

She stared at him. "Are you saying you want me to learn how to shoot and ride *while* wearing this?"

"Of course." He seemed to think her question was utterly ridiculous. "If you can master that, you'll be a terrifying force against the enemy."

"But I won't be wearing this stupid thing against the enemy."

"Did you hear what I just said? Are you even listening?"

Coxani desperately wanted to kick him—hard. In the groin. "Fine, let's get on with it!" she yelled. She fastened her belt, from which hung her sheathed bow and quiver of arrows, around her waist and struggled to mount her horse again.

Tikran slipped into a similar cuirass and jumped on his horse easily. He pulled his bow from his hip and looked at her. "Forget almost all you know about archery. A mounted archer must not only be a master of the bow, but also a master of the horse. Simply aiming at a target isn't enough. You need to consider the horse's stride, the ruggedness of the terrain, and the direction and strength of the wind. You must use both your hands to shoot and therefore control your horse with the pressure of your legs alone. I know you can ride without holding the reins, I've seen you do it. Now, only loose your arrow when your horse is in flight, meaning all four legs are off the ground." He indicated the gourds that hung from poles at the far end of the training grounds. "Those are your targets. Remember that in battle, your targets will be moving too, making it even harder to strike."

Her anger faded away as she listened attentively, wondering if she could master this without embarrassing herself too badly. He must have sensed her anxiety, because he said, "A lot of this will come naturally to you, Coxani. You'll see." He squinted at the gourds. "I'll show you." He began to canter toward the targets, then abruptly turned and galloped back toward her. As he approached at full speed, he twisted in his saddle and loosed his arrow behind him. They heard the gourd burst in the distance, and Tikran slowed, turning again, smiling at her.

Show off! She began to ride toward the gourds herself, pulling an arrow from its quiver. It took her several tries before she began to grow somewhat accustomed to shooting while jostling, waiting for the moment when she and her horse were weightless to loose an arrow. To make things worse, the cuirass weighed her down, making her movements slower. By the time she ran out of arrows, she was panting and drenched in sweat. Tikran called to her and she began to ride toward him when her vision began to shimmer. Tikran's voice was muffled and she couldn't make out the words. Before she had time to grasp what was happening, she began to slump forward and everything faded away.

She was brought back to consciousness when a shock of cool water gushed over her head. She gasped, sitting straight in a jerk of movement. Tikran hovered over her, holding his flask. "Welcome back," he said. "Let's get this hot metal cuirass off you." He helped her slip out of the armor then asked, "Can you walk to the shade?"

She nodded but stood up too quickly and nearly collapsed. Tikran swept her up in his arms and carried her to the shade beneath a big tree. *This is so embarrassing. Holy Cenk.* As he set her down, she squirmed to get out of his grasp. He sat next to her in the grass and held out her flask. "Drink," he commanded. He didn't have to tell her twice. She emptied the flask, tilting it to ensure she got every last drop. He watched her and said, "Coxani, I have to admit, I'm really impressed with you. You have determination and stamina."

She lay back against the tree trunk, still feeling woozy. "You're just saying that to make me feel better for passing out."

"Is that so? You've gotten to know me over the course of a month. Do I strike you as the type of man who would spout compliments to ease anyone's ego?"

She shook her head. "Not really."

He offered what was left of the water in his flask. "Here. Drink the rest."

"What about you?"

"I'm fine. I'm not exerting myself like you are." She took the flask gratefully and drained it in several swift swallows. Tikran was smiling.

"What? Does my face look like a tomato?"

"It does, but that's not why I'm smiling." He leaned back in the grass. "Tell me. How did you scare off that nobleman at the choosing party you attended?"

The question did not help ease the redness of her face. "Oh. You heard about that, did you?"

"Mago told me."

She looked away. "I'm not sure, to be honest. I guess I... befriended him."

He raised his eyebrows. "Befriended? How?"

"I don't know. I was candid with him and told him I didn't want a protector, that I wanted to become a Manzakar, and then I made him laugh with my stories." She shrugged.

Tikran scowled. "It doesn't sound like you scared him off at all."

She sat in stunned silence. Was he expressing... *jealousy*?

She didn't know how to respond, so she sat there with her mouth ajar.

"Anyway." He stood. "Are you feeling well enough to get back in the saddle?"

Still tingling with surprise, she tried to smile. "Without that awful cuirass? I think so."

CHAPTER 5

King Delger's annual Fire Festival was one of Anzor City's main events. As spring began and the weather turned warm, everyone—from prince to peasant— stopped their daily work shortly after midday supper, donned their most festive attire, and watched the king's elite class of slave-soldiers compete in tournaments and perform daring feats of skill. Ostensibly, it was to honor Cenk and celebrate the return of life, but in actuality it was a way to showcase the Manzakars' military prowess in front of ambassadors from the northern kingdoms and, in particular, the southern kingdom of Dilovar.

Coxani had always looked forward to it. It was in large part what had made her decide to become a Manzakar. This year, however, was even more exciting than usual for her, because Tikran was competing in the mounted archery tournament. Two months into her training, he'd finally acquiesced and begun to teach her mounted swordplay. She'd been training with the lance, her least favorite weapon. She knew that, to a Manzakar, knowing how to wield one was as important as having expert horsemanship, but she felt awkward using it. The only move she enjoyed with the lance while on horseback was tucking it under the stirrup leather and grabbing her bow.

"You aren't going to the festival in *that*, are you?" Ola's hands were on her hips and she regarded Coxani's cadet uniform with something akin to horror.

Coxani frowned. "It's a military festival. I'm training to join the military. Why is it so scandalous that I wear my uniform?"

"Child," Ola replied, her gold bracelets tinkling as she gesticulated her frustration, "I understand that you want to be a soldier. But you must still look for a husband. And I can guarantee that you won't find one while wearing a cadet's uniform."

Struggling to hide the annoyance from her face, Coxani sighed. In addition to being headmistress of the girls' school, Ola was the concubine of one of the king's many advisors and the wife of a Manzakar. With caramel-colored hair that complemented her dark skin and eyes, Ola was a lovely woman. Now she stood before Coxani looking every bit the high-class courtesan in her crimson gown with wide tapered sleeves that had gold-edged bands around the cuffs and hemline. Over it, she wore a matching wrap that covered her shoulders and hair just enough to seem modest.

"The problem is," Coxani said, deciding honesty was the best approach, "that I love beautiful gowns just as much as any girl, but I most definitely *don't* want to attract a husband or, Cenk forbid, a protector." She wrinkled her nose in distaste.

Ola rubbed her temples. "Coxani. How many times in my lifetime, and yours, will we have this discussion? It's exhausting. How about we look at it differently then." She smiled. "You've been among men—handsome men, not to name names—all these months, looking and behaving like them.

What would it hurt for them to see you looking like a beautiful woman for a change?"

Coxani flushed. "I don't care if they see me," she insisted. "But ok. I'll change my clothes, Mistress. Just for the festival."

Ola looked relieved to have won this battle. "Good girl."

Twenty minutes later, Coxani joined Ola, the Gohari girls, and their attending eunuchs to descend from the palace and walk to the hippodrome, which was also within the Citadel's walls. The festivities had already started, and people milled all around, drinking wine or ale, eating honeyed nuts and dried pears, and waiting for the spectacle to officially begin. The king had not yet entered his gallery, so Coxani asked Ola, "May I run to the stables to wish Tikran luck?"

"Please do not run," the headmistress replied, raising an eyebrow. "But yes, go wish him luck. We got you dressed up, after all, for his eyes." She smiled.

Coxani turned away before Ola could see her face redden. That was *not* why she'd dressed up... for the most part.

"Oh, and Coxani," Ola added, "Take Alp with you. For propriety's sake. We certainly don't need any more tongues wagging over you."

The pale eunuch stepped forward, bowed dutifully at the headmistress, then looked disapprovingly at Coxani. The eunuchs were distinguished from other slaves by their shaved heads and, typically, judgmental expressions. Alp in particular had spent much of his time chasing after Coxani, and she didn't doubt he had no love for her. She made a face at him as they began to walk to the royal stables. The crowd was thick, however, and when Alp was distracted, she snuck away, weaving between boisterous revelers, running as quickly as her slippered feet would carry her.

Two hundred Manzakars readied themselves and their horses in the cool shade of the stables, outfitted in their armor, looking like gods of war. The most stunning among them were the fifty Aslan Manzakars, the king's personal warriors and the upper echelon of the Manzakars—the elite of the elite. The Aslans never failed to take Coxani's breath away, even after all these years, and she was certain Tikran would join their ranks someday. They wore full iron lamellar cuirasses, as well as plated shoulder and leg armor. And of course, those much-coveted maroon riding boots. Their gilded, domed helmets covered the nose and had layers of cloth-covered mail hanging in the back, and their intricately tooled leather belts carried their sabers, daggers, and war axes. These soldiers rarely sullied themselves with battle unless the king himself was threatened, and they were selected carefully from among the best of the Manzakars. Often, it turned out that those chosen were admired not only for their military skills, but also for being pleasing to look at. Unsurprisingly, Haydar had once been an Aslan before he became a durai—a landed, retired Manzakar—and advisor to the king himself.

Every Manzakar, Aslan or otherwise, wore a colored jacket beneath his armor with embroidered panels on the upper sleeves that revealed a heraldic emblem—which didn't indicate his family's origins, since he was a slave, but instead illustrated his reputation as a Manzakar. Coxani briefly wondered what Tikran's emblem would be when he became a Manzakar. Maybe something with a bow or sword...

"What's a pretty thing like you doing wandering around soldiers unattended?"

Coxani turned to see a Manzakar with a swarthy Gohari complexion, black mustache, and small, pointed beard staring down at her. He was older, likely in his thirties, with a criss-cross pattern of fine scars on the bridge of his nose and across his right cheek. She said, "My companion eunuch was right behind me. He must have gotten lost."

The soldier leered at her. "You're one of Haydar's little playthings, aren't you?" His gaze swept over her from head to toe, making her skin crawl. "He loves to collect little girls and boys to train. Perhaps the more appropriate word is 'groom,' eh?"

She recoiled. "That's disgusting."

He laughed. "I agree. But he knows how to pick the pretty ones, doesn't he?"

"Nasch," another Manzakar said as he walked past. "You're needed in the armory."

The soldier, Nasch, nodded but kept his eyes on her. "Watch me win the archery tournament, sweetheart. Then tell Haydar that I could teach you a thing or two." Before walking away, he winked at her.

Coxani shuddered and continued to hurry through the vaulted halls, maneuvering her way between heavily armored men and horses, peeking into every stall. She found Tikran in the very back of the stables, since he was still a cadet. But he was dressed like a Manzakar, wearing a velvet jacket lined with steel scale armor, a fluted helmet, and the yellow riding boots. He lacked the heraldic emblem but otherwise looked every bit the elite soldier. He was armed with a saber, dagger, and full archery equipment. Envy and admiration battled within Coxani as she approached and said, "Well, I suppose you clean up nicely."

He turned from his horse, which was likewise armored in leather covered by a gold-edged quilt and an intricately decorated steel chamfron. "I wish I could say the same for you," he replied with a playful grin.

Oh. Her cheeks burned.

"I'm teasing, Coxani. You look very nice." He cleared his throat and returned to tacking his horse.

"I just wanted to wish you luck out there." She hugged her

waist, suddenly hating her fitted cream-colored gown. It didn't matter that she wore a blue kaftan, sash and veil over it—she felt utterly naked. Why hadn't she just insisted on wearing her uniform? "I admit to being incredibly envious."

"With your determination and skill, I don't doubt you'll be competing in this very tournament one day soon." He flashed her a quick smile that slowly turned mischievous as his gaze shifted over her shoulder. She spun around to see an indignant eunuch stalking toward them. Tikran lowered his voice and said, "It looks like you're in trouble for wandering alone among us lecherous soldiers. Better run."

WITH A BLAST of horns and a beating of drums, the crowd hushed to watch King Delger, Queen Adiyiku, Prince Vazha and the three princesses enter their gallery, followed by the five royal mages. Below in the portico, Tikran, his fellow cadets, and the Manzakars paused their preparations to stand at attention. The king and queen sat on their thrones, flanked by their children. Prince Vazha walked with a cane and wore a mask and gloves to cover the lesions the disease had wrought. The princesses, still children, watched excitedly as the mages approached and, after bowing, moved toward the balcony that overlooked the arena.

Tikran and other senior cadets resumed helping the three Aslan Manzakar initiates, Jan, Kazbek, and Naran, get ready for the grand entrance—the Fire Game. Their armored jackets were covered in talc and black powder cartridges. The cartridges were also put on their helmets, horses, and the poles they were to carry across their shoulders. Tikran smiled at Naran. "Are you ready?"

Naran shrugged, attempting to look nonchalant as he was

turned into a human torch. "Only, what, three Manzakars have been badly burned in the last decade? I imagine my odds are decent. It does, however, feel every bit like a suicide mission." He grinned at Tikran as he mounted his horse. "Fear not, your turn is next."

Only the newly initiated Aslan Manzakars were chosen for this role, and it was viewed as something of a rite of passage. It was also used as a scare tactic during battle. Tikran grinned back. "Fear is for the weak." It was an inside joke between the two of them, as they'd been very afraid together more times than they cared to count, and they'd never even been in battle

Naran and the others lined up, and when the lance-master gave the signal, they rode out into the middle of the hippo-drome as the crowd thundered with approval. They stopped as high above in the king's gallery, one of the mages stepped forward, cloaked and hooded in deep red, with a veil covering her nose and mouth. The crowd held its collective breath as she closed her eyes and raised a hand, making symbols in the air. In a great *whoosh*, the powder cartridges on each of the three Manzakars caught fire from right to left, the flames licking high into the twilight sky. The crowd was a deafening roar as the Manzakars began galloping in three different direc-tions, standing on the saddle arches and spinning their poles above their heads.

The horns and drums echoed again through the arena marking the start of the games. The fiery Manzakars rode back into the portico, where they were doused and extinguished. Naran fell off his horse and onto Tikran deliberately, knocking the cadet to the ground and laughing. "Didn't burn to death. Your turn."

"Not yet," Tikran replied, grinning. "Aren't you up again in the tilting tournament?"

Naran groaned, dragging his hands through his blond

plaits. "That's right. Guess I should go win that really quickly." He changed into a red, flamboyant silk tunic beneath his armored vest and caparisoned his mount in similar colors. Tikran watched in admiration as Naran rode out into the hippodrome once again, in formation, while the mages above lit fireworks into the darkening sky. By firelight, the lancers divided into two teams and fought one-on-one, filling the arena with the clangor of lance striking lance and armor. True to his word, Naran won the round and returned, a victorious smile on his face.

It really was Tikran's turn now, and he slid his hand down the hard maple, horn, and sinew of his composite bow. It had been a gift from Haydar when Tikran had commenced his military training, and it was beautifully crafted, decorated with patterns in gold leaf and red paint. He was competing against men who'd been Manzakars for years, but he'd qualified to compete and knew he was up to the challenge. Naran winked at him and said, "I'd wish you luck, but you won't need it."

With a quiver full of arrows at his hip, Tikran mounted his horse and followed the other competitors out to the arena grounds, which were brightly lit with torches. No doubt the mages ensured they glowed brightly enough for a mounted archery tournament in which the goal was to hit four gourds that hung from the tops of increasingly taller poles. At the top of each player's last pole hung a golden birdcage. The aim was not to strike the bird within it, but to hit the latch that would open the door and set the bird free.

The rules were thus: the players weren't allowed to prepare their shot until their horses were in full gallop, and only two runs were allowed for the opportunity to strike every gourd and the birdcage. The first player who struck all was the winner.

Tikran had done it before, just not in front of the king,

queen, and well, pretty much all of Anzor City. His nerves hummed as he tried not to look into the sea of spectators rising on all sides.

"What's a cadet doing here?" One of the competitors, an older Manzakar that Tikran had seen on the training grounds but had never met, turned in his saddle and grimaced.

"They say he's good, Nasch," another answered. "He qualified, in any case."

The grimacing Manzakar, Nasch, replied, "Good, is he? We'll see about that." He flashed Tikran a smile that was more of a showing of teeth—and clearly an assertion of dominance.

Tikran narrowed his eyes at the fellow, looking him over and assessing him as competition. Nasch looked to be in his thirties but, like most Manzakars, had a body that aged very slowly thanks to the intensive military training. What were the chances the man had more ability and skill than Tikran himself with a bow? Tikran's gaze fell to the embroidered heraldic symbol stitched to Nasch's sleeve as the signal sounded for them to line up at the starting line. It was a silver chalice topped by a gold flame on blue.

He'd seen that insignia before.

The noise of the arena, as well as the voices of the Manzakars, faded into the background. His vision blurred. All he heard was his heartbeat swishing. Then, his mother's voice:

Promise me you'll hide yourself and your sisters, Tikran. No matter what happens, stay hidden. Do you promise?

Holding Bruneta and Evren's little hands and flattening against the earth. Making them close their eyes, giving them Wig to squeeze tightly. Hearing his mother arguing, then screaming, and peering from under the rigid canvas, his heart pounding. He saw the flaming chalice on blue, then...

Swish. Swish. Swish.

He could hear his name, as if from far away. Someone was

shouting at him. Naran. Naran was shouting expletives at him. Violently. Tikran's vision returned along with the booming thunder of the crowd. He sat at the starting line, watching as the four other Manzakars galloped off at full speed, shot arrows at their targets, then turned around and came back.

Nasch glowered at Tikran as he returned and reined his horse around. "You must have shit for brains. You can't possibly believe you have a chance to win now."

Tikran blinked. None of the others had hit all their targets in the first round. Nasch had hit all his targets but one: the birdcage at the very end.

The dust had settled. The horns sounded again. This time, Tikran moved instantly. As his horse reached a gallop, the sequence of movements came naturally to him, thanks to years of daily practice and a fierce determination. Dropping the reins, he drew an arrow from his quiver, nocked it to the silk bowstring, locked his right hand to the string, drew it taut to his cheekbone, aimed while accounting for the jostling of his mount, and released.

Nock... Draw... Anchor... Aim... Release...

Each step blended together in one continuous flow, lightning fast, smooth, and calculating. His focus on the gourds was razor sharp as his arrows struck every one, exploding them with a loud crack.

The golden birdcage was his last target. *Nock... Draw... Anchor... Aim...* At the very last millisecond, he swiveled at the waist and pointed his arrow directly at Nasch's birdcage rather than his own.

...Release.

Tikran had taken a gamble, betting that Nasch would take his time shooting his last arrow, since, in his mind, he was the definitive winner and there was no hurry. Tikran was right. His arrow hit the latch as Nasch's arrow followed, a fraction of a second too late. With a loud *clink* the cage opened and the bird a bright blue kingfisher, flew out and into the evening sky.

The din of the crowd was deafening. Nasch's face was beet-red and he was shouting at Tikran, who silently rode back to the starting line, indifferent to the consequences of his actions. He didn't know if he'd won or lost, and at this point, he didn't care.

But he knew one thing for sure: Everyone in Anzor City understood that he was not to be trifled with.

CHAPTER 6

Anzor
Three Years Later
Year 220 of the Dark Age

The enormous doors to the great hall slowly swung open. King Delger was pacing, deep in discussion with his advisors, many of whom were retired Manzakars who'd become durais. Among them was Haydar, who turned toward the doors and smiled.

Tikran sucked in his breath and walked in, flanked by two Aslan Manzakars. The great hall was also the throne room, and it was a grand sight—it was octagonal in shape, its ceiling and columns finished with carved and painted woodwork and had twenty-four clerestory stained glass windows. The light beamed through the colored glass, giving the room an other-worldly atmosphere. As Tikran approached, the king saw him and beamed.

"Tikran, good to see you, my boy." There was no mistaking Delger for anything but the king in his long, purple silk tunic embroidered with gold thread and his matching turbaned cap embellished with pearls.

Tikran knelt before Delger, bowing his head. "The honor is mine, Your Highness."

"Stand, soldier," Delger commanded, then took Tikran's hands in his own. "Do you know why I've asked you here today?"

Tikran's eyes darted quickly to Haydar and back. Haydar's expression revealed nothing, as usual. "No, Your Highness."

The king turned and walked to his throne, sitting on its edge and leaning his elbows on his knees. Delger was everything Anzor—fair-skinned, light-haired, blue-eyed. He was a stocky, well-built man who sported a beard that these days was more silver than red. He must have been approaching fifty but still had the vigor of a younger man. It was well-known that, in his youth, he had begged his father to let him train with the Manzakar cadets. His mother had been appalled by the idea of her prince training with slaves. His father, however, understanding the admiration young boys had for Anzor's elite caste of slave-soldiers, allowed it off and on. As such, Delger had something of a fighter in him, even though engaging in battle was beneath him. War was the reason Anzor imported slaves from Gohar to fight, so the blue-blood Anzori wouldn't have to sully their hands with the blood of their enemies.

"Tikran, in a month I must make the journey across Gohar to Dilovar, for diplomatic reasons," the king said, examining his immaculate nails. "As you well know, things are tense between Anzor and Dilovar. I have intelligence that King Bilguun has been sending troops creeping into northern Gohar, violating the terms of our truce." He raised his head to meet Tikran's gaze. "This is mostly a friendly visit, and I think I have a bargain I can make with him that will keep discord with Dilovar at bay, at least for the time being. That said, I do want the best of my Aslans to accompany me, if for no other reason than to strike some fear into Bilguun's heart. Anzor's Manzakars beat his fierce warriors once, and they can certainly do it again, if need be."

Tikran digested this information and was still puzzled. "Yes, Your Highness?"

Delger smiled. "How long have you been a Manzakar, Tikran?"

"A full two years, Highness."

Delger straightened. "Two years." He chuckled. "I remember the Fire Festival of 217 vividly still. I don't think anyone who witnessed what you did has forgotten it. Eight and a half seconds. By Cenk!"

Tikran's face grew hot. He hated remembering the tournament but had been forced to daily since. He had become a celebrity of sorts, both among the Manzakars and the people of Anzor City. Everyone thought he had been showing off, deliberately waiting a full round before beginning to shoot his arrows, then shooting his competition's birdcage rather than his own. They thought him a braggart, but one clearly deserving of the win. The truth was that, despite his clear, skilled actions, he'd been in a haze of fury and pain and confusion, reacting to emotions that terrified him. No one knew the truth about what had happened, not even Naran. Tikran preferred it that way. He hadn't been able to interpret his inopportune flashback, and he tried not to dwell on it. He had more important matters to attend to—like his training, as well as Coxani's. Under his tutelage, she was becoming a flight archer to be reckoned with.

"It was luck, Highness," Tikran insisted, looking down.

"Tikran, come now, don't be modest," the king said, smiling. He pointed to the heraldic symbol stitched to Tikran's sleeve: a blue kingfisher escaping a gold cage. "I'm clearly not the only one who was impressed, Tikran of the Caged Kingfisher."

In front of anyone else, Tikran would have winced. He most certainly hadn't wanted *that* as his emblem. He'd hoped for something like Haydar's insignia— an arrow in the shape of a lightning bolt. But tradition was tradition, and his teachers and fellow Manzakars had unanimously decided the caged bird best suited him. As such, "Caged Kingfisher" had become his Manzakar name.

"Your kind of mettle is rare. It's what I need at my side. *You* are what I need at my side." Delger stood. "I know it is unusual, but I am making you an Aslan Manzakar in the next several weeks and taking you to Dilovar with me. Hang the exams. I know what you are capable of."

Tikran blinked. Before he could process what Delger had said, he bowed and said by rote, "I am honored, Your Highness." *What?* Aslans were usually chosen from Manzakars who had served at least two years, and only after careful examination and a series of tests. This was definitely unusual. He was to become an Aslan *now*? And in part because of that bloody archery tournament! Tikran swallowed hard.

What followed was a blur. Handshakes, bows, smiles. "Lord" and "Highness" and standing stock still, his hands behind his back. He was offered wine and he partook, toasting to Delger, Cenk, and Anzor, in that order—the proper order.

When he was finally dismissed, Haydar accompanied him back to the barracks. Much to Tikran's chagrin, a small crowd of people—all inhabitants of the Citadel, and therefore mostly of the merchant and upper classes—awaited him outside the palace. *They're here to meet the Caged Kingfisher.* Tikran stopped dead in his tracks, contemplating turning around. Running into crowds of fans had become commonplace, unfortunately. For the past three years, he'd found himself taking alternate routes and hiding in alleyways, behind carts, trees, barrels. Haydar touched his elbow and said in a low voice, "I know how you hate attention, lad, but remember that it's part of being a Manzakar, especially a very good one."

Great. For some reason, when younger Tikran had imagined the fame of a Manzakar, he hadn't considered having to actually interact with fans. He swallowed and fixed a smile on his face as he approached the crowd. He shook hands with the men and bowed his head to the ladies, discomfited by the look in many of the women's faces. *Like they want to make a meal of me.* The only fans who genuinely made him smile were the children. He crouched down to face the smallest of them, smiling at their wide, glistening eyes.

"You're my favorite Manzakar," a boy of about five years old with golden curls said to him.

"Tell your mother to bring you by the hippodrome during the afternoon lance training," Tikran said. "I'll let you sit on my horse and hold a bow." He couldn't help but laugh when the boy immediately dashed off, calling for his mother.

When finally Tikran had greeted everyone who'd sought to speak to him, he and Haydar continued on to the barracks. Tikran let out his breath, relieved to be away from the crowd. They walked in silence for a bit, Haydar looking up at the stars, bright in a dark sky. Finally, he said, "You're surprised by Delger's decision to make you an Aslan."

Tikran's brow furrowed. "Yes, my lord. I'm not sure I deserve such an honor." He also felt somewhat cheated of the opportunity to prove himself worthy and possibly do something more amazing than the tournament of 217, so that people would stop bringing it up every time they looked at him.

Haydar continued to look at the stars. "Tikran, you earned this. Be proud."

"Yes, but—" Tikran caught his thought mid-sentence, then

continued. "Sometimes things happen that I can't be sure I can recreate." *Or want to recreate.*

Haydar looked over at the young Manzakar gravely. "Don't doubt your skills, lad. You earned those by working hard. And they will come to your aid when you need them."

For a split second, Tikran considered telling Haydar everything. But something stopped him. What would he say? *My lord, during the tournament, Nasch's insignia triggered a memory involving my mother's death that I had completely forgotten...* He would sound crazy, or worse, disloyal. Then again, there was a good chance that he had seen something that simply *looked* like Nasch's symbol during that harrowing moment... Still, Haydar was too close to the top. Haydar had once been an Aslan Manzakar to Delger, and after twenty years of service, Delger had made him a durai—a property-owning member of the gentry in his own right. Regardless of the freedoms associated with becoming a durai, Haydar would always be the king's vassal. As much as Tikran loved and admired him, it was unwise to tell Haydar too much, particularly something that seemed to implicate one of their own, either in actuality or in Tikran's mind.

Then he thought about Mago. Perhaps he could tell Mago when he saw the merchant next. Mago had been nothing short of a parent to him. And yet... Mago hadn't shared much about his Gohari ward's childhood, even when Tikran's questions were simple ones he was sure Mago knew, such as what his father looked like, or what words had been exchanged on that fateful day. Why would Mago continue to be silent even as Tikran reached adulthood? The only explanation was that he knew something that he didn't want Tikran to know. So how could Tikran trust that the old slave trader wouldn't lie to him?

There was, of course, Naran. While he would have been the best choice as a confidante a couple of years ago, Tikran worried that Naran's life as an Aslan Manzakar had changed him, maybe hardened him. Tikran closed his eyes briefly, breathing steadily. For some reason, one person stood out in his mind as the best option: his pupil, the only person who could possibly understand his inner turmoil—because she had shared so much of her inner turmoil with him, and he knew she would hear him out without judgment.

Tikran's training of Coxani had lasted far longer than the six months he'd initially anticipated. But Haydar had been right—the longer he trained her, the better his own skills became, both as a warrior and a leader. "I am taking Coxani to Tenzin in a few days to finish the last segment of her Level Three training," he said.

"Good. I will notify the king and we will delay your induction into the Aslan ranks until you return." Haydar put his hands behind his back and looked at the ground. "I'm pleased that her training has gone so well. It has been thanks to you."

"Not entirely, my lord. Coxani is a fast learner, and you were right about her skills with a bow. She will make a formidable Manzakar."

The durai looked at Tikran. "You have a good relationship with her, I can tell. When I decided you would be the one to mentor her, I knew that although you both have strong personalities, a harmony could happen with time."

Tikran nodded, unsure of what to say.

"You know," Haydar continued, smiling with mirth, "my intentions—as well as Mago's—in having you train her were not entirely honorable."

Tikran looked at him then, bemused. "My lord?"

"I admit we hoped—still hope—for a love match," he replied, still smiling. "What strong young warriors the two of you would produce! Not to mention beautiful."

Tikran could feel his face flush a dark red beneath his tanned skin. He was at a loss for words. He managed an, "Oh."

"I know she's your charge, and you've taken your duties very seriously and behaved honorably, as you should, and as neither Mago nor I had any doubt you would. But..." He winked at Tikran mischievously. "Consider this my, ehm, granting you permission to pursue a romantic relationship with her, if you are so inclined."

"I... ah..." Tikran stammered, thunderstruck. What in Cenk's name was he supposed to say to that? *Thank you?* It seemed wholly inappropriate, especially considering Coxani was not part of this decision. What if she had no desire to have a romantic relationship with *him*?

"You needn't respond, lad." Haydar laughed, reading his mind. "Just take my blessing to Tenzin with you. And return ready to accompany the king on a diplomatic mission to Dilovar—as an Aslan Manzakar."

CHAPTER 7

The smell of the ocean tinged the air long before Tikran and Coxani saw water. They rode side by side on their geldings at a comfortable clip toward Tenzin, Anzor's sleepy seaside town. It was the third day of their journey, and they would arrive at the military outpost shortly after midday supper. At night, they had been making camp in the woods just off the well-traveled road rather than staying at an inn, which would have caused quite the scandal. Not only were the pair unmarried and unchaperoned, but Coxani was clearly a Manzakar cadet. The combination would have drawn attention that neither of them wanted.

Now, as they approached Anzor's coast, Tikran looked at his charge sidelong. "Are you nervous?" he asked.

Coxani's expression betrayed no emotions. "*Nervous* is an understatement. I'm both ecstatic and terrified. Every body of water I've ever seen has had land on the horizon."

Tikran smiled. He'd come to appreciate Coxani's openness, her willingness to be vulnerable with him. It had, to an extent, relaxed his own inclination to keep every emotion buried deep.

It certainly helped keep his mind off his unexpected and imminent induction into the Aslan ranks. "It's overwhelming at first, I won't lie. But once you get used to it, it's quite relaxing."

Snapping him a look, she said, "Relaxing? Maybe when you aren't in the water. What about all those... *things* under there? The thought certainly isn't relaxing."

"Coxani, learning to swim is part of a Manzakar's training. You want to become a Manzakar, no?" Despite his words, Tikran understood her reluctance. Gohari slaves likely never saw the ocean, since their lives were confined to Anzor City and the Citadel. The last segment of Level Three training was the first time most Manzakar cadets ever laid eyes on the vast stretch of water.

"Well of course I'm going to do it." She rolled her eyes. "But I certainly don't like it. Besides, Anzor has never been attacked by sea. It's training time wasted."

"I thought we covered this." Tikran rubbed his face. "What would you do, little Miss Manzakar, if we *were* ever attacked by sea? Hmm? An entire empire falls because its oh-so elite caste of soldiers can't swim. Is it worth the risk? Or, for that matter, the embarrassment?"

"Do *not* call me that," she retorted, shooting him a dirty look, then falling quiet for several minutes. Out of nowhere, she exploded with laughter.

"What in the name of Cenk...?"

"I'm just imagining," she said through her laughter, "all of us idiots sinking to the bottom of the ocean in our armor."

Tikran cracked a smile. "Yes. It's absolutely hilarious."

They reached Tenzin at the hottest part of the day, but the ocean breeze was cooling and pleasant. As they finally came into view of the water, Coxani stopped her horse. Shading her eyes with her hand, she gaped at the endless expanse as it gradated from the darkest blue to a bright, crystal turquoise and eventually ended in white crested waves on the shore. Ships with curved prows and lateen sails dotted the horizon, and the water itself rolled and breathed beneath them. Dolphins leaped ahead of one ship in a beautiful formation of eight. "It's *alive*," she whispered, in awe.

They finally arrived at the fort and the soldiers watched Tikran with a mixture of admiration, envy, and resentment. Most were Gohari slaves who had not been able to complete the required Manzakar training or for some reason had been discharged dishonorably. They watched Coxani, on the other hand, with mostly contempt—they were likely put off by the fact that she had traveled with a man, unattended by a eunuch, and, to make things worse, was clearly training to become a Manzakar.

"Intolerable brutes," Coxani grumbled to Tikran as they led their horses to the stable. "They can't stand seeing a woman succeed where they couldn't."

"I think," Tikran said with a chuckle, "it's more that I can travel with a beautiful woman without a eunuch breathing down my neck."

Coxani looked at Tikran in shock. He saw her expression and paused, confused. "What's wrong?"

"Nothing." She raised an eyebrow and smiled. "Except that you think I'm beautiful."

He blinked. "I didn't say that."

"Yes, you did."

"No, what I meant was that the *soldiers* think you're beautiful," he insisted, tethering his horse in the shade of the mews, his heart increasing its pace ever so slightly. Haydar's words had been replaying in his head since the night of his audience with the king in spite of his attempts to push them from his mind. And at eighteen, Coxani was nothing less than stunning. Her face had caught up with her nose and sculpted cheekbones had emerged from the baby fat. Her eyes were as large and green as ever and her mouth was wide, with full lips shaped like, well, a bow. He knew that underneath her cadet's attire she was most definitely a woman (the vision of her in that fitted gown at the Fire Festival of 217 was seared permanently into his memory), but personal experience on the training grounds had taught him that she did not lack muscle either. Her ability to embrace both the feminine and masculine sides of herself enhanced her beauty all the more.

But... something about initiating an intimate relationship with her felt wrong. What if she relented, not out of desire for him, but simply because he, as a man and her trainer, had more power than she did? Coxani was not afraid to assert herself, to be sure, but... The idea didn't sit right with him. Moreover, he didn't want to feel the sting of rejection in the case that she was not interested or worse, repulsed.

"All right." Coxani frowned and turned away. "As if it would cost you anything to admit it."

Tikran laughed out loud. "Coxani, you are my charge, and a woman to boot. Surely you understand what it would cost me."

She grinned. "Then you *do* think I'm beautiful?"

Tikran rubbed his face to avoid looking her in the eyes. "Let's unsaddle and feed these horses, then go learn how to swim, shall we?"

Not long after, the pair made their way down from the fort's perch on a rocky cliff to a secluded pebble beach below, where Coxani stripped down to her shirt, which was layered over her chemise, and breeches. It was high tide, and the waves, while not large, were aggressively reaching inland. He could see the fear in her eyes as she waded knee-deep into the water. She turned to look at him. "There must be a better way."

He smiled. "This isn't really a swimming lesson, Coxani.

It's just to get you used to the pull of the ocean. Remember not to fight it. Let it pull and push you, and use it to move where you want to go."

She cocked her head at him. "Would you care to demonstrate?"

"No."

"Well then, I don't believe you know how." She grinned mischievously.

Why did he always take the bait? More specifically, *her* bait? He'd hoped to stay mostly dry for the first lesson. Muttering oaths, he yanked off his turbaned cap, shed his sword belt and boots, and stripped down to his drawers. Then he marched resolutely into the water and dove into the waves, emerging with a shake of the head.

She ventured further into the water, smiling broadly. "Go deeper. Surely you can still touch the floor from there."

He was treading water. "I can't," he said. "That's the thing about the ocean floor. It will suddenly—"

In an instant, Coxani disappeared into the waves. He sucked in his breath and dove. Within seconds, he'd pulled her to the surface and dragged her to shallow waters. She sputtered and coughed, frantically trying to wipe the wet hair from her eyes. "The bloody water stings!" she cried.

Tikran battled the urge to laugh—until she stood up in the lapping waves, dripping and frustrated. His desire to laugh vanished, along with most of his coherent thoughts. Those curves he remembered all too well were on display under the wet, clinging clothes. He suddenly realized that he hadn't thought this whole excursion through thoroughly. He and Coxani had fallen into such an easy rhythm over the course of three years that he hadn't considered the implications.

No, he hadn't thought this through at all.

Once again, Haydar's words rushed back to him. Once again, he forced them from his mind.

He stood as well and said, "You've had a long day of travel. Maybe we begin fresh tomorrow morning?"

She glared at him, blinking the salt water from her bloodshot eyes. "I'm not tired. I want to try again."

Well, shit. He'd known it would be her answer. It was always her answer. He raked his wet locks from his face with his fingers and said, "All right. You know where the floor drops now. Stay in the shallow waters for the moment, as you acclimate to the feel of the waves."

She tried twice more to keep her head above water beyond the drop. Twice more, he had to dive down and bring her back up. Finally, as the sun had nearly completely sunk beneath the sparkling horizon, she said, "By the end of this training, I will have either drunk or breathed in half the ocean. I'm done for today, I think."

Thank Cenk! It wasn't that Tikran was tired of teaching her. Rather, he needed a few hours to collect his thoughts and prepare himself for the sight—and feel—of Coxani's body, minus her armor and most of her clothing. He was a soldier, after all. He knew how to shut distractions out and focus on the task at hand... regardless of how beautiful those distractions may be. He'd been doing it successfully for three years.

Back on the beach, Tikran unrolled two cotton sheets and handed one to Coxani. She looked furious. He said, "Go easy on yourself. This isn't going to happen in one afternoon."

"I would be able to do it if..." She huffed, exasperated. Then she dropped the sheet he had handed her, yanked her soaking shirt from over her head, and pushed the breeches down into a puddle at her feet. In the twilight, she stood in her chemise and underpants, looking like an angry goddess of the sea. The thin, gauzy material left nothing to the imagination—not the color or size of her nipples, nor the fact that she had a patch of darkness further down, at the juncture of her legs. She said, "I am wearing *twice* as much as a male cadet would be wearing to learn how to swim. It's simply not fair."

Tikran breathed evenly, keeping his eyes fixed on hers. He lifted her sheet from the ground and held it out to her. "Before you make a scandal of us both," he said, his voice low, "perhaps you should wrap yourself in this."

She snatched it from him, grumbling. "Cenk forbid men learn to handle the sight of a naked woman without losing their minds. Cenk forbid women be given the same permissions as men."

When she was finally wrapped in her sheet, he let out his breath slowly. "I don't disagree with you. But right now isn't the best time to make a statement."

"Is there ever a good time?" she retorted.

He was quiet for a moment before answering, "I suppose not." He couldn't resist grinning at her and adding, "A better time would be when I'm not around."

She rolled her eyes. "Coward." After a moment, she said, "That's one of several things the Anzori could learn from us lowly Gohari."

"What's that?"

"In Gohar, women are just as respected as the men," she said. "One of the few things I remember about our people is the huntresses. They were not separated from the hunters. They were fierce and treated with esteem."

"That is true," Tikran conceded. His own mother had been one of them, hunting alongside his father often. He chose not to tell her that this "equality" extended beyond hunting. He remembered seeing unmarried youths copulate practically out in the open—boys with boys, boys with girls, girls with girls. His mother had explained to him what they were doing and called it "learning love." This unrestricted sexual exploration obviously scandalized the Anzori to no end, as only a man and woman could be bound under Cenk, and only men were allowed to seek sexual pleasure outside of marriage—and definitely *not* with other men, *or* out in the open.

Tikran had dreaded the endless lectures on morality that he and his fellow cadets had received in class as their teachers attempted to wipe the Gohari influence from the boy slaves—particularly their homophile tendencies. Tikran smiled inwardly at the futility of it all. Someone should have told them that keeping adolescent girls sequestered from adolescent boys while encouraging close male bonds within the barracks was hardly helping their cause. In fact, it was a recipe for "learning love" between men.

The group baths certainly didn't help, either.

Despite their condemnation of same sex relations, however, the Anzori tended to turn a blind eye to what went on in the barracks, so long as it was discreet. Tikran had only had a couple relationships himself, with Manzakars and other cadets, and they had been very covert. Since open displays of affection between men were impossible, his relationships had also been primarily sexual. From a soldier's perspective, he'd convinced himself that this worked well, since it allowed him to avoid any emotional entanglements that might derail his training.

They trudged back to the fort, draped in sheets and carrying their clothing in bundles beneath their arms. A woman—an innkeeper—waited for Coxani just outside. Coxani would stay at the inn a mile away while Tikran would stay at the hold with the soldiers. As they approached, they could see the glowering look of disapproval on the innkeeper's matronly face. It was a familiar look to them and they mostly shrugged it off. People who had issue with the arrangement could take it to Lord Haydar, if it upset them so.

"I will be ready tomorrow morning," she said to him, that look of determination he had come to know so well furrowing her brow and gleaming in her eyes.

He grinned. "I don't doubt it. Until tomorrow, soldier."

As she headed off to the inn with the discontented innkeeper, he leaned against the rough stone of the fort.

She would be ready. He had to be ready too.

True to her word, Coxani was ready the following morning at dawn, waiting for Tikran in shallow water. Tikran too was ready—or so he believed.

"The water is cold in the morning," she said to him as he waded into the water toward her.

"Indeed," he said. He dove into a wave and reemerged seconds later, wiping the salt water from his face. "Did you never go to the Damla River back in Gohar?" The river separated Gohar from its mountainous eastern neighbor, Dilovar.

She rolled her eyes. "You seem to forget I was four years old when I left Gohar. I hardly remember a river, let alone whether it was cold or not in the morning."

"You're right," he conceded. "I do forget. In any case, the river's water was always cold, no matter the time of day. But on a winter morning, it was icy. I know because when I was around five years old, I was fishing with my mother and fell in. I think I went into shock, it was so cold. Luckily, I was in relatively shallow water and my mother was able to grab me quickly. Her hands warmed me immediately. It could have been disastrous, since neither she nor my father could swim."

"You were definitely lucky." She bobbed in the water to

avoid a wave in the face. "I admit it's probably a valuable skill to have. It's just..." She grimaced. "Every time something slimy brushes against my legs, I have to resist the urge to bolt to dry land."

He smiled. "It's most likely seaweed." He reached down to the bottom and felt for a slimy patch, then pulled the green, blade-like algae out of the water to show her. "It's harmless. And tasty, or so I've heard."

She wrinkled her nose. "I'll pass, thank you."

"In that case," he replied, tossing the seaweed back into the water, "shall I teach you how to float?"

For the next hour, Tikran lifted Coxani gently with one hand as she lay on her back, tilting her chin upward and breathing slowly. Finally, Tikran grinned at her. She kept her head level but rolled her eyes in his direction. "What?"

"I'm no longer holding you," he replied, backing away. "You're floating on your own."

She grinned at the sky. With renewed confidence, she ventured out into deeper water, learning to float on her stomach with her face submerged. A couple more hours passed, then they took a break and had lunch on the beach, in the shade of a tall date palm.

After devouring her share of bread, cheese, and fish, Coxani leaned back on her elbows and looked out over the water. "It's beautiful here. I could see myself living near the ocean."

Tikran shook his head. "You've chosen the life of a Manza-kar. We are horsemen of the steppe, bred to survive dry, desolate lands." She made a face and he asked, "What?"

"That word," she answered. "*Bred.* As if the Gohari are animals."

"If we were animals, the Anzori wouldn't hold us in such high regard."

She shifted to face him. "Do they hold us in high regard?

Perhaps like prize horses?" She sighed deeply and shook her head. "We are slaves, Tikran."

"I don't think of it as slavery as much as... patronage. We can do what we want with our lives in Anzor."

"Oh, *can* we?" The color crept into her cheeks and he knew she was getting worked up. "Can any of us marry an Anzori, should we choose to do so? Can we leave the Citadel freely? Can we leave Anzor freely, for that matter? Can I, as a Gohari woman, choose *not* to marry or have children? Can I choose not to become a courtesan if an Anzori noble decides he wants me? Can I choose to open a shop in the city and live alone if it's my preference? An Anzori woman can. But a Gohari woman? No. I have no choices." She curled her lip. "Even as a Manzakar, I will never become a durai and own property, and I must eventually find a husband to provide for me and be forced to bear his children."

"I'm not sure a Gohari man has choices either, Coxani," Tikran said. "If a male slave shows no inclination to become a soldier, he is limited to becoming a servant, or worse, a eunuch."

"Indeed!" The color was bright in her cheeks now. "And you say we aren't slaves. Ha! Even for you Manzakars, it's an illusion of freedom."

Tikran draped his arms over his knees. "But what kind of lives would we have in Gohar? One of desperate poverty, landless, homeless, chasing our food and dying of illness."

She huffed and crossed her arms. "Don't tell me you believe that shit about Anzor 'saving' the Gohari from Archil's heresy."

"I don't know what I believe. But I do know what my lot is in life, and I'm determined to make the best of it."

Coxani shook her head in frustration. "Tikran, I hope you realize that if you were a woman, your *lot* would be as a man's property. You would be forced to open your legs to whichever man—or men—chose you, whenever the urge struck him. And if you resisted, those men would have the right by law to beat you senseless. You would always be a slave, no matter how they dressed you up and fed you and had you bear their children. And they'd expect you to be forever grateful to them for saving you, lowly Gohari woman that you are." She was breathing hard now, her eyes blazing with passion.

Tikran held up his hands in defeat. "I admit, I've never considered it from a woman's perspective. That certainly sounds like slavery to me. Coxani, I'm on your side, I swear it."

Her expression softened, her shoulders relaxed. Looking down at her hands, she said, "That's one of the things I've always loved about you, you know."

A frisson of discomfort ran through him. As usual, he felt out of his depths in the realm of emotions. He tried to jest about it. "What? My lack of conviction in what I believe?"

"No." She met his eyes. "You may be a fierce Aslan Manzakar destined for glory, but you will never be a brainless killer."

Tikran started. "Wait. How did you know...?"

She sighed, smiling. "Oh, Tikran. Word travels quickly in our world." She cocked her head. "Are congratulations in order, or...?"

He took a deep breath and gazed out at the waves, squinting. This was his chance to open up to her. "I'm not sure. I think I was promoted to Aslan prematurely by King Delger because of that bloody Fire Festival. And I'm not sure that's a good thing." He paused, collecting his thoughts. "You probably wondered why I hated talking about it, hated hearing people rave about what I did." He scratched his chin. "It's hard to explain, but it had to do with Nasch."

She snorted. "But of course, he's known for being a real

asshole. He made my flesh crawl that night. I was thrilled that you beat him."

He shook his head. "It wasn't the taunts that got to me. That kind of thing doesn't bother me, I can handle it."

"So what was it?"

He licked his lips. "We were getting ready at the starting line, and I looked at his mark—you know, the silver chalice with the flame—and I was suddenly back in a memory I'd completely blocked out. I'm certain it was the day of my mother's death. She told me to hide myself and my sisters, she made me swear I wouldn't come out once we were hidden. Of course, I did what she wanted. I was a child. I was terrified. But as we hid, there was a... an altercation of some sort. I heard men's voices as well as my mother's, which got shriller until it was a scream. I held my sisters' hands and told them to close their eyes and not open them until I said to. I tried to see what was happening, and that's when I caught a glimpse of it."

Coxani's eyes were enormous. "Nasch's symbol?"

He took a deep breath. "Yes. Or something that looked just like it."

"Did you see men? Your mother?"

"I can't remember anything beyond what I've told you." He set his jaw. "As for the tournament, I didn't start with the others only because I was consumed by this lost memory. When I finally became aware of the world around me again, my competitors were returning from the first round and readying themselves for the second. The memory, it triggered a —madness in me. My mind was suddenly crystal clear, and I just..." He sought for the right word, landing on, "...performed. Better than I ever have."

Her hand was suddenly on his. It was warm and damp from the sea. "Oh, Tikran. I don't know what to say. How could

Nasch have been there the day your mother died? Or worse—been somehow involved in it?"

"I don't know. Maybe I've gone crazy." He chuckled.

She bit her lip pensively. "You're not crazy. You were a boy who was traumatized by his mother's death. You suppressed the memory, and for some reason, Nasch's emblem made you remember."

"Yes. Well." He moved his hand out from under hers and stood. "There's still plenty of daylight left. Would you like to learn how to tread water?"

She stood, a peculiar look on her face. "Remember when I said you'd become an asshole?"

"Compared to when I was seven?" He grinned. "How could I forget."

"Well, I was wrong." She smiled up at him. "You're much more than the pretty brute I initially thought you were."

He raised an eyebrow. "Er, thank you?"

"There's a depth to you that..." she stopped, looked away, and shrugged. "...that I just hadn't seen yet." She said suddenly, "Let's go tread some water before I lose my nerve."

———

By the time they left Tenzin two weeks later, Coxani could swim. More or less. At the very least, she knew how to *not* drown.

They packed their belongings and began their three-day journey back to Anzor City. Coxani had a lot on her mind. She was struggling with a torrent of feelings that she had never felt, nor knew how to manage.

Tikran was becoming a problem.

Over the course of eleven years, she'd often wondered what became of the sweet boy who had been her greatest comfort at a very difficult time—for both of them. She'd kept Wig in her arms almost continuously for two years, sewing him up when his seams fell apart, washing him gently when he fell in the dirt. These days the rabbit sat on her shelf, amidst her favorite books and trinkets, like a holy relic. When she and Tikran were reintroduced and he began to train her three years ago, she'd felt immense disappointment. The boy she had adored at the age of four had become... one of *them*.

A man. A soldier. A lackey.

But what had she expected? Tucked away in the barracks, learning to fight and kill in the name of Cenk, to die protecting the king...

At some point early in her training with him, she'd accepted it and decided to use him to her advantage. She, after all, did not want the fate of a Gohari woman in Anzor. And she was willing to do whatever it took to ensure that her fate was different. Tikran was her opportunity, her way out of that fate, and Haydar had been more than willing to grant her access to him. She would learn to become a warrior if it killed her, and Tikran would teach her. If she was destined to be a slave, she would be a dangerous one.

Of course, she would not be human if she hadn't admitted to herself that the beautiful boy had grown into a beautiful man. This, she was willing to concede. And she'd be lying to herself if she didn't admit that watching him was enjoyable, not just because he was beautiful, but because his skills in mounted archery, horsemanship, and swordplay were unsurpassed. She'd become content with her situation, despite the fact that Tikran had turned out to be, for the most part, just another exceptional soldier. But over time, as she got to know him better, she began to realize that this man had self-awareness, and layers, and even insecurities that he was willing to expose to her. He'd listened empathetically when she ranted about how unjustly Gohari women were treated in Anzor, and when he'd told her the story about the tournament and his flashback, he'd been utterly vulnerable.

And over the course of three years, to her dismay, she found herself not just liking him but *wanting* him. Now more than ever. She did not need that complication right now—or ever. She would never be a wife, if she could help it. She would most certainly never be a courtesan to one of those intolerable Anzori noblemen. She would never bring children into this world of slavery, regardless of how opulent it seemed. She would sooner die.

But holy Cenk, seeing Tikran in nothing but his drawers and completely wet... The man was nearly six feet of lean, firm, masculine beauty.

"So," he said, drawing her out of her thoughts. "What was it like, growing up at the girls' school?"

She considered for a moment, then said, "Boring."

"Ha. Tell me more."

She looked at him, perplexed. It was as though he'd read her thoughts and decided to confuse her further by showing interest in her life. *Curse you, Tikran.* "Well, we spent a lot of time learning about and worshipping Cenk."

"I believe we both endured quite a bit of that," he said. "What else?"

"We learned etiquette—how to dress, hold polite conversation, eat, sit, walk..." She chose not to tell him that they were schooled in certain bedroom manners as well, including how to undress oneself in front of another, how to flirt without seeming to flirt, how to read the nuances of body language... "We also learned calligraphy, painting, sewing, and cooking. My painting isn't bad, but I'm an awful cook. I nearly burned the kitchens down once or twice."

"Why am I not surprised?"

She ignored him, squelching the urge to smile. "We read poetry and literature. We were taught how to make conversation on philosophy and religion. We had elocution classes to beat the Gohari accent out of us."

"That last bit sounds familiar as well."

"We learned to play the lute and sing. I discovered very quickly that I am definitely no nightingale. I've been asked to *stop* singing more times than I can count."

He laughed. "Let me hear you."

"Absolutely not." She still didn't look at him. "It was just all so... infuriating. I was not cut out for any of it. Compared to the other girls, I felt clumsy and awkward."

"Clearly, you were not meant to be one of them. You were meant to be a Manzakar."

A warmth suffused her chest. She turned to find him smiling at her, his eyes twinkling. He was determined to make things much, much more difficult for her. *Curse you, Tikran...*

Coxani was quieter than usual the first two days of their journey home, which Tikran should have counted as a blessing, but in fact, it bothered him. Her chattering about everything and anything under the sun had grown on him—had begun to give him a level of comfort, even. He stole looks at her contemplative face as she stared absently ahead. Something was clearly preoccupying her, and he worried a bit, but also hoped it had nothing to do with him.

"Coxani."

She turned to look at him as if coming out of a dream. "Yes?"

He cleared his throat. "It's getting dark. We should stop for the night."

She hesitated before answering, "Yes, all right."

Within the shelter of their leather tent, Tikran paused before blowing out the candle of their lantern and looked at Coxani. She lay turned away from him on her unfurled bedroll, a wool blanket over her legs.

"Coxani," he said. "Are you all right? You have me worried."

She turned to look at him, her mouth set in a line and her brow creased. "May I ask you a personal question?"

Oh, no. He swallowed and replied, "Maybe?"

She pursed her lips before asking, "Have you ever had sex?"

Oh... shit. "Ah... Coxani, this is hardly appropriate—"

"We are friends, aren't we?" There was an almost demanding tone to her voice.

He took a long, deep breath, looking up at the folds of leather above them, one hand behind his head. "Not with a woman, but yes."

She lifted herself up on her elbow, contemplating his words. "Would you ever... *want* to with a woman?"

He suddenly had a feeling he knew where this line of questioning was leading. His body tingled. "Perhaps."

She looked down, biting her lip, high color in her cheeks. Quietly, she asked, "Would you want to with me?"

He froze, unable to think properly. All the blood from his brain was flooding his groin. He finally stammered, "But young women who... How will you find..."

Coxani smiled. "I have no desire to marry or have children, if I can help it. I will become a Manzakar any time now. My life is as much mine as I can make it." She licked her lips. "The only real question is, do you want me as much as I want you?"

His heart thumped in his ears. He had no idea what to say. Haydar's words played in his mind yet again. The durai hadn't been cryptic—this was exactly what he'd meant. *Take my blessing to Tenzin with you...* And now, *she* was the one initiating intimacy.

Tikran met her gaze and held it. Of course he wanted her. He'd wanted her for far longer than he cared to admit. He was just very good at reining in his thoughts and feelings, at taming his base urges and focusing on what needed to be done. Those Manzakars who did not learn that discipline rarely climbed to the top—and most certainly didn't stay there for long.

She must have seen the ardor in his eyes, because she stood and, very slowly, as if to give him time to protest, began removing her shirt and breeches, then her chemise and underpants. She kneeled beside him, all smooth, taut, golden skin, and unbraided her hair, letting her thick brown curls cascade over dark pink nipples. Her movements were fluid and sensual, almost like a dance.

Tikran's brain may not have been functioning, but his body most certainly was. He sat up, cupped her face between his hands, and brought her lips to his. She opened her mouth against his, flicking her tongue against his lower lip and, taking his hand, placed his palm on her breast. Tikran broke the kiss abruptly, his eyes wide. "Wait... have *you* ever...?"

She smiled coquettishly. "Not with a man. But yes."

He ran his thumb ever so lightly over her nipple. "So this will be a first for both of us."

She sucked in her breath at the sensation, then began unlacing his breeches, grazing him with her fingers and making him gasp in return. Leaning in to kiss him, she whispered, "Promise me that after this, nothing changes."

"I promise," he muttered, wrapping his arm around her waist and pulling her down with him.

CHAPTER 8

Coxani squeezed through the crowd of onlookers to the royal stables, where a hundred Manzakar cavalrymen, including the Aslans, were loading their supplies for the long journey to Dilovar. They were dressed in their armor, their gilded helmets and shields glittering in the sun. She shaded her eyes and scanned the soldiers for Tikran, finally spotting him with Mago.

"Did he come bearing date cookies?" she asked as she approached them. She embraced Mago enthusiastically, nearly knocking the portly old man over.

"He did. I needed a whole batch of them for the trip," Tikran teased.

Mago gazed at him, pride shining in his face. Coxani felt a twinge of envy. "I always knew you'd end up among the guardians of the king himself, my boy," Mago said. "How do you feel?"

"As a soldier, I feel ready," Tikran answered. After a pause, he added, "As a Gohari, I feel a bit apprehensive about returning to Gohar after so many years."

"Hmm." Mago nodded. "I know, lad. Rest assured, that's quite normal. Just remember, without the Manzakars, Gohar would have fallen into chaos a long time ago."

Tikran nodded, exchanging looks with Coxani when Mago wasn't watching. Gohar had become an Anzori colony one hundred years after the death of Archil and the onset of the Dark Age. While the Anzori did not settle in Gohar—for it bore very few natural resources—they set up garrisoned outposts throughout Gohar and "maintained the peace" between the various Gohari tribes, as well as imported slaves to serve in Anzor's renowned military. Anzor also regulated the use of magic in Gohar ruthlessly, claiming that the Essence would be devastating in the hands of the Gohari, possibly annihilating all of mankind. Any Gohari found to have the Essence was taken to Anzor to serve the king. If they refused, they would be imprisoned or, in some cases, executed. Luckily, having even a little bit of Essence was rare, and having a lot even rarer.

But this was where Coxani's knowledge ended. She and Tikran had discussed it at length, and he knew no more than she. Other than the grand fire displays of the mages at the various Anzori festivals and the reassurance that Cenk's Essence maintained peace and prosperity, neither of them had any real sense of what the Essence was, or what having it meant. She doubted anyone but those closest to the king knew.

Mago set a hand on Tikran's shoulder and smiled. "During the months that you are gone, I will watch over Coxani."

Before Coxani could express outrage, Tikran laughed and said, "Mago, I have been training her for three years now, and I can guarantee you that she most definitely does not need anyone watching over her."

"What a compliment," Coxani said, beaming. Her smile slowly faded. He would be gone seven months. Three months to travel there, one month in Dilovar, and three months to get back—assuming all went smoothly. She would miss him. "So you're really off, then, eh?"

He shrugged. "It certainly seems like it."

"I wish I could go with you." What she wouldn't give to be journeying across Gohar as a real Manzakar!

"Your turn is coming." He winked at her and desire rushed right through her, leaving her feeling hungry for him. Since their trip to Tenzin, she and Tikran had shared several more intimate encounters—under the trees at the training grounds, in the straw of an empty horse stall, against the wall of a garden and under the cover of night... And yet, as he'd promised, their relationship remained the same, their camaraderie unchanged. They'd agreed that an official "romance" would create expectations that neither one of them desired to meet, and so kept their dalliance secret. She was very careful to track her cycles and ensure that she and Tikran did their best to avoid certain devastating consequences. In spite of her initial reservations, the arrangement was perfect for the both of them, at least for the time being.

"I'll leave you two to your goodbyes," Mago said with an impish, gap-toothed grin. "Safe travels, my boy, and return to us safely!"

Mago turned and disappeared back into the crowd, and Coxani said, "Do you ever get the feeling Mago is trying to make a love match of us?"

Tikran looked away. "Not really. Why?"

"Manzakar, at attention!" A tall, broad-shouldered Manzakar swaggered over and glared at Tikran. The soldier couldn't keep the fierceness on his face for long and broke out into a grin. He looked at Coxani and cleared his throat, addressing Tikran. "Soldier, aren't you going to introduce us?"

Tikran rolled his eyes. "Naran, this is Coxani, the cadet I've been training. Coxani, this is Naran, the junior commander of the Aslans and the biggest jackass you'll ever meet."

"*You* are Tikran's charge?" Naran's eyes widened in astonishment.

Coxani crossed her arms, immediately on the defensive. "Yes, why?"

Naran stepped closer, bowed, and smiled at her, a deep dimple in one cheek. "Your idiot teacher somehow failed to mention that, in addition to being one of the best flight archers he's ever seen, his pupil is also unbelievably gorgeous."

Tikran groaned and Coxani blushed in spite of herself. Naran was a big man—taller and broader than Tikran. His long, straw-colored ropes of hair were tied back in a queue and his eyes were amber-colored, which were striking in contrast to his deeply bronze complexion. Unlike Tikran, he was not what one would call beautiful, but something about his strong features made him attractive. Also unlike Tikran, this Manzakar looked her over brazenly in admiration, his eyes meeting hers unabashedly.

She returned his smile, suddenly feeling uncharacteristically bashful. "I've seen you many times before," she said, looking up pointedly at his yellow locks. "You're hard to miss." She glanced at his heraldic insignia—a pacing lion with a full, bright yellow mane—and stifled a smile. It was utterly fitting.

"No doubt." He chuckled. "When do you graduate?"

"In the next couple weeks."

"Your mentor will be missing your graduation?" Naran looked back at Tikran.

"It's not a big deal. This is far more important," she insisted.

"I'm still sorry to miss it," Tikran said, looking at her fondly. "I am incredibly proud of you."

Coxani felt the heat returning to her face. She needed to say her farewells quickly before she inadvertently revealed too much of what she was thinking and feeling. "Well," she said, "I suppose this is goodbye for now."

Naran watched in obvious amusement as she and Tikran faced each other, unsure of what to do. Then Coxani punched Tikran playfully in the arm and, in an attempt to sound tough, said, "Try not to get yourself killed." Before he could respond, she hurried off, weaving her way out of the stable.

THE MANZAKARS RODE SURROUNDING the king's carriage, as well as those of his entourage of servants and advisors, as the royal party of two hundred left Anzor City behind. Naran and Tikran were a part of the banner-guard and led the way, occasionally undertaking reconnaissance ahead of the party. Tikran had caught a glimpse of Nasch among the rearguards, protecting the supply train. He was commander of a squadron of Manzakars that was responsible for ensuring supplies reached the garrison towns and for generally keeping the peace between the various tribes in Gohar, and so was often out campaigning. Since that fateful tournament, Nasch had not avoided Tikran, but had not sought him out either. Occasionally when they were in the same company their eyes locked and Tikran knew, without a doubt, that Nasch had neither forgotten nor forgiven. He was certain that, if given the chance, Nasch would try to bring him down several notches.

Try being the operative word. Tikran feared him like he feared a gnat buzzing around his head.

As the royal party approached the Anzor-Gohar border, Tikran's stomach tightened in anticipation. Unbidden, his father's words returned to him: *When you are a powerful Manzakar, you will send for us and we will come to you.* He shook his head, smiling sadly to himself. What horseshit his father had fed him to make selling his son into slavery easier. Even if Tikran wanted to, how could he "send for" his father and sisters? They were nomads with no formal identities under Anzori law. It would be like looking for needles in a haystack—assuming those needles were even still alive.

The transition from Anzor to Gohar was much starker than Tikran remembered. As they left the heavily guarded border behind, the landscape quickly changed from green to brown, from fertile to barren. Rocky, flat-topped hills punctuated a sea of dry grass that stretched as far as the eye could see, whispering with hidden life. There were no trees, no splashes of color within the grass, and the sky was clear of clouds. The paved stone road that connected the garrison towns had been built by the Anzori and was the only one in Gohar. It weaved through the plains, a river of gray.

"Ah, home sweet home," Naran muttered under his breath.

Tikran stole a look at his friend. "It's very strange, seeing Gohar again. It's a lot like I remember it."

"It doesn't change," Naran replied, his expression sober. "The winters are bitterly cold, the summers scorching hot. Water is scarce, and food is scarcer. How anyone survives out here is beyond me." Naran's story was one of the more brutal ones Tikran had heard from his fellow Manzakars. Naran had been the same age as Tikran at the time of his enslavement, hunting antelope on the steppe with his older brother, when unfamiliar horsemen approached. One of them asked for directions, claiming they were lost. As soon as they were close enough, Naran was snatched up and his brother speared through the neck. The slave traders who had captured Naran were nothing like Mago—Naran remembered being bound and gagged with three other boys through most of the journey to

Anzor, only occasionally being allowed to stretch, eat, and relieve themselves.

"The slavers would hit us just hard enough to hurt us, but not hard enough to leave a mark. They wanted to get paid well for their human commodities," Naran had shared with a sardonic laugh.

Tikran turned in his saddle to study the Manzakar faces around him, all of them men who'd had appalling beginnings like himself and Naran. Their expressions were downcast but resolute. No doubt they believed, as all of them had been taught, that this was all because of Archil, the heretic. Archil was why the Gohari people suffered—even *deserved* to suffer. The Manzakars—particularly the Aslans—had been the lucky ones, the ones who were granted a new and infinitely better life in Anzor. And since they were the elite protectors of the crown, unless the king himself was in danger, their lives were not forfeit, and they would eventually become property-owning durais. They would die in wealth, honored by the king they served.

"Tik." Naran bumped his leg against Tikran's. "Are you okay? You have that look on your face."

"What look?"

"The one you get just before you start spouting existential shit," he replied, the corner of his mouth quirking in a half smile.

"Ha." Tikran chuckled. "You know me too well."

"I do," Naran agreed. "But I'd be surprised if you're the only one getting existential riding through this place."

As they traveled eastward toward the infinite, bleak horizon, they began to see signs of human life. Here and there, they'd pass a cluster of yarms, the round, portable dwellings made of bamboo and animal skins, and small herds of scrawny goats and sheep. In the long sheepskin vests typical of the

Gohari, the nomads stood and gaped silently as the royal party, surrounded by the legendary Manzakars, rode past. Two adolescents in fur-lined caps, bows tied to their waists, sat astride a horse and watched from the side of the road. A bearded man stood outside his yarm, holding the hand of a skinny little girl with a dirty face and a tangle of black hair who waved timidly at them. Tikran made eye contact with a woman who was herding her sheep, clicking her tongue, her black hair escaping the scarf around her head. For a split second she resembled his mother and his heart stopped. He looked away, his muscles tensed.

"What are they thinking, I wonder?" he muttered.

Naran scratched his chin. "The children are awestruck. The adults? Not so much, I imagine. I was old enough that I remember my father cursing Anzor, Cenk, and especially Delger." He shrugged. "I guess he felt like Anzor wasn't doing enough to help."

"Delger sends caravans of food to the garrison towns several times a year," Tikran pointed out. "And in spite of it, the nomads have begun attacking Anzori outposts, as if the king wasn't doing what he could to help."

"Gohar is a big place," Naran said. "It'll never be enough."

They both fell quiet then, watching the swathe of long grass across the steppe undulate in the wind. Gohar, it seemed, was doomed.

At nightfall they stopped to rest, feed and water their horses, and allow the king and his retinue to sleep. Canopies and tents were pitched, trunks and rugs unpacked, and cooking fires started. This was no regular military encamp-ment—there were professional attendants, baths with warm water, and even latrines. The nights in Gohar were drastically chillier than the days regardless of season, so members of the king's retinue donned fur-lined hats and velvet robes. Naran and Tikran had volunteered for the second half of the night watch, so they ate a quick meal of lamb, olives, and bread, then slept in the soldiers' tents while everyone socialized around the fires. After four hours of rest, when all was quiet and everyone slept, they mounted their horses and readied their weapons as the Manzakars who had been on duty crawled under their blankets.

Tikran was stringing his bow while Naran brewed strong coffee for them. Nighttime in Gohar brought back powerful memories Tikran had all but forgotten—Da teaching him to hunt at night, using only the moonlight to see; Mama caressing him to sleep while singing an old lullaby; sneaking out of the yarm with his sisters to count the stars.

"Coffee?" Naran rode up beside him, holding out a steaming tin cup.

Tikran took the cup and thanked his friend, sipping carefully and looking out into the utter darkness of the steppe. A burrowing owl screamed in the distance and the grass rustled rhythmically. "It's actually peaceful out here. Perhaps even *too* peaceful."

Naran grunted in agreement and the two Manzakars gazed out into the night for several silent minutes. Then he said, "So... Coxani. What's the story?"

Tikran blinked. It wasn't at all what he'd expected Naran to say at that very moment. He shifted uneasily in his saddle. "What? I don't understand the question."

Naran shrugged. "I find it strange that you've been training her for three years and I only just met her. It's almost like you've been hiding her. It makes me wonder about the nature of your, er, relationship."

"Don't be ridiculous. I haven't been hiding anything." Tikran took another sip of coffee only as an excuse to avoid eye contact. Naran knew him far too well for even the least bit of it.

"She's my student. Lord Haydar insisted I train her. She excels at archery. That's it."

Naran's jaw dropped. "By the hairy balls of Cenk. You two are fucking!"

"*Naran.*"

The yellow-haired Manzakar removed his helmet and raked his fingers through his dreadlocks. "I'm sorry. That was crude of me. But you *are*, aren't you?" When Tikran said nothing, Naran laughed. "The boy who cannot lie has become the man who cannot lie." He stared into the distance for a few moments. Finally, he said, "I won't lie this time either—I'm incredibly envious. She's stunning. And brave, and clearly skilled." He gave Tikran a sidelong look. "Would it bother you if I were to show interest in her?"

Tikran snapped his head around to glare at his friend. Naran's sexual appetite was notoriously voracious. As a cadet, he'd found creative ways to sneak around the eunuchs and have sex with both men and women, Anzori and Gohari, by the time he was barely fifteen, *and* gotten away with it. "You can't be serious. *You.* The man who can snap his fingers and have anyone naked in his bed within minutes?"

"Yes." Naran raised an eyebrow. "What's your point?"

Tikran struggled to find the words, he was so exasperated. "Can't you just... leave Coxani alone?"

A broad smile slowly spread across Naran's face. "Oh? Are you *possessive* of her? What—"

A clatter behind them made them both swivel around—coffee cups discarded, Naran's saber drawn, Tikran's arrow knocked and bowstring drawn tight, their eyes razor focused. A woman had emerged from one of the royal tents wearing a long, red hooded robe that was folded over the chest and buttoned beneath the arm. She had accidentally kicked a tray of tin cups that lay on the ground beside the extinguished campfire. She held up her hands. "Don't shoot, please. I only seek a cup of wine."

Both Manzakars immediately relaxed and bowed their heads, turning their horses to face her. "Our apologies, my lady," Tikran said.

She approached slowly. "No apology needed. You're just doing your job." She was perhaps in her late thirties, with caramel-colored skin, high cheekbones, and wide-set phoenix eyes that were a remarkable lavender color.

Had she been Anzori, the conversation would have ended then. Manzakars were forbidden from fraternizing with Anzori women unless it was in an official capacity. But she was clearly Gohari and very attractive, so she was fair game—as far as Naran was concerned. He squinted an eye and rubbed his chin, as if in thought. "If I had to guess, I would say you're the king's interpreter."

"No. An interpreter is unnecessary in Dilovar in any case, as most of their aristocracy speak Perchuhi." A smile danced on her lips as she peered up at him from underneath long eyelashes. "Try again."

Naran made a couple more incorrect guesses, causing her to giggle. Finally, she said, "My name is Saltanat. I am the king's head mage."

Two pairs of Manzakar eyes widened. Naran said, "Apologies, my lady. We've only ever seen you wearing a veil, so we didn't know..."

She waved her hand. "Once again, no apology needed. Delger is very protective of his mages. He likes to keep our identities hidden to the public. But you are Aslans, so it matters little." She smiled at Naran. "And who are you?"

Naran straightened. "Naran, junior commander of the Aslan Manzakars." He nodded at Tikran without taking his eyes off Saltanat. "He's a nobody."

Saltanat's eyes lit up as she looked at Tikran. "Hardly so! You are the Manzakar of the Caged Kingfisher!"

Despite the strong desire to cringe every time someone referred to him by his official name, Tikran couldn't help but smirk at Naran. "I am. My name is Tikran." He bowed his head again. To avoid talking about the tournament, he quickly asked, "Have you been His Highness's mage for long?"

"Oh, yes. When I was taken to Anzor at the age of nine, I was tested for the Essence. It was so strong in me that I was immediately bought by the king and installed as an apprentice mage."

"And does the king always travel with his mages?"

"Just myself." She brushed a stray strand of black hair from her face.

Tikran had a million questions he wanted to ask but knew she would likely decline to answer them. The mages' roles and duties were kept very secret, as was the power of the Essence. They were only ever told that the mages served primarily as clerics, working "in the service of Cenk." With a calculated but playful smile, he settled on, "Are you here to light our campfires?"

She tilted her head back and laughed, her voice like a bell. "No. Although I do that as well." After a moment, she shrugged. "I imagine you'd learn this anyway, so I can tell you. I travel through Gohar often, with and without the king, to detect those who may have the Essence."

Tikran blinked. "You can tell?"

She smiled slyly. "Indeed. The Essence in me is powerful enough that I can detect it in others."

Naran leaned forward, a wicked gleam in his eye. "What else can your Essence do?"

If he'd meant to make her blush, he failed. She met his gaze straight on with a mischievous one of her own. "Much, my fine

Manzakar." She swirled her robe around her legs and said, "Now, even a woman who is a mage shouldn't be seen with men while unescorted. So if you would kindly point me in the direction of the correct barrel..."

Naran dismounted, shooting Tikran a puckish look before saying to Saltanat, "Let me find you some wine, my fair lady, so that you can return to your tent."

THEY REACHED the garrison town of Eter after two weeks of travel. Tikran was immediately struck by how dismal Gohari "towns" were. Considering the Gohari were nomadic people, many of them chose to settle in them out of desperation—it was where the food was, after all. But at their core, these towns were military outposts, centering around a fort made of lumber that had been brought in from Anzor.

As the regal procession entered the gates, at least a hundred Anzori troops greeted them. Natives came out of the ramshackle houses and lined the side of the road, some waving Anzori flags, most watching somberly. Tikran wondered if, in an attempt to put the town's best foot forward before the king, the soldiers had ordered the Gohari townspeople's presence.

The party made camp within the gates while King Delger climbed out of his carriage and made his way to the town square before the fort, where the food would be distributed. The garrison commander kneeled before the king while several of Delger's Aslan Manzakars, Tikran and Naran included, stood like a protective wall around him. After some time, the king turned and summoned Nasch, who materialized immediately. Delger spoke softly to him, causing Nasch to bow and signal to his squadron. The Manzakars promptly began unloading the food they had brought from Anzor.

The Aslans stood at perfect attention, their eyes on their king. But Tikran had learned how to see without watching: although his eyes looked forward, he saw the Gohari natives approach eagerly.

No. *Desperately.*

They emerged from their dilapidated houses—men, women, and children. Hundreds of them. Nasch's Manzakars held them back as the food was placed in carts guarded by soldiers. Tikran heard Nasch say to the crowd, "Each of you will receive your fair portion if you follow regulations."

Delger then turned to his Aslans. "Let us return to camp." He nodded at the Aslan senior commander, a fellow named Ayaz whom Tikran didn't like very much. Ayaz motioned for his Manzakars to follow the king back to camp.

Tikran could hear Nasch's voice delivering orders. His heart thumped faster against his chest. He wanted to stay, to see the distribution of food. But his job was to guard the king with his life, at all times.

So he followed.

The king slipped into his tent and the Aslans divided into two halves around it, facing outward. Tikran deliberately positioned himself facing the center of town, his eyes seeking the line of people awaiting their food. Even from a distance, he could hear Nasch yelling.

"Psst."

Tikran blinked but didn't move.

"Tik." Naran took a deep breath quietly. In barely a whisper, he said, "Go and watch. I'll cover for you."

Tikran looked at Naran, whose expression was earnest. Naran growled, "Well go on, neophyte. I know what it's like to have the shits on the road. Entirely unpleasant. Relieve yourself downwind from here and return promptly. Mind you don't get your ass bitten by snakes. Oh, and for the love of Cenk, wipe properly this time!"

Tikran almost cracked a smile as he hurried off. He wasn't sure how Naran knew what he'd been thinking, unless Naran had been thinking it as well.

As he approached the fort, he could see the line of Gohari families that snaked out of the square and through the town. He saw the horses and donkeys tethered to a hitching post and knew that many of the nomads had traveled here specifically for this reason. In order to remain inconspicuous (or as inconspicuous as possible, considering he was decked out in the finest Manzakar armor), he stopped several yards away and leaned against the rough wood of a house, watching from against the wall.

As each individual or family reached the cart, they were handed a relatively small bundle of food items, particularly for the larger families. After receiving their bundles, Nasch's soldiers herded them away efficiently. While most of the people receiving food stayed quiet and accepted their portions without issue, some tried to haggle, even beg, for more food. One elderly woman began to sob to one of the Manzakars distributing the food, wailing that her son and his wife had recently died from a fever and left her with four mouths to feed, and the baby was sick now, and couldn't they spare a bit more?

Nasch quickly intervened, putting his hand on her bony shoulder and pushing her along. He said, "Now, ma'am, that wouldn't be very fair to the others receiving food, would it?" Her appeals became increasingly frantic, and Nasch had two garrisoned soldiers haul her off. She crumpled in their hands, letting them drag her as she wept and continued to plead. Nasch dusted off his hands as if touching the woman had sullied them, then turned back to oversee the distribution.

Where were they taking her? What would they do with her if she continued to beg? Tikran was feeling increasingly tense, unconsciously rubbing the curved pommel of his saber with his palm. His eyes swept over the line of people and were suddenly drawn to movement from the corner of his peripheral vision. He looked to the left where a boy, probably ten or eleven years old, crept around the side of a wall, his eyes fixed on what looked like an apple that had been left on a post, likely by one of the troops. The soldiers were fully engrossed in giving out food, so the child was taking the opportunity to snatch the apple.

As his small, dirty hand curled around the fruit, Nasch turned and looked directly at the post. *Hurry!* Tikran tensed his jaw. But the boy was a fraction too slow. Nasch took two long strides, grabbed the boy by his jacket, and yanked him off his feet, bellowing, "Thief!" Everyone stopped what they were doing to turn and watch as Nasch dragged the boy to the middle of the square and motioned to two Manzakars, ordering they remove his clothes and tie him to the back of an ox drawn cart. The boy was sobbing his apology, but to no avail. Tikran's hand was working the pommel of his saber again. He was intimately familiar with this form of punishment. He knew it wasn't uncommon for peasant children to be tied to carts naked and birched for the purpose of humiliating them. This cart, it seemed, was commonly used for that exact purpose. He had anticipated this sort of discipline for the boy, but... the bones of his ribcage protruded under his skin, his shoulder blades unprotected by layers of muscle or fat. A harsh beating could very well kill the child.

Nasch pulled a three-headed switch from the cart and began whipping the boy's back, bottom, and legs with cruel competence. The child's cries got louder as welts rose on his skin. Tikran waited for the whipping to end but Nasch continued, using significant force with each swing. When droplets of blood bloomed and began streaming down the boy's back, Tikran moved without making the conscious decision to move. He was standing in the square within seconds. In a flash, he grabbed Nasch's arm and twisted it behind his back, forcing the switch to fall from his hand. Before Nasch could register what had happened, Tikran released his arm and stood aside.

"I think the boy has had enough, Commander," Tikran said calmly.

Nasch looked up in startled anger, his eyes widening as he recognized Tikran. The expression on his face grew murderous. "*You.* How dare you interfere with my command?" His hand was on the hilt of his saber.

Tikran kept his hands in front of him and his voice calm. "The boy tried to steal an apple. He's likely starved. You can't beat the survival instincts out of him."

Nasch's nostril's flared as he took a step closer, his hand still at his saber. "Once again, I will ask: How fucking *dare* you interfere with my command?"

"What in Cenk's name is going on here?" Ayaz marched over, looking from Nasch to Tikran.

Nasch pointed at Tikran and said, "You need to keep your men in better order, Ayaz. This piece of shit in particular. He's interfering where he has no business or authority."

"The boy stole an apple. The commander here was going to beat him unconscious," Tikran said.

"And so what?" Nasch snarled, the veins in his neck bulging. "I've been campaigning in Gohar for fifteen years. You have no idea what these savages can be like. This is *my* domain. Go back to the palace and look pretty, little girl. You're no warrior."

Tikran's face darkened. "I didn't realize beating children senseless made you a warrior."

Ayaz moved between the men and held his palms out to each of them. "Enough." He looked at Nasch. "We will go."

"Not if he continues beating the boy," Tikran said.

Ayaz gaped at Tikran. "Are you defying my orders?"

"Commander," Tikran implored, "if we leave and let him resume, he'll take his anger at me out on the child."

Ayaz considered, looking back at the limp, bloody form of the small thief. He said to Nasch, "I think the boy has had enough."

"You have no—"

"I will take this to the king himself if you continue," Ayaz interrupted, his tone firm.

Nasch was silent for a moment, his jaw working, before turning to his men. "Untie the boy and return him to his family. Tell them they have forfeit their food for the year."

Ayaz grabbed Tikran's arm and hissed, "We go. Now."

Tikran yanked his arm away. "Not until I've seen them untie him."

Ayaz's face was purple with rage, but he waited with Tikran until the boy was untied and carried away. As they walked back to the royal camp, Ayaz said, "For the record, Tikran, the next time you need to take a shit while standing guard, you'll wait or do it in your breeches. Period."

CHAPTER 9

Savages.

Tikran could hardly keep the look of disgust from his face. "He called the Gohari savages. Every single Manzakar has Gohari blood running through his veins." He could tell Naran was doing his best to keep his expression neutral despite Tikran's words.

"One could argue, however," Naran said, "that Anzor made us who we are, and without its influence, we would be savages too."

"Bullshit!" Tikran glared at his friend. "And I know you don't believe that. I *know* you don't believe that."

Naran smiled. "Look at you, getting all worked up. The quiet, disciplined boy has passion!" The smile became mischievous. "Not that I didn't already know that."

"Naran, I'm not in the mood for your twisted sense of humor."

"Are you ever in the mood for it?" After a chuckle Naran added softly, "I know, Tikran. I've done this a couple years longer than you have. It isn't right."

Tikran rolled his shoulders tensely. "I'm constantly expecting a blade in my back. I can feel Nasch's eyes like daggers."

Naran whistled. "I don't blame you. He fucking *hates* you." After snickering to himself for several seconds and getting a dirty look from Tikran, he said, "No one's throwing a blade between your shoulders, Tik. Not if I can help it."

The pair had ridden ahead of the party to ensure its safe arrival into Dilovar. The Damla River lay ahead and jagged, forbidding mountains loomed darkly on the horizon. As they approached, they could see the Dilovari forts along its foggy banks and Damla Bridge stretching across the river with its pointed arches. Unlike Anzor's military outposts in Gohar, these were solid stone forts with wide bases that tapered to narrow battlements at the top and towered over the dark blue waters of the river.

"What do you know about Dilovar, other than what we were taught in school?" Tikran asked his friend as they approached the Gohari side of the river.

"You mean other than the fact that the Dilovari also worship Cenk, so they're better than the Gohari?" Naran replied with a sneer.

Tikran rubbed his chin. "After the Akmaral War, Anzor allowed Dilovar a handful of children with strong Essence to take back with them, under the condition that the Dilovari stay out of Gohar and refuse to allow the Gohari people entrance into their kingdom."

"Yes," Naran sighed. "How many times did we hear that bedtime story in the barracks?"

"As far as we know, they've kept their side of the bargain for over a hundred years. But now," Tikran continued, "Dilovar has been caught venturing into Gohar, violating the peace treaty." He looked at Naran. "The most logical explanation is that they're running out of the Essence. Whatever the magic does, they need—if for no other reason than to keep Anzar from becoming more powerful."

"We know what the Essence does, remember?" Naran's voice dripped with scorn. "It does the work of Cenk. Oh, and it lights fires."

Tikran remembered the prayers they had learned those early years as cadets. *Cenk's Essence blesses mankind with life... It is light, it is water, it is food and shelter...* Out loud, he said, "You would think the Gohari would have figured out how to use the Essence to their advantage, since they're the ones who have it." He quickly added, "And please, don't spout that religious rhetoric about Cenk punishing the Gohari for the sins of Archil. A god that punishes innocent people for the sins of one man is no god of mine."

Naran's jaw dropped but his eyes lit up gleefully. "When did you become such a firebrand, Tikran? I like it! It's that Coxani, isn't it? She strikes me as the type to defy authority." He grinned. After a thoughtful moment, he added, "But Tik, if anyone heard you..."

"Well, we're out here all alone, aren't we? I wouldn't have said it otherwise," Tikran muttered.

"Hmm. In any case, you and I both know there's more to the magic than just having the Essence," Naran commented. "You saw how the mages make signs in the air and did fancy shit with their hands. They have to know spells in order to use it."

Tikran shook his head. "It's a shame that only the oldest Gohari still remember the story of Archil, if at all, at this point. I have a feeling it would hold some answers."

Naran rumbled deep in his chest. "Don't go asking those questions, Manzakar. It'll land you in hot water—and quickly."

Squinting at the riverbank, Tikran said softly, "I think I see someone approaching."

Three Dilovari warriors emerged from the fog, closer than the Manzakars had anticipated. Tikran sensed Naran stiffen at his side and both men felt for their weapons discreetly. The Dilovari rode their warhorses slowly, their silhouettes nothing short of intimidating. They wore the heavy cavalry lamellar armor like the Manzakars, but brightly burnished and adorned with strips of bone and bird feathers. Their iron helmets had broad brims and spikes at the top from which black plumes of hair hung. They carried lances, maces, compound bows, and quivers of thirty arrows that were fletched with eagle feathers. As cadets, Tikran and Naran had heard incredible stories about the Dilovari soldiers—that they were tied to horses at age two and three to learn how to ride; that they slept in their saddles while on campaign when speed was essential; that they drank horses' blood to stay strong.

Both Manzakars had learned some of the Dilovari language, Erdem, specifically for this purpose. Naran cleared his throat before uttering, "Greetings. We come ahead of King Delger of Anzor to announce his arrival." One of the soldiers, the one in the middle, turned his head and spoke to the other two. As the two turned and trotted back to the river, the soldier who was apparently in command approached. He spoke in heavily accented Perchuhi. "Welcome, Manzakar. We have been expecting you."

Naran whispered to Tikran, "Did that sound threatening to you, or am I on edge?"

"You're on edge," Tikran hissed back.

As the soldier came close, his face came into view. Tikran had never seen a Dilovari before. He was awestruck by the man's face—his skin was fair, fairer than that of an Anzori, but his hair was the blackest black, and he had long, narrow eyes.

The soldier spoke again in broken Perchuhi: "We have informed the gates. Tell your king. You may cross the bridge."

"Thank you," Naran replied. He nodded at Tikran and the pair turned and galloped westward, toward the royal train.

As the royal Anzori procession came into view, they slowed their horses to a trot and Tikran mused out loud, "The creation of the Manzakars was a boon to Anzor, wasn't it? It was the reason they were able to defeat Dilovar in the Akmaral War. I can't imagine the Dilovari warriors have forgotten that."

"They most certainly have no love for us," Naran agreed. "We are about to enter unfriendly territory, brother."

———

THE JOURNEY from the Damla River to the city of Ogedei was more difficult than any other part of their journey so far. They traveled through a mountain pass and over a ridge as the temperatures dropped and the wind blew fiercely. From the ridge they could see Dilovar's capital nestled in a green valley, and after what seemed like an eternity, it finally grew closer as they descended further down from the mountains. The people of Dilovar were primarily pastoral nomads, with the exception of the wealthy, who lived in large, sparse cities. Ogedei itself was a city of cool, gray stone, contrasting starkly with the greens and browns of the countryside. It was more fortress than city, with those tapering towers that rose above the high city walls, lit a glowing orange. While Anzor City was meant to inspire awe, Ogedei was clearly meant to inspire fear.

They entered the city gates and saw that the citizens awaited their arrival, a hushed murmur undulating through the crowds. As the banner-guard, Tikran and Naran led the way, their backs straight, their faces stoic. Tikran could hear the whispers of "Manzakar" as they passed, and for a moment he swelled with pride. This was, after all, what he'd worked so hard to accomplish—to be the best of the king's warriors, feared and respected throughout the land.

And yet... there was a niggling doubt he couldn't explain, a strange feeling that a game was being played in which he—and Coxani and Naran—were expendable pawns... a game they had not agreed to play...

King Bilguun awaited them within the palace walls, high on a hill. Two stone lions guarded the gates to the palace, and a large, gilded fountain sculpted in the shape of a tree adorned the entrance. The tree had silver fruit hanging from its branches and three dragons twined about its trunk, water flowing from their open mouths. As the gates closed behind them, Delger and his advisors emerged from the royal carriage, looking worn from the long journey across the Continent. Bilguun greeted Delger cordially, if a bit aloofly. Bilguun himself was not a tall man, but his poise was nothing short of regal. He was slim with a pale face and watchful eyes. He was at least ten years older than Delger but somehow looked younger than the Anzori king.

"King Delger," Bilguun said in his accented but clear Perchuhi, "Welcome to Dilovar. You must be exhausted after such a journey. Please, have your retinue come inside, my men will tend to your horses. You have arrived just in time for evening supper and my cooks have prepared a special banquet in your honor."

Five of the Aslan Manzakars—Tikran and Naran included —stood at the king's back during the banquet, unmoving save for their eyes. They would have to wait until the king retired before they could eat, but that was to be expected. Musicians and dancing girls entertained the royal party as they ate their roast wolf soup and skewers of venison, washing it down with enkh, fine fermented mare's milk. The Dilovari were a handsome people, without a doubt. Their aristocrats wore long, silk tunics with standing collars that were delicately embroidered and shimmered in the light. The women wore their hair away from their faces and down their backs, and the men shaved their faces clean, with neat queues that fell to their shoulder blades. Bilguun's eldest son, Orxan, heir to Dilovar's throne, sat at his father's side. He was an enormous fellow compared to his father, with the look of a man who spent all his time training in the arts of killing and defending Dilovar's northern frontier. At the moment, he seemed to have little interest in anything other than eating the food that was piled high before him.

Delger took a sip of his soup and looked at Bilguun. "How goes it in the north? Do the Haldorans still raid your borders?"

Bilguun nodded gravely, barely touching his food. "Orxan spends much of his time there, fighting them off. They are ever persistent."

Frowning, Delger said, "The nature of their god's power is similar to Cenk's Essence, is it not?"

The Dilovari king grunted. "It is. But... I wonder if they're enhancing the magic in some way."

Delger grew still. "In what way?"

"I don't know." Bilguun looked up at the ceiling, as if the answers were above him. "I suspect they have been able to cross the Dzud Mountains. We have found evidence on the border, along the Damla River."

Delger took this in for a moment, then drained his cup of fermented horse milk and turned to lighter subjects.

Tikran frowned as he listened to the kings' conversation. The Dzud Mountains separated all of Anzor, Gohar, and most of Dilovar from the kingdoms to the north, including Kalevi, Taranis, and Haldor. The mountains were impossible to cross alive. No life, as far as anyone knew, could exist there. It was too cold, too barren, and violent storms swirled over them almost constantly. No one who ventured into the range was ever seen again. Not even the formidable, metal-encased Haldorans could survive a crossing...

Still processing the information Bilguun had shared, Tikran's eyes fell on Saltanat absently, who was unveiled and sitting on one side of the king, her eyes scrutinizing Dilovari faces, one at a time. He snapped out of his contemplative trance. *She's looking for the Essence.* Naturally, Bilguun had his own mages, and Tikran guessed the five individuals with the red conical hats and similar probing gazes were they. He continued to peruse the banquet attendants with interest, trying to determine who was who and what their roles were in Bilguun's court.

One individual sat as quietly and observantly as Saltanat at the end of Bilguun's side of the table. He was young, perhaps Tikran's own age, perhaps a bit older. He had the straightest, blackest hair and, unlike the other men, wore it loose. His skin was much lighter than Tikran's but not quite the typical alabaster white of a Dilovari. His eyes were a pale gray, almost colorless, under straight dark eyebrows. He had arranged himself comfortably in his chair, leaning back casually with a goblet dangling from his hand, and surveyed the banquet with a bland expression, as if none of it interested him in the least. Quite unexpectedly, he met Tikran's gaze and smiled. Tikran startled without moving. It was as though the man had known he was watching all along. The smile transformed the man's expression from bored and nonchalant to almost taunting. He raised his goblet in Tikran's direction before taking a sip.

Tikran nodded once in acknowledgment but did not return the smile. *Is he challenging me? Mocking me?* They might have glared at each other indefinitely, waiting for the other to look away first, if suddenly the banquet attendees hadn't risen to their feet in prayer to Cenk, breaking the two men's line of sight. After the prayer, Tikran noticed the man was gone, his seat at the table empty.

FROM ATOP A ROCKY CLIFF, Tikran surveyed the landscape of Dilovar. The mountainsides were blanketed with forests of larch, pine, and cedar trees, and the valleys were grassy and dotted with hundreds of sheep, cattle, and goats. "It's a beautiful kingdom," he commented, half to himself.

Naran watched as an eagle soared overhead. "I wonder how their soldiers trained, with all these mountains? It makes me nervous."

Tikran looked back at his friend. "Why?"

"Tik, they have the benefits of training on treacherous land. We don't."

"Gohar is pretty treacherous."

"Not rocky and windy and... high up like this."

"It doesn't matter. We're not at war with them."

"Not yet."

Tikran sighed. "Even if war were to happen, it wouldn't be here. It would be in Gohar."

"It doesn't matter." Naran stalked moodily toward his horse. "They've been training and fighting in the mountains—the Dzud Mountains no less, if they're to be believed." He shook his head. "They have one on us."

Tikran said, "They haven't been training in the Dzud Mountains. That's impossible. And if they've been fending off some powerful horde from the north, then we're the least of their worries."

Naran shook his head. "You're missing the point."

"Oh, that's right." Tikran laughed, rolling his eyes. "The

point is to be the greatest warriors of them all, not to prevent unnecessary war."

Naran tilted his head, giving Tikran a strange look. "Since when have you been concerned with preventing war?"

Tikran opened his mouth to reply, but the sound of approaching horses stopped him. Both Manzakars instinctively tensed, feeling for their weapons.

As the Dilovari troops appeared, ascending toward them, Orxan, at the head, held up his hand in peace. Tikran heard Naran mutter some concerned oath as the prince of Dilovar drew near with five of his soldiers.

The Manzakars bowed their heads and Naran spoke immediately in Erdem, as if he'd prepared for this: "Your Highness. We are honored by your presence. How may we be of assistance?" He snuck a look at Tikran and winked.

Orxan, whose face was not disposed to happiness in any situation, smiled broadly. In crisp Perchuhi, he said, "Do you hear that, men? The Manzakars are honored by my presence."

Tikran did not relax his grip on his saber. He knew Naran didn't as well.

The Dilovari prince continued to grin. "I have studied you my whole life. As a boy, you were what I aspired to be. As a man, you are what I aspire to surpass."

The Manzakars exchanged looks of surprise. The fierce Prince Orxan was a fan. "We're flattered, Your Highness," Tikran said. "Especially considering we studied the Dilovari military as well and are likewise in awe of you."

Orxan straightened. "I am pleased to hear it. I would very much like to challenge you to compete—in horse racing, archery, and sword fighting. But not today, unfortunately. I come to summon you back to the palace, Manzakars."

Tikran and Naran followed the prince back to the palace, where King Delger was preparing to meet with Bilguun over important matters—*the* matter, in fact. He needed his Manzakars around him, bolstering him and intimidating all who watched.

Goblets were filled with wine and the kings sat across from each other, each flanked by his advisors. Orxan and a few of his men stood behind Bilguun while Delger's ten Aslans—heads held high, backs straight, hands at their sides—watched from the shadows. Tikran positioned himself so that he could hear Delger clearly and see Bilguun's face. Delger began, "My men in northern Gohar at the garrison town of Sitora have reported sightings of Dilovari troops on the steppe."

Bilguun said, "Yes. I sent them. Gohar's northern border also meets the Dzud Mountains. As I told you, we suspect the Haldorans have been penetrating the mountains and we believe there to be a passage or tunnel on our shared border allowing them to cross."

Delger shifted in his chair. "If the Haldorans were entering through Gohar, my men would likely know. We have several outposts along the northern border."

"Why don't you speak your mind, Delger?" Bilguun said, narrowing his eyes. "You think we are searching for the Essence and breaking the truce."

Delger smiled faintly. "How old are your mages now? You must be anxiously wondering how you'll replace them when they die, assuming they don't have children with the Essence themselves."

"Only one of my mages has a child with the Essence, and it is weak at that. Without access to the Gohari, we cannot replenish the Essence in Dilovar."

Delger nodded, drumming his fingers on the table. "I do not wish to be unjust to Dilovar, Bilguun. You have held up your side of the bargain for a hundred years." He paused, Bilguun waited. "I may have a proposition for you."

Bilguun inclined his head. "I am listening."

The Anzori king's expression guttered briefly, sadness in his eyes. "As you likely know, my son, Vazha, is afflicted with leprosy. It began several years ago, and while the illness is progressing slowly, there is no question that it will eventually take his life if it persists."

"I had heard that, yes." Bilguun frowned. "I'm sorry for you, Delger."

"I've been told you have a doctor here in Dilovar who has been able to treat several illnesses successfully, including the plague." Delger met Bilguun's eyes.

"My royal physician, yes," Bilguun answered. "But he has never cured leprosy. It is believed to be incurable."

Delger rubbed his chin. "Perhaps. But I will try anything." He straightened. "If you allow me to take your physician back to Anzor with me and let him try his hand at curing my son, I will grant you access to Gohar to find and bring back nomads with the Essence until you've replenished Dilovar's supply." He considered. "Six months should be enough."

Bilguun sat back in his chair. "I accept your proposition." He turned to an attendant. "Bring Damir to me."

Tikran scanned the faces of the Dilovari noblemen. They seemed pleased with the agreement and their goblets were refilled with wine. Within a few minutes, the attendant returned, the man with the pale eyes following him. Dressed entirely in black, Bilguun's young physician moved with a lazy grace, like a leopard after a meal. His ebony hair was tied back this time, revealing high, broad cheekbones and a chiseled jaw. He bowed before Bilguun, then Delger.

"Damir," Bilguun announced, "you will be returning to Anzor with King Delger to attempt to cure his son, Prince Vazha. The prince is dying of leprosy, and it is of utmost importance that you do everything you can to rid him of the cruel disease."

Damir bowed again. In a deep, silky voice, he replied, "I will do everything I can, Your Highness."

The meeting became something of a celebration at that point, and all the nobles were called to the great hall for drinks and food. The Manzakars observed the revelry in amusement, which carried on well into the night. Delger finally retired and dismissed all but two of his Aslans, allowing them free time. No doubt he would call on Tikran and Naran to guard him in the dead of night, so they headed back to the Dilovari barracks, where they'd been installed for their stay, to get some sleep. On their way, Orxan and several soldier friends of his intercepted them.

Orxan's face was flushed and it was clear that he had been drinking—quite a bit. "Manzakars," he said. "Join me and my men for some enkh and a bit of shooting, eh?"

Tikran and Naran exchanged looks. Orxan was the prince and they were his guests, so they had no choice but to accept— and try to stay as sober as possible. Tikran was running on nervous energy, feeling both comfortable and ill-at-ease all at once. He certainly wasn't a lightweight when it came to alcohol, but he rarely, if ever, partook. Naran, on the other hand, was a practiced heavyweight and could hold his own regardless of the beverage. He leaned toward Tikran and mumbled, "You should have gone drinking with me all those times. I have a feeling you're at a disadvantage here."

"Naran, I'm not a kid," Tikran snapped. "Besides, fermented mare's milk has next to no alcohol in it."

Naran shrugged. "Suit yourself. But I'm not carrying your drunk ass to bed."

They followed Orxan and his men to a training area beside the barracks, which was nicer than the regular training area and clearly where the soldiers of noble blood practiced, apart from the regular troops. It had a covered pavilion which was used by the elite warriors to make merry and entertain. Goblets and jugs were brought out by eager servants. Dilovar did not have the luxury of importing Gohari slaves, so their servants were Dilovari as well.

"Sit, Manzakars!" Orxan roared as they reached the pavilion. "Let's toast to the renewed peace between our people!"

The pair dutifully sat and accepted their goblets of enkh. No fewer than five toasts later, Tikran wondered if the beverage they were drinking was *regular* enkh. His head was beginning to swim and his joints felt looser than usual. Much to his frustration, Naran seemed completely unaffected.

"Caged Kingfisher," Orxan said, drawing Tikran out of his thoughts. The prince, a hard glitter in his dark eyes, was staring at him. "I want to see you do what earned you your name. Tonight."

Shit. Tikran replied steadily, "I'm not sure I'd be able to, Your Highness, after three goblets of enkh."

Every man in the pavilion stopped and gaped at him. Orxan said, "What soldier cannot fight and win after a bit of booze?" His men didn't bother to stifle their laughter.

Naran could hardly contain his glee. He spoke from the corner of his mouth. "You're fucked, Caged Kingfisher."

Tikran stood, his cheeks hotter from the alcohol than the embarrassment. "Where's my mount, then?"

The Dilovari cheered their enthusiasm as a groom brought Tikran's horse from the stables, complete with his bow and arrows. It was dark and even though torches lit the grounds, Tikran had to squint to see the cages hanging at the far end of the arena. He turned to Orxan. "What are the rules?"

"Same as they were during your tournament," Orxan

answered. "Two runs. Four gourds and a cage to strike. No arrows loosed until in full gallop."

Tikran nodded. "And my competition?"

Orxan smiled. "Me."

The alcohol was working some magic on Tikran. He was not a social creature, not smooth and debonair like Naran, and yet he grinned, leaned forward, and said softly, "Now, Your Highness, you realize if I beat you, I put myself in quite the quandary, don't you?"

"No excuses," Orxan said. "And you won't beat me, Caged Kingfisher." He chuckled, clearly enjoying himself.

Tikran and Orxan dressed in their full lamellar cuirasses and armor and jumped on their mounts as the other men continued to drink, becoming more raucous. Naran approached Tikran, a mildly concerned look on his face. "Tik, you sure you want to do this?"

"Of course," Tikran answered, half wondering if the enkh had made him lose his mind. "He set this up. He got me drunk. And now he's going to lose."

Naran backed away with a quick salute, unable to keep himself from grinning. In the back of his mind, Tikran wondered if he could actually win under the circumstances. As he and Orxan lined up, he closed his eyes briefly and remembered the Fire Festival that had given him his name. He relived the terror of his seven-year-old self, of hearing his mother's screams, of Nasch's symbol, and finally, of Nasch whipping a small, starved Gohari boy to ribbons for trying to take a half-eaten apple.

It was all he needed.

One of the Dilovari soldiers blew a horn and they were off in the blink of an eye. The gourds swung gently in the light of the torches, the shadows and flames dancing hypnotically across their hard beige skins. With nearly inhuman speed,

Tikran dropped the reins, drew an arrow from the quiver, nocked it to the silk bowstring, locked his right hand to the string and drew it taut to his cheek, then released.

Nock... Draw... Anchor... Aim... Release...

He could feel Orxan at his side, maybe even ahead of him, releasing his arrows speedily, smoothly. As Tikran finally reached the gilded birdcage, he didn't allow himself to think before acting. He immediately swiveled and loosed his arrow at Orxan's cage. Orxan, in the meantime, did likewise at Tikran's cage. With a resounding clink, both cages opened simultaneously, releasing the birds into the blue-black, star-speckled sky.

By the time he reined his horse around, Tikran was feeling fairly sober. The cheers of the men echoed across the arena, and as he returned and dismounted, he was rushed by Dilovari soldiers—and not in the way he'd ever imagined. Orxan elbowed his way through, beaming, and embraced Tikran fiercely. "You are worthy, Caged Kingfisher," he said, holding Tikran by the shoulders. "And now, we celebrate!"

Naran laughed as they dragged Tikran back to the pavilion and refilled goblets to the brim. Tikran wanted to ask for water but fell quiet as yet another toast was made: "To the combined forces of Anzor and Dilovar against the enemy Haldorans!" Naran widened his eyes at Tikran and shrugged.

Once again, Tikran lost count of the number of times his goblet was refilled. He downed the contents thirstily, knowing full well they would only make him thirstier. His head began to swim again and he quickly felt boneless in his armor. He excused himself no fewer than three times in an hour to empty his bladder. Then, mercifully, Orxan acknowledged they should get to bed, as the morrow held a full day for all of them. *Thank Cenk*, Tikran thought, beginning to slump in his chair.

"As a gift, Manzakar, I give you women this evening, to

comfort you into blissful sleep," he said, a wide, mischievous grin on his face. His men hooted as two beautiful Dilovari women materialized at his side, smiling coyly. Orxan said to Tikran, "You may take them both for yourself, or share them with your friend. They don't speak Perchuhi, so no need for conversation—just get down to business!" He laughed then, thoroughly satisfied with his own generosity.

"Well." Naran could barely keep the look of mirth from his face as he glanced at Tikran. "Are you up for the final challenge, soldier?"

"Yes. No. What?" Tikran stood suddenly and his head spun. The women approached him, smiling and wrapping their arms around him, and began leading him back to the barracks.

"Are you going to share or what, brother?" Naran yelled at him from behind, laughing.

Tikran may have been drunk, but he wasn't so far gone that he didn't realize how irked Naran must have been at that very moment. He smiled and draped an arm around each of the women, saying, "Maybe. Maybe not. I'm feeling especially virile tonight." He was lying through his teeth. All he wanted was a few full flasks of water and a bed. Had Coxani been there, he likely would have gotten it up despite the copious amounts of booze he'd ingested and his utter exhaustion. But two strangers? It didn't matter how beautiful they were, there was zero chance—even if he'd been sober.

They entered the barracks and suddenly a cool, slender hand slipped under his cuirass and down the front of his breeches. "Naran! Wait," he cried.

Naran leaned against a wall several steps behind, his eyebrows raised. "Yes?"

Tikran smiled faintly, swallowing. "Help?"

Naran laughed deep in his chest. "Of course, Caged King-fisher." He held his hands out to the courtesans and said in

Erdem, "Ladies, may I interest you in *my* bed, which is right over here..."

The women let Tikran go reluctantly and followed the charming Naran down the corridor. Tikran heaved a sigh of relief and drank an entire jug of water, knowing that Naran had learned to say that exact phrase in Erdem just to seduce Dilovari women. *That dog.* Grinning and shaking his head, Tikran landed on his bedroll still dressed in his armor and was snoring instantly.

CHAPTER 10

The journey out of Dilovar was no less treacherous than the journey in. Several emergency stops to fix carriage wheels and get fresh horses delayed them, and they were now facing a difficult journey as winter arrived on the Continent. In Dilovar, the wind howled through the mountains and snow began to fall, slowing their progress back to Anzor. Even Gohar was bitterly cold; that, however, Tikran could handle. The steppe in all its weather was in his blood.

When they would make camp for the night, the fires were kept burning until morning while the Manzakars stood watch. No doubt Saltanat was kept busy ensuring the flames never went out. The truth was, Tikran enjoyed the silence and solitude of the night watch. Even when he stood watch with Naran, a comfortable silence would inevitably fall upon them, and Gohar would whisper to them by moonlight.

One such night, Tikran replaced Naran for the night watch. Squeezing his friend's shoulder, Naran mumbled good-night and slipped into his tent to sleep. It was late at night and the camp was silent as Tikran sat on his horse, breathing in the sharp air.

He'd been dwelling on the Essence since Delger had struck a deal with Bilguun. Dilovar must have had mages that could sniff out the Essence as well. He had to know what the Essence did, and how. He was tired of being left in the dark. He'd been taught that Anzor had saved him—had saved all the Gohari who'd been bought as slaves. But Coxani had helped open his eyes to certain things... certain inconsistencies... certain injustices...

He was becoming increasingly convinced: *Something* could be done to help the Gohari people. The question was not one of possibility, but of desirability.

"Little wonder you don't freeze to death out here, sitting still for hours on end."

Tikran brushed the pommel of his saber with his gloved fingers but made no movement otherwise. The voice... deep, soft, utterly bored... He knew who it was. Without looking, he said, "Shouldn't you be asleep, doctor?"

Damir laughed softly. "How did you know it was me? I must have left an impression."

"I'm a Manzakar," Tikran replied with satisfaction. "I'm trained to notice everything involving the king."

"Ah, yes. The Manzakars. The elite lapdogs of Anzor."

Tikran's head spun in the Dilovari's direction. "There's nothing keeping this elite lapdog from driving his blade right through you. So maybe show a bit of respect, eh?"

Damir raised his hands in defeat but continued to smile audaciously. "You win. Although I don't think your king would be too pleased with that turn of events." He held out his hand. "My name is Damir. You are...?"

Tikran eyed the outheld hand suspiciously for a moment. Then, "Tikran."

The two men shook hands.

"Good to meet you, Tikran," Damir said, a smile still dancing on his lips. He looked out into the darkness that enveloped the steppe. "Tell me, is Gohar always like this?"

"You mean desolate and foreboding?" Tikran chuckled. "Always."

"I will admit," Damir said, "the Anzori knew what they were doing when they recruited the Gohari into their armies. You are a formidable lot."

"How would you know that?" Tikran asked.

"I don't," Damir confessed. "It's what I've heard. But if you can successfully survive this without the Essence, then you must be."

Tikran respected the man's honesty. He observed the doctor briefly. He was as tall as Tikran and had the lean build of a man who could, if he were so inclined, become quite muscled. His striking face could have been sculpted from stone. In addition to his near-colorless eyes and dimpled chin, he had the look of a brooding intellectual, of someone who searched through tomes by candlelight. Tikran ventured, "I hope this isn't too forward of me, but are you full Dilovari? Your complexion and certain facial features are, well, different from the Dilovari I've seen."

Damir raised his eyebrows. "Perceptive of you, Manzakar. I am only half Dilovari by blood, on my father's side. But I never knew my mother and my father raised me, so I haven't known any other way of life. As such, I think it's safe to say I am a product of Dilovar."

Tikran wanted to ask about Damir's mother but felt he would be prying, so he changed the subject. "Do you think you can cure the prince?" Tikran asked.

Damir crossed his arms over his chest, drawing his fur-lined coat tighter around him. "I have no idea. I've never tried to treat a leper before. I am a royal physician, so I treat the afflictions of those who live well in Dilovar. And generally speaking, leprosy is found among those with little means." He looked up at Tikran. "That a prince has it is highly unusual."

"I don't know how he contracted it, but I will say that the royals of Anzor like to play soldier," Tikran said. "They will roll in the mud with the rest of us."

"They roll in the mud with the rest of you until the real fighting starts, eh?" Damir shook his head. "It's different in Dilovar. Bilguun was once a fearsome commander, and Orxan is following in his footsteps."

Tikran heard Damir's unspoken words: *They don't take slaves from the steppe to do their dirty work.* He cleared his throat. "I admire that in a king. But it does raise the likeliness that your king and his heirs will meet an untimely death."

"That it does." Damir glanced back at the campfires that were still burning strong. "Your mage. Saltanat, is it?"

"She's not *my* mage. But yes, that's her name."

"She likes you Manzakars."

Tikran snorted. "Is that so."

"Yes." Damir smiled. "I've seen her flirting with one of you quite a bit. A mustachioed fellow with a silver goblet on his sleeve." He began to turn away, meeting Tikran's startled gaze. "I bid you good night, Manzakar. Until tomorrow." With that, he swept back to his tent.

LYING on a cold bedroll in all but his armor, Tikran tried to fall asleep.

He'd never in his life had trouble sleeping. For as long as he could remember, his body would hit the bed—or floor—and he'd be out within seconds, usually in a deep, dreamless sleep. But lately, it had been different. As exhausted as he was when it was his turn to get some rest, he could not stop his mind from churning. Sometimes, he wasn't even sure what was keeping him awake—he wasn't consciously thinking of anything. He simply couldn't shake this undercurrent of tension, of anxiety.

He missed Coxani. He missed her nonstop talking, her laughter, her sharp observations, her stubbornness, her rage. It wasn't so much that he wanted to have sex with her—although Cenk knows, he wanted that too. It was more that he missed her strength, her ability to fearlessly take on the world. He had a feeling that she would know what to do, that she would know where to go for answers... about Nasch, about the starving Gohari people, about the Dilovari king, about the judgmental doctor.

He flopped over to his other side, exasperated. He had all of three hours to sleep before he was on watch again. Why couldn't he shut the noise out of his head? *Think of the ocean. Think of the waves, going back and forth, back and forth...*

His eyelids began to droop.

Back and forth... Back and forth...

Manzakar at arms... Manzakar at arms...

"Manzakar at arms!"

It was as though someone had dropped a bucket of ice-cold water on him. He scrambled for his armor and weapons along with the other soldiers, his foggy mind unable to determine who—or what—they would be fighting out in the middle of Gohar. Surely not the Dilovari... Then who? There was only one possible answer...

Tikran emerged from the tent and ran to his horse as a volley of arrows soared toward the encampment, drumming rapidly as they landed around him. He looked at an arrow that was embedded in a satchel nearby: short, light, with small fletching and a bone tip.

Gohari arrows.

Ayaz was screaming, "Aslans to the king! To the king!"

The Aslans encircled the king's tent, raising their circular, domed shields and arming their bows. Tikran's mind was racing. *They have no chance.* Another volley of arrows rained down, beating rapidly against iron and steel.

"Have you seen them?" Naran asked from beside him, peering out from behind his shield.

"No," Tikran answered. "Do you think there are many of them?"

Naran shrugged. "There must be. I imagine they're the sorriest looking group of archers we've ever seen."

The arrows fell again and this time one embedded itself in the shoulder of Tikran's cuirass. He yanked it out and said, "Well, they have skill, that's for certain."

Beyond the camp, Gohar lay dark. The arrows would fly in from the black sky, visible only when they were illuminated by firelight and mere yards away. Engaging the Manzakars would have been foolish of the Gohari attackers, and they were smart enough to know that. So they remained in the darkness, sending their arrows and hoping to strike. It would only be a matter of time before they ran out of arrows and retreated.

But then Ayaz grabbed Tikran and Naran by the shoulders from behind and said, "King Delger orders you give Saltanat safe passage to the front lines immediately!"

Exchanging brief looks, the two Manzakars lifted their shields and opened the flap to the royal tent. The mage slipped out, hooded, and put one hand on each of their arms. They moved carefully past the tents and toward a line of Manzakars on the cusp of the darkness—Nasch's squadron.

As they reached the soldiers, Saltanat squeezed between Tikran and Naran, pushing aside their shields. She closed her eyes, her mouth moving soundlessly, her fingers swirling in the air above their heads. In a sudden gust of air, a fire ignited in the dry grass in the distance, burning quickly and forming a semicircle of flames. They heard screams and saw the silhouettes of horsemen, their horses rearing, unsure of where to run. About fifty of them were trapped within the circle of fire, and the Manzakars raised their shields in the nick of time. A hailstorm of arrows descended on them. Tikran and Naran closed their shields over Saltanat, backing away slowly from the onslaught.

The mage touched Tikran's sleeve. "Wait," she said. "I must wait to see."

Tikran peered around his shield. The horsemen who were trapped within the ring of flames began to fall, one by one, as Nasch's Manzakars attacked them with arrows, lances, and swords.

Saltanat cried, "Stop! They're here!"

Nasch looked over his shoulder in her direction briefly then called off the attack. "Bring the rest of them!"

As the fire continued to blaze, seventeen Gohari men and women were brought, bound and beaten, before the mage. Blinking in the smoky haze, Tikran realized that they were, in fact, little more than children—the youngest must have been thirteen at most, and the oldest no more than eighteen. And Naran was right, they were a sorry sight. Bedraggled, beaten, skinny... and utterly unafraid. The fierceness in their eyes was as bright as the fire around them, and they each sported lines of brown paint across their cheekbones and down their chins.

Saltanat stepped toward them, her lavender eyes narrowed. She looked at each of their faces, searching. Then she stopped and smiled, approaching one of the older captives, a girl in her late teens with brown, matted hair and skin to match. "This one," she said in a silky voice. "But she's much too old, unfortunately." Shrugging, Saltanat returned to Tikran and Naran, her Aslan protectors.

Nasch nodded once. "Take them into the field!"

Wait. What are they doing? What are they going to do with them? As Tikran tried to follow, Naran's hand came down on him—hard. Tikran snarled, "Get your hands off me! What—"

"Brother," Naran said, his eyes wide and face bloodless, "think. Think! Before you do something epically stupid, just *think.*"

Tikran would have snapped back if Saltanat hadn't been there between the two of them, watching with interest. *Breathe.* He said, "You're right, Naran. Let's get the lady back to safety."

As they rushed back toward the royal train, Saltanat turned and briefly closed her eyes, moving her slender fingers in the air above. Out of nowhere, thunder sounded, and with a suddenness that left Tikran reeling, rain poured down on them, just long enough to put out the fire.

They returned the mage safely back to the king's tent. Tikran turned with urgency only to have Naran pounce on him. They both slammed into the ground, now muddy from the rain. "Tik, you're not thinking! Tikran! Think!"

"You already said that," Tikran said, spitting mud from his mouth. "I'm thinking, Naran. I'm thinking about those stupid kids who are about to be—"

Screams shattered the night and Tikran slumped. The two Manzakars lay on the ground, panting, horrified. Soldiers hurried about, checking on the royal retinue. Tikran could hear them speaking in hushed tones about the attack by "those Gohari savages."

"Why?" Tikran's voice cracked as he let his head fall back in defeat. "I don't understand. They posed no real threat. Why...?"

Naran gripped the neckline of Tikran's cuirass and shook him hard. "I don't know. I don't know. All I know is that you need to keep it together. You are an Aslan Manzakar, remember? Your first and foremost duty is to protect the king." Tikran met Naran's unrelenting eyes. Naran said, "Don't make me knock you out. Please."

They were drenched and filthy. Naran stood and hauled Tikran up with him. As if in a dream, Tikran nodded and stepped toward the king's tent, where several other pairs of Manzakar eyes watched him. He turned his back to them, planting his feet into the sludge. He wasn't afraid of Naran's blackout punches. They'd felled him before and he'd survived. *My duty is to protect the king. First and foremost.* He focused on the smoke that rose from the wet, singed grass in the distance, trying not to scream.

Because every fiber of his being wanted to *scream.*

"Tikran." Ayaz approached, his eyebrows drawn together and his lips tight. "His Highness would have a word with you." There was no mistaking the threat in his eyes. *Don't fuck up,* they said.

Sucking in his breath, Tikran turned toward the entrance to the royal tent. He was most certainly not in the right head space to speak with anyone, let alone the king. His heartbeat still thumped in his ears. Without looking at Naran (for surely he would get yet another ominous look), he ducked in between the flaps of canvas and kneeled before Delger, his head bowed.

Delger sat on a stool, looking older than usual. The bags under his eyes were dark, the corners of his mouth sagged further. He rubbed his hands together. "Tikran. I am told you were disturbed by what was done to the raiders tonight."

Tikran kept his head bowed but shifted his eyes in the

direction of Saltanat, who sat in the shadows. He thought carefully before speaking. "Yes, Your Highness. I don't think they deserved to die."

"Do you second guess His Highness' decisions?" Saltanat's voice was sharp .

Delger raised his hand to her. "Let him speak his mind. I select some of my closest advisors from the Aslan ranks, and I will hear him out." He sighed. "Please sit, Tikran."

Tikran obeyed, sitting on a stool across from the king. He raised his eyes and met the king's gaze steadily. "They were hardly older than children. Yes, they did something incredibly stupid, but—"

"What do you remember about the Gohari?" Delger interrupted. "Have you forgotten that your own parents sold you into slavery?"

Tikran resisted the urge to flinch. "Of course not, Your Highness. But they were starving. They had no choice."

Delger shook his head. "There is always a choice, lad. I, for one, would sooner die and see my children die than sell them for a pouch of coins."

Stiffening, Tikran remained silent, waiting for the king to make his point. His mind flooded with a dozen responses. *You can't even begin to fathom being in their shoes. And you are the one who encourages an exchange of a pouch of coins for a child instead of providing his family with enough food.*

"What I'm trying to impress upon you, Tikran," Delger continued, "is that the Gohari are innately savage. I was under the assumption you learned as much in the barracks, but it clearly needs reinforcing. Without the firm hand of Anzor, Gohar would be a place of chaos, of lawless, godless debauchery."

"Your Highness," Tikran said, "I am Gohari."

Delger chuckled and shook his head. "Oh no, Tikran. That

is where you are utterly mistaken. Everything you are is Anzori, from your speech, to your beliefs, to your morals. We take these discarded children of the nomads and turn them into civilized human beings." He sighed. "It's a shame the rebels were too old to be molded; they were already very much Gohari—even the girl with the Essence. Such a waste! And as much as it pained me to kill a group of foolhardy youths, I must ensure the nomads recognize the consequences of their actions and stay in line. Do you understand?"

Tikran remained quiet for a moment, then answered, "I do, Your Highness." There was nothing he could say that would make a single bit of difference, except to get him in more trouble than he was already in. And the truth was, he *did* understand. All too well. The king stood and Tikran followed suit.

Delger placed a hand on Tikran's shoulder and smiled. "The fact that you have such empathy is in itself evidence of how fully Anzori you are. Don't worry, we will go back to Anzor and you likely won't be faced with such things again. I let this kind of work fall to Manzakars like Commander Nasch, who are seasoned soldiers and understand the imperatives of peacekeeping. You are an Aslan, after all. You belong at my side."

"Thank you, Your Highness. I am honored, as always." Tikran bowed and turned to leave. He paused and looked at Saltanat. "You can make it rain. And make it stop."

She smiled. "Indeed."

"Cenk's Essence is powerful in Saltanat," the king confirmed. "We are blessed to call her Anzori."

Tikran emerged from the tent and resumed his position between Naran and Ayaz. He didn't look at either of them. His eyes focused on the scorched landscape ahead and the daylight that was beginning to creep into the horizon. He was grappling with several troubling thoughts, two of which were realizations. The first was that all of Anzor, and perhaps Dilovar as well, saw the Gohari as subhuman, and any "charity" shown to the nomads had only selfish intent—to acquire slaves and the Essence.

The second realization was that, beyond any doubt, Nasch and his men had killed his mother, and by order of the king.

CHAPTER 11

Holding ten arrows in her bow hand, Coxani squinted in the sunlight at her target, 200 yards away. Her goal was twofold: speed and accuracy. She wanted all her arrows to hit the target as vertically as possible. She smiled at her beautiful blue and silver bow—a graduation gift from Haydar—and wondered what Tikran would say when he saw it.

This morning, couriers had reported that the king's caravan had entered Anzor. They had been delayed two months but had finally made it home. Tikran would be here any moment now. She couldn't wait for him to see what she could do.

She nocked her first arrow, looked directly upward, and took a deep breath. Then: *Draw... Anchor... Aim... Release... Nock... Draw... Anchor... Aim... Release...* Her movements were fluid, just as Tikran had taught her. An arrow would leave her string and she would smoothly nock the next one, watching as the dust of her arrows rose in the air. When she'd shot all ten arrows, she jogged toward the target. All of them had hit the mark.

Sajo, a fellow Manzakar graduate and a young man she suspected was fairly besotted with her, followed her over. He said, "All perfectly vertical, Coxani. Amazing, as usual." He smiled, his eyes filled with admiration.

She beamed. "Tikran is much better at this. I have to keep practicing."

His smile faded and he cleared his throat. "Speaking of Tikran... I suppose you won't be training with him anymore when he gets back."

She had begun unstringing her bow. "I don't know about that. I think we both benefit from it." She shrugged, as if unconcerned, but desperately hoped she was right. She hadn't realized how much his guidance had helped her until he was gone. And of course, it wasn't only his guidance she missed, but his company, his friendship. Besides, how would they spend time together if he wasn't training her? How would they manage to spend *alone* time together? She felt her cheeks flush.

Sajo must have noticed. He suddenly looked sullen. He said, "Well, I suppose you two will have to get married."

Coxani laughed. "Oh? And why is that?"

A mean glimmer came into his eyes. "All that time you spent with him, unsupervised. It's nothing short of a scandal, you know. If you don't marry him, you've ruined your chances at having any sort of respectable life."

She leveled a threatening look at him, her eyes narrowed, her lips pressed in a line. "He was training me. That's it."

Sajo raised his eyebrows innocently. "I mean no offense, Coxani, but from what I've heard, that's definitely not *all* he was doing with you."

Her blood boiled at the same time that her stomach

dropped. *He's full of shit. No one knows.* They had been as discreet as possible, and Tikran was most certainly not the type to brag about anything, let alone seducing his student. Besides, *she* had seduced *him*. She thought to shove Sajo, to provoke him into fighting her so that she could sink a fist into his gut and wipe the smugness off his face, but horns sounded in the distance. *They're back.* Coxani turned and walked away with purpose. The asshole wasn't worth it. And suddenly, he didn't matter at all.

It seemed as though every inhabitant of Anzor City lined the main road awaiting the return of their king. Coxani suspected that a majority of the spectators awaited the return of the Caged Kingfisher just as eagerly. She and the other Manzakars stood at attention just outside the gates of the Citadel, watching as the train wound its way through the city and over the moat. Coxani's heart jumped when she recognized Tikran and Naran at the forefront, bearing the king's banner. As they approached, she could see how worn and weary they were; their armor was dull, their horses trudged at a snail's pace, and their faces beneath their helmets were drawn. Even so, as he rode past her, Tikran looked over, the ghost of a smile on his lips.

When finally they were allowed to help the returning party take the tired horses to the stables and unload the wagons, Coxani rushed over to where Tikran stood, helmet and armor off, removing the tack from his horse. "Tikran." He turned and she tackled him. He let out an *Oof!* at the impact and tottered back. Her head was against his chest, her arms wrapped around his waist.

The sound of his chuckle vibrated against her ear. "By Cenk, Coxani, I almost drew a weapon on you."

She pulled away just as suddenly, taking two steps back and putting her hands behind her back, aware of the several scandalized onlookers. "It's good to see you," she said, flushed and panting slightly.

He grinned at her, his eyes saying what his mouth could not. "It's good to see you too."

As she searched his face, it struck her that he looked... different. It was obvious from the shadows under his eyes that he was exhausted, and the hug had revealed that he had lost some weight. But there was something beyond that. Something about him had changed, under the surface. "You look like you could use a good meal and a bed," she said, trying to keep the concern from her voice. She leaned forward, sniffed, and wrinkled her nose playfully. "And definitely a bath."

"Most definitely," he said. "All three of those."

She hesitated, desperately wanting to ask him questions. They stood there looking at each other, not speaking.

"Ah, teacher and student reunite!" Naran walked over slowly, grinning. He too looked bone-weary and thinner, but he seemed to be the same man otherwise.

Coxani smiled at him. "Welcome back, Stalking Lion."

Naran's expression became mischievous. "Thank you..." he leaned to the side to look at her heraldic mark. "...Leaping Dolphin!"

Tikran tried to hide his smile unsuccessfully. "I swear I had nothing to do with that choice."

"Nothing?" Coxani asked, rolling her eyes. "Really?"

"Well, perhaps a little." Color returned to Tikran's face for a moment as he shrugged boyishly.

Coxani laughed. "Well, I for one, think it's utterly appropriate. The dolphin represents joy, balance, and harmony. I am honored."

Tikran avoided her gaze while Naran said, "That's good, because from what I've heard, you aren't exactly swimming like a dolphin."

She crossed her arms. "Not yet. Give me time."

As Tikran walked back to the wagons to help unload the royal retinue's luggage, Coxani approached Naran. "Is he okay?" She asked.

The laughter left Naran's eyes. "He's fine. This was his first campaign. I think, perhaps, things were not as he expected."

She peered up at the big Manzakar. "In what way?"

"That's a question you should ask him."

Coxani hesitated for a moment, then said, "You love him."

Naran looked down at her and smiled. "Of course. Always have, always will." He considered her. "And you, Dolphin?"

The heat began to creep up her neck. "Of course I love him."

Raising an eyebrow, he asked, "As a... brother?"

She looked away. "I don't know what it means to love a brother, I had none."

Naran looked over to where Tikran was carrying a large trunk. He said, "You should know... I asked Tikran if I could show interest in you."

A jolt of surprise ran through her. "You did?"

"Yes." Naran met her startled gaze and flashed a covetous smile. "He didn't seem too keen on the idea." He shrugged, turning to walk toward the wagons. "For what it's worth."

She was unable to speak to Tikran even semi-privately until the following afternoon, while he was feeding and brushing his gelding in the stables. She had just returned from the hippodrome and decided to walk by his stall. "If I didn't know better, I'd say you were avoiding me," she said.

He turned, surprised. "Avoiding? Not at all. Lest you forget, I'm an Aslan now. I spend at least half my time attending to the king."

She tilted her head. "You say it as though it were a bad thing."

"Would you like to grab a fresh horse and ride to the tree with me?" The large oak tree was near the training grounds outside the city, where they'd done most of her training. They often sat in its shade during their breaks.

"Yes," she said hurriedly.

As they rode through Anzor City and out the gates, Coxani told him about the graduation, her time spent training without him, and how she was adjusting to being a Manzakar. "I'm not blind, you know," she said. "I understand that, as a woman and Haydar's charge, I'm treated differently. Unless I insist otherwise, the officers go easy on me and exclude me from many activities that occur in the barracks. It used to bother me. But now, I just shrug it off. I'm a flight archer, after all. I will likely never be on the front lines wielding a lance against the enemy."

Tikran looked straight ahead. "You wouldn't want to be, trust me."

"Tikran," she said, "what happened out there? You're... changed."

He put a finger to his lips. "Let's get to the tree."

By the time they arrived, the sun was beginning to set. Coxani dismounted quickly, tethered her horse, and flopped down under the tree in a cloud of dust. "We're here. Now talk before I burst with impatience."

Tikran followed, sitting with his back against the gnarled bark of the old tree. As he rested his head, he let his breath out slowly. "Coxani. You were right."

"What about?"

"Everything." He ran his fingers through the grass. "Not only do they see the Gohari as lesser, but they don't even see them as human." He met her gaze. "Anzor is not 'protecting' or 'guiding' Gohar—it's exploiting it." He told her about the food rationing, the boy who stole the apple, and finally, the ambush by the youths and their ultimate fates.

Coxani was pale, her stomach queasy. "Holy Cenk. I never imagined..."

"Neither did I. And the worst part is that I had no power to get involved. Being an Aslan is..." He grimaced in disgust. "We're over-trained, glorified cupbearers and occasional performers. I've spent more time looking like one of the king's ornaments than I have doing anything else since becoming one."

"It's better than being the Manzakar ordered to campaign in Gohar," she replied. "Unless you're like Nasch, that piece of shit."

"I've been rendered powerless." Tikran grit his teeth.

She felt rage blossom in her chest. "We should do something."

"Ha!" Tikran shook his head. "Us and what army? Anzor holds all the cards, Coxani. They've been exceptionally clever. They manage to convince the nomads to sell their children in exchange for next to nothing. They bring the children to Anzor and celebrate them, transforming them into objects of sexual pleasure for their aristocrats and soldiers to fight their wars. They brainwash them into believing that Anzor has done the Gohari—those 'savages'—a service and continues to do them favors by providing food at the garrison towns. They trap the Manzakars in this life of... lavish servitude."

Coxani stared toward the sunset, the full gravity of Tikran's words sinking in. "What do we do?"

"I'm not sure we can do anything." The fire that glowed in his eyes was one that Coxani had never seen. In a soft voice, he said, "I'm convinced Nasch killed my mother."

She swallowed. The thought had occurred to her as well.

"But why would he kill her? Was she rebellious? Were you near a garrison town?"

"No to both those questions." Every muscle in his body seemed to tense. "The king's favorite mage... Her name is Saltanat. She told Naran and me that she often accompanies the Manzakars on campaign in Gohar because she can detect the Essence in others."

Coxani blanched. "It's how they find those with the Essence?"

"Yes. One of the Gohari who attacked the royal train was a girl Saltanat singled out as having the Essence. They didn't try to take her, however, because she was too... Gohari. So she died with the rest of them." He finally looked at her. "My mother must have had the Essence. She had to know they were coming for her. They found her and maybe tried to talk her into returning to Anzor with them, or maybe they just killed her because she was too old. Nasch may not have killed her with his own hands, but he gave the order—an order that came from the king himself. I'm certain of it."

They sat in contemplative, horrified silence for several minutes as the sun sank into the horizon, leaving a pink and purple sky behind it. At some point, Tikran reached over and pushed a stray tendril of hair from Coxani's face. "I thought about you often, you know. I wondered what you would do, or say, if you'd been there. I believe you would have handled it all better than I did."

Coxani smiled sadly. "I would have been so enraged that I would have definitely gotten myself suspended and possibly killed. I don't think that would have been handling it better." She looked at him then, hoping her desire wasn't showing on her face. "I thought about you too. A lot. I worried that you would return and I wouldn't be able to spend time with you, now that you aren't training me."

"The training doesn't have to end." An almost bashful smile tugged at his lips. "I'll see if Lord Haydar can arrange it so it doesn't."

She leaned forward, put her arms around his neck, and kissed him full on the mouth, hungrily. He responded in kind, his hands roaming up her hips and under her tunic. As quickly as was humanly possible, they tugged their clothes away or off, eager to feel skin against skin. Tikran lowered himself over her in the grass, their bodies intertwined. He braced his arms on either side of her head and kissed her desperately, his tongue seeking hers. Every other time they'd had sex, he'd been extremely gentle, as if afraid she would break, and as quiet as a mouse with his pleasure, emitting barely a gasp.

But this time was different. He wrapped her curls around his hand and tugged at her scalp. "Look at me," he demanded. She obeyed, her entire body shivering with anticipation. His eyes were like embers as he began to thrust hard inside her, and a deep groan escaped his lips. She heard rapturous noises emanate from her own mouth as pleasure overtook her.

Yes, his return to Gohar had changed him.

"Coxani," he said breathlessly. "I need you." She wrapped her legs around him and pulled him deeper, feeling his desire and anguish course through him, wishing she could save him, save Gohar, save herself.

———

Tikran ran his fingers through his damp hair and bound it back neatly in a queue. He tied the sash around his waist over his sword belt and put his turbaned cap on his head, tossing the loose end of the cloth across his neck over his shoulder. Dressed in uniform, he left the barracks and walked to the palace. Since getting back from Dilovar several days ago, he'd fallen into something of a daily routine. From dawn until mid-morning, he trained in the hippodrome; then he bathed, dressed, and attended to the king until mid-afternoon, serving as everything from a ceremonial guard to a secretary to a page. Unless the king was having an audience in the evening, Tikran would spend the rest of the day training some more, sometimes with just Coxani, sometimes with both Coxani and Naran, and sometimes alone.

He entered the palace and strode to the throne room, where the king was meeting with his advisors. Naran and the other Aslans were on rotating duty, but not Tikran. No, the king wanted Tikran by his side every day.

It's a great honor. I am what every Manzakar aspires to be.

Ignoring the nagging doubts in his mind and heaviness in his chest, he bowed to the king before taking his place to the side, awaiting orders. They had been discussing Vazha, since a minute later Delger summoned Damir. The Dilovari physician entered the room shortly thereafter and bowed deeply, his eyes flicking briefly to Tikran.

"I hope you find your accommodations in the palace satisfactory, doctor," the king said. "If you feel adequately settled in, I would like for you to examine Vazha today."

"Of course, Your Highness," Damir replied. "I am ready to see the prince whenever it best suits you. I only need to prepare my bag."

"Good," Delger said. "Prepare your bag and I will have Tikran take you to Prince Vazha's chambers in an hour."

Damir bowed again. "I will be ready, Your Highness."

When Damir was gone, Delger turned to Tikran. "I want you to keep an eye on him. He is, after all, Bilguun's personal physician. While I don't think he has ill intentions, I want assurance that he doesn't get any foolish ideas about his place here. He is not to attend Vazha without your presence."

"Yes, my king."

After an hour had passed, Tikran took his leave of the king and walked to the guests' quarters. He rapped against the door of Damir's room and the doctor promptly answered, raising an eyebrow at Tikran. "Good afternoon, Manzakar."

Tikran nodded curtly. "Good afternoon. Are you ready?"

"As I'll ever be."

Tikran felt Damir look at him as they walked through the palace. "I've changed my mind about you," Damir said.

Tikran blinked. "I'm sorry?"

"I said that the Manzakars were the lapdogs of Anzor." Damir looked forward. "I saw how you reacted to the execution of those young Gohari raiders. You are no lapdog."

His ears hot with embarrassment, Tikran cleared his throat. "It's unfortunate that it took a crisis for you to change your mind."

Damir smiled. "It's unfortunate that it took a crisis for you to reveal who you really are."

Tikran's muscles flexed. *What does he want with me?* The man clearly enjoyed provoking him. "Doctor, you have no idea who I really am. And I'd appreciate it if you'd stop making assumptions about me."

The physician shook his head but said nothing more.

They entered Vazha's chambers to find him standing at the window, his back to them. His mask and gloves were off, and he leaned on his cane, looking decades older than his twenty-six years.

"Your Highness," Tikran said, "I have brought the Dilovari physician at your father's request."

Vazha turned, his manner listless. "I don't see the point, but if my father wills it, there's no changing his mind."

Damir bowed. "Prince Vazha, if you would remove your clothes and lie down, I would like to examine you."

The prince's attendants, wearing gloves and cloth about their mouths, helped the prince disrobe down to his breeches and lie back on the overstuffed pillows of his bed. Damir pulled up a stool and sat at the bedside, his face tight with concentration, his gloveless fingers gently touching the scaly patches and nodules that covered the prince's torso, arms, and legs. Damir asked, "Can you feel my touch?"

"Only in some places. Not in others. Certainly not in my right foot."

"Do you feel any pain?"

"No. Tingling, sometimes burning."

"How is your vision?"

"Sometimes hazy."

Damir moved up to the prince's face, which was marred by the red patches. He repeated the process with Vazha's nose and mouth, then ears and neck. Finally, he sat back and reached into his bag. He retrieved a small bottle and motioned to the attendants. "Fill a bath with warm water and five drops of this tincture. Have him soak for thirty minutes." He looked at Vazha and smiled. "Your Highness, I have a treatment plan in mind, if you and your father will allow it."

"I'll allow anything," Vazha said. "I'm almost certain my father will too, at this point."

"I will discuss it with him at his earliest convenience and hopefully we can begin your treatment soon."

As they left and shut the door behind them, Tikran asked, "What's in that tincture?"

"It's a blend of sage leaf and calendula flower." Damir sighed. "It's no cure, but it will help ease any discomfort he feels from the lesions."

Tikran looked at him curiously. "You touched him with your bare hands. Aren't you worried you'll catch it?"

Damir dismissed the concern with a wave. "No. You can't

catch it from merely touching a leper. I've known many physicians who've handled lepers and never contracted it. I suspect —as do many of my fellow physicians—that it is passed from the fluids of the nose and mouth, and only after long periods of contact."

Tikran digested this. "What will your treatment plan involve?"

"I was reading the medical texts I brought with me last night. There's a shrub that is native to Gohar. It grows in the central steppe and bears a round purple fruit with black seeds that the Gohari nomads have traditionally used to treat a variety of illnesses, not least of which is leprosy." Damir looked down thoughtfully. "I don't know if it still exists, but anecdotally, it has cured more than a few lepers."

"I know what shrub you mean," Tikran said, stopping suddenly and turning to look at the doctor. "As children, my sisters and I were often tasked with plucking the fruit for my mother. She crushed the seeds and took the oil. She used it for all kinds of ailments. We didn't eat them. My sister and I tried once, out of hunger, and it was disgusting—very bitter. We had stomachaches for days afterward."

Damir smiled. "Then they still existed as of fifteen years ago."

"But how will you get it?"

Shrugging, Damir said, "I believe that is up to the king."

They walked back to the throne room, where the king ordered silence to hear Damir's assessment of Vazha. "I regret to report that he is no longer in the early stages, Your Highness," Damir said with a frown. "As you know, he has lost most sensation in his right foot, his eyesight grows weak, and he risks losing sensation in his left hand. Much of his skin burns or tingles. The disease has progressed more quickly than usual."

Delger made a tight fist. "And? What do you propose?"

Damir repeated what he'd said to Tikran about the shrub in Gohar. Then he said, "I request permission to travel to Gohar —with Tikran. He remembers where it grows."

What in the name of Cenk? Tikran opened his mouth to protest but the words wouldn't come out.

The king looked at him. "Is this true, Tikran?"

"I remember harvesting the fruit of the shrub for my mother, Your Highness."

"And you know where it grows?"

Don't lie! "Yes, Your Highness. It's a place our clan went often."

Delger stroked his short beard. "I will consider it."

With that, he turned back to his advisors, and Tikran knew they were dismissed. He led Damir out of the throne room and down the hall. Through his clamped teeth, he said, "I don't know where it grows, Damir. I was no more than seven years old."

The physician walked with casual indifference, cat-like and infuriating. "But you didn't object."

When there was no one nearby, Tikran stopped, turned, and shoved Damir up against the nearest wall, his forearm pressed into Damir's chest. "What game are you playing at, Doctor?" His voice was husky, his pulse pounded in his ears.

Damir looked startled but not afraid. "No game, Manzakar. I'm trying to cure the prince. You are the only man I trust to take me into Gohar."

Tikran didn't let go. "You can't know enough about me to trust me."

The haughtiness fell from Damir's face long enough for him to say, "But I trust you anyway."

Releasing him suddenly, Tikran continued to walk. His mind was awhirl. He'd been mildly aroused by Damir's nearness and it confounded him. He said, "Well, I don't trust *you*."

"That's fair. But give me the chance to prove I am worth trusting."

"Why?" Tikran glared. "Why do you want me to trust you?" He raised a finger. "Be careful, Doctor. I'm watching you. Do not underestimate me."

"I know," Damir answered, his face unreadable. "And I don't."

The two men didn't exchange words when they finally arrived at Damir's chambers. The door shut behind the doctor and Tikran headed once again back to the king, wondering, for the first time in his life, if Naran had enough wine stashed away for him to get drunk later.

A WEEK LATER, Tikran entered the throne room to find Delger and Haydar together, deep in discussion. "Tikran," the king said. "Just the man we wanted to see."

Haydar dismissed the other Aslans in the room so that it was only the three of them. Tikran bowed and wiped his suddenly sweaty palms on his tunic. Delger tapped his lips with his forefinger before speaking. "I have decided to grant Damir an escort into Gohar to find this shrub. A couple of my advisors—Lord Haydar included—have heard of it and, while they weren't aware that its fruit was used to treat leprosy, they confirmed that it is used by the Gohari and that it cures a variety of ailments." He paused. "I wanted to send the doctor with Commander Nasch, as he and his squadron will be heading back into Gohar in a couple weeks, and I have reservations about sending you. I fear that you might be... *unreliable* if faced with aggressive nomads."

Tikran tightened his jaw.

Delger continued. "However, Lord Haydar seems to believe you are the best man for the job on account of your familiarity with where the shrub is located. He also argues that judging you based on your very first campaign is unfair and that he is willing to vouch for you this time around."

"Yes, Your Highness."

The king relaxed and smiled. "Haydar will share the details of our plan with you later. But first, it has occurred to me that since your induction into the Aslan ranks was rushed, you have not been formally honored. Since the Fire Festival is only two weeks away, you will leave afterward—as a proper Aslan."

"I am touched and honored, my king."

That evening, Haydar invited Tikran to his home in the Citadel to discuss the pending trip into Gohar with Damir. Durais typically had two homes, one in the Citadel and one in the countryside, where they were granted land by the king. They were also allowed the temporary right to collect tax revenue from the land by dividing it into fiefs. In return, the durais maintained their own household of up to two hundred Manzakars for the king. When he was younger, Tikran had secretly hoped to belong to Haydar's household, since Haydar himself was the boy's idol. But Haydar had made it clear that serving the king directly was the greatest honor bestowed on a Manzakar, and ultimately, young Tikran wanted nothing more than to please Haydar.

He arrived at sundown, and a Manzakar let him in through the front gate. He walked through the garden to the door, inhaling the scent of the roses and jasmine flowers that perfumed the air. A Gohari slave girl, wearing a loose cotton dress and several braids in her hair, greeted him at the ornately carved and gilded door. She led him through the house, over marble mosaic floors and under beautifully painted ceilings, to the central courtyard, where a fountain spilled water gently into channels that ran into the house. The girl directed him to a small table and chairs beneath an orange tree.

"Lord Haydar will be with you momentarily," she said, then padded back into the house.

Sitting in one of the pearl-inlaid chairs, Tikran looked about him. *Someday all of this will be mine too.* He expected the heaviness in his chest to lift, but it didn't.

"Welcome, Tikran," Haydar said as he walked into the garden, smiling. He wore a thinly quilted cap, a linen shirt, cotton breeches, and soft leather slippers. Tikran stood and bowed. "Please sit," Haydar said, and settled comfortably in the opposite chair. "So tell me. How are you feeling?"

Tikran considered. "In general? Or about going to Gohar?"

Haydar's smile grew. "Let's begin with in general."

"Fine. Good." He couldn't think of anything more to say on the matter. "I'm great." How much did Haydar know about what went on in Gohar, he wondered? As one of the king's top advisors and a former Manzakar himself, he had to know how the nomads were treated.

The slave girl returned, bearing a tray of refreshments and delicate pastries. She set it down on the table and poured two glasses of rosewater and honey. "That's good to hear," Haydar replied, taking a sip from his glass. "How are things with Coxani?"

The back of Tikran's neck and the tips of his ears grew impossibly hot. He should have expected the question. "Fine. Good. Fine."

Haydar's laughter echoed through the courtyard. "Not one to kiss and tell, are you, lad? I expected nothing less of you." He took a bite from one of the pistachio-topped pastries. After swallowing, he added, "You do realize, Tikran, that there will come a time when Coxani will have to marry.

She can't live in the women's quarters forever, nor can she live in the barracks. As a Gohari woman, she cannot earn money or own property. She must have a Manzakar husband and she must bear his children. It's the law. It increases the chances that the Gohari who have the Essence are born in Anzor, and therefore reduces our need to go into Gohar to find them."

Tikran frowned. Coxani was right—a Gohari woman's life was not in any way her own.

Haydar leaned back in his chair and lowered his voice. "Unfortunately, your relationship with her is presumed to be physically intimate by most, and not without reason. Let's just say that one or two witnesses have... corroborated this presumption."

Oh, fuck. Tikran closed his eyes, his face burning with shame. He sucked in his breath and opened them. "Holy Cenk. Lord Haydar, I don't know what to say. I'm sorry. We thought we were being discreet, but clearly we were mistaken."

"Tikran, you are a grown man. Coxani is a grown woman. You made adult decisions. You owe me no apology. I'm only trying to provide guidance." Haydar sighed deeply. "I admit I am complicit... responsible, even. I gave the two of you more freedom than I likely should have, and I did, ultimately, encourage you to woo her. But I did so with the expectation that it would lead to a more serious commitment. Of course, as an Aslan you have the rare privilege of being able to choose to not marry. But I'll be honest, at this point anything short of marriage between the two of you would cause a scandal that would likely follow her for the rest of her life."

Tikran's pulse increased. "That's entirely unfair to her." His voice had an edge that caught him off guard.

The durai's eyebrows drew together. "She's a woman. While it's unfortunate, it's the way of things."

Not in Gohar, it's not. But then the Gohari were "savages," weren't they? Tikran clenched his jaw.

Haydar took another sip of his rosewater. "Coxani knows very well what the rules are for women in our society. They no doubt have been drummed into her from the time she was small. Nevertheless, she made her choices. She'll be hard-pressed to find a Manzakar who will marry her, considering. And while several Anzori lords have expressed great interest in becoming her protector, we already know how she feels about that sort of arrangement. Her best course of action would be to marry the man with whom she's been caught... frolicking."

Flustered, Tikran said, "I will marry her if that's what she wants. But I don't think it is."

"And what do *you* want, Tikran?"

"I don't know."

"Do you love her?"

"Yes, of course." As the words came out of his mouth, he realized he meant them. Admitting it felt natural, as if it had always been so. *I've loved her my whole life.* Still, it didn't change the truth of what he said next: "I just don't think I'm the marrying kind, to be honest. I'm certain Coxani isn't either. That said, I would marry her to save her from judgment, humiliation, or a loveless marriage to someone else."

Haydar's eyes softened. "You remain the kind-hearted boy, lad." He paused. "I think with a bit of encouragement from you she could be swayed."

Tikran took a gulp of rosewater in the hope it would cool him off, then said, "I can... suggest it. But she must come to the decision on her own."

Haydar sat quietly, a pensive look on his face. Finally he said, "I suppose that's good enough for the time being." The smile returned and he shifted in his chair. "Now. In regard to escorting the Dilovari doctor into Gohar. Your thoughts?"

After draining his glass in two large swallows, Tikran set down his glass and said, "I'm not entirely sure. I don't trust him. But if the shrub will cure Prince Vazha, I will escort him regardless."

Haydar nodded. "I do genuinely believe you are the best man to do this, Tikran. I would feel that way even if you didn't know where to find the shrub."

Tikran kept his eyes level and his face composed even as his stomach flipped. "I'm honored, Lord Haydar." He'd been struggling with his decision to go along with Damir's lie. Why had he done it? And why had he lied to the king outright himself? At the time, he had no idea what compelled him. Now, however, he realized that he wanted to go back to Gohar. He wanted to see what was happening there with his own eyes and... *do* something. What he could possibly do as a single Manzakar amidst hostile natives was beyond him. But his conscience wouldn't let him rest.

Haydar continued. "As for the king's reservations about you... We all make mistakes. And you were thrust into the role of Aslan unexpectedly, so you had little time to prepare for what awaited you. Not to mention, it was your first campaign. There was a lot of pressure on you. I think the king accepts all of this now."

Again, Tikran wondered whether Haydar condoned Anzor's treatment of the nomads. *We all make mistakes.* Haydar had to believe the Gohari were savages too, then. A feeling of desperate sadness settled over Tikran. "Thank you for your support, my lord."

"Of course, lad." Haydar's eyes brimmed with affection. "I've always believed in you, and I always will." He leaned forward and rubbed his hands together. "So the plan is to have you enter Gohar as a Gohari. A Manzakar would draw attention, some of which would no doubt be negative, so having you play the part of a humble nomad guiding a Dilovari doctor will allow you to find the shrub and return without any unnecessary harassment. Hopefully you remember the Gohari dialect?"

"Some. I would have to practice it."

"You have a good two weeks to brush up on it. That should be enough time." The men stood and Haydar clapped Tikran on the shoulder. "I am proud of you, Tikran. You are becoming every bit the man I expected."

"Thank you, my lord." Tikran's throat clenched. He suddenly had the strange urge to cry. *Get a grip, man.* "I hope to always make you proud."

Instead of walking back to the barracks after bidding Haydar good night, Tikran went straight to hippodrome and hacked furiously at felt-covered clay with his saber well into the night.

CHAPTER 12

Anzor's flag would have blended seamlessly into the bright blue sky if not for the golden scepter in its center as it flapped in the cool spring breeze. Coxani breathed in the fresh air deeply as she faced the bustle of the Citadel. It was once again the time of year when the great gates were thrown open and Anzori commoners thronged the clean, paved streets, gaping in awe at the white terraced homes and sumptuously draped carriages of the aristocrats. The carriages were a rare sight even for Coxani, as the nobles used them primarily to avoid interacting with the lower classes. They bumped down the thoroughfare toward the hippodrome, parting the crowd like a sea.

Coxani looked forward to competing in the mounted archery tournament in this year's Fire Festival and hoped her queasy stomach wouldn't interfere. She knew she could never match Tikran's 217 performance, but she had worked hard to qualify and knew, deep down, that she could win.

"A lady Manzakar!" a young Anzori girl cried, her eyes wide and darting from Coxani's navy jacket to her white turban as

Coxani brushed past, trying to squeeze through the crowd. Coxani smiled and winked at the girl, who promptly turned and beamed at a boy around the same age. "I *told* you they were real!"

Still smiling, Coxani strode into the royal stables where Naran was preparing Tikran for his rite of passage as an Aslan: the Fire Game. She watched, her hands on her hips, as Naran attached the black powder cartridges to Tikran's talc-covered jacket. "This is child's play for you, isn't it?" she asked Tikran.

Tikran shrugged. "I wouldn't say that. I'm not sure anyone would consider being lit on fire child's play."

Naran held up a hand. "Depends on the child. I, for one..."

"You must have been a nightmare of a child," Coxani said, shaking her head.

Naran chuckled. "You have no idea, Dolphin." He finished affixing the last cartridge and slapped Tikran on the back. "You're all ready, Tik."

"Let's get this over with." Tikran smiled at Coxani. "Are *you* ready?"

"To watch you catch fire? Always."

"No, smartass. To win the tournament." He winked at her. "I know you can do it. Remember what we practiced."

"Yes, yes." She gave him a playful shove. "I'll remember." He'd told her all about his pending trip to Gohar with the Dilovari doctor. She'd have been lying if she didn't admit to being worried. The way he'd come back after his first trip to Gohar... And she didn't blame him. She knew deep down that she would have handled the whole thing much worse.

He tilted his head at her. "Are you okay, Coxani? You seem... off."

"I'm great," she lied. At some point soon she had to talk to that Dilovari doctor—alone.

The lance-master motioned to the Aslans to line up and she backed away. "Light up the sky, Tikran."

"I don't think I have a choice." He slipped on his helmet and rode to wait beside the other two Aslans. At the lance-master's signal, they rode out to the middle of the hippodrome to a roar of cheers.

Coxani rushed to the entrance of the portico to better see and Naran came up beside her. The mage—Saltanat, Tikran had said her name was—stood at the balcony, her hand moving through the air. For a moment, it felt as though all the air was sucked from the sky. Then the three Manzakars ignited from right to left. The crowd thundered. The newly initiated Aslans rode to a gallop and stood on their saddle arches, twirling their flaming poles. The fire swirled like ribbons over the Manzakars' heads, dancing in synchrony with each flick of their wrists. Coxani kept her eyes on Tikran, the Aslan on the right. Even from a distance, there was no mistaking him. His posture, the ease with which he moved, his confidence...

She realized with a start that his flames blazed brighter and licked higher than the others, leaping like tongues of orange light. The crowd noticed as well and cheered louder. If she hadn't known any better, she would have assumed he was showing off.

But she *did* know better.

Tikran abruptly dropped his pole, dove to the ground, and rolled. Naran flashed past her. With her stomach roiling, she was right behind him, her mind in a panic. From a distance Tikran was a ball of fire, and in spite of his rolling, the flames persisted. Coxani began to scream when, out of nowhere, clouds surged into the sky and a gush of water soaked the earth. It was so powerful that she fell to the ground twice trying to reach him. She made it as Naran was lifting Tikran into his arms and the other Manzakars arrived with a stretcher.

Naran helped to lay his friend upon it and yelled at the others to hurry.

The rain stopped almost as suddenly as it started while they rushed through the portico, out of the hippodrome, and to the barracks, where Tikran was stripped down to his breeches. The skin of his left arm and shoulder was badly burned, causing Naran to slump and Coxani to cover her mouth. Angry red blisters at least three inches wide ran from his wrist to his neck, edged with a raw pinkish white. As Coxani desperately tried to keep from sobbing, Tikran said, "It's okay. I can't feel it."

As if he meant to make her feel better.

The Dilovari physician suddenly materialized beside her with a large cloth soaked in something that smelled herbal. He laid it gently on Tikran's wound, shooing everyone but Naran and Coxani away. He then held a cup of something to Tikran's lips, coaxing him to drink in a soft murmur. Tikran drank and moments later his eyelids drooped, then shut. Coxani spread her arms across Tikran's legs and said to Damir, "If you remove me from here, I will hunt you down." She saw the doctor's lips quirk in amusement.

At some point Haydar appeared. He tossed a cotton sheet to Naran and draped another around Coxani's shoulders. She heard him speaking in a low voice to the doctor. Then he rested one hand on Tikran's sweaty forehead and the other on Coxani's back. "Coxani. You're going to miss the tournament. Why don't you change out of those wet clothes and get ready?"

Even though she knew she spoke to Lord Haydar, she snapped, "Absolutely not. Hang the tournament. I'm not leaving him." After a bit of thought, she added, "My lord."

The doctor began cleaning the wound gently, careful not to wake his patient. Tikran grimaced with pain in his sleep. She watched his chest rise and fall with each uneven breath for what felt like hours. At some point she must have dozed, her head resting beside Tikran's knee. She awoke abruptly. The festival had long ended and the night outside the window was quiet as the city slept. Tikran slept peacefully, normal color restored to his face. Naran was sprawled on a bench beside him, snoring. Sitting next to the cot on a stool, the doctor kept quiet vigil, watching his patient. It suddenly occurred to her that he was young—and attractive in an icy, unapproachable way. She asked, "Will he be okay?"

Damir nodded, dark smudges under his eyes. "Yes."

"The wound..."

"It will leave a significant scar and he won't be able to feel anything that touches it, as the fire burned through the skin and into tissue beneath. But thankfully it did not reach his tendons or muscles. He will keep full function of his left side."

She slumped with relief. If it hadn't been for the sudden storm... "The rain came out of nowhere. The mages must have had something to do with it."

Damir averted his gaze. "No doubt."

She slept for a short time and only awoke because she heard movement. Haydar had returned. He said to the doctor, "Go and rest. I will ensure that the king's doctors take care of him. We will summon you if we must."

"As you wish, my lord." Damir bowed and left, somewhat reluctantly.

Coxani jumped up after a moment and followed. She heard Haydar say her name but kept moving. This was her chance. She rushed out into the moonlight and saw Damir walking down the road back to the palace. She ran behind him. "Doctor," she panted. "Wait."

He stopped and turned, frowning. "Yes?" She skidded to a stop, catching her breath. He said, "Coxani, is it?"

She nodded. "Yes. And you are Damir."

He bowed his head. "At your service."

Looking around to make sure any errant passers-by weren't close enough to hear their conversation, she said, "I need your help."

"Yes?" There was a slight shift in his expression.

She looked up at the night sky and squeezed her eyes shut in humiliation. She was standing in the middle of the street, in a soldier's still-damp uniform, her hair streaked with mud, and about to utter words she'd never dreamed would come out of her mouth—to a complete stranger. "I'm pregnant."

Damir was very still for several seconds. "I'm assuming you don't seek congratulations."

"No. Not at all." She tried to keep the desperation out of her voice.

"Does the father know?" The look in his pale eyes told her that he knew very well who the father was.

"He can't know." She shook her head. "He has too much on his plate at the moment. He would worry and feel immense guilt... and Cenk forbid he feel some sort of obligation to marry me..." She lifted her chin, her mind set. "He can never know."

Inhaling sharply, Damir said, "I can help you if you're certain that you—"

"I'm certain. If word got out that I'm with child, I'd be immediately removed from the Manzakar ranks and forced to keep it. And the father... he'd likely be demoted and forced to marry me." She met his gaze directly. "I'm hoping for your complete discretion, Damir. While my fate as an unwed pregnant woman might be bad, my fate as a woman who ended her pregnancy would be much worse."

Damir nodded slowly. "You have my word. I have no desire to meet the fate of a doctor who abetted you. Meet me in the palace gardens tomorrow just before midday supper. I'll give you something that will likely be quite unpleasant and indispose you for a bit, but should do the trick."

Relief washed over her. "Thank you."

He bowed. "Good night, Manzakar. Take care." Then he turned on his heels and continued on down the road, his long, black robe fluttering behind him.

SALTANAT HURRIED through the palace halls. Ice cold fear trickled through her veins as she remembered the events of earlier that night. Everything had been going perfectly. Nasch had tampered with the insolent Aslan's jacket, dusting it with flour instead of talc. He'd ridden out and she'd lit the cartridges, ever so subtly increasing and fanning the flames on his. The crowd had believed it to be part of the show, as she'd intended. As the left side of his jacket caught fire, he leaped from his horse and tumbled into a roll. But she kept the fire blazing, coaxing it to burn hotter.

Then the rain had come, pouring down in sheets.

It hadn't been the other mages; of that she was certain. She could sense when they used the Essence. No, this had come from somewhere else within the hippodrome...

The Aslans guarding the throne room opened the heavy doors for her without question. She swept in, dismayed to find Lord Haydar with the king. She had wanted to speak with Delger privately.

"Saltanat!" the king cried, his arms open. "My lady, you are the heroine of the night!"

The mage forced a smile and bowed deeply. "Your Highness flatters me."

Delger clasped her shoulders between his hands. "I do not. Without your thunderstorm, Tikran might have died."

"He speaks only truth, my lady," Haydar said from where he sat perched on the edge of a table.

Saltanat struggled to keep smiling. "I only did what I had to do to save him. Any of the other mages would have done the same in my shoes."

Shaking his head, Delger said, "You are being modest, but very well. What matter brings you to me tonight?"

She hesitated, choosing her words carefully. "My king, there is someone with the Essence in Anzor City—someone I failed to detect."

The king's smile dissipated. "How do you know this?"

"Someone made Tikran's fire grow so he would burn." She licked her lips. "But for some reason, I did not feel their Essence until it happened."

"How is that possible?" Haydar asked.

"I don't know," she answered. "The only explanation is that this person was able to mask their Essence."

"Is that even possible?"

She crossed her arms tightly against her body. "I cannot do it. But I have heard, at least by word of mouth, that it has been done by those with very powerful Essence. But this would have been at least a hundred years ago."

"By Cenk." Delger looked at Haydar, who seemed to be deep in thought. "We must find this criminal."

Haydar nodded grimly. "Most definitely."

The king spun around to face Saltanat. "Search every home, every alleyway, every wagon in the Citadel. If you find nothing, go into the city. Take the mages and as many Manzakars as you need with you. This... abomination must be found."

Saltanat bowed again. "Immediately, Your Highness." She turned and walked briskly from the throne room.

She would find—and kill—this abomination.

CHAPTER 13

Naran's opponent, a tall, beefy Manzakar who had rage issues, hacked furiously at Naran, their blades crashing together at an almost even cadence. Other than Tikran, Naran had beaten every other Manzakar at tactical fencing with a saber. It only took a couple seconds for Naran to realize that his opponent had no strategy—he seemed to believe that brute strength and anger would win him the bout. *Big, dumb bastard.* It made Naran smile. Literally. He was smiling as he parried the attacks with ease, which incited his opponent even more.

The beat of the clashing sabers increased until Naran decided he'd had enough. He stopped a cut from above, stepped forward while sliding his blade to the side, then seized his opponent's hilt with his left hand. He shoved the hilt down and swung his blade around, its blunted tip pressed firmly against the beefy Manzakar's chest. Naran's smile grew. "You're dead, my friend."

His opponent threw his weapon to the ground like a petulant child and Naran laughed while shaking his head. He removed his helmet and walked back to the portico, exhausted. Constant drilling was the only thing that kept him from worrying about Tikran. It was also the only thing keeping him from dwelling on a particular pair of big green eyes. The moment he was at rest, those eyes were all he could think about—along with the bow-shaped mouth, and golden skin, and captivating laugh, and sharp wit, and shapely ass...

He huffed in frustration. *She loves Tikran. Get over it, you idiot.* But he couldn't. The more time he spent with her, the more convinced he became that she was the woman of his dreams. Admittedly, other than his numerous but brief dalliances, he didn't know many women. He certainly didn't know any women *well*. His own mother had died when he was an infant and he had no sisters. His Manzakar upbringing hadn't given him the opportunity to know any women—quite the opposite. Until Coxani, he'd seen them as a different species—smaller, prettier, gentler, and with brains that worked very differently from his own. Flirty banter aside, he'd never really been inclined to have any conversations with them.

Coxani was turning everything he thought he knew about women on its head. She was definitely smaller and prettier, but everything else was a surprise: she was whip-smart, had a wicked sense of humor, swore like a soldier, and could definitely hold her own on the training grounds. She was fearless, joyful, mischievous... She made him see women in an entirely new light, and quite honestly, he was embarrassed by his past behavior with them.

He waited in the portico for Coxani to join him for some mounted archery. Since he and Tikran had gotten back from their trip to Dilovar, the three of them had started training together. Now, however, Tikran was injured, so it would just be the two of them. It made him nervous. Coxani was Tikran's girl. He absolutely had to keep from flirting with her, especially considering Tikran couldn't be there.

Tikran's accident had jarred him. Tikran was always the lucky one. *The favorite.* Sure, Naran struggled with envy on occasion. He was human, after all. But he loved Tikran and saw him for who he was—a man with a heart of gold destined for success. Naran felt this need to protect him. If he had been any other kind of person, Tikran's injury would have seemed fortuitous. But Naran couldn't imagine a world without Tikran, even if it meant pining for Coxani for the rest of his life.

He heard someone say his name and turned to face a young eunuch. "Commander Naran, Coxani regrets to inform you that she is unable to train with you today. She is unwell."

Naran's heart sank. "Is she okay?" he asked. "Wait, aren't you one of Lord Haydar's servants?"

"Yes," the eunuch answered. "Miss Coxani is staying at my lord's home until she recovers."

Naran frowned. It must be serious, if Haydar had taken her in. "What's wrong with her?"

"I'm not sure, Commander."

"Well," Naran muttered, "I'm going back with you."

They returned to Haydar's home where Naran was surprised to see Damir, the Dilovari doctor, leaving one of the bedrooms—presumably the one where Coxani was staying. His chest tightened. Something had to be very wrong. "Doctor Damir," Naran said, "what's happened to Coxani?"

The doctor looked curiously at Naran. "You are Tikran's good friend, no?"

"Yes. What's wrong with Coxani?" They could have formal introductions another time, as far as Naran was concerned.

Damir seemed to consider him before answering. "She has an inflamed appendix. It's causing her abdominal pain, nausea, vomiting, and other unpleasant symptoms. I have begun administering a serum that will hopefully reduce the inflammation and prevent it from rupturing, which would require surgery."

"That sounds awful," Naran muttered. "May I see her?"

"I will ask her," Damir said, turning back toward the door and disappearing inside briefly. He emerged again and said, "Yes, you may."

"Thanks, Doctor." Naran let out a laugh. "Between the prince, Tikran, and Coxani, you're staying busy, huh?"

"I am indeed." One corner of Damir's mouth curved up. Naran noticed then that, though his eyes were uncanny, the doctor was a handsome man.

"I'm sure King Delger has doctors who could help," Naran said, scratching his cheek as he wondered why the Dilovari doctor was suddenly everywhere.

"They have no idea what they're doing," Damir replied, wrinkling his nose. "I am the best man for the job. And I don't mind it." The Dilovari straightened, relaxing his expression. "I'll return tomorrow. In the meantime, make sure she gets plenty of water and rest. If she worsens, call for me immediately."

"Will do," Naran said and slowly entered the room. Coxani lay in bed on her side, a blanket pulled up to her shoulders. She was facing the door, her eyes half open, her face drained of color. She looked at him and smiled, making his stomach flutter. "First Tikran, now you? What the fuck, Dolphin?" he said softly, smiling back.

This made her giggle. "Stop," she said. "It hurts to laugh."

He sat on the chair beside the bed and leaned his elbows on his knees. *She's still so gorgeous.* He cleared his throat. "I stopped by to see Tikran this morning. He was trying to convince Damir to let him train with us today. Damir was having none of it."

"That sounds like Tikran," she said, continuing to smile. "Damir told me his wound is already beginning to heal."

"Tikran will be healed and back in the saddle in no time. Nothing can stop him."

"I think Doctor Damir probably can."

Naran chuckled. "The doctor doesn't seem to mess around. Maybe Tikran has finally met his match."

Coxani's smile faded. "Naran, I'm worried about Tikran going back into Gohar. He told me what happened on the journey to and from Dilovar. With the boy who stole the apple and with the Gohari warriors. It's... horrific."

Naran looked at his hands. "Yeah. Even I was shocked by what happened. I was worried, though. Tikran was getting really fired up, saying things that would land him in prison if the wrong people heard him say them. I was as angry as he was, but I felt like I had to temper him." He shook his head. "Since we've been back, we've both been grappling with it. Here we are, Aslan Manzakars, something both of us have dreamed of becoming practically our entire lives. And suddenly we're finding out that we're, well, the bad guys."

Coxani shifted, pushing the blanket down to her waist. "There must be something we can do."

He raised his eyes to look at her. Her brow was furrowed, her lovely mouth drawn tight, a fire in her eyes. She looked so beautiful he wanted to smile but thought better of it. "Problem is, we don't really have any power. Tikran's right. We only have the illusion of power."

She huffed. "We're soldiers, aren't we? We—"

"Coxani, you're sounding exactly like Tikran," Naran warned. "I can't decide if you're rubbing off on him or if it's the other way around."

She relaxed a bit and smiled. "Obviously, *I'm* rubbing off on *him*."

Naran grinned. "No doubt, Dolphin." He held her gaze for a fraction of a second too long. She blinked and looked away, a tiny bit of color returning to her face. *Well, at least I'm helping her circulation.* Frustrated with himself, he frowned at the floor. "Is there anything I can do to help you get better faster?" he asked. "Other than visiting you every day, which I'm going to do regardless?"

The smile returned. "I would like that, Lion. Just keep an eye on Tikran."

"I would do that anyway, you know."

"Yes, I know." She looked at him, her eyes shining.

Fuck. He had to get out of there before he professed his undying love for her. He stood. "Manzakar, your duty at the moment is to get better as soon as possible. Understood?"

She giggled and winced again. "Yes, Commander. You fucker."

He snorted in spite of himself. *I definitely love this woman.* "I'll be off, then." He turned and walked out of the room without looking back. After shutting the door behind him, he wilted just a bit but continued to walk, massaging the ache in his chest with his hand.

THE GIFTS and flowers that were piling up in the hospital were all addressed to Tikran—and mainly from women he'd never met. Coxani snickered as she opened the notes wishing him a quick recovery. "Oh, this one's good." Her voice was several octaves higher as she read, "Dearest Tikran, I almost died when I realized you were actually injured during the Fire Game. I wish I could nurse you back to health. Please enjoy these cookies—I baked them with utmost love. Yours forever, Tarana." Coxani wiggled her eyebrows at Tikran as she bit into one of the cookies. "With utmost *looooove*. The ladies certainly lust after the Caged Kingfisher," she said through a mouthful.

Tikran winced with embarrassment. "Coxani, please stop." Two weeks after the accident and the day before he and Damir were to leave for Gohar, Tikran had to admit the wound looked worse. But the doctor had reassured him that it was all part of the healing process. As he finished cleaning his wound, the edges stung like fire. He yelped aloud.

Coxani set down the unfinished cookie. "Tikran, you should let me or Naran go in your stead."

Tikran gently placed a strip of poultice-smeared gauze up his arm, across his shoulder, and against the side of his neck. He said, "Look Coxani, I know how to dress my wound without help. I certainly don't plan on doing any fighting. On top of that, I will be traveling with a doctor, for Cenk's sake."

Coxani shook her head and stood. "You are a stubborn man, Tikran."

He began wrapping a thicker strip of cotton over the gauze and around his arm. "I committed to doing this. I won't let a minor injury keep me from it."

She snorted. "If that's a minor injury, I don't want to see what you consider a major one."

Tikran wasn't worried. It certainly was a nuisance, but once it healed it would become a mere inconvenience. In truth, he was more worried about Coxani. She'd been bedridden with an inflamed appendix for a week. He and Naran had been at her bedside every chance they got, and Damir had insisted on visiting her several times to check on her even though he hadn't been called on. Tikran had become ambivalent about the doctor. Between the way he'd worried after Coxani and had tended to Tikran himself, the Dilovari doctor had shown compassion and patience, which conflicted with the haughty, snide man Tikran had initially judged him to be.

"How are you feeling today?" Tikran asked, noting that Coxani looked thinner. Although she had recently resumed her daily activities, he could see the toll the sickness had taken on her.

"Oh, much better." She straightened. "Almost at a hundred percent."

"Good." He had his doubts. He finished dressing his wound and slipped carefully into his shirt. "You should take it easy until you're fully recovered, though. I can see that you don't have your usual energy."

"Don't worry about me." She smiled. "Worry about your wound festering while you're out in the middle of the steppe. It's definitely what *I'm* worried about."

He chuckled. "Well, stop worrying. It's a waste of energy, and you need every bit of yours." He paused, remembering his promise to Haydar. They were alone for the moment, and now was as good a time as any. He cleared his throat. "Coxani, have you thought about your plans for the future?"

She blinked in surprise. "Where did that question come from?"

He shrugged and wiggled into his tunic. "It's just something I've been thinking about. Usually girls leave the women's quarters by the time they're eighteen under the protection of either a husband, an Anzori lord, or a master. You just turned twenty. They won't let you stay there forever."

She crossed her arms defensively. "I'll figure something out." She knitted her brow. "I was planning on approaching the king to ask if I might get a Manzakar's salary like the men. I know Haydar will support me."

"As will I," Tikran said. "But what if he denies your request? It would be a major break from the norm, after all. And even if you were to earn a salary, you would still have to marry and your money would become your husband's."

She looked down. "I haven't thought that far yet."

He pretended to study his bandaged arm as heat prickled his ears and neck. *Here goes.* "What if we were to be married?"

She flinched. "What?"

"Obviously, it wouldn't be a traditional marriage," he continued in a rush, still not looking at her. "We would be equals in everything. None of this wife being the husband's property bullshit. Nothing would really change, except that we would live in the same house." He knew he was beginning to ramble but couldn't stop himself. "I'm looking to buy a house when I return from Gohar. I need to move out of the barracks. We could—"

"Tikran." He looked up. Her eyes were a limpid green, shimmering with emotion. "Is that what you really want?"

He stepped closer, reaching out and touching her cheek with his fingers. "I want you to be happy. That's what I really want."

She took his hand in hers and pressed it to her face. "And what do you think would make me happy?"

He smiled wistfully. "To be free."

She reached up and quickly swiped the tears that had welled up in her eyes before they could fall. "You know me well."

He cupped her face in his hands. "You know I love you, don't you? I don't think I've ever told you. Marriage may not be right for either of us, but that doesn't diminish my feelings for you."

"Stop it," she demanded, the tears streaming freely now. "You brute, look what you've done. I'm a mess." She wiped her face on her sleeve, sniffling. "You know I feel the same about you."

Voices echoed in the hall, approaching. He took a step back

and let his hands drop. "If you change your mind, just know... my offer stands. Think on it."

Coxani smiled, wiping her face again quickly. "Oh, but how devastated the women of Anzor would be if their favorite Manzakar got married! Their chances of bedding him would certainly dwindle."

Tikran opened his mouth to answer when Haydar strolled into the room, looking Tikran up and down. "Just stopping by to see if you're still determined to make the journey, lad."

"Yes, my lord."

"Coxani hasn't been able to talk you out of it, eh?"

Coxani veiled her face with her curls. "He's stubborn as a mule."

"Everyone is making a big deal of it," Tikran said. "I'm a Manzakar, for Cenk's sake. I can do this."

"The people who love you will worry about you, there's no stopping that," Haydar said.

The corner of Coxani's mouth lifted in a half-smile. "I just wish he wasn't so flammable."

LATE THAT NIGHT, Tikran sat in the stables, feeding his gelding, cleaning his weapons, and preparing the items he might need —besides extra drawers, undershirts, and stockings which would be bundled in a sack, he would carry money, a quill, the king's official orders, and a spoon in a leather purse that hung from his belt. He would have two daggers, one on his belt and the other in his boot, as well as a bow on his back and a quiver of arrows at his hip. He would not take the beautiful bow Haydar had given him, since it practically screamed "Manzakar." Instead, he would take a Gohari bow, which was plain but just as effective.

Since his accident, he'd practiced shooting as often as the doctor would let him. While the worst part of the wound itself didn't hurt, its periphery of singed, pink flesh did. Other than that, however, the injury hadn't affected his abilities. There was simply no reason he couldn't escort Damir into Gohar, and he refused to even consider not going.

"Changed your mind?" Naran leaned against the entrance of the stall, his eyebrows raised.

Tikran grinned. "Not a chance."

"I didn't think so." The yellow-haired Manzakar walked in and began rubbing the horse's neck. "Well, is there anything I can do for you while you're gone?" He smiled slyly. "That is, other than flirt shamelessly with Coxani?"

Tikran was quiet as he wiped the blades of his daggers with an oily rag. After a minute, he asked, "How do you feel about marriage?"

Naran didn't seem startled by the question. "With the right woman, I'd certainly do it."

Tikran's jaw dropped. It wasn't at all what he'd expected Naran's answer to be. "Really? *You?*"

"Yes, really." He looked at Tikran. "Why do you ask?"

"Coxani won't marry me." He tossed the rag down and slipped the daggers into their leather-covered, wooden sheaths. "Neither of us wants to get married. But I would do it to ensure she has money and a place to live without having to get into some other asshole's bed."

Naran looked downright horrified. "Tikran, no wonder she won't marry you!" He rubbed his face. "Is *that* how you asked her? 'Hey, look, I don't really want to marry you, but I'd do it to keep you out of trouble?'"

"That is *not* what I said."

Naran let out a laugh. "Brother, I can guarantee that's what she heard. This is Coxani we're talking about." He began to pace back and forth across the stall. "By Cenk! You really fucked that up."

"I wanted to be perfectly honest with her."

Naran stopped pacing. "You really *don't* want to marry her, do you?"

"I want her to be happy. She would not be happy married to me—or anyone."

"I absolutely disagree."

Tikran stopped fiddling with his daggers and glared at Naran. "Oh? And you think you know her better than I do?"

"In some ways, yes."

"Is that so? And in what ways are those?"

"Man, are you blind? She's passionate and brilliant and... the things she's accomplished against all odds... She's stronger than both of us put together." Naran's cheeks were several shades darker than the rest of his face.

Tikran gawked at his friend. Naran did not blush. It was simply not a thing he did. Not in sixteen years had he seen the big Manzakar ever... "Holy *shit*. You're in love with her."

The blush graduated into a full-on flush. He looked Tikran in the eyes. "I hope you know that I would never overstep the boundaries you've drawn."

Tikran's mouth hung open as he processed this unexpected revelation. "All this time, I thought you just wanted to add her to your long list of conquests. Why didn't you tell me?"

Naran snorted. "Tik, the two of you are a... thing. Can you imagine if I just randomly declared my love for the woman you're actively, er, having relations with?"

Dragging his hands down his face, Tikran plopped down in the straw. "Does she know?"

"I certainly hope not."

Bracing himself for the answer, he asked, "Do you think she feels the same way about you?"

"No. I don't think so." Naran shook his mane and laughed quietly. "She thinks I'm funny and strange, and she definitely likes how I always watch your back."

Tikran looked up at his friend, an idea dawning on him. "Those boundaries... they're gone. You're free to show interest in her."

For a moment, Naran looked stricken. "Tik, I think *you're* the one she loves."

"Yes, she loves me, and I love her. There's no denying that. But..." Tikran scratched his head. "She won't marry me. Maybe I'm not... what she deserves."

Naran rolled his eyes. "Oh for fuck's sake. And *I* am? Get a grip, man."

"Brother." Tikran jumped to his feet and took two steps so that he was inches from Naran. He laid the hand of his good arm on his friend's shoulder. "I'm serious. She has to marry eventually, it's the law. It may as well be one of us. It may turn out that you're just what she needs. I mean it when I say that I just want her to be happy."

Searching Tikran's face, Naran's suddenly softened. "All right, then. If you're sure. But if I express interest in her and she turns me down because she's in love with you, you better not break her heart."

"I promise I won't."

With force that made Tikran's wound sear with pain as though it had just split open, Naran embraced him. "I love you, Tikran." His voice was muffled, his face buried in Tikran's good shoulder.

Tikran grinned even as he desperately hoped the hug would end soon. "I love you too, asshole."

CHAPTER 14

They left Anzor City on a beautiful spring day, just on the cusp of summer. Tikran dressed as a simple Gohari nomad in a long sheepskin vest over a tunic and breeches, and Damir wore the clothes of a middle-class Dilovari, in a long robe that folded across the chest and buttoned under the arm. They both wore felt hats with broad brims that folded up. After saying their farewells, they rode through the gates and down the road that eventually led into Gohar. At night they set up camp just off the road alongside many of the other travelers—mostly slave traders. Tikran wondered if they would run into Mago, whom he hadn't seen in a while.

When they resumed their journey, Damir was silent and pensive, and Tikran didn't feel the need for discourse. Each was deep in his own thoughts, speaking only when one of them had immediate needs or when they were agreeing on where to stop. Then, the first night they stopped in Gohar, about a week into their expedition, Damir initiated conversation. They were sitting around a small campfire cooking the birds Tikran had killed. The sun was setting and the heat of the day had begun to dissipate.

"So tell me," Damir said, leaning back casually on the ground, his legs crossed before him. "Have you made many enemies in Anzor?"

Tikran chuckled at the question, twisting the skewer of bustards—flightless birds that were a Gohari favorite—over the fire. "Just one, as far as I know. Why? Have you made many enemies in Dilovar?"

"Oh, many," Damir answered with a smile. "I'm exceedingly good at making enemies."

"You sound proud."

"Only when they're the right enemies," the doctor answered. "And most of them are, I believe." He looked at Tikran. "And yours? Is he—or she—the right kind of enemy?"

"Yes." He answered without hesitation.

"How so?"

Tikran's lips tightened. He lifted the skewer from the fire and blew on the now-cooked birds. "He has no conscience. He thinks beating and killing those much weaker than he is makes him powerful."

"You speak of the Manzakar who murdered those young nomads on the way back from Dilovar," Damir said, pulling a bird from the skewer. "That man is definitely the right kind of enemy."

They ate their dinner in silence, listening to the crickets' song as the sun disappeared behind the horizon. Then Damir said, "He's romantically involved with the mage. Saltanat."

Tikran wiped his mouth with his sleeve since he had nothing else. "I couldn't give a shit about their love affair, Doctor."

Damir rolled his eyes. "My name is Damir. And I'm

suggesting she may have been helping him take out some form of revenge on you the night of the Fire Festival."

Tikran processed this, pulling a chunk of meat off a thigh bone. "You think Saltanat had something to do with my uniform catching fire?"

The doctor shrugged, frowning into the campfire. "I was watching. Those flames rose higher than the rest and persisted despite your attempts to put them out."

Tikran suddenly lost his appetite. "Then who made it rain? I know for a fact she can make it rain."

Damir chuckled. "Why are you so impressed with her parlor tricks? Any decent mage can make it rain. It could have been any of the others."

Turning to stare at the doctor, Tikran said, "So do all the Dilovari know the ways of the Essence? Or are you, as a royal physician, privileged? Because I can tell you that likely no one in Anzor except the mages and the king fully understands what it does."

A slow smile crept across Damir's lips. "I suppose I must be privileged, then."

Tikran stood suddenly. "I'm going to sleep."

Damir cleared his throat. "We need to change your dressing first."

"I *just* changed it."

"That was three days ago."

"It can wait."

"No, it can't." Damir shot Tikran a look. "I made a promise that you would return to Anzor alive and with both arms intact, if I could help it. So sit down and let me do my job."

Tikran glared at the doctor, his nostrils flaring. Finally, he approached and sat down. As Damir unwrapped his wound, Tikran said, "To whom did you make that promise?"

"The king's main advisor," Damir replied.

"Lord Haydar."

"The big Manzakar with the orange hair."

"Naran. And it's yellow."

"And your—Coxani."

"Holy Cenk." Tikran dragged the fingers of his good hand through his hair. "Even a foreigner who's been in Anzor for just five weeks knows all about my personal life."

Damir carefully wiped the wound with a tincture-soaked cloth. "Why don't you marry the girl?"

"Why don't you mind your business?"

Damir continued to clean the wound silently as Tikran watched. The doctor's hands were strong and masculine, but also gentle, with long, graceful fingers. The unwelcome notion of those hands touching Tikran elsewhere made his entire body tingle. *Where did that come from?* Tikran held still for as long as he could while Damir laid a poultice-covered gauze over his wound and bandaged it. Then he snapped, "Are you done?"

The doctor lifted his translucent eyes to look Tikran in the face. "Yes, Manzakar. I'm done."

In an agitated state he couldn't understand, Tikran crawled into the tent and flopped onto his bedroll. He fell asleep before he had time to contemplate any of the evening's conversation.

The next morning, he awoke with the memory of the Fire Game alive in his mind. What if Damir was right? The flames had been uncontrollable. And his jacket had caught fire almost instantly, as if no talc covered it at all... He'd noticed Nasch and the mage behaving familiar with each other in a few instances, so it was completely in the realm of possibility that they'd conspired to get rid of him.

But there was one problem with the theory. Saltanat was not just the king's favorite mage; she was the head mage.

Would one of the other mages interfere when she was the one controlling the flames and hence, the Fire Game? If one of them rained on her parade, so to speak, they'd have to undoubtedly deal with the consequences of interfering with her leadership. Besides, she must have intended to put out the fire at some point, since not doing so would implicate her. She had probably been waiting until she was sure he'd been thoroughly cooked to bring on the rain.

The pair continued their journey to the central steppe—a vague destination, to say the least. There was only one garrison town, Areg, in that area, so Tikran thought it would be a good place to get fresh horses and replenish their food supplies. Even though summer had not yet begun, the sky was void of clouds and the sun shone hot on the vast, brown expanse that was Gohar. As they crossed the plains, they saw a few scattered yarms and sheepherders with their sheep. When no yarms or people were within view, they came across a herd of saiga antelope, grazing in the dry grass and watching them warily.

"Other than humans," Damir said, eyeing the antelope, "are there any predators we need to worry about out here?"

Tikran looked over and smiled. "Lions and other big cats can be a problem, although they generally avoid humans." He pointed at the dagger he'd given Damir to wear on his belt. "Can you wield any weapons, Doctor?"

"Not the way you mean." Damir shrugged. "I'm not even sure what I'd do with this dagger if faced with an enemy or predator. Perform surgery on it, I suppose."

Tikran chuckled. "Maybe I should take it back, then."

Damir said, "Well, I may not be handy with a weapon, but I'm a challenging opponent in hand-to-hand combat, believe it or not. I've trained in wrestling since my youth."

"Is that so?" Tikran raised his eyebrows. "Maybe I could test your abilities at some point."

"I may not be a Manzakar, but I can grapple with the best of them." Damir grinned.

Unbidden, Tikran imagined wrestling Damir to the ground and pinning him down. A frisson of pleasure rushed through him. *Holy Cenk, what's wrong with me?*

They fell back into silence until later that day. Tikran said, "As followers of Cenk, the Dilovari believe he brought on the Dark Age because of Archil as well, eh?"

"Indeed." Damir tilted his head. "Do you not believe that, Manzakar?"

"I didn't say that." Tikran snapped a look at the doctor. "Stop putting words in my mouth, Damir."

"Apologies," Damir said, sounding not in the least bit apologetic. "Our traditions may be different, but our beliefs are the same."

"So the mixing of Dilovari and Gohari bloodlines is forbidden in Dilovar?"

"Yes."

Tikran knitted his brow. "I assume the Dilovari see the Gohari as savages as well, then?"

Damir sighed. "Most do, yes."

"Do you?"

"I do not."

Surprised, Tikran asked, "Why not?"

"The Gohari are a devastated people, struggling to survive in a world that has no interest in helping them." He looked at Tikran, a hard glimmer in his eyes. "The Manzakars are much more savage, in my experience."

"You would think that, Dilovari," Tikran replied. He thought of Nasch beating the boy for stealing an apple, of his fellow soldiers executing the Gohari youths. *But I don't disagree.*

The days passed thus, and in under two weeks, they reached Areg. The town was even more pitiful than Eter, which Tikran hadn't thought possible. Very few Gohari wandered about, probably because there was no food being distributed Tikran approached one of the Manzakars keeping guard at the front of the fort. He saw the soldier grip his sword. Tikran said "I come by order of King Delger. I am Tikran of the Caged Kingfisher, Aslan Manzakar to the king. I request to speak to your commander." He pulled the official papers from his purse and handed them to the guard.

After a cursory look, the guard nodded. "Wait here." He walked briskly into the fort.

Damir stepped closer and murmured, "Tikran of the Caged Kingfisher?"

"It's the way Manzakars identify themselves to each other, since we have no family names," Tikran replied.

"Interesting." Damir smiled. "Tikran of the Caged Kingfisher." When Tikran frowned and shifted uncomfortably, Damir said, "You don't like it. Why?"

Luckily for Tikran, the soldier returned with his superior, a fellow named Oter, before he had to answer Damir's question. Oter held the documents out. "Greetings, Tikran. I am honored to welcome you and your guest." He turned to his men and ordered them to take the horses, then led the travelers into the fort. Tikran recognized some of the Manzakars from his graduating class when they approached him, their eyes brimming with admiration.

One of them, a large fellow with red hair named Tural, grasped Tikran's hand and shook it vigorously. "We knew you'd become an Aslan after our first year as cadets," he said as several other Manzakars nodded in agreement. "You were always the best."

Tikran was caught off guard by their deference and tried to

be gracious without looking uncomfortable. "Thank you. I'm truly flattered."

Oter invited him and Damir to sit and dine with him in his chambers, which overlooked the town square. As they ate a veritable feast of roasted meats, cheese, bread, and vegetable stew, Tikran couldn't help but think of the starving Gohari and his appetite dwindled. He focused on the conversation instead. "This shrub is said to grow in the central steppe, which as you can imagine, has not made it any easier to find," Tikran said, holding out a drawing Damir had made of the plant. "Any chance you or your men have come across it in the wild or seen anything like it in the hands of the natives?"

Oter chased a bite of food with a swig of wine, then shook his head. "I will ask around, but not to my knowledge. I'll be honest, your best bet would be to ask the nomads directly."

"Yes, that's the plan," Tikran said.

"My squadron covers only a part of the central steppe," Oter said. "The Manzakar who has the most experience campaigning throughout Gohar and is most likely to have happened upon this shrub is Commander Nasch. Surely either he or his men would know of it. He is to visit Areg in the next couple weeks during his next campaign." Oter sat back in his chair. "I can mention your mission to him."

"That won't be necessary," Tikran replied, whatever appetite he had left quickly vanishing. "I discussed it with him at length back in Anzor and he had no memory of the shrub."

"Well, we will keep our ears and eyes open here in Areg," Oter said, patting his stomach and signaling to a slave. "For dessert, I asked the cook to make a rice pudding in the Anzori style, with cardamom and pistachio. A sweet reminder of home!"

Later that night, as Tikran and Damir retreated to their

tent, Damir said, "I suspect you haven't spoken at length with Nasch about the shrub."

"You would be correct," Tikran replied.

"The irony isn't lost on me, you know." Tikran looked at Damir inquisitively, who said, "The fact that Manzakars are Gohari but consider Anzor—the land of their enslavement—home."

Tikran sat and began unwrapping his bandage. "Most Manzakars were very young when they were enslaved," he said. "So young that they hardly have any memory of their lives in Gohar. On top of that, their impressionable minds were fed half-truths and lies about the Gohari from the moment they were brought to Anzor. They really believe that they were saved by the king." He carefully peeled away the old gauze from the still-raw flesh of his arm. "Then they return to Gohar as pampered, celebrated soldiers of the Anzori and feel no kinship whatsoever with the natives."

Damir soaked a cloth in an herbal concoction and began to wipe Tikran's wound. "A clever game of deceit and manipulation, I'll give the Anzori that," he said. "Clever... and dangerous. How is it that you turned out differently from the others?"

Tikran shrugged, deliberately looking away from Damir's hands. "Did I turn out differently? I'm not sure. I suppose I was surrounded by the right people—or wrong people, depending on how you see it."

Damir applied a healing ointment to Tikran's wound and helped him wrap a fresh bandage around it. "You're able to see and accept what most of your comrades don't. That speaks volumes for your character."

Unsure of how to respond, Tikran remained silent. He still didn't know what Damir was about, and despite the man's qualities, Tikran couldn't shake the feeling that he was hiding something.

When they were done, they lay on their respective bedrolls to sleep for the night. Shortly after Tikran put out the light, Damir said, "Caged Kingfisher. I know how you got the name. I asked the red-haired Manzakar. Impressive, what you did. What I can't figure out is why you don't like it."

Tikran rolled away from him and grunted. "Good night, Doctor."

TIKRAN SHADED his eyes with his hand and squinted out onto the plain. He could see the five yarms more clearly now and noticed that they were clustered together. "They must be a clan," he told Damir. "Clans are groups of a few families who work and travel together. They usually have a leader. There are many clans in a tribe, and all the clan leaders answer to the chief."

Damir blinked in the morning sunlight. "Which tribe is that one from?"

"I can't tell from here." His horse stomped its hooves in the grass. "Probably the Sachin or Davlat tribes. They're the largest."

"None of those tribes are... aggressive, are they?"

"The Gohari I remember are very peaceful unless attacked. But things seem to have changed since I was a child," Tikran said. "That said, I suspect they would only show aggression toward Anzori or Manzakars."

They approached slowly on horseback, and as a man rounded one of the yarms and spotted them, Tikran raised a hand in greeting. The man, likely the head clansman, raised his hand in return and watched them curiously as they came close. Tikran spoke. "Good day, friend. My name is Jasur. I was wondering if you could help us."

The man, who was likely middle-aged, had a sad, weather-beaten face and wore a soft felt cap over his long gray hair. The only weapon on his person was a dagger tucked in the woven belt around his waist. He shook his head. "We can hardly help ourselves, lad."

Tikran dismounted. "I'm sorry to hear that. How many are in your clan?"

"Twenty-seven counting the infants," he replied. He looked Tikran over. "You're a townsman, aren't you?"

"How can you tell?"

"We can always tell."

Tikran cleared his throat. "I've just come from Areg, where my friend and I were able to get food. I may have enough to share with your clan, if you can share the information we're seeking."

The man's eyes widened. "How did you manage to get that much food?"

"A bit of negotiation, we'll call it." Tikran grinned. The truth was, it had been difficult convincing Oter to give him food for the nomads. It wasn't distribution time, the commander argued. It would cause hordes of them to come to Areg begging for food. And Tikran's favorite: It was going against Nasch's strict orders. Ultimately, it was a plea on behalf of the leper prince that made Oter relent.

Tikran and the doctor began unloading the bundles of food from the backs of their saddles. Suddenly there was a crowd of people hovering about and watching, their eyes wide and mouths ajar. Tikran locked eyes with Damir, who was evidently as startled as he was. Dirty-faced children with eyes like luminescent orbs stared hopefully. Adults who were probably all too familiar with the gnaw of hunger watched in disbelief.

"Psst."

Tikran looked at Damir, who motioned with his head toward a group of young men and women that watched the proceedings suspiciously from a distance. They were a menacing-looking lot, no question. There were around ten of them in total, and they stood separately from the rest, their faces blazing with barely restrained anger. They were as armed as they could be, with daggers and bows and quivers full of handmade arrows. Like the raiders from the king's visit to Dilovar, their faces were painted—or tattooed— with brown lines across their cheekbones and down their chins.

The food was not like the fancy meal they'd had with Oter. It consisted of bread, cheese, lentils, rice, and a small quantity of minced lamb. To the nomads, however, it was a veritable feast. The Gohari welcomed the strangers to join them in the center of the yarms and eat with them. Even the wary group of young adults couldn't resist but to partake, and they sat quietly on the fringes of the circle, devouring their food. Tikran saw several depictions of a lynx painted on the yarms and immediately knew the nomads were from the Sachin tribe. *Amazing, how the memory works.* Tikran hadn't remembered the lynx was the Sachin's emblem until he saw it.

"My name is Donaba," the man said as he finished his food, thoroughly licking his fingers. "I am the head clansman. What tribe do you hail from, Jasur?"

"Iroda," Tikran answered. He had talked at length with Oter about the various tribes and chose a small, obscure tribe that tended to live in the south and closer to Dilovar, hoping it would raise fewer eyebrows.

One of the "warriors," a young woman with black hair and a clever, sharp face, spoke up. "Iroda? I didn't think there were any of them left after what happened."

Uh oh. Oter had failed to mention anything happening to

the tribe. "A few of us made it. Which is why I am now a townsman."

The woman crossed her arms and narrowed her eyes at him. She clearly hadn't bought his story. "That must have been a harrowing experience, watching your tribe slaughtered by the Manzakars. Tell us how you escaped."

Slaughtered by the Manzakars. Before Tikran could open his mouth, Donaba said, "Stop harassing him, Bruneta. He brought us food, by Archil!"

Bruneta. Tikran suddenly felt dizzy. What were the chances...? Bruneta was a common Gohari name, after all. He tried to study the girl's face surreptitiously. She had the same deep-set brown eyes as he did, the same olive-toned skin...

"How can we repay you for your kindness, Jasur?" Donaba asked." You mentioned something about seeking information?"

Forcing his mind away from the woman, he said, "Yes. I'm trying to help this Dilovari doctor, Damir, find a shrub with purple berries that grows in the central steppe. Several of his townsfolk across the Dalma have contracted leprosy. He's heard the shrub can help treat it."

"It's illegal for you to be here," Bruneta said to Damir.

Damir said, "I was granted special permission because of the fear that the disease will continue to spread."

Bruneta raised her eyebrows. "Well, isn't your Perchuhi fancy, doctor."

Damir smiled coolly. "I learned the Anzori dialect to pursue my studies."

"Bruneta," Donaba warned, then sighed. "Many of our medicinal shrubs and plants have died off in recent years on account of the droughts. I haven't seen the one you speak of in over a year."

"I think I know where you might still find some." Bruneta

stood and looked back at the other armed nomads. "We can take you there. Donaba, if we find it, we'll bring some back for the clan as well."

"We would be very grateful," Tikran said, standing too. Damir followed suit, an apprehensive look on his face. The pair mounted their horses and waited for the nomads. There was no tack to prepare so they leaped nimbly onto the horses' backs and approached. At this point, Tikran understood that Bruneta was the leader of the pack. He asked her, "How long of a ride will this be?"

"We should be back before sundown," she said, then began to lead them eastward.

Aside from some quiet banter between the young men who rode in the back, they traveled in silence, each thinking their own thoughts. Tikran, for his part, was noting how the nomads surrounded them, as if preparing for a flank attack. The Manzakar in him began to plan counterattacks, and he suddenly wished he had his lance and saber. *What's wrong with you? They're not going to attack you. Or are they?* They likely would if they knew his true identity. Bruneta had said the Iroda had been slaughtered by Manzakars. Was that true? After what he'd witnessed with his own eyes, he had to admit it was a possibility. He felt ill. He took a long, deep breath and considered striking up a conversation with Bruneta, then remembered how she'd wanted to grill him about his backstory. *Maybe not.* She rode slightly ahead and he took the time to look her over. She had a beautiful bow strapped to her back and he wondered if she'd made it herself. No doubt she had. Her long dark hair was adorned with colored beads and tied haphazardly in the back, an eagle feather tucked in the knot. She rode gracefully, occasionally turning her head so he could see her profile—confident and earnest, with sharp cheekbones and a firm chin. She was familiar in a foreign way, and as he gazed at her he became increasingly convinced that the young woman was his sister.

My sister. And if she was, where was his father and Evren? They might have been among the clan, but he hadn't had a chance to really look. He probably wouldn't recognize them, in any case.

"So Jasur," Bruneta said, drawing him out of his thoughts, "how did you end up helping the doctor?"

"We were both in Areg at the same time, and I asked him how he was in Gohar legally," Tikran said. "He told me why he was there and I decided to help him." Tikran knew he was a terrible liar and hoped she didn't begin poking holes in his story.

"Really?" She turned to frown at him. "You just decided to help a Dilovari stranger for no reason? Don't you have kin to take care of?"

"No, I don't. And... yes, I just decided to help him. I guess I took a liking to him."

At this, Damir looked over at Tikran, his eyebrows raised as if to say, *Oh, really?*

Once again, Bruneta narrowed her eyes at him and turned back around. "What happened to your arm?"

For once, Tikran felt he could be truthful. "I was burned in a fire."

She said nothing in reply, and silence once again befell the group.

In the afternoon, they reached a stretch of rolling brown hills surrounded by low shrubs. Bruneta hopped off her horse and looked at Tikran and Damir. "If the plant still exists, it will be here."

They dismounted and followed Bruneta into the shrubbery while the other nomads watched. After rummaging through spindly branches and brittle leaves for half an hour, Damir signaled to them. "I think I've found it." They huddled around to peer at the purple fruit in Damir's palm. He crushed one between his fingers to reveal several black seeds.

"That's it," Bruneta confirmed. "My siblings and I used to gather them for my mother. They're not to eat, though. When I was very little, my brother and I ate some. We had aching bellies for a while afterward."

It's her. Tikran knew it in his bones. Shock vibrated through him.

They began to fill sacks with the berries while his mind raced. So what did it matter if she was his sister? He couldn't reveal his identity. He was still a Manzakar on a mission for the King of Anzor, and revealing himself would cause complications—not to mention possible conflict.

Having plucked as much fruit as they could carry, they prepared to head back to the clan's encampment. Tikran had just tied a third bag to his saddle when he heard Damir mutter, "Well, shit."

He turned to see Bruneta holding her bow, her arm drawn, an arrow nocked and pointed right at him. The others stood behind her, at the ready.

"Who are you?" she demanded.

Tikran slowly raised his hands. "I've told you who I am."

"You're lying." She motioned her head and one of the young men came toward Tikran, reaching inside his vest and pulling his dagger from its sheath on his belt. The young man took several steps backward and held it up. Tikran realized with a jolt that he'd brought his actual dagger, not one a nomad would have used. "What kind of Gohari carries a bronze-handled dagger? Only Manzakars carry daggers like that. I'll ask you one more time. Who *are* you?"

"Bruneta." Tikran sucked in his breath. "It's me, Tikran."

She didn't move. "I don't know a Tikran."

"You did. Long ago." He struggled to remember something she would recognize. She was Coxani's age, and like Coxani, had loved his rabbit. He said, "I still have Wig, if you can believe it. Well, I gave it to a girl, but she still has it."

Her eyes widened and she wavered. Still, she kept her arrow pointed at him. "My brother Tikran was sold into slavery."

"Yes. And he became a Manzakar."

Through clenched teeth, she said, "Why have you come back? To slaughter more of us?"

"No. I'm one of the king's personal Manzakars. We don't do the slaughtering." He swallowed. "I was sent by King Delger to find the shrub. Prince Vazha is dying of leprosy. Damir, the royal doctor of Dilovar, was tasked with treating him and believes the shrub can help."

"Why should we believe you?"

"If I was going to make up a story, it wouldn't be this one."

"Bruneta," the warrior holding the dagger said, "we could ransom them."

Tikran shook his head. "Don't do that. You know they'll destroy you and your families without a second thought. They hold all the power."

Bruneta still didn't move. "They'll destroy us anyway."

Tikran said nothing. He knew deep down that she wouldn't shoot him. Even angry as she was, even after the life she'd had, even with all the resentment she must have felt toward him. He just *knew*.

Abruptly, she lowered her bow. "Let's go. It's getting late." She looked at the young man. "Give the Manzakar his fancy dagger back."

"But—"

Bruneta glared at him. "Don't you dare start with me, Omid. Give the fucking dagger back now."

The warrior, Omid, was not pleased, but passed the dagger back to Tikran.

They began the journey back as the sun was beginning to set. Damir looked at Tikran then looked meaningfully at Bruneta, as if to say, *go talk to her.* Tikran nodded. He trotted up beside her. "What happened to the Iroda?" he asked.

She didn't look at him. "As if you don't know, Manzakar."

"That's the thing, Bruneta. I really *don't* know. They brainwash us in Anzor, then keep information from us so we stay loyal to them. I had no idea that the Anzori weren't actually taking care of the Gohari until just a few months ago." He yanked off his hat and dragged his fingers through his hair. "I've been kept close to the king, so I know even less than the other Manzakars. I've never fought in a battle. This—all of this —is a shocking realization. My life has been a lie."

She looked at him then, and the steel was gone from her face. She was quiet for several moments before saying, "The Iroda attacked the king's train as he was traveling back from Dilovar. The Gohari warriors who attacked were all caught and executed. They were young and had acted without consent of the chief or the elders. Still, the whole tribe paid for what happened. The Manzakars set fire to their yarms, executed the men and children, raped the women, then executed them too." She waved a fly from her face. "The Iroda are no more."

Tikran felt like drawing in a breath had suddenly become difficult. "Holy Cenk."

"Cenk is a piece of shit," she snapped angrily. "Your god is a piece of shit, Manzakar."

"He's not my god. He never was." Tikran grimaced. "I don't know what to say."

"There's nothing to say."

He breathed slowly until his heart stopped pounding in his chest. Then he said, "Where is Da? Evren?"

"Both with Mama," she answered matter-of-factly. "Da died ten years ago, from tumors in his lungs. Evren died five years later, of the white plague."

Tikran fell silent. He'd spent his life imagining his father and sisters alive and well. In his child's mind, he'd been sold to save them. He'd become a Manzakar to save them. He'd been the martyr in his mind.

His whole life... was truly a lie.

CHAPTER 15

Coxani was tired of smiling.

She'd smiled to get access to Haydar. Then smiled at Haydar to get permission to access to the library. Then smiled at the guards to physically get into the library. She was a Manzakar, for Cenk's sake. She shouldn't feel the need to smile. And yet, she did.

Finally inside the library, she stopped smiling. She walked straight to a certain bookshelf—the bookshelf she'd been browsing last she was there—and began to search. She had left the book peeking out and its gilded spine caught her eye. *Theology of the Continent.* Even though the library was virtually empty save for the occasional cleric, she looked over her shoulder to make sure no one was watching her. Instead of sitting on one of the couches in the middle of the sanctuary, she retreated to the back of the library and sat on the floor in a corner, sliding down against the wall.

Since Tikran and Damir had left for Gohar a couple weeks ago, she'd been searching for information on the Essence. She believed that if only she knew the extent of what it could do, she'd be able to figure out the truth about Anzor's relationship with Gohar. What would she do with that information? She hardly knew. But she had to find out.

Unfortunately, clear information on the Essence was impossible to come by. Its effects were deliberately obscured, which made acquiring the knowledge even more enticing to her. So far, she knew there were three gods involved in the creation of the Continent: Cenk, Ing, and Ahti. The gods divided the Essence among themselves evenly, and each created kingdoms that would serve them. Cenk, as the oldest god, created Anzor, Gohar, and Dilovar. Ing created Taranis and Haldor. Ahti, as the youngest god, created Kalevi. *And with their Essence they created life, allowed it to thrive.* This, of course, was true so long as their followers didn't make them angry. The gods bestowed Essential abilities to only the most devout clerics, to use only as the king dictated. The king, of course, was his respective god's greatest apostle. The clerics who were lucky enough to earn the power of the Essence became the king's mages.

Everything was going well, presumably, and the gods did not meddle in the affairs of humans. They clearly had better things to do. That is, until Archil. He'd been bestowed with powerful Essence, and as such served as a mage in Gohar. But rather than doing the king's bidding, he began doing the people's bidding. When the king would order his mages to punish his people for some wrongdoing, Archil would defy him. So the king prayed to Cenk for help. And here is where the lore got vague: Archil somehow "stole" the Essence from Cenk. When the Anzori and Dilovari armies came after him, he killed himself by fracturing into light and scattered his Essence throughout Gohar. As such, a rare few Gohari were born with the Essence each generation—some with very little, some with a lot. And to use it, one with the Essence had to learn certain spells—spells kept safely locked away by the mages.

Coxani stopped and re-read: *When the king ordered Archil to punish the people for violating his will, Archil refused.* She tapped the page with her thumb, thinking. How did the mages use the Essence to punish people? How was this reconciled with: *Cenk's Essence blesses mankind with life... It is light, it is water, it is food and shelter...* Funny, they'd never been taught how the Essence could be used to punish. Granted, since she knew the mages could light fires, she could see the possibilities. But surely the kings didn't punish their own people by incinerating them?

Unbidden, the memory of Tikran rolling, consumed by flames, rushed back to her, and for a moment, her heart stopped. Was it possible the mage had something to do with it? But why would she do that?

"I knew I'd find you hiding in here." Naran leaned against a pillar casually, smiling at her. He must have just gotten done attending the king, because he looked sharp in his long jacket with the standing collar, his polished boots, and turbaned cap. His dreadlocks were neatly tied back and his amber eyes were bright in his dark face. He gestured to her book. "Brushing up on your religious studies?"

Coxani stood. "I guess you could say that."

He tilted his head. "Is something wrong?"

A cleric appeared among the book stacks several yards behind Naran. She nodded. "Perhaps we can speak later."

He rubbed his chin. "Would you care to go hunting this afternoon?"

She opened her mouth to accept then stopped. "Alone?"

Naran raised his eyebrows. "Why not? You can be alone with Tikran but not me?"

"Naran," she said, feeling her face warming, "I'm already in hot water for that, you know. Everyone seems to think..."

"Who cares what they think?" He scowled.

"Easy for a man to say!" She crossed her arms. "If I'm caught alone with you, my reputation will go from bad to worse in a heartbeat."

Naran huffed in frustration. "All right. Then bring a eunuch. Not sure how freely we'll be able to talk, though."

Coxani said, "I'll figure something out."

An hour later, they met at the royal stables, and Coxani had a eunuch in tow. She said to Naran, "This is Bolat. He's deaf but can read lips." She smiled innocently.

Turning his head away, Naran muttered so she would hear, "Clever woman."

They rode out of Anzor City and into the nearby woods to, at least ostensibly, hunt wild boar. They had two saluki hounds ahead of them and wore armor on their lower bodies to protect from the potentially fatal thrusts of an angry boar's tusks. Bolat rode a short distance behind them, seemingly uninterested in their conversation. Coxani said, "I never thanked you, by the way."

Naran asked, "For what?"

"You were very attentive while I was sick," she said.

He shook his head. "Don't thank me for being a decent human being. That should be a given."

As Coxani had gotten to know Naran, her respect for him had grown. Initially, she'd judged him to be a superior soldier, like Tikran, but with little else occupying his mind besides sex. She'd heard the other Manzakars tease him about his innumerable conquests, often enviously, and Naran seemed to enjoy it. She'd admitted to herself that she was attracted to him physically; she very much doubted there were many women who weren't. Naran was the portrait of male virility. Throw in a boyish, dimpled smile and two mesmerizing amber eyes... Nonetheless, physical attraction wasn't enough for Coxani to be more than vaguely intrigued.

But during her illness he had visited her every day, sometimes for over an hour, and they had talked about everything under the sun. She was surprised to discover that he had much more depth to him than she'd given him credit for. Naran was intelligent, kind, and had Tikran's moral compass. Now she felt guilty for being attracted to him. She likely shouldn't have accepted to go hunting with him, but she *wanted* to be around him. She said, "You were probably spread thin, worrying about Tikran, and then me..."

"I wasn't so worried about Tikran," he said with a smile. "I told you. He always bounces back."

"I wonder how he's faring in Gohar. I'm worried about him." She stole a look at Naran's profile.

His expression became grim. "Yeah, like I've told you, it's shocking to finally understand what's going on there. I'd only been on one other campaign into Gohar, and while sad, it wasn't as... violent as that one was." He looked at her. "I was worried they'd put a target on Tikran's back if he kept interfering with orders."

"A target on his back?" Her brow was furrowed. "What do you mean?"

"I don't mean it literally," Naran said. "He'd risk getting kicked out of the Aslan ranks. Maybe get a mark on his record. He'd make becoming a durai that much harder."

She chewed on her lip. "What about Nasch? You don't think he would do anything... literal, do you? I mean, Tikran humiliated him. Twice."

"He better not," Naran said. "Besides, I don't think he'd risk the punishment." He considered. "Now, if he thought he could get away with it, I wouldn't put it past him."

With a jarring bay, the hounds were abruptly off, and the large, bristly back of a boar burst from the thicket and rushed away. The Manzakars pulled their lances and followed, galloping after the dogs while Bolat tried to keep up. They knew when the boar turned, because the dogs bayed again.

Naran leaped off his horse, growling, "I'm not letting it kill my dogs!"

Coxani was right behind him, lance in hand. The boar rushed and she flung her lance at the same time Naran did. Knowing that boars became more dangerous after the first strike, she pulled her bow and saw Naran, several paces ahead, draw his sword. As they approached, they could see that the boar was injured—and furious. It squealed terribly and charged through the bushes, its tusks glistening in the sunlight. Both Manzakars ran to meet the animal. Before it could reach Naran, Coxani had released at least five arrows—directly into the boar's back. It screamed and continued to charge, and Naran suddenly jumped and drove his sword, double-fisted, into the base of the animal's skull.

Then silence, save for the dogs.

As Coxani reached Naran, panting, he grinned. "That was a group effort if I ever saw one." He looked about, then said, "The eunuch isn't here yet. May I kiss you?"

She startled, moving back. *Is he serious?* "What? But... What would Tikran..."

"Tikran gave me his blessing to pursue you before he left. Still, I'm sorry." He looked contrite. "The excitement of the kill must have gotten to me."

Tikran had given Naran his blessing to pursue her? She stiffened, looking down at the dead boar at her feet in consternation. Part of her was slightly hurt, but another part was thrilled. Driven partially by defiance, she said, "Yes, Naran. I'd like to kiss you." As she spoke the words, she realized how true they were.

A fire lit in his golden eyes and he took two long strides toward her. "Are you sure?"

Quivering with anticipation and a sense of urgency, she stepped closer to him, smelling his perspiration and a hint of musk. "Yes."

He wrapped his arm around her waist and pressed her to him, looking down into her face. "I can't believe this is finally happening. I never thought it would." Slowly, he put his mouth to hers. His lips were soft, warm, insistent. They parted slightly and she responded by parting hers. His tongue slid across her lips, probing gently until it touched hers. Its sly, soft caress touched every part of her body and she felt herself unravel, lost in his kiss. Then he pulled away and stepped back, his eyes still aglow.

At that moment, Bolat arrived, motioning excitedly at the dead boar. She blinked. *Oh yes. We killed a boar. Almost forgot.*

They tied the beast to the back of Naran's saddle and began the ride back to the city. Coxani's heart was pounding, and not from the hunt. But a small voice in the back of her mind whispered sobering rebukes. *Only fit for a courtesan... unchaste... wanton...* Her exhilaration faltered.

Naran broke the silence. His voice was low. "Kissing you had quite the effect on me. If not for the armor, Bolat might have thought I really, *really* like to kill boars."

She blushed. Without looking at him, she asked, "What did you mean when you said Tikran gave you his blessing to pursue me?"

He shrugged and looked at her bashfully. "I've had a thing

for you, Coxani. But I had to get clearance from him. He's my friend and he loves you. I would never want to do something that would hurt him."

"I would never hurt him either."

"Of course you wouldn't."

She was gripping the reins tightly. "Naran, I'm not some sweet, innocent girl."

He let out a laugh. "Thank Cenk! I'm not a fan of sweet, innocent girls. Never been, never will be."

"I'm not interested in becoming another notch in your belt, either."

He looked at her. "Coxani, I can understand why you would think that my interest in you is, er, carnal, and I would be lying if I said that wasn't a part of it, but it's so much more than that. You're... amazing."

His eyes shone with admiration and she felt shame overwhelm her. *Tell him now.* When she felt certain Bolat couldn't see her face, she said, "I didn't have an inflamed appendix."

"What?"

She stared firmly ahead. "I ended a pregnancy."

Naran was quiet for a moment, then said, "Tikran's?"

She nodded.

"Does he know?"

"No. Please don't tell him."

"I won't." He paused. "That must have been awful for you to grapple with." When she didn't respond, he said, "Coxani, look at me." Reluctantly, she dragged her eyes to his face. The admiration was still there. "It doesn't change how I feel about you. In fact, I'm even more in awe of your strength."

Tears flooded her eyes, but she willed them not to spill. "Really? You like me that much?"

He chuckled, his cheeks darkening. "Yeah."

She didn't know what to say. A lump was lodged in her

throat. Naran must have sensed it, because he changed the subject. "I look forward to dining on that boar with you. I think I'll request that the cooks prepare it in a spiced wine sauce with fruit and almonds. What do you think?"

She felt the tension leave her body and smiled. "That sounds delicious."

CHAPTER 16

The clan remembered him.

Once Bruneta told the rest of the clan that Jasur was Tikran, the older brother sold into slavery long ago, their walls came down and they treated him like family. Despite the treatment they had suffered at the hands of the Manzakars, most of them welcomed him with happy tears and open arms. The exceptions were the warriors, particularly Omid. They kept watchful, wary eyes on him.

Tikran had no memory of most of them, but something in their ways—their hugs, the lilt of their Gohari accents, their hand gestures—was deeply familiar to him.

"I was very close to your father," Donaba told him as they sat around the fire that night. "Hanno was so proud of you. It broke his heart to have to do what he did. And to be honest, he considered selling the girls too. He saw no future for the three of you in Gohar. And he believed that, despite being slaves, you would have much better lives in Anzor."

"Donaba, what happened to our mother?" Tikran asked.

Bruneta, who was sitting nearby, said, "She was murdered

by Manzakars. That night you made us hide, Tikran. Do you remember?"

Tikran swallowed. "Yes. But just pieces of it. I don't remember exactly what happened or who was involved. Did she have the Essence?"

Donaba nodded gravely. "And unlike others who have it, Gamze knew she had it."

"How?"

Donaba shrugged. "I have no idea. It's very unusual, from what I hear."

Damir, who had been staring broodingly into the flames, suddenly spoke. "Her Essence must have been very powerful. Only those with much of it can feel it." He looked at Donaba, then Tikran, with pale eyes that were bright in the firelight. "One of our mages in Dilovar claims to have known long before it was detected."

"Saltanat said she could detect the Essence in others," Tikran said.

"Yes," Damir confirmed. "All mages can."

"Can she also detect how powerful the Essence is in someone?"

"I believe so."

Tikran locked eyes with Bruneta. "I have a memory of something else from that day. A silver chalice with a flame on a blue background."

"Oh yes," Bruneta replied, a rageful grimace on her face. "Commander Nasch. He and his men murdered Mama. They're King Delger's henchmen. They scour Gohar, terrorizing clans to keep them afraid and quiet. There isn't a Gohari who doesn't know who he is."

Tikran slowly made a fist. "Do you remember anything else from that day, Bruneta?"

"One other thing. You told us not to look, but I peeked. I

saw a beautiful woman in a red robe, wearing a veil over her mouth." Bruneta curled her lip. "The mage Nasch sometimes travels with to sniff out the Essence. She's as brutal as he is."

"Saltanat." Tikran closed his eyes. The idea that she might have conspired with Nasch to get rid of him was becoming a real possibility. He stood and went over to sit next to Bruneta. She looked at him coldly. He said, "I'm sorry for all you've been through. I wish Da had sold you and Evren with me."

"I don't," she said. "I hear the girls become playthings to rich men, have no rights, and are forced to bear children. I'd rather die of starvation than become one of them." When he said nothing, she continued, "So I guess now that you've found the medicine for your precious prince you'll leave and think of us on occasion, shake your head sadly and sigh, then hurry off to wipe Delger's ass, eh?"

He put his head in his hands, linking his fingers in the back. "I have to go back with Damir. As for the rest of it... I feel helpless, Bruneta. If I take my rage over what's happening here to the king, he'll punish me by demoting me, but he won't listen. If I persist, he'll have me flogged and thrown into prison but still won't listen. Then he'll send Nasch to punish you for putting ideas in my head. Ultimately, many of us will lose our lives, and Anzor wins."

"You don't get it, do you?" She shook her head in amazement. She stood and loomed angrily over him. "What in your life have you ever fought for, Tikran? Other than yourself?"

As she stormed off, Donaba sighed. "Tikran, you've been generous with us. Don't worry. We realize you are just one man and a slave."

A slave.

Tikran promised to return the following day with more food, then he and Damir rode back to Areg. The heaviness in Tikran's chest was unbearable as his sister's words replayed in his head. What *had* he ever fought for, other than himself? What would he ever fight for, other than a bigoted, ruthless king? He would likely never fight in a real battle, in any case—he'd entertain Anzor with his useless skills and spend most of his life as a royal attendant until the king deemed it appropriate to grant him land which, in the end, would still not truly be his. He was, as Donaba had so succinctly put it, just a slave.

"Tikran," Damir said softly. "I'm sorry about your mother, father, and sister. I can see you're being hit by one revelation after another, and none of them is pleasant. All of this must be difficult to take in."

The sincerity in Damir's voice was comforting.

"It's mind-numbing, to be honest," Tikran said. "I just can't afford to process any of it right now. My primary concern at the moment is feeding those starving people."

"You're a good man, Manzakar." What Tikran saw in Damir's face surprised him—his eyes were brimming with admiration and tenderness.

Tikran looked away, feeling heat creep up his neck. Every additional moment he spent with Damir made him reevaluate his harsh appraisal of the doctor. In truth, Tikran was beginning to enjoy Damir's company. No, more than that. He was genuinely grateful for Damir's presence as he navigated these shocking discoveries about his family, his life, his very identity. He finally said, "I think you overestimate me."

"I'm certain I don't," Damir answered.

Once again, Tikran was unsure of how to answer so remained silent. A part of him wished he could rest his head against Damir's chest, feel the doctor's arms around him, and listen to the vibrations of his resonant voice. He blinked hard, shaking his head quickly. He had to stop with these ridiculous thoughts. The man was the royal doctor of Dilovar, for Cenk's sake. He was not to be trusted.

As they rode through the town gates and toward the fort, Tikran recognized a green wagon stopped to the side. He hopped out of his saddle and walked around the wagon to find Mago talking to Oter. Mago didn't recognize him at first and looked away.

"Mago." Tikran smiled.

Finally, Mago's eyes widened with delight. "My boy! What are you doing here?" He clasped Tikran tightly to his chest.

A large lump formed in Tikran's throat. "Doing the king's bidding." He explained his mission and introduced Damir. "Damir, this is Mago..." This was about to get awkward. "...the slave trader who bought me from my father and sold me to the king."

Damir's eyebrows were practically at his hairline. "A pleasure."

Mago beamed proudly at Tikran. "I always knew you'd become something special, lad."

Tikran felt nauseous. "And you? What are you doing in Areg?"

"What else? The Gohari see my wagon and know my trade. They come to me with their children when they're ready."

Tikran turned to Oter. "I would like to request more food to take to the same clan tomorrow. They helped me find the shrub and I'd like to reward them."

Oter set his hands on his hips and shook his head. "I'm afraid I can't do that."

Tikran's body tensed. "Why not?"

"You've already given them food, which I wasn't supposed to allow in the first place. And now you want to give them more?"

Damir said smoothly, "Commander, doesn't it benefit you to have a clan in the area do your bidding in return for a trivial amount of food?"

Oter stiffened. "It's against strict orders. I'll hear no more." Then he stalked back into the fort.

Tikran felt the fury rise from his belly when Mago laid a big hand on Tikran's sleeve. He smiled vaguely and murmured, "Let's take a walk, eh? The doctor may join us." They strolled away from the fort as Mago talked nonsense about the weather. Finally, he said, "The storeroom guard lets me in for food on occasion. I can get some for you."

"How do you manage that?" Tikran asked.

Mago waggled his eyebrows. "I bribe him with aspers, of course! What else?" He chuckled. "How much food do you want? I'll load it into my wagon tonight and help you take it to the nomads first thing tomorrow."

"You would do that?"

Mago frowned. "Of course, boy! Nothing frightens this old slave trader."

True to his word, Mago was waiting with his wagon at dawn. "Lead the way, boys. And hurry!"

They left Areg without incident and arrived at the cluster of yarms by late morning. There had been little road for the wagon to tread on, but it survived the bumpy trek if only by the sheer force of Mago's will. The nomads emerged from their yarms hopefully. Bruneta and her gang stood aside, watching with more interest than suspicion. Mago hopped off the wagon and began unloading. As he helped, it occurred to Tikran that the merchant had taken a lot of food, and some of it high quality lamb, beef, vegetables, fruit...

"Mago..." Tikran looked at the old man in disbelief.

Mago winked. "Don't worry, lad. I've known Oter for a long time. He won't miss it."

What happened next was nothing short of a celebration. Cooking fires were lit to grill the meat, pots were hung to make vegetable stew, hunks of bread and cheese were passed to each person in turn. One of the older women, her silver hair dressed with feathers, sat down and began playing a lute. The children laughed and chased each other around the yarms. Even the young warriors were smiling. A warmth blossomed in Tikran's chest as he watched the nomads come alive, dispelling the cold heaviness that had resided there for months. At some point, every single nomad save for the warriors approached Tikran for a handshake or an embrace.

When I leave, all this will end. They'll go back to starving. The thought was devastating.

The food was cooked and a bowl was passed to everyone, brimming with everything the nomads hadn't eaten in a very long time... or at all. As they ate, Damir chatted to a group of women, smiles on all their faces. Mago laughed heartily with Donaba.

An old man came and sat beside Tikran on a worn rug, crossing his legs in front of him. He wore a faded, yellow felt cap over his bald head and was wrapped in a heavy cloak that was fringed and beaded along its hem. His voice, when he spoke, was gravelly with age. "I'm Beg Sone. You probably don't remember me. I'm old enough to remember what Gohar was once like. I was born just a few years after the Akmaral War. Gohar was still vibrant and the life hadn't been choked out of it yet." He chuckled, revealing mostly toothless gums. "You have brought back a bit of that today, young man."

Tikran remembered that "Beg" was a title of respect given to the elders and chieftains. He turned to face the old man with interest. "I'm glad, Beg Sone. What was Gohar like then?"

Beg Sone looked about with cloudy eyes, seeing something other than what was before him. "The land provided. The people were joyful, strong, united. "His gnarled fingers stroked the rug beneath them. "The Gohari used to weave glorious rugs. I remember traders coming from faraway lands to acquire them. Weaving is only done for necessity now. The art is lost."

Tikran touched the plain, rough wool, wondering what Gohari rugs had once looked like. But he had more important questions to ask. "What do you know about Archil? As a child, I remember my parents avoided speaking about him, even discouraging me from saying his name. In Anzor, we're taught that he was a heretic who stole Cenk's magic."

The elder turned his foggy gaze to Tikran. "It's dangerous to speak of them. It was even worse when I was a child, since Gohar had just become an Anzori colony. The Manzakars roamed the steppe, punishing anyone who dared to mention their name. But you *are* a Manzakar, so I guess it's all right." He smiled, his eyes crinkling into crescent-shaped moons. "Archil hailed from the Davlat tribe. It's said they had incredibly powerful Essence. As head mage of Gohar, they lived humbly and walked among the nomads, using their Essence to provide for those who needed it—the elderly, the orphans, the sick."

Doesn't sound like someone who would steal anything. Puzzled by the old man's use of pronouns, Tikran decided it was a feature of the Gohari dialect that he'd forgotten. He leaned forward, waiting for the old man to continue. "And?"

Beg Sone laughed. "That's as much as I know, lad. The rest is folklore."

"I'd love to hear the folklore sometime," Tikran said with a kind smile, realizing how late it was. The feast had lasted all day and the sun was beginning to set in a spectacular wash of orange, pink, purple and blue. The nomads were storing the extra food in their yarms when Tikran approached Damir. "We should head back to Anzor."

Damir nodded. "Your people are good, Manzakar. I—" His smile quickly dissipated and his eyes darted to something behind Tikran.

Tikran spun around as the music stopped and the nomads fell quiet. In the distance, horsemen approached, black against the sunset. There was no mistaking the dome of their helmets or the flash of their armor. "Go into your yarms!" Tikran yelled. "Take the children. Stay there!" His heart hammered against his chest. He noticed that Bruneta and her warriors remained outside, discreetly pulling out their shields and preparing their bows for battle. He turned to her. "No. We are not shooting arrows. Do you understand?"

Bruneta bared her teeth. "If they even *look* like they're about to shoot, we shoot. Period." She handed Tikran a round, handmade shield. "You'd be smart to take this."

Mago shook his head resolutely. "No, no, no... there will be no fighting today." He walked out to greet the Manzakars, Tikran hot on his heels. He had no idea what the slave merchant was thinking. The soldiers stopped and Tikran could see their lances and sabers and battle axes and maces. Mago yelled, "Oter! Stop this madness. You want to blame the nomads when it was I who took the food! Come now, surely we can settle this in a civil way."

Oter rode forward. "Mago, you deceived me and stole from the king. Do you realize—"

A single arrow—handmade, with small fletching and a bone tip—bounced off one of the Manzakars' cuirasses harmlessly. In immediate response, an arrow flew from the troops. Tikran flinched. Mago stood several feet before him, teetering. He crumpled to the ground and Tikran lunged to catch him. An arrow protruded from his chest, directly over his heart.

"It's fine, boy," Mago said, his eyes wide with shock. "I'm fine! Stop this silliness."

Kneeling, Tikran held the slave trader's hand in his. Everything outside of Mago faded into the distance. "You'll be okay."

Tikran heard himself say several times as his eyes darted over the wound frantically. *He won't be.*

Damir was suddenly there, his arm around Mago. "I have him."

It was all Tikran needed to hear. That clearness of mind derived from a certain madness drove him as he held the shield over himself, Damir, and Mago. He pulled his bow and several arrows from his hip and, as if coming out of a dream, abruptly heard the whistling of Manzakar arrows as they descended, raining down them. Amidst the hailstorm, his eyes zoomed in on one Manzakar after another.

Nock... Draw... Anchor... Aim... Release... One down.

Nock... Draw... Anchor... Aim... Release... Two down.

Nock... Draw... Anchor... Aim... Release... Three down.

Manzakars were well-trained in shooting while shielding themselves. Moreover, since the lamellar armor of the Manzakars was nearly identical to the ones the Dilovari wore, Tikran knew exactly where the weaknesses were so he could strike to injure or kill. He'd studied it, perfected it. He tried to aim as best he could for openings in the armor at the armpit, the neck, the back of the arms and legs, and the face. And of course, he could always shoot the horse to unsaddle his enemy, then shoot the soldier while he was down, even though he preferred not to do that. The only thing limiting him was his arrows. He would eventually run out. He also didn't have any other weapon save his dagger. Still, he continued.

Four down. Five down. Six down.

He heard screams from the nomads behind him as the arrows whistled past his head. One embedded in his thigh with a searing flash of pain. He shot his arrows faster.

Ten... Eleven... Twelve... Thirteen...

Deep inside, he knew it was a lost cause. And yet, he'd

somehow accepted that, if this was how he died, he would not have died in vain. It was a strange but liberating feeling.

Their numbers seemed to remain steady even as he disabled one after the other. There were just too many. Just as he'd accepted that they were done for, a fire ignited and raced through the dry grass between the nomads and the Manzakars—well, most of the Manzakars. Some were caught in the flames and fell screaming from their terrified horses. Tikran's mind raced. *Saltanat.* Was she here? The fire had been too instantaneous and spread too quickly to have started without magic. *If not her, then who?*

As the flames licked higher and higher, the Manzakars retreated and finally vanished. Tikran turned to Damir, who cradled Mago in his arms. The look in the doctor's eyes was despairing. Tikran uttered, "No."

Mago was still alive, bleeding profusely despite Damir's attempts to staunch it. The slave trader's eyes were glassy, his face colorless, his breathing labored. He saw Tikran and almost smiled. He gasped, "Tikran. Love you." Then his struggle ended, quietly.

Tikran didn't even realize it was raining until he was drenched. Next to him, Damir gently closed Mago's eyes. The rain slowly stopped. Bruneta crouched beside Tikran, grabbing his shoulders.

"Tikran. Tikran!" She shook him hard, her wet, beaded hair slapping against them both. "You need to leave. Now. They'll come for you."

He looked up. "I can't leave. They'll come back and slaughter you all."

She yanked him by the vest. "If you stay they'll definitely come back and slaughter us all—including you." She stood. "If you want to help us, then leave."

He had no idea what to do. His mind raced. How many

Manzakars had he injured or killed? *Holy Cenk.* He was in deep trouble.

"Tikran, she's right. Let's go," Damir said.

The men stood and hurried to their mounts, Tikran limping.

"Wait." He half turned and Bruneta touched his face, her eyes a storm of emotion, her face slick with rain. "Take care, brother." Then she turned and ran back toward the yarms.

As he and Damir mounted their horses and kicked into a gallop heading westward, the clouds parted, revealing a full, bright moon.

Tikran had an arrow protruding from his thigh.

Pain shot through his leg with each bounce of the horse's stride. But they couldn't stop yet. He knew what he was looking for: an area of hills and low shrubs to hide and find water. By the time their mounts grew tired, Tikran and Damir had easily covered four miles westward. Slowing to a trot, they continued another half mile before Tikran spotted the shadows of hills on the dark horizon. They rode into the tenebrous hollows between the hills and found a cluster of shrubs just large enough to hide in. They checked the underbrush for snakes then draped a canvas sheet over top the branches, creating a small canopy.

"Let's find some water," Tikran said.

"Manzakar," Damir protested, "you have an arrow embedded in your leg. Let me get it out and dress the wound first."

Tikran shook his head. "I'm not bleeding. I saw animal prints and midden back there. There has to be some shallow groundwater in the area." He grabbed their flasks and they wandered off between the hills, following a set of fox prints by moonlight. Where there were animals and plants, there was bound to be water. Tikran crouched to the earth in what looked like a dried creek bed. "Shit," Tikran said. "I was hoping it would still be wet."

Damir kneeled and buried his fingers in the sandy dirt, feeling for moisture. "Here. Help me dig."

"Damir, there's no way we'll hit water that way. It will be at least ten feet before we find any," Tikran said, trying not to lean on his injured leg.

"So little faith," the doctor muttered, scooping the earth and dumping it to the side.

They needed water. Their horses needed water. They wouldn't make it very far at all unless they found some. Out of desperation, Tikran got down on his knees beside Damir and the two men shoveled through the earth with their hands. They had dug a mere foot when, to Tikran's astonishment, water began to collect between their fingers. Tikran remembered helping his father dig for groundwater—finding it had most certainly not been that easy.

They returned to the makeshift canopy with full flasks. Tikran's leg throbbed. He crawled carefully beneath the canvas, where Damir lit a lantern. Without a word, the doctor began cutting Tikran's breeches away from the shaft of the arrow.

"I don't think it's deep," Tikran said. "It's a course-winged iron arrowhead. It's what we use against unarmored enemies."

The arrow's shaft was surrounded by tight skin. After breaking off the protruding end of the arrow, Damir pulled a scalpel and a wire instrument with a loop at its end from his bag and began cleaning them, and his hands, with alcohol. "I don't think it's hit bone. It can be extracted. Have you ever had an injury like this before?"

Tikran shook his head. "Have you ever treated an injury like this before?"

"Orxan has provided me a few opportunities, yes." Damir held up his scalpel. "Ready?"

Tikran nodded. "Ready."

Quickly and adeptly, the doctor cut an incision at the entry site. He immediately felt the base of the iron arrow tip. He inserted the loop of the wire instrument into the wound. Tikran grunted, clenching his teeth as sweat rolled down his face and neck. Damir maneuvered the loop around the tip of the arrowhead and, grasping the broken end of the shaft, pulled the entire arrow out at once. He examined the tip to ensure it hadn't broken, then cleaned the wound and used a needle threaded with silk to swiftly stitch it closed. Finally, he smeared it with honey and wrapped Tikran's thigh in gauze and a cotton bandage. Tikran's labored breathing slowed as he blinked, trying to stay lucid.

"This will help ease the pain," Damir said, mixing drops of an herbal tincture with a cup of water. "You got lucky, you know."

Tikran drank deeply then said, "You're telling me. A few inches up and to the left and they'd have made a eunuch of me."

Damir offered a wry smile. "A few inches up and the arrow would have hit a major artery and killed you."

"In that case, I suppose becoming a eunuch isn't looking so bad." Tikran's mind was slowly clearing. "That fire. The one that stopped the Manzakars back there. It was ignited with magic. I'm certain of it. The question is, who ignited it? It couldn't have been Saltanat or one of Delger's mages because the fire was started to protect the nomads. The way it lit along the line of Manzakars... But it couldn't have come from the nomads because even with the Essence, none of them would have known how to use it so well."

"That's not necessarily true," Damir said as he cleaned his instruments.

"What do you mean? Even someone with strong Essence needs to learn how to use it."

"Again," the doctor said, "I think you've been deliberately misled to believe that. One with strong Essence can learn to use it without spells. You should also know that it's possible for one with very powerful Essence to hide it, so that mages like Saltanat can't detect it."

"How do you know this?" Tikran frowned. "You know, Damir, if I didn't know better, I'd think *you* were the one to light the fire."

Damir flashed a quick smile. "I'm flattered."

Tikran rubbed his face with his hands. "The Manzakars will go after the nomads if they believe one of them has the Essence." He glared at Damir. "Since you seem to know so much about it... do you know what the bloody magic does other than set fire to things then quench them with rain?"

Damir scrubbed his hands with alcohol. "Only as much as you do."

Tikran let his head fall back. "How convenient." After a pause, he said, "I just injured and possibly even killed Cenk knows how many Manzakars. When I get back to Anzor, I will likely have to stand trial for treason."

The doctor sat cross-legged and helped Tikran wiggle out of his tunic and shirt to check his burn injury. "You did nothing wrong. It was self-defense. Here's the story, and Oter can corroborate it: You asked for more food to reward the nomads. They helped us find the shrub that might save the prince, which is no small thing. Regardless, Oter said no. Mago stole the food and brought it to the clan. You thought he'd gotten permission, since he's friends with Oter. When the Manzakars started to attack, you defended yourself and me, the doctor who might save the prince. And," Damir added, "in a moment of anguish, you reacted to Mago's death, the man who was like a father to you."

At this, Tikran's chest constricted. He lay down and rolled to his side, away from Damir. *Mago.* Like a crashing wave, grief hit him. The merchant had been alive and laughing just a few hours ago, and now he was gone. *And it's my fault.* If he hadn't let Mago help him... He said hoarsely, "We need to leave in a couple hours. Let's get some rest." Damir snuffed out the light and all went dark, save for the moonlight that shone through the branches holding the canopy.

Tikran waited for as long as he could, feeling the pulsing pain in his leg subside from the herbal tincture Damir had given him, breathing evenly. Finally he let out his breath and tears began to stream from his eyes. As a child, he'd perfected the skill of crying silently. *Mago, Da, Evren...* They were really gone.

He felt Damir's hand on his back. "I'm so sorry, Tikran. I'm so very sorry." Damir's whisper, to Tikran's surprise, was like the soothing balm the doctor had spread on his wounds, except this wound was deep inside him. Tikran wiped his face and rolled over toward Damir, seeking... something. Sympathy? Kindness? He wasn't sure. In the slices of moonlight that filtered down on them, the Dilovari's eyes were silver and lambent with warmth... and desire. A shiver of excitement zipped through Tikran. *Am I going crazy?*

Damir smiled ever so slightly. Tikran automatically focused on Damir's mouth. It was shapely and almost sensuous, and he wanted to feel it against his. As if hearing his thoughts, Damir propped himself up on his elbow and leaned over him. Gently, the doctor brushed his lips against Tikran's. Need welled in Tikran's body despite being battered and exhausted. He reached up and wrapped a hand around the back of Damir's neck, pulling him into a deeper kiss. He parted Damir's lips demandingly, encouraged by how Damir leaned into the kiss, matching his hunger. Tikran's fingers wandered down, seeking the buttons to Damir's robe. He quickly found and unfastened them, then slipped his hand inside, sliding his palm across Damir's chest.

Damir broke the kiss, breathless. "Tikran. Wait."

"Why?" For a brief, horrifying second, he feared he'd misread Damir's intentions.

Damir's skin had taken on a rosy hue and his gaze was lidded with lust. "I've imagined this moment a hundred times, Manzakar. But you need to sleep. You've been through a lot today."

"Right now, I don't want sleep," Tikran said. "I want you."

Damir hesitated for just a moment before shedding his robe, revealing a lean, sculpted torso devoid of hair and smooth as marble. When Tikran tried to lift himself up, the doctor gently coaxed him back down. "You've done enough for one day." He smiled. "Let me please you."

Tikran obediently leaned back down as Damir ran his warm, beautiful hands down Tikran's chest, over his stomach, and to the drawstrings of his breeches. The doctor untied the knotted laces with deft, quick fingers, then slowly slipped his hand underneath them. A deep, guttural sound escaped Tikran's throat at Damir's touch. He closed his eyes, let his head fall back, and forgot about his physical pain and emotional agony, losing himself to the sensations of Damir's hands and mouth on his body.

Later that night, as the two men lay wrapped in each

other's arms, fading into sleep, Tikran clasped Damir's hands to his chest and marveled that, for one ludicrous moment, he felt like everything would be okay.

CHAPTER 17

Coxani and Naran's hunting trips—under the careful supervision of Bolat, of course—had become an almost daily occurrence, much to the exhaustion of the deaf eunuch. The royal kitchens couldn't process the kills quickly enough; the two Manzakars were creating a glut of meat. There had not been any opportunity for more stolen kisses, much to her chagrin. But as they spent time in each other's company, the desire for more kisses grew exponentially.

Coxani was in the royal stables on a sunny afternoon preparing for another hunting trip with Naran. The sound of giggling made her peek between the slats to the next stall. She saw the mage, Saltanat, and Nasch, talking. She overheard Nasch say softly, "...you in my bed tonight."

Coxani pulled back, wrinkling her nose. She would have preferred not to have heard that. What did the woman see in that pompous, murderous asshole? How awful did someone have to be to—

She froze, her heart suddenly racing. Something about a

romance between those two sounded alarm bells in her head. Why?

What about Nasch? You don't think he would do anything... literal, do you? I mean, Tikran humiliated him. Twice.

He better not. Besides, I don't think he'd risk the punishment. Now, if he thought he could get away with it, I wouldn't put it past him.

Again, the memory of Tikran engulfed in flames flashed in her mind. Was it possible Nasch had conspired with the mage —his lover—to try and kill Tikran? Coxani chewed her lip. If so, then who had made it rain? Tikran had said Saltanat had made it rain to put out the fire in Gohar. Perhaps one of the other mages had done it, then.

"Hello, beautiful." Naran strolled into the stall and glanced around hopefully. "No Bolat yet?"

Coxani held her finger to her lips and gestured for him to follow her. As they left the stall and walked quickly through the stable, Coxani whispered, "Naran... the mage and Nasch... are having an affair."

Naran raised an eyebrow. "That's an interesting match."

"You said that if Nasch thought he could get away with hurting Tikran, he would."

"What are you saying, Coxani? I'm not following."

Coxani swallowed. "The Fire Game."

Naran considered, his eyebrows drawn together. Then he looked at her abruptly, his eyes wide. "You don't think...?"

Bolat appeared at that moment, looking dismayed. He motioned to the two Manzakars urgently. They followed him out of the stables and toward the hippodrome, where Haydar was speaking with a circle of commanders. Haydar saw them and said, "A moment, please." He walked over to the pair, his face somber.

Somehow, Coxani knew it had to do with Tikran. *Oh,*

Cenk... "Lord Haydar, what's happening?" she asked breathlessly.

Haydar set his hands on his hips. He spoke softly. "There's been an incident in Gohar. While no one is certain of exactly what happened, Tikran was involved in a confrontation between a clan of nomads and Areg's Manzakar squadron. He was injured by an arrow to the leg but was otherwise unharmed." Haydar paused and looked at the two horrified faces before him. "He took down eighteen Manzakars with his bow."

"Fuck." Naran's face was bloodless. "Pardon my language, Lord Haydar."

Coxani could barely hear her own voice over the rapid swishing of her heart. "There must be an explanation. He wouldn't just—"

"Even with a good explanation, he will have to answer to the king," Haydar said. "And he will no doubt be punished."

"Where is he now?" Naran asked.

"We're not sure. He's with the Dilovari doctor. If he's smart, he'll come back to Anzor immediately."

Coxani felt dizzy. She gripped Naran's arm to steady herself. "What was the confrontation over?"

"Stolen food. But I don't think that's what compelled Tikran to fight."

"What did it, then?"

Briefly, Haydar's face betrayed him and he looked devastated. "Mago was there. He was killed by a Manzakar's arrow."

THEY WERE QUICKLY APPROACHING ANZOR.

Tikran and Damir had been traveling a little more than a week. Tikran had gone from anxiously anticipating what awaited him, to stoically preparing to face the consequences of his actions. He'd replayed the events of the confrontation in his mind a hundred times, and he always came to the same conclusion: He had made a fatal mistake by involving Mago and he would never forgive himself for it. But he also had no regrets for stealing food to feed the nomads, nor for fighting back. Something had to change in the way Anzor treated the Gohari and he was determined to be Gohar's voice.

He would sway Delger to reason or die trying.

Tikran stole a look at Damir's profile as they rode in silence. Since that first night, Tikran had tried initiating intimacy again only for Damir to invent all kinds of excuses why they shouldn't—he'd be violating some code of ethics regarding doctors' involvements with their patients; sexual relationships between men were frowned upon in all the southern kingdoms; there was no point in growing attached to one another since he'd eventually return to Dilovar...

Tikran would be lying if he said he wasn't hurt. Had he just imagined Damir's passion for him? By Cenk, he could have sworn it was very real. Perhaps the intensity of the day had simply gotten to the doctor, although that didn't seem in line with his cool, composed behavior in the face of danger so far. Moreover, he was getting to know Damir well enough to doubt that religion had anything to do with his reluctance.

The only possible explanation was that he'd simply changed his mind.

They didn't talk about it. Tikran wasn't sure what the purpose would be to bring it up, since he doubted anything would happen between them once they returned to Anzor. How could it? Ultimately, he decided to behave like it never happened. The ache in his heart would eventually pass... he hoped.

It was a warm summer morning when they reached the

border between Anzor and Gohar. Tikran said to Damir, "Remember what we decided."

"What *you* decided." Damir shook his head in frustration. "If it were up to me, I'd have you lie through your teeth in every way possible to save your skin."

"I'm done lying. I'm done looking away." He smiled sardonically at Damir. "I'm done being an elite lapdog."

As the guards on the wall caught sight of them, a cry went up. Both men raised their hands in surrender. Soldiers spilled from the battlements, and Tikran realized with a jolt that he was very much a wanted man. *They've been watching for me.* The two fugitives were ordered from their horses. Their hands were tied and they were shoved into a covered wagon with a black slash of paint across its side. Tikran knew the wagon all too well—it was the wagon in which the Anzori transported their criminals. As a cadet, he'd watched the wagon pass with rage, determined to protect Anzor from such villains.

The irony almost made him smile.

From the sounds outside, Tikran could tell when they entered Anzor City and crossed the moat into the Citadel. As the wagon slowed, Damir said, "Tikran..." He swallowed, his slate-colored eyes gravid with emotion. For the first time, Tikran saw real vulnerability in the doctor's face. Then the wagon door swung open, and the Manzakars led Damir out. Before the barred door shut behind him, Damir looked at Tikran, the vulnerability gone. "Good luck," he said solemnly.

The wagon bumped on to the prison. Anzor had several prisons for various types of crimes and prisoners. While he awaited trial, Tikran was put in a holding cell within the Citadel itself. He'd never been inside the actual prison in the Citadel, and was dismayed at how dirty it was compared to the rest of the fortress. The Manzakars who led him to his cell were men Tikran had trained with, and they avoided looking him in the eyes.

His cell was small and comparatively clean, with a cot and a basin. A wool blanket covered the cot and the basin was full of fresh water. A narrow opening high on the wall allowed light to filter in and illuminate the barred enclosure. He winced as he sat, his leg aching with every movement. Within minutes of sitting, he heard a clatter and two familiar voices. His heart leaped in his throat.

Naran and Coxani were flanked by two guards as they approached his cell. Upon seeing him, Coxani rushed to the bars. "Tikran. Holy shit, Tikran."

Tikran stood and took two strides to the bars, then grasped Coxani's hands in his. "Mago..." He couldn't formulate the words without choking up.

"Lord Haydar told us," Coxani said, her eyes filling with tears. "What happened? We've heard so many different stories."

"It's all my fault." Tikran pressed his forehead against a bar. "I shouldn't have let him get involved. I wanted more food for the nomads who helped us find the medicinal shrub. He was trying to help me—"

"Tikran, Mago was a grown man and I am convinced he knew exactly what he was doing," Coxani said. "You can't carry that burden."

"It's more than just Mago," Tikran said, squeezing his eyes shut. "My actions will likely result in the deaths of a whole Gohari clan."

"Brother," Naran said, wrapping his rough fingers around Tikran's through the bars. "You were trying to feed them."

Tikran opened his eyes. "The Manzakars. Did any of them die?"

Naran sucked in his breath. "You hit eighteen of them. Two died from their wounds. The arrows were definitely yours."

"Tikran," Coxani insisted, "you were defending yourself and Damir. Your defense is self-defense."

"No," Tikran said. "I was defending the Gohari and in a desperate fury over Mago. I was shooting with intent to injure or kill Manzakars."

Coxani blanched. "You absolutely cannot say that before the judges. They'll—"

"I'm sick and tired of being complicit in the destruction of an entire people," Tikran said, his voice rasping with anger. "In retaliation for the attack on the king's train, we exterminated an entire tribe. The Iroda tribe no longer exists. We have been abetting this with our silence. I've had enough. I will not look away anymore."

Coxani and Naran stared at him, their mouths ajar, a mixture of admiration and horror on their faces. Coxani finally said softly, "Tikran, please don't be a martyr. I—we—need you."

Tikran shook his head. "I can't go on pretending to not know what I know. It will eat me from the inside out. If I'm martyred for it, then so be it."

"I don't think Delger would do that—not yet, anyway," Naran said.

"How can you be so sure?" Coxani asked, her voice shaking.

"Because there would be repercussions for martyring the Caged Kingfisher." He smiled. "Anzor's favorite Manzakar."

Coxani's eyes suddenly widened and she looked at Naran. "The Caged Kingfisher is definitely loved by the Anzori. They would likely stand by him if they knew he had tried to feed starving Gohari when he was attacked by Manzakars and had to defend himself, the doctor, and the nomads."

Tikran groaned. "I'm definitely not a hero and I don't want extra publicity, please."

"Tik, Coxani's right," Naran said. "Public support can help your cause. If anything, it'll ensure Delger doesn't attempt to... do away with you."

Tikran looked down at his feet. He suspected they might be on to something, as much as he hated the idea.

"We have a plan, then." Coxani stood on her toes and, slipping a hand through the bars, turned Tikran's head toward her. She kissed him on the mouth then pulled back and looked him in the eyes. "We'll get you out of here."

"Hmm." Naran eyed Tikran in mock suspicion. "Considering how the women love you, maybe I should be happy you're locked up." He wrapped his hand around the back of Tikran's neck. "Try not to fuck up any more than you already have, eh?"

A laugh escaped Tikran's lips. "I'm not sure I could."

After Naran and Coxani left, Tikran felt like a weight had been lifted from his shoulders. They didn't hate him for what he'd done. They wanted to help him. *I'm not alone.* He would have lain on the cot and sobbed with relief if a mere five minutes later he hadn't heard someone else approaching. When he recognized the voice of Lord Haydar, he instantly felt sick. What would he say to the durai? Tikran had failed his mentor—his idol—in every way possible. How would he look Haydar in the eyes ever again?

Haydar approached the bars of Tikran's cell, looking older than he had a few weeks ago. He looked Tikran directly in the eye, betraying no emotions. The silence stretched endlessly until Haydar said, "Tikran. Would you please explain to me— in your own words—exactly what happened?"

The vision of Mago crumpling to the ground, an arrow through his heart, flashed through Tikran's mind. Bruneta's words replayed, yet again: *The Manzakars set fire to their yarms, executed the men and children, raped the women, then executed them too.* He felt that now-familiar outrage well up in his chest. His thoughts were suddenly crystal clear.

Tikran took a step toward Haydar, meeting his gaze fully. "I'm guilty. Of all of it. I wanted to reward the nomads with food for helping us find the plant, because they're fucking starving. All of Gohar is fucking *starving*, Lord Haydar." The edges of Tikran's vision were tinged with red hot fury. "And we're just pretending to help. That alone is enough to drive me to fight Manzakars. But that's not all. We aren't just starving the Gohari. We're annihilating them because we see them as animals and not worthy of living." Tikran was breathing hard now. "I will not be a part of this. Do what you will to me, but I will not just stand by quietly and let this happen."

Tikran's leg ached. His arm and shoulder burned. He couldn't remember the last time he'd eaten or drunk anything. He could feel himself fading. But by sheer force of will, he stood as straight as he could, his eyes locked on Haydar's. The world began to swirl around him. Perhaps he just imagined it, but something in Haydar's face flickered. It was a glimpse of something so starkly different from what he expected that he had to lower himself to the floor, certain he was about to lose consciousness. As everything began to go dim, he set his head on the cold stone floor of his cell.

His eyes began to close. He saw a blurry Haydar turn and heard him call to the guards.

Then everything went black.

He felt Damir's gentle, skilled touch as he returned to consciousness. He opened his eyes to find himself lying down in his cell, with Damir seated beside him and Haydar standing at the foot of the cot. Relief flashed across both men's faces as he tried to sit up. "I don't know what happened," he said.

"You have two injuries, you haven't had water or food in over a day, and you've just been arrested for treason." Damir smiled dryly, handing him a cup of water and setting a bowl of lamb stew in his lap. "Drink and eat."

Leaning against the wall, Tikran drained his cup and began eating, the smell of the food stimulating his appetite. Damir said, "Both wounds are healing well, thankfully. We should be able to remove the bandage on your burn completely in the next day or so. I will visit daily to check your leg for festering and administer a tincture that will help relieve the pain." Tikran nodded, meeting Damir's gaze. Emotion flashed in the doctor's gray eyes briefly.

"Thank you, Doctor," Haydar said. "The king has agreed to let you visit Tikran every morning until he is fully healed. You may take your leave until tomorrow."

Damir stood and bowed to Haydar. "Of course, my lord." He gave Tikran a detached look. "Until tomorrow."

The door clanged shut behind the doctor and Haydar took his place on the stool beside Tikran's cot, his arms crossed on his chest. "Tikran. Your trial is set for a week from now. I highly recommend you claim self-defense against the accusations of treason. According to Damir, you were, in fact, shielding him and an injured Mago during the skirmish. As for the accusations of grand theft, your best defense is lack of intent."

Tikran set the now-empty bowl down. "I was defending Damir and Mago, you're right. But I was also fighting with the nomads and defending *them* as well. As for the theft, I very much had intent to give stolen food to the clan."

Haydar lowered his voice. "Lad, the penalty for treason is

death. If you go to trial and repeat what you just said to me, you will hang at best, be drawn and quartered at worst."

"I know," Tikran said. He hesitated before adding, "What I can't figure out is why you're trying to help me. I've just admitted that I'm a traitor, and your duty as a Manzakar is to the king, first and foremost."

Haydar frowned. "I love you, boy. You may be a traitor, but I don't want you to die for it."

A lump quickly formed in Tikran's throat. Haydar had never said those words to him. He'd expressed pride and admiration, but love? He struggled to compose himself. *You absolutely cannot start crying now. Get a grip.*

Haydar continued. "I want to speak to the king on your behalf, but I certainly can't make any sort of compelling case to spare you if you refuse to defend yourself against the charges. I implore you to reconsider."

Tikran tightened his jaw. "I want to stop living a lie. The lie that I saved my family, the lie that I'm not a slave, the lie that everything I stand for by wearing a Manzakar's armor is just and benevolent and... heroic."

Haydar stood. "Do you want to stop living a lie? Or stop living altogether? If there's something you believe in fighting for, you have to at least live long enough to actually fight for it." He motioned to the guard that he was done and to let him out. The door shut behind him but before walking away, he turned and looked at Tikran through the bars. "Remember that if you die, your message dies with you."

Tikran sat quietly in the darkness of the cell for a long while after Haydar left, trying to make sense of why the durai had said what he said. Haydar was *the* king's man. Was he saying those things about fighting for one's beliefs or living to send a message because he was merely trying to convince Tikran to defend himself? Or were those things he actually believed? Nothing Haydar had ever said or done implied he believed them.

He stood and began pacing the length of his cell. One week. How was he going to endure this place for one week? He wondered if Coxani or Naran could help him find out what happened to his sister's clan. Every time he considered the possibilities, he felt sick. If Nasch decided to go after them, it—

The sound of clanging doors and footsteps meant someone was coming to see him. He heard no voices but desperately hoped it was one of his friends. When the red-robed, lavender-eyed mage emerged from the shadows, he braced himself. The lower half of her face was veiled but he could clearly see the hostility in her slanted eyes. Hostility and... fear? She would not approach the bars, but chose to stand several feet away, her hands clasped behind her back. Tikran stayed silent, waiting. He couldn't begin to imagine what she wanted with him.

"Manzakar of the Caged Kingfisher," she said. "What are you hiding from me?"

Tikran sighed deeply, shooting her a look of utter disinterest. "Why don't you just ask me what you want to know? Because I have no idea what you're talking about."

Her eyes narrowed at him and she yanked off the veil to reveal a snarl. "Believe me when I say I will destroy you if you continue this charade. You're already on the road to execution. All I have to do is make sure everything goes through." She smiled. "And I can do that easily."

He was genuinely trying to figure out what she was saying, with little success. Charade? He took a deep breath and said, "My lady, what charade? Please forgive me—I'm a little disoriented at the moment, what with the injuries, arrest, and pending death sentence."

She seemed to become angrier by the second. She stepped forth and wrapped her hands around the bars of his cell. "Oh, you're good, Caged Kingfisher. Play the noble hero while you can. Just rest assured that you will die. And when you do, you will fight for your life to no avail, and your secrets will be plain for all to see."

After she said this, Tikran dwelled on his secrets. *Does she know something I don't know?* Other than his relationship with Damir, he couldn't think of a single thing about himself that was still a secret—and for all he knew, that wasn't a secret anymore either. Maybe the fact that his sister was among the clan he'd fought with? That might be it, but it would be something that would bring her glee, not this blatant rage. So what in the name of Cenk was this mage insinuating?

"Saltanat, once again, I have no idea what you're talking about."

"Keep your tongue then!" she snapped. "Regardless of how powerful you think you may be, the full power of the mages of Anzor can and will defeat you. I will relish watching you die, Manzakar." With that, she turned, the hem of her robe swirling across the dirty stone floor, and marched away with the guards hurrying behind her.

When she was gone, he dropped down on his cot, exhausted. Whatever secret she thought he was hiding from her, it was apparently enough for her to summon all the mages to—

Wait. He sat up suddenly. Was it possible?

You should also know that it's remotely possible for one with very powerful Essence to hide it, so that mages like Saltanat can't detect it.

It was the only thing that made sense.

Saltanat thought he had the Essence—and was masking it from her.

CHAPTER 18

The word spread quickly and easily.

Coxani had started in the exact right place—the women's quarters. From there, it disseminated throughout the Citadel, the barracks, and trickled across the moat and into the mouths and ears of the bakers, blacksmiths, fish wives, and tailors: The people of Gohar were suffering mistreatment at the hands of King Delger, and the Manzakar of the Caged Kingfisher was accused of treason for defending them.

She and Naran had snuck into town and left handbills with Tikran's heraldic symbol in public spaces, like markets and squares. *Free the Caged Kingfisher.* And the Kingfisher was, in fact, caged.

The following afternoon, Lord Haydar requested that both Coxani and Naran meet him on his way back from his manor in the country and join him on a hunting trip. As the pair saddled up, Coxani said, "We're in trouble."

Naran chuckled. "What's new? But it would be strange if

Haydar is angry at us for trying to help Tikran. Tik's like his son."

As they rode out to meet Haydar on the outskirts of Anzor City, Coxani said, "Haydar bought you for the king as well, didn't he?"

"Yes. I love the man." Naran smiled. "I think every boy bought by Haydar to serve the king worships him. He could shoot a bow on horseback and wield a saber just as masterly as Tikran when he was younger. For all I know, he still can. And just like Tik, the women continue to go crazy for him."

"That's what I heard as well," Coxani said. She gave Naran the side-eye. "But from what I can tell, the ladies go crazy for you as well, Lion."

Naran flashed his dimple at her, making her stomach flutter. "Yes, but I put myself out there, you know? I like the attention. Tikran hates attention. Always has. He's dived into bushes to avoid an encounter with his adoring fans on more than one occasion. And yet, they continue to be obsessed with him."

"Tell me about it," Coxani said with a laugh. "When did you two meet?"

Naran rubbed his chin. "Oh, pretty much right after Tikran came to the barracks. He was seven and I was nine. We took to each other right away. I guess you could say I played big brother to him." The dimple returned, along with a bit of color in his cheeks. "Well, for a little while, at least, until we hit puberty."

"What happened when you two hit puberty?"

Naran shook his head. "Nothing. We just deviated from the whole brotherly relationship thing."

"You grew apart?"

"Ha! Hardly."

Coxani narrowed her eyes. "Then what do you mean?"

"Forget it, Coxani."

"Naran, now you *have* to tell me."

"Fine, fine." He blew out his breath, his cheeks coloring further. "You know, we were teenage boys, isolated together in the barracks, spending every waking and sleeping moment together. Things... happened."

"What *things*?" Coxani's voice was louder, her eyes wider.

"Holy Cenk, woman," Naran mumbled. "You really want me to spell it out for you? We became lovers." Coxani's jaw dropped. When she didn't speak for several seconds, Naran laughed and said, "A lot of the boys got intimate with each other. We were Gohari boys with all these urges and no outlet. It was kind of... normal to turn to each other. And the eunuchs tended to turn a blind eye unless the relationship was overt."

Coxani sputtered. "How old were you? How old was he?"

A broad, white smile spread across Naran's face. "Are you getting worked up over this?"

"No, I'm just... startled." Her face grew warm. Tikran had implied that his previous lovers had been men. She just hadn't expected one of those men to be Naran. Two beautiful men— *her* men—had been lovers at one point.

"I guess Tik must have been fifteen? It was when he began his military training and we were suddenly around each other all the time again. By Cenk, he was pretty. I was sixteen or seventeen and already had quite a few exploits under my belt by that time, but none had been much of an emotional experience for me. It was somewhat different with him."

"Holy shit," Coxani muttered. "You were *in love* with him?"

"Eh." Naran scratched his chest. "I don't know if I'd call it that. None of the cadets were really given the chance to, you know, fall in love with each other. Besides, we were young. We were best friends, first and foremost. I can tell you though, I do love him and always will." He grinned. "Just not as a lover."

"How long did the... physical aspect of the relationship last?"

"A year, on and off. But eventually it became more of a very close friendship and the sex just kind of fell by the wayside."

Coxani stared ahead without seeing. "I need a few minutes to process this."

Naran frowned. "Are you upset over it?"

"No, no," she assured him. "Just shocked. The more I think about it, though, the more it seems... just as it should have been."

Naran cleared his throat. "I can tell you that for the last couple months, I've longed for only one person to share my bed." He looked at her then, his amber eyes luminous with yearning.

A shiver of delight raced through her, pebbling her skin and making her heart race. She was uncomfortable expressing her desire for him out loud, so she simply looked at him, hoping he could read her answer in her eyes.

They reached Haydar shortly thereafter, and Coxani's elation dissipated quickly. She couldn't help but notice the lack of attendants as they ventured into the woods. Apprehension crept up her spine. *This is deliberate.* She loved Haydar and trusted him. But she also knew something was amiss. She could tell that Naran had sensed the same. His hand touched the pommel of his saber, the fletching of his arrows.

"Thank you for joining me this afternoon, Manzakars," Haydar said as he rode between them, looking straight forward, his handsome face austere. "I've asked you here to discuss Tikran in some privacy, as you might have expected." He sighed and shook his head in disappointment. "You both know how much I love him. I will do everything I can to help him avoid execution, but he has committed unforgivable treachery. No one feels it greater than I do, except perhaps for King Delger. It is like a dagger to both our hearts."

Coxani felt like a weight was pressing against her chest, like she and Naran were walking into a trap. She saw sweat bead Naran's brow, the base of his neck. Anger began to brew within her—anger and pain—at the thought that Haydar, of all people, could not see the justice in what Tikran had done.

Haydar continued. "There is no question that the crimes Tikran has committed should be punishable by death. King Delger is, as always, wise in understanding that a firm hand is necessary when it comes to treason, without exception. But I am hoping I can sway him to be merciful in regard to the Caged Kingfisher, beloved by Anzor City." He looked at Coxani and Naran in turn, his expression grim. "However, last I spoke to the lad, he seemed intent on pleading guilty of the crimes rather than defending himself. Doing this will make it much harder to convince the king to spare him. King Delger will no doubt see Tikran's admission of guilt just as he means it—as defiance."

"We couldn't try to talk him out of it even if we wanted to," Naran said stiffly. Coxani could see the outrage in him. "They won't even let us see him."

Coxani could keep silent no longer. She suddenly understood what Tikran had meant when he'd described that sharp clarity emanating from a certain madness... Her voice was steady and firm even as her heart raced. "What he did was no crime, Lord Haydar. He responded to the crimes of King Delger, which include deliberate starvation and systematic extermination of the Gohari people. I am appalled—and broken-hearted—that *you* don't see that."

Haydar reined his horse to a stop and glared at Coxani, his face fierce. "Those are treasonous words, Coxani. I command you to retract them, or else I will be forced to have you arrested."

She could feel the bow at her hip beckoning to her. She sensed Naran go perfectly still, as if preparing for an attack. She inhaled sharply. *We're done for.* "No."

Haydar swung his head to look at Naran. His voice was calm, which made the entire exchange all the more terrifying. "You agree with her, I assume?"

Naran held the durai's gaze steadfastly with his. "One hundred percent."

The silence that stretched over several seconds lasted an eternity. Haydar's eyes flicked between them, then he slowly nodded. "I see." The hints of a smile began to curl the corners of his mouth. "Then you are both ready to join me." As the two Manzakars gaped at him in stunned silence, he glanced around the forest and said casually, "Let's kill something before we head back to the Citadel, shall we? It would be highly suspicious if three exceptional Manzakars returned from a hunting trip empty-handed."

THE YOUNG GOHARI slave woman bowed after knocking gently on the study door. "My lord, Doctor Damir has arrived. He is waiting in the courtyard."

"Thank you, Dihya," Haydar said, rising from his desk. He slipped into his linen kaftan and walked across the hall to the open doors of the courtyard. Haydar had been dwelling on what he planned to do next for quite a while. He knew there was a serious risk in his course of action, but it was one he had to take. He would deal with Bilguun when the time came. As for the doctor... Haydar prayed his instincts were correct. He arranged a friendly smile on his face and stepped out into the garden. It was a beautiful summer evening and the Dilovari doctor sat comfortably watching butterflies dance from violet irises to a jasmine bush. He rose when he saw Haydar approach.

"Lord Haydar, thank you for inviting me tonight," Damir said, bowing gracefully. He looked about him. "You have a beautiful home. One feels at peace in this garden."

"Thank you," Haydar said. "The courtyard is indeed my favorite spot in this house. It allows for some meditative thinking." He gestured to the table. "Please, sit." As they sat, the slave girl slipped a tray of refreshments between them. Haydar lifted a blue bottle from the tray and began pouring a clear liquid into small, enameled glasses. "Have you ever had xew, doctor?"

"No, my lord, I don't believe I have."

Haydar set one of the glasses before Damir. "It is an Anzori liquor made primarily from the seeds of the anise plant, but also contains grapes, dates, and figs. I admit that it's an acquired taste, however it complements the cheese Dihya chose to accompany it beautifully."

Damir lifted the glass and smiled at Haydar. "To your health, my lord."

Haydar lifted his glass. "To Prince Vazha's health, Doctor."

After taking a swallow, Damir said, "Interesting. It's... very strong. Must be at least seventy percent alcohol." He cleared his throat. "I think I'll have some cheese."

Haydar laughed. "Indeed! No doubt it's as strong as what you use to clean wounds. It certainly isn't something you drink very much of, unless you wish to lie in bed nursing a throbbing headache and churning stomach for the next day or so." He sipped from his glass then said, "You're probably wondering why I asked you here tonight. You likely suspect it has to do with Vazha's shocking recovery, for which you are solely responsible."

Damir shook his head. "I am honored, Lord Haydar, but I couldn't have done it without Tikran's help. He alone knew where to find the shrub, and with the help of the Gohari clan, we were able to procure enough of it."

Haydar took another sip of xew, staring at Damir over the rim of his glass. He sat back. "Yes, of course." He examined his hands and sighed. "I'm sure you've heard that Tikran is something of a son to me."

Damir met Haydar's gaze evenly. "I have heard that, yes."

"His treasonous actions hurt me greatly," Haydar said, scowling and shaking his head. "I trusted him implicitly, and he betrayed that trust."

"My lord, if I may." Damir licked his lips and leaned forward. "While I do understand how Tikran's actions may appear treasonous, I can vouch that his intentions were to protect the slave trader from the onslaught of arrows. He was very distraught by Mago's death. Surely that means something to Anzor's court of justice."

Haydar watched Damir carefully as he said, "It would, but... Unfortunately, Tikran intends to plead guilty to the charges and refuses to defend himself on any grounds, including those of self-defense."

Damir's eyes flickered, his lips tightened. The moment was brief, and he composed his features quickly. "That is quite unfortunate. Because I can testify to what I saw, how his primary concern throughout the trip was Vazha, and how desperately he hoped the shrub would work."

Haydar weaved his fingers together in his lap. "You seem to have taken a liking to him, Doctor."

Damir straightened, then leaned back in his chair in seeming indifference. A haughty smile hovered on his lips.

"Liking? Well, yes. Who doesn't like a man so singularly devoted to his king's bloodline?"

Haydar smiled back. *He's good.* "You know, it's funny. Tikran was quite unwell those first days in prison. Nearly delirious, at certain points. During one of his episodes of delirium, he told me that, somehow, a fire ignited just as he thought all was lost during that treacherous battle. It tore through the Manzakar line, and he's certain it wasn't naturally created. I'm curious, since you were there. What are your thoughts on it?"

Damir considered. "I admit that my first thought, as a doctor, you see, is that I wasn't called during these moments of delirium."

Haydar continued to smile. *He's very good.* "Apologies, Doctor. We were absorbed in thought over the words he spoke. We were certain he would come to no harm."

The doctor lifted his glass and drained it in one swallow. "I saw nothing unnatural about the fire. One of the nomads must have lit it."

Haydar shrugged. "I would believe you, except... King Delger's head mage has disclosed that she believes someone with strong Essence is among us and masking it. Can you imagine? I never would have thought such thing was possible." He took another slow sip of xew and a bite of cheese. "She seems convinced it's Tikran himself."

It was then that Haydar saw a flare of emotion in the doctor's eyes. Damir's gaze locked on Haydar's. "I think you already know it's not Tikran."

Haydar finished his cheese, then looked up at the evening sky. "Why would Bilguun send a mage disguised as a doctor to Anzor?"

"I *am* a doctor," Damir said through his teeth. "And Delger asked for me, in case you've forgotten."

"Forgive me," Haydar replied. "Why would Bilguun not reveal to Delger that the doctor he was sending to Anzor is also a very powerful mage? The only logical explanation is that he saw an opportunity to send a spy, someone to sniff out the strength of Anzor's Essence. Or perhaps to venture into Anzor and do some reconnaissance. Or why not both?" Haydar leaned forward once more, his elbows on the table, tapping his chin in thought. "One of the more confounding questions is how a Dilovari has the Essence. Only one with Gohari blood could possibly have any trace of it. And looking at you, Damir, I can see the possible hints of the nomad in the color of your skin, your eyes, the shape of your brow. I suspect there must have been some illegal procreation involved. And what a windfall for Bilguun! To have a young, powerful mage just as the Essence was beginning to dwindle in Dilovar." Haydar tilted his head to the side. "Am I on the right track, Doctor?"

Damir's body language spoke of a man who was utterly unconcerned with what he was hearing—he leaned back casually, his legs crossed, his right hand dangling over the arm of the chair. But a dangerous storm brewed in his gray eyes. "I would be careful with your speculations, my lord. Share them with the wrong people, and you could have another Akmaral War on your hands."

"Indeed," Haydar said. "And I'll be honest, the choice of whether to share my speculations would be fairly cut and dry, if not for the most confounding piece of it all." He looked at Damir for a long few seconds, searching the doctor's impassive face. "Why would a powerful Dilovari mage save Tikran's life —twice?"

Damir leaned forward across the table, bringing his face closer to Haydar's, his dispassion falling away briefly. Color suffused his cheeks as his eyebrows drew together and his lip curled over his teeth. In a low, threatening voice, he said,

"Tikran is Anzor's only redeeming quality. If you destroy him, I promise to do everything in my power to goad Bilguun into a war Delger has no chance of winning."

Haydar lifted the blue bottle and tipped more xew into Damir's glass. He then lifted his own and, with a dazzling smile, said, "Let's toast to Tikran, then, and get him out of this mess."

HAYDAR'S COUNTRY manor was enormous—and empty. As Coxani peered about the high, painted ceilings and intricate mosaic floors, she said, "I used to wonder what you did here, all alone. Now I understand that you weren't really alone at all."

Haydar's laughter echoed and as he led her and Naran to his study. "This is where my real work takes place—and it has only some to do with collecting tithes and managing fiefs."

"Who else is involved in... this?" Naran asked.

Haydar closed the door behind them. "It's better that I not name names. I will tell you, however, that this effort is spear-headed by myself, other durais, and Manzakars. I would say roughly a third of the Manzakar troops are on our side. And I can assure you that we have allies in all places. We use a combination of certain phrases to identify ourselves to one another and carrier pigeons to communicate over long distances. Please know that my household staff, though sparse, is utterly trustworthy."

"How long has this been going on?"

Haydar sat behind his desk. "Oh, it's been thirty years. Something like this requires extensive planning and prepara-tion. Some durais have been at this longer than I have. I've spent decades very carefully selecting and monitoring Gohari children, including yourselves, for this exact purpose."

"Holy Cenk," muttered Coxani. "That explains so much—why you bought me a bow when I was little, encouraged me to become a cadet, reunited me with Tikran..."

"You deliberately made sure Tikran and I were always training together, didn't you?" Naran asked.

Haydar nodded. "Everything has been very thoughtfully planned out." He looked at Coxani. "Including the visits to the library, and the books I hid in the stacks for you to find." He leaned back. "My goal was to show you the injustices done by cloaking them in religious righteousness and hoping you saw through it. Which is why I chose children with intelligence, empathy, and an independent spirit."

Naran grinned. "You mean rebellious spirit. And we're flattered."

Coxani stared at Haydar thoughtfully. "You have bigger plans for Tikran. You've always had bigger plans for him."

A smile hovered on Haydar's lips. "In Tikran, I see a better version of myself poised on the precipice of change. If he is willing to lead, people will follow him."

"What if he isn't?"

"Come now, Coxani. You know Tikran better than any of us." Haydar looked out the window at the vast fields beyond. "When faced with iniquity, he can't stop himself from acting. He may not want to lead, but he will if it means fighting for the oppressed."

Naran chuckled softly. "He sure will."

Haydar stood and began to pace, his hands on his hips. "So here comes the hard part. In order to convince Delger to let Tikran live, I will have to make some suggestions that will be difficult for you both. Are you willing to suffer to free Tikran and fight for the cause?"

A chill rushed down Coxani's spine. The cause. *To overthrow the king.* Without hesitation, she said, "Yes."

Naran nodded. "Absolutely."

"Good." He stopped pacing. "Tomorrow, I will have you both arrested for inciting a riot by dropping handbills around the city in support of Tikran. Your fates will likely be used as leverage in persuading Tikran to claim self-defense and publicly apologize. As a matter of fact, I will encourage it. The two of you will then be stripped of your Manzakar ranks. I imagine Tikran and Naran will be sent to remote outposts while you, Coxani, will become a low-level cleric in Cenk's temple in the Citadel, if Delger follows my recommendation." He paused, looking them each in the eyes. "After hearing all that, can I still rely on your full commitment?"

"Holy shit," Naran mumbled. "Excuse my language once again, my lord. But yes, you can rely on me."

Coxani nodded, feeling light-headed. "And me as well."

"I will prepare you to find allies wherever you are and keep you abreast of any plans or news by visiting the Loom—it's the name we've given the Crooked Street Inn on the east side of Anzor City. You two will be instrumental in helping us mobilize. When you need to send a message to me through an ally, refer to me as 'Enlil the Weaver.' My identity must remain secret from everyone but a very select few." Haydar perched himself on the edge of his desk, his hands folded in front of him. "I wish I could tell you that this phase will be quick, but I can't know that for certain. It depends on a number of factors, including whether we have enough arms, enough Manzakars, full buy-in from key durais and noblemen, and, perhaps most importantly, Tikran's full involvement."

"I wouldn't worry about getting Tik's full involvement," Naran said. "He will definitely get involved. I'd worry about him doing something on his own before he knows about your plan, Lord Haydar. The man has the bad habit of acting before he thinks."

Haydar smiled. "He acts without thinking when something he regards as truly unjust occurs. That's part of the reason I think he'll be able to see this through when no one else can."

"Lord Haydar." A terrified excitement was building in Coxani's chest. "What happens... after?"

The sound of far-off thunder as raindrops began hitting the windowpane punctuated Haydar's answer. "Justice for the Gohari people, in Anzor and Gohar."

Coxani and Naran left Haydar's manor very late that night, during a pause in the rain. Haydar would return to the city a day later, before the trial. It was then that he would have them arrested and taken to court alongside Tikran. They rode side by side, both jarred by everything they'd discovered that day, both ruminating on what the future held.

"Poor Tikran," Coxani said. "He has no idea any of this is happening. He'll be horrified when he sees us at the trial."

"Hopefully he does what Haydar predicts he'll do and not lose his shit," Naran said.

"If our lives are at stake, he will do whatever it takes," she replied sadly. "I know he will."

"Coxani." Naran's face was outlined in the moonlight. "We may not see each other for a while."

Her heart sank as she realized he was right. "I think I was mentally ignoring that part."

"Before we get back, can we stop so that I can get a proper kiss?"

She inhaled. "Yes, please."

They dismounted and Naran tethered the horses to a tree. Her heart was pounding in anticipation as he turned and smiled at her, then led her by the hand under the cover of some low hanging branches. He pulled her against him and tilted her face up to look at him. "I keep dreaming about doing this. I'm not sure there's anything I want more." She stood on her toes to meet his lips as his hands slid up her back. Once again, she found herself sinking, melting as his mouth teased hers, his kiss slowly becoming deeper. Her entire body was ablaze. She couldn't stop her hands from wandering over his chest, his arms, and down to the bulge in his breeches.

He broke the kiss, his breath coming quickly. "Be careful what you start, Coxani. It'll be torture to stop."

She moved her hand away, embarrassment warming her neck. "You're right."

He held her wrist and let out a low chuckle. "That said, I don't *want* you to stop."

She pulled her body from his and took a step back, her eyes downcast. "I'm sorry, Naran. I'm not ready for... that yet."

He took a deep breath and reached for her face, tipping her chin up so that he could look into her eyes. "Coxani, I understand. I'm happy to wait."

Tears prickled her eyes. "Are you sure?"

He smiled tenderly. "You don't get it, do you? I'd wait for you forever."

Coxani willed the tears back into her head and smiled back shakily. She didn't know what to say. Naran sensed it and looked toward the horses. "Well, I guess we should get back and get this whole rebellion thing going."

They rode the rest of the way to Anzor City while Naran regaled her with stories about growing up in the barracks, making her laugh and feel more hope than she'd felt in a long time.

CHAPTER 19

The now-familiar clanging of iron doors made Tikran pause his back-and-forth pacing. It was the early evening and he knew his visitor must be Damir. As the doctor entered the cell with his doctor's bag, Tikran suppressed the urge to clasp Damir to him in a tight, desperate embrace. But then he remembered the promise he'd made with himself. *He's a doctor, that's it.* Tikran removed his shirt, tugged down his breeches and sat down on the cot, awaiting examination.

Damir paused as he approached, tilting his head. "You're like a caged lion, pacing back and forth, aren't you?"

Tikran had little energy for trite conversations. He wanted answers—answers to what was happening outside this prison, to what Coxani and Naran were thinking and doing... His trial was a night away, and he'd become increasingly doubtful that admitting guilt was his best course of action. It wasn't that he feared death—that was the last thing he feared, at this point. What he feared was that, after his trial, things would return to as they were, and the Gohari would be mostly killed off, becoming a race of mages and slaves, slowly dwindling into extinction.

He looked at Damir, desperate for human interaction. "How is Prince Vazha?"

Damir unwrapped Tikran's leg wound first. "He's better every day. The treatment is working."

Tikran let his head fall back against the stone wall behind him. At least that was working in his favor. He hesitated a bit before asking, "When do you return to Dilovar?"

"Not until the prince is fully cured, which will likely be another week." Examining the arrow wound, he added, "You're healing well. How does it feel?"

Tikran shrugged. "It still throbs, but I can walk on it without limping."

"Good. The tincture is working." He cleaned and rewrapped the leg wound, then moved to the arm.

Tikran watched Damir nimbly unwrap his burn wound and couldn't help but remember the feel of his hands as they worked in a non-medical capacity. *Stop it!* The last thing he needed at the moment was an erection. Damir had made it abundantly clear that he wanted nothing to do with Tikran in *that* way. He sucked in his breath and stared at nothing against the back wall, dragging his mind back to his current situation —about to be found guilty of treason and sentenced to death.

Damir smiled. "There is no longer a need for a bandage. The burn is healed."

Tikran looked at his arm. A pale pink trail of leathery skin ran from his wrist, up his arm, across his shoulder, and disappeared as it reached halfway up the side of his neck. He chuckled without humor. "Just in time for my execution."

Damir's smile was gone in an instant. Tikran could tell he wanted to say things. Instead, he released his breath slowly and said, "I will request that you get a bath and a good shave before your trial. You look terrible."

This made Tikran smile. "Thanks, asshole."

It was then that Damir's wall fell away, for just an instant, and he grinned back, something akin to affection in his eyes. He composed his face quickly and said, "I will visit you tomorrow at the same time, as usual." He stood and looked at Tikran somberly. "Good luck, Manzakar." Then he promptly turned and left.

Tikran slowly slipped back into his shirt and breeches. He still had no idea what he would do. What he wouldn't give to talk to Coxani, Naran, or even Haydar. As the sun set and the night grew ripe, he decided to stick to his original plan. If Delger chose to make a martyr of him, the king would no doubt pay the consequences. As Tikran settled on his cot, he heard the iron door open again. Hopeful, he sat up.

The shadow of a large man, surrounded by Aslans and a bevy of attendants, approached the cell. Tikran's heart sank. *Oh, shit.* The door was opened for King Delger, and Tikran immediately stood and bowed. "Your Highness."

Delger turned to his Aslans and the guards. "I wish to speak to Tikran in some privacy. Please remain outside." He looked at Tikran and pointed to the stool beside the cot. "May I sit?"

"Yes, of course." Tikran pulled the stool out for the king.

Delger sat and leaned on one knee, frowning at Tikran. "I can't begin to tell you how devastated I am by this turn of events, boy. Both Haydar and I had such high hopes for you. We gave you everything. You could have become so much more." He sighed deeply. "But instead, you chose to betray us. I can't fathom why you would do such a thing. I thought, at first, that you simply didn't understand. But reasoning didn't work with you. I see now that you aren't fit to be in any position of power, and it truly breaks my heart."

Tikran had slowly sunk down on the cot and was listening silently. When the king paused and appeared to expect some response, Tikran said, "Betraying you was never my intention, Your Highness."

Delger's expression darkened. "And yet, betray me you did. Now, thanks to your meddling friends, I am having to contend with a protesting mob, insisting on mercy for the Caged Kingfisher."

Shock vibrated through Tikran. He hadn't imagined their plan would work. He held his breath.

The king sat up straight. "I have decided to break from tradition in this instance and preside over your trial myself, rather than let the clerics serve as judges. And this is what you will do on the morrow when you are brought in, Tikran. You will plead self-defense, then publicly denounce your actions. You will confirm that the nomads were in the wrong and apologize for the Manzakar lives lost by your arrows. Then, you will swear to make it your mission to hunt down the clan that caused Anzor such grief."

Is he kidding? Tikran scratched his cheek. "Your Highness, what makes you think I'll do this when not even the threat of death is enough?"

Delger smiled. "The threat of *your* death is not enough."

An icy tingle spread through Tikran's veins, slowing the beat of his heart. He felt, for a brief moment, like his spirit had left his body and was watching the proceedings from above. He heard himself say, "You can't do that."

Delger laughed. "I'm king, boy. I can do whatever necessary to protect my kingdom. Of course, your friends are not innocent either—they're complicit in fanning the flames of treason. They would stand trial regardless."

Tikran's voice sounded foreign to him, as though someone else was speaking. "If I do what you ask, what will happen to them?"

Delger shrugged. "They will be stripped of their Manzakar rank, but they will live." He paused. "Be forewarned, Tikran. If at any point from here on out you decide to go rogue, so to speak, your friends will pay the price. Understood?"

Tikran wasn't sure if he nodded. He must have, because Delger stood. "I want you to know, boy, that it pains me greatly to have to do this. But ultimately, you brought it on yourself. I hope you eventually come to understand why I had to force your hand."

Later, Tikran couldn't remember if he stood and bowed as the king left. What he did remember, however, was leaning over the basin and emptying the contents of his stomach in a violent retch.

———

THE FOLLOWING MORNING, a razor blade glided across Tikran's jawline, taking tufts of hair with it. The eunuch wiped the razor and continued to shave off Tikran's two-week-old beard. Tikran sat in a tub of soapy water with his head tipped back, exposing his throat as the eunuch slid the blade under his chin. He'd finally gotten approval from Damir to soak his injured leg and he was thoroughly relishing his first bath in weeks. The eunuch finished shaving him and he sank into the tub, submerging his head briefly. He surfaced to see Damir standing over him, a faint smile on his lips.

"That's much, much better," Damir said, walking around and sitting on the stool recently occupied by the eunuch. "How does the leg feel?"

"Fine," Tikran answered, not looking at the doctor.

"Tikran." Damir sighed. "Things are not as dismal as you think they are."

Tikran looked at him then, grimacing. "Are you crazy? You have no idea..." He trailed off, his eyes on the backs of the guards several paces away. He said softly, "This is worse than death. I've ruined my friends' lives, my sister's life, and ended Mago's life. And now, I will live with the repercussions of my actions until I die, which will likely be sooner rather than later."

Damir sniffed. "Do you regret any of it?"

Tikran stared miserably into the bathwater. "I just don't know that I've done any good. If anything, I've made things much, much worse."

"If Coxani or Naran heard you say that they would be devastated, wouldn't they?" Damir crossed his arms, his voice barely a whisper. "They put everything on the line for you because they believe you did the right thing."

Tikran suddenly stood up, water sluicing down his body and sloshing from the tub. He glowered at Damir. "Can you grab me the sheet on the cot, please?" Damir stood and retrieved the sheet. He held it out and kept his eyes level with Tikran's, his face a distinct pink. Tikran took the sheet, stepped out of the bath, and moved closer to Damir—close enough that droplets splashed from him to Damir's robe. He lowered his voice and said, "I find it ironic that after a week of being alone with me, treating my wounds while I lay practically naked and clearly hard for you, it's watching me get out of a bath that makes you blush."

Damir swallowed. "I'm a physician, Tikran. I'm strictly focused on treating my patients' medical conditions."

"Then why the blush, doctor?"

The pupils of Damir's eyes were large, leaving just thin rings of gray iris around each one. "I'm visiting you as a friend, not a doctor. Moreover, you are an exceedingly attractive man who is standing very close to me, wet and naked."

Tikran turned away and wrapped himself in the sheet. "I'll see you later."

Damir stood quietly for several seconds before turning and striding out of the cell. "Good luck, Manzakar."

Tikran dried off and dressed in the white uniform of a prison inmate. On the back of the tunic were two large eyes—the eyes of Cenk, watching. He pulled his wet hair back with a leather thong and sat, hands folded, waiting. He didn't have to wait long before the Manzakars arrived to take him to the palace. Their faces were expressionless as they bound his hands in chains and accompanied him to the waiting wagon outside. *I grew up with these men. They know me.* And yet, they had been trained to show not even the tiniest bit of emotion.

At the palace, they led him to the great hall, which was packed to the rafters with maroon-clad aristocratic spectators. *Holy Cenk, they're here to see a show.* His heart beat faster. He would have to apologize for his actions in front of all these people. He closed his eyes briefly, summoning up his courage, before they nudged him forward, over the threshold and into the hall. The crowd grew quiet, all eyes on the renegade Manzakar as he was led to his seat before the throne. He sat and stared down at his chained hands, mentally blocking out the hushed whispers of the people around him. When King Delger was announced, he stood with everyone else.

The king swiftly walked to his throne and sat, Lord Haydar and Saltanat close to his side. Tikran couldn't bring himself to look at the durai. Instead, he fixed his eyes on his new enemy: the king he'd sworn to protect and die for, no matter what.

King Delger motioned for the spectators to sit. Tikran, as the accused, remained standing. Haydar held out a sheet of parchment to Delger, who began to read Tikran's offenses slowly, articulating each word and scanning the crowd ever so often. Treason... Grand theft... Sixteen Manzakars injured... two dead... Delger looked at Tikran. "Before you speak on your own behalf, Caged Kingfisher, I want to bring out your accomplices."

Tikran sucked in his breath as Coxani and Naran were brought out, their hands bound, wearing the same inmate's uniform. As each was guided to flank him on either side, he met Coxani's eyes and saw a familiar glimmer in them. It was the same look she'd given a hundred times before, when she'd felt at ease and mischievous. He glanced at Naran, who was staring forward, and likewise saw that familiar arrogance and bravado. Tikran looked front again, feeling overwhelmed and confused. *It's like they knew this would happen.*

"Caged Kingfisher," Delger said. "What do you have to say for yourself?"

Tikran could hear his heart pounding in his ears. "I made a mistake, Your Highness." *...in dragging poor Mago into this.* "My actions against the Manzakars were all in self-defense." *Self-defense—protection of Damir, Mago, Bruneta, and my clan.* "I will find those nomads and ensure they get what they deserve." *Justice—to be able to live without fear.* He realized how silly it was, but in his mind, he had to justify his words to himself in order to live with their impact. He was, after all, as Naran often said, the boy who could not lie.

Delger was not stupid, unfortunately. Tikran could see the hard glitter in his blue eyes. The king sat back in his gilded throne and brought his steepled fingers to his lips thoughtfully. After several painful seconds, he smiled. "I appreciate your honesty. And it breaks my heart that someone so dear to me would so ruthlessly deceive me. But, you did bring back the shrub that is curing the prince, and I am grateful for that. As such, I will spare your life."

The crowd sighed and gasped and even clapped. Tikran wanted to roll his eyes but instead kneeled and bowed his head. He was supposed to say something about the king being merciful, but he couldn't bring himself to say it. Instead, he remained silent.

"Rise, Caged Kingfisher," the king said. Tikran rose, wishing all this pomp and circumstance would end as soon as possible. Delger said, "Because of your honest confession, I will send you instead to Areg to finish your revenge against those savage nomads who killed the slave trader and forced you to defend yourself—after twenty lashes. You will remain a Manzakar until you have completed your mission, then stripped of your rank. I will also spare your friends, Naran of the Stalking Lion and Coxani of the Leaping Dolphin, from imprisonment for life. Instead, I strip you, Naran, of your Manzakar rank and, after twenty lashes, assign you to the northern outpost of Otebek as a sentry to guard the northern border of Gohar."

Tikran felt his throat clench. He desperately wanted to look at Naran but resisted.

"And you, Coxani," Delger said with a smile that chilled Tikran to his core. "Lord Haydar suggested I make you some lowly cleric of Cenk, but I have a much better idea." Every muscle in Tikran's body was tensed and ready for battle. He could feel Naran's nervous energy as if it were his own. Delger continued, "I strip you of your Manzakar rank, and order that you will be married immediately. Luckily for you, Commander Nasch has generously offered to marry you in the eyes of Cenk, that you may bear his children and live a moral, proper life as a mother and wife. As for the lashes, I will defer to your future husband to punish you as he sees fit."

Tikran didn't hear what the king said next. A roar in his head made him dizzy. Every muscle in his body wanted to move, to act. Instinctively, he opened a palm out in Naran's direction. He could feel his friend's anguish match his own... maybe even surpass it. Coxani stood stock still, her head high, unmoving. Only someone who knew her well would have noticed the color drain from her cheeks or her fingers convulsively open and close. Tikran felt his stomach churn. *He's punishing me and Naran through Coxani.* Delger turned to Haydar and said something, to which Haydar nodded. The durai directed the Manzakars, "Take them away."

Coxani was led in the opposite direction from Tikran and Naran. Both men turned, unspoken words on their lips, to see Nasch standing at the far end of the hall, his arms crossed, a smug smile on his face. Naran jerked at his chains, resisting as the soldiers tried to pull him forward. "I need to see her," he said with a rasp. Naran's rage was catching—Tikran, too, began to resist the Manzakars' increasingly aggressive pulls and shoves.

"Please brothers, don't fight us. Please." Tikran looked at the face of the Manzakars who held them and recognized Jan and Kazbek, two Aslans he and Naran had befriended as cadets. "We'll ask Lord Haydar if he can get you a moment with her," Jan said. Tikran had his doubts, but this seemed to appease Naran somewhat. They were taken to the temple and left in the capable hands of the temple guards and clerics. In a ritual they remembered all too well, the men were stripped and washed in holy water, then tied side by side to posts before Cenk's altar.

Two large, muscular clerics readied their heavy, multi-pronged whips as Naran turned his head to look at Tikran. "Soaked in holy water and about to get our bare asses whipped. Just like old times," he muttered.

Tikran said, "I'm so sorry, Naran. This is all my fault."

"Shut up," Naran said. "Stop saying that shit. I'm a grown

man and Coxani is a grown woman. We chose to stand by you, regardless of the consequences. We *believe* in you, Tikran. Period." His face against the post, Tikran felt his eyes moisten with emotion. Naran smiled humorlessly. "You should probably save those tears for the next few minutes."

At the exact same moment, both men received their first lash, and they both grunted on impact. In perfect synchrony, the whips fell across their backs, mere seconds apart. By the tenth lash, Tikran wasn't making any noise. He could feel the knotted tips blaze across his back like knives of fire. He was aflame in a pain worse than when he'd actually been burned by fire. He felt blood run down the back of his thighs and calves. By the final lash, the blistering, blinding pain was all-encompassing, all he felt, saw, and heard. He didn't remember his legs crumpling under him, but abruptly realized he was hanging by his wrists against the post, his breath ragged. Slowly, his vision returned and he turned his head to look at Naran. His friend wasn't faring much better than he was—Naran was also slumped against his post, strips of flesh laid open, rivulets of blood running down his back. He blinked as if trying to clear his head, then said hoarsely, "That was worse than I remember."

The next half hour passed in a haze of pain as they were unchained, dragged to another room, and laid face down. Tikran's cheek was pressed against the cool stone beneath him as he panted, waiting for the agonizing throb to ease. The pain was bad enough that it didn't seem to get worse when a wet sheet was laid across his back. He heard a deep, smooth, familiar voice say, "Tikran. Naran."

Tikran opened his eyes. Damir stood between them, a tender look on his face. He sighed and said, "You are determined to keep me busy, aren't you, Manzakars?"

Naran didn't smile but his sense of humor was clearly still

intact. "We figured your life in Dilovar wasn't exciting enough, Doctor. You can thank us later."

Before Damir could answer, Haydar was standing in the room, looking down at them, unable to hide his distress. He kneeled between them, his head hanging.

"Coxani," Naran said. "Lord Haydar, you have to change the king's mind. She—"

"I tried, Naran," Haydar answered, looking up. "He won't hear of it."

Tikran's anguish threatened to choke him. "You may as well kill her," he said, trying to move. "I'm sure it's what she'd prefer."

Naran's eyes were glazed. "We can't let that animal have her. I can't—" He tried lifting himself up, crying out in pain before sinking back down.

"Soldiers!" Haydar snapped angrily, high color in his cheeks. "Listen to me. Both of you. Coxani is strong and a trained Manzakar. She would be enraged to see you two behaving as though she can't handle herself." He gave Naran a long look, then turned to Tikran. "You trained her well, Tikran. Have faith that she can do this."

"I didn't train her to handle a dangerous asshole just in case she ended up married to one," Tikran replied. "Holy Cenk, I should have insisted she marry me. If he hurts her..."

Naran lay listless, looking more devastated than Tikran had ever seen him. "Can we at least speak to her before..." He clenched his teeth, unable to finish.

"I'm sorry, Naran," Haydar said, regret written all over his face.

"My Lord Haydar," Damir said, "would it be possible for me to relay messages to Coxani on behalf of these two? I am, after all, a doctor, and one who has treated her before when she was ill."

"If Nasch will allow you to tend to her—and I don't see why he wouldn't—of course you can," Haydar said. He looked between his battered protégés. "What do you two think of that?"

"It's not enough," Tikran muttered, grimacing.

Naran remained silent for a moment. As a tear trickled from the corner of his eye and over the bridge of his nose, he looked at Damir. "Tell her I love her madly. Forever."

CHAPTER 20

This is temporary.

You are suffering for a cause.

Tears streamed down Coxani's cheeks as she rode flanked by two Manzakars, following Nasch to his home. She wasn't crying for herself. She was crying for the two men she loved more than anything, who were presently being brutally flogged. *You have it easy compared to them*, she told herself.

But by Cenk, she'd rather be flogged and sent to a remote outpost any day over this.

They'd been married in an extremely succinct ceremony immediately after the trial while her hands were bound. If ever she'd imagined her wedding day, it was definitely like this— catastrophic, grim, and involving chains. She worried that Naran and Tikran would do something stupid on her account, something that would make it much harder for Haydar to accomplish what they'd set out to do. She worried about Tikran more than Naran, because at least Naran knew of the grander plan. He knew this was hopefully temporary.

Tikran had no idea. And yet, the entire success of their plan relied on him.

She tried to focus, tried to prepare for the next few moments, hours, days. But her mind kept racing back to the flogging. She couldn't stop imagining their agony as they were hit repeatedly with those heavy, knotted, nine-tailed whips. She'd seen firsthand what those things could do. All of them had, during public floggings. King Delger had probably decided not to make Tikran's flogging public because of how loved he was in Anzor and chose to spare Naran for the same reason.

Coxani was so lost in her thoughts that she didn't realize they'd arrived until one of the Manzakars said her name. Nasch's home, not surprisingly, abutted the barracks. The last time she'd been in the barracks was when Tikran was in its hospital after having been set on fire... probably in part because of Nasch.

The man to whom she now legally belonged.

She slid out of her saddle and followed the men into the terraced home, where she came face to face with her new husband. She glanced down at her chained wrists. "Dearest," she said, her voice dripping with disgust, "at what point will you unchain me?"

Nasch grinned. "I knew I had to marry eventually, you know. The idea never appealed to me. But after hearing you say those words, I'm thinking I should have married sooner." He nodded to the soldiers and they left quietly, leaving the newly-weds alone. Then he said, "I think we'll keep the chains on for a bit, eh?"

"Are you serious?"

"Oh, absolutely, my dear wife," Nasch replied with a chuckle. "The last thing I need right now is a knife in the back —and on my wedding day." He removed his turbaned cap and began walking toward a low table surrounded by reclining cushions. He turned and looked at her. "You must be tired and hungry. Won't you join me?"

I will not! No! She wanted to scream and fight and die on the spot, until she remembered why she was there. It was a game of deception—one that she had to play or forfeit her life, and possibly the lives of Naran, Tikran, and Haydar. She took a long, deep breath, then followed him to the table, where a servant had left various bowls of beef, lentil rice, and pickled beets. She sat opposite him and watched as he poured her a small glass of xew.

"To a fruitful marriage," Nasch said, smiling at her over the rim of his glass before tossing its contents into his mouth.

"That's repulsive." She refused to drink. The food smelled good though, and she was hungry. She held up her chained wrists and said, "Can't you unchain me long enough to eat?"

Nasch chuckled, scooping a spoonful of rice into his mouth. "Absolutely not."

Coxani huffed. "Nasch, seriously, call in a horde of Manzakars to watch. I swear to you, I just want to *eat*."

He poured himself another glass of xew, considering. "If you promise to behave yourself."

Holy Cenk, did she want to drive her dinner knife into his jugular. "I promise."

"Hold up your hands." She complied and he removed the chains, setting them down nearby. He sat back down and held up his glass, a smile on his lips. "Cheers, wife."

She scowled in response.

They ate in silence. She tried to assess him as an opponent as he ate, avoiding eye contact. Tikran had shied away from teaching her hand-to-hand combat, since he was concerned it would raise eyebrows. Now she wished she had insisted, since those eyebrows were already permanently raised when it came to her. He'd taught her how to wield a dagger—how to hold it when faced with an attacker, how to open a target by slashing at the chest and knocking the attacker off balance, then stabbing the forward leg. Unfortunately, that required her to have a dagger. Tikran had also shown her how to defend against blows from both fists and legs. She remembered his words of wisdom: "In a weaponless fight against a man, you will always lose if you take the offensive. He's bigger and stronger. It's just a fact. So your best bet is to use your smaller size and agility to dodge and escape."

She stole furtive peeks at Nasch. If he'd been a Manzakar commander on campaign when Tikran's mother was killed, he must have been at least twenty at the time. Which meant he was somewhere in his late thirties now. He was easily six feet tall, with that V-shaped build of a Manzakar. She would most definitely need to take Tikran's advice if he attacked her. If she didn't know what a soulless villain he was, she wouldn't think him unattractive, she supposed, save for his eyes—a shark's eyes, black and emotionless. She shuddered and continued to eat. When she was done, she met his gaze. "I'm finished."

He stood, lifting the chains. "Please understand that this is a precautionary measure for the time being. You won't always be chained—so long as you behave."

She stood, her voice like acid. "How kind of you."

He said, "Before you are bound again, I've found the best ladies' attendant to help you bathe and do all the things women do to beautify themselves in preparation for their wedding night." He paused, looking over her shoulder. "I think you've met Saltanat, no?"

Coxani's heart stopped as she slowly turned to face the beautiful mage with the lavender eyes. She stammered, "I don't think we've ever formally met, no."

Saltanat smiled and took the chains from Nasch. Coxani

had never seen the mage unveiled and with her hair unbound. She was indeed beautiful—and apparently corrupt to her core, just like Nasch. She said, "Coxani. Come. Let me help you prepare for the consummation of your marriage."

Coxani swallowed hard. *They're enjoying this. It's a game to them.* She sucked in her breath and followed the mage out of the courtyard and into a room with a large bathtub and two young Gohari servant girls. The tub was filled with hot water and smelled of jasmine. The girls helped her undress and unbraided her hair, then guided her into the bath.

In spite of everything, Coxani sank into the water with a deep sigh, closing her eyes as the warmth enveloped her and the aromas soothed her. She submerged her head for a moment, breathing deeply after she broke the surface. She opened her eyes to see Saltanat perched on the edge of the bathtub, a small smile on her lips. "Girl Manzakar," she said, her voice like silk. "Which of the two strapping lads do you favor? Or were you fucking them both?"

For some reason, Coxani was not surprised by the question —revolted, but not surprised. She replied flatly, "I'm shocked and offended, my lady. Everyone knows I'm as chaste as they come."

Saltanat threw back her head and laughed. "I like you already, Coxani." She examined her long, painted fingernails. "The Caged Kingfisher is shy with women. But the Stalking Lion..."

Oh, Cenk, no. Coxani braced herself. She knew Naran had gotten around. She shouldn't have been surprised.

"...The Lion is quite spectacular, isn't he?" Saltanat grinned widely.

Coxani began to count the seconds between her inhales and exhales. "As I said, I wouldn't know," she replied.

Saltanat gurgled with laughter. "I'm sure you wouldn't."

She signaled to the servant girls, who immediately began scrubbing Coxani with scented oils and soaps. One of the girls massaged her scalp while washing her hair and Coxani let a gratified sigh escape. The mage watched with interest, her eyes scanning Coxani's length. "A tad muscular for his taste, but you'll do."

Coxani bit down on a venomous response. *Inhale. Exhale. Bitch.*

When the servants were done with the ministrations, Coxani stood, wrapped herself in warm sheets and stepped out of the tub, exhaustion suddenly hitting her. The girls dressed her in a wispy gown and brushed her wet curls. Saltanat watched carefully, her eyes darting over every detail. Then she locked the chains around Coxani's wrists and said, "Don't fight him, girl. He enjoys the struggle and he will break you. But if you simply accept it and succumb, he can bring you immense pleasure."

I'm going to vomit. "I suppose sharing him doesn't bother you."

Saltanat waved her hand dismissively. "Not at all. There is no romance between us. We use each other to get what we want, and that includes sexual pleasure."

"That's so sweet," Coxani said drily. Her mind raced. What would she do? What could she do? She considered the options. If she fought him, he'd beat her senseless and ultimately have his way with her in any case. Her wrists were chained, for Cenk's sake. If she just let him, he might eventually think she'd accepted her situation, and his vigilance might falter. Her breath came fast.

Saltanat must have noticed, because she touched Coxani on the shoulder and whispered, "Maybe the Caged Kingfisher will come and rescue you."

Coxani caught her breath, the hairs on her arms rising. Was

this a trap laid for Tikran? Every fiber in her being wanted to fight. She just wasn't convinced that it was the smart thing to do. She couldn't help Naran or Tikran if she was indisposed because Nasch had beaten her into submission. Coxani sucked in her breath.

She'd made her decision.

———

TIKRAN SAT on the floor in the middle of his cell, his arms hanging over his bent knees, deep in thought, watching as a trail of ants marched from his half-eaten meal to a crevice between the stones. The second their wounds had been cleaned and bandaged, he and Naran had been put in separate prison cells. Tikran had had plenty of time to think when Haydar entered. The durai pulled up a stool and sat next to him. "How's your back?" he asked.

Tikran didn't look up. "What do you care?"

"You sound like a sullen schoolboy." Haydar sighed.

"Lord Haydar, I *will* kill Nasch on Coxani's behalf. So if you'd like to save yourself some trouble, you should probably have me executed now." Tikran met the older man's eyes.

Haydar stroked his beard. "I understand how you feel. But Coxani is a fighter. She will manage."

Anger flared in Tikran's chest. He stood up in one clean movement, ignoring his back's painful protest. "How can you be so cavalier about this? This is her *life* we're talking about! She's bound to this monster... she is his property..." He raked his hands through his hair and gnashed his teeth. He turned on Haydar. "You pledge your life to a king who would do this to her? To Naran? To me? You aren't the man I thought you were, Haydar. The man I grew up idolizing would not stand by and let such gross injustices be done—not just to the three of us, but to the Gohari people." Furious tears flooded his eyes. "I've spent my life desperate to please you, to make you proud, to... not disappoint you." He didn't bother wiping the tears away as they flowed down his cheeks. "Well, my lord, *you* have disappointed *me*."

He paced to the wall, leaned his arms against it, and hung his head, watching as the tears dripped down against the stone. When he felt like he'd gotten control of himself, he turned back toward the durai. "And don't think I don't know what's happening. Delger and his mage think I have the Essence and that I've somehow blocked her from sensing it. It could be that Saltanat is lying to Delger about my having the Essence but wants to get rid of me. Either way, it means Delger needs to do one more thing before he can close this messy chapter of his reign." Tikran smiled grimly. "He must do what he did to my mother before me, and he must do it without raising the ire of the Anzori people. So he's either going to goad me into doing something brash that would prove to everyone that I am a criminal, or he's going to make my death look like an accident, just as Saltanat and Nasch attempted at the Fire Festival. In fact, Delger may have conspired with them to set a trap for me with Coxani as bait. It would be easy business, between Saltanat and Nasch. And I would fall into that trap willingly if I didn't think Coxani would pay the price as well."

Tikran glared at Haydar. "Go tell your precious king everything I've said here. Go. Let him know that, even though he'll probably kill me quietly once he's sent me out to Gohar where no one but his men can witness it, I see him for what he is—a bigoted, egocentric piece of shit with no respect for human life." He turned away again. "Leave, Haydar. Just leave. If you don't, I may punch you in the jaw and enjoy it."

He didn't move until he heard Haydar rise and walk away, waiting for the clang of the door closing behind him. Shortly after, he crumpled to the ground and moaned, racked with sobs until he was spent. Exhausted, he lay down on his side atop the stone floor and fell into restless sleep, the wounds across his shoulder blades throbbing.

He awoke the following morning to a sharp rebuke.

"Manzakar, why in Cenk's name are you on the floor? Are you actively *trying* to infect your wounds?"

Tikran opened his eyes to see Damir scowling over him. "Stop calling me that. I'm not a Manzakar," he croaked, his throat dry and eyes swollen from crying.

Damir rolled his eyes and helped Tikran get off the floor. "You are, perhaps unwillingly, still a Manzakar. Come on."

Tikran pulled away. He was perfectly capable of getting to the cot without assistance. He moved to the cot and sat down. At least this wound required Tikran to face away from Damir, unlike the other two. As the doctor carefully peeled the poulticed gauze from his back, Tikran asked, "How's Naran?"

"His back will heal," Damir answered, then hesitated. "His heart will take longer to recover."

Tikran hung his head. "When can you go see her?" He was unable to bring himself to say Coxani's name without feeling a nauseating guilt.

"I will go this evening, assuming Nasch allows it. It will be my only chance before we set off for Areg."

Tikran spun his head to the side. "*We?*"

"Yes," Damir said, gently dabbing the angry, raw streaks that ran from Tikran's shoulders down to the small of his back. "Prince Vazha is fully recovered. My services are no longer needed. I will accompany you to Areg and continue on to Dilovar."

"Areg is a bit out of the way, isn't it?"

"No matter. It will save Delger the trouble of sending me

back separately. The same Manzakars who guard you can accompany me."

Tikran sucked his breath through his teeth in a sharp hiss, his back pulsing with pain. When he was able to exhale, he said, "Does Naran leave for Otebek tomorrow as well?"

"I believe so."

As Damir spread a layer of fresh poultice to his wounds, Tikran said bleakly, "It isn't safe for you to travel with me."

"Please." Damir chuckled. "After our last journey through Gohar, I've realized that being around you will always be dangerous. I willingly accept the risks." When Tikran remained quiet, he asked, "What message would you like me to relay to Coxani?"

Tikran rubbed his face and let out a tormented groan. "Oh, Cenk, what is there to say? Words can't convey how broken I feel... how guilt-ridden..."

"I doubt saying any of that will inspire her to stay strong," Damir muttered.

"Inspire her? Very well." Tikran tensed his jaw. "Tell her that as long as I'm alive, my mission will be to make her a widow."

CHAPTER 21

P rince Vazha sat before a polished silver mirror, gazing at his reflection as he turned his head from side to side. "By Cenk, Damir. You did it. The lesions are completely gone."

"Yes, but I'm afraid much of the nerve damage in your foot can't be repaired," Damir said as he helped Vazha dress after a full examination. "You will always need a cane to walk, Your Highness."

"You've done more than I could have ever hoped for," Vazha said. "If that is the price I pay for an otherwise full recovery, I'll take it." He glanced at himself in the mirror again and grinned. "You've made me beautiful again, after all."

Damir smiled. No one, not even he, would have guessed that beneath the disfiguring patches of rough, raised, red skin was a face that resembled Delger's, only younger and more handsome. After only two weeks of treatment, the lesions on Vazha's face and body had completely resolved. Clear vision and full sensation in his left hand had returned. Only the nerve damage in his right foot was any indication that the prince had suffered from leprosy at all.

"I must convince my father to offer Bilguun something in exchange for you," Vazha said. "You must become Anzor's royal physician." He smiled. "*My* royal physician."

Damir busied himself by packing his bag. "I'm flattered, Prince Vazha, but I don't think Bilguun would be willing to give me up."

"Not even for, say, one of the king's mages?"

No, not even that. Damir shrugged. "I don't know. I suppose that's something only King Bilguun can answer."

Vazha dismissed his attendants and reluctant Manzakar guards so that he and Damir were alone, then stood and leaned on his cane. "Must you leave so soon?"

Damir cleared his throat. "My work here is done, Your Highness."

"Why won't you just call me Vazha? I keep asking you to."

Damir met the prince's eyes. "And I keep telling you it isn't appropriate, Your Highness."

Vazha stepped closer. "Damir, I love you."

Well, shit. He'd had a sneaking suspicion this would happen. Damir licked his lips. "No, Your Highness. You don't. You only think you do. It's called erotic transference. Doctors experience this sort of thing often. Because I treated you, listened to you, and ultimately cured you, you believe you're in love with me. But you aren't really. The feeling will dissipate after I leave, I promise. And you will go on to meet a beautiful woman, marry her, inherit your father's throne, and have several heirs to continue Anzor's royal bloodline."

Vazha let out an uncertain laugh. "You go right to the heart of the matter, don't you?"

"There's no reason not to. It helps... keep things in perspective."

"I see." Vazha's smile faded. "I suppose it's safe to assume you don't feel the same way about me."

The doctor kept his gaze steady. "I'm afraid this has happened to me often enough that I've learned not to even consider developing romantic feelings for my patients."

Vazha pondered this, looking crestfallen. "So you've never fallen in love with one of your patients?"

Damir felt a sharp pang in his chest and stiffened. "I have."

"What happened?"

The pain didn't subside. "I suspected their feelings for me were a result of erotic transference, so I ended any hint of mutual affection."

Vazha tilted his head. "But what if they had been real? It isn't always transference, is it? Sometimes it must be real love."

Damir wanted the conversation to end. "I don't think it was." *I can't take the chance that it isn't.* He lifted his bag, smiled, and bowed deeply. "It has been a great honor, Your Highness. I pray for your bloodline, may it prosper for centuries."

Vazha gave a brief nod, hurt plain in his eyes. "Thank you. Goodbye, Damir."

"Goodbye, Your Highness."

As he turned to leave, the prince said, "Just once. Call me by my name just once."

Damir paused. "Goodbye, Vazha."

He left the palace and headed to the barracks, where he was redirected to the royal stables. Damir wandered through the stables in awe, gazing up at the vaulted ceilings, pausing to peer curiously at the beautiful hawks in their cages, and watching a tanner sell his beautifully crafted leather belts to noblemen and Manzakars. His smile waned as he approached a group of soldiers, one of which was Commander Nasch.

The commander was showing his men a newly minted

saber, its steel blade and bronze quillons glinting brightly. Damir cleared his throat. "Commander Nasch?"

Nasch turned, looking Damir up and down with little interest. "Yes?"

"I am Doctor Damir, the Dilovari doctor who has cured Prince Vazha," Damir began, enjoying how the Manzakar's mood visibly changed. "I'm leaving on the morrow to return to Dilovar and would like your permission to visit your wife, Coxani, to supplement her medicine."

Nasch quickly dismissed his men and turned to face Damir fully. "Supplement *what* medicine?"

"I'm not sure if you're aware, but Coxani was very ill several weeks ago. I treated her." He met Nasch's gaze evenly. "It's a highly volatile illness. If I don't give her additional medicine, she might relapse. And that would be life-endangering."

Nasch jutted out his chin and frowned, setting his hands on his hips. "Aren't you the doctor who traveled with that piece of shit traitor Tikran? The doctor who tended to his wounds while out in Gohar?"

"I am, Commander. I was trained as a doctor, and I am required to treat the ill or wounded." He smiled. "It's part of the doctor's oath."

Nasch bared his teeth. "You should have let him rot."

Damir's expression didn't change. "I am a visiting doctor from Dilovar and I do not involve myself in Anzor's politics."

Nasch's shark-like eyes scanned his face. "So why do you care what happens to Coxani?"

"I would rather not earn a bad reputation in Anzor with her untimely death, particularly after treating the prince. Plus, she's a lovely person."

"That's sweet of you." Nasch held out his hand. "Give me the medicine and I will ensure she receives it."

"I wish it were that easy, Commander. I need to examine

her in person in order to know what kind of supplemental treatment she needs."

"Oh." Nasch's expression turned sinister. "I see. You want to *examine* her." He laughed. "Fat chance."

Damir sucked in his breath and closed his eyes, struggling for patience. "Save your jealous rage for the Caged Kingfisher, Commander. Just so we're clear, I tend to prefer cock."

That made Nasch deflate instantly, much to Damir's delight. Scowling with disgust, he said, "Holy Cenk. Fine. Go and deliver your medicine. Saltanat will be there to keep an eye on you. Then hurry back to Dilovar, because we in Anzor want nothing to do with your type."

"Of course, Commander Nasch." Damir bowed and turned, struggling to keep in his laughter as he walked out of the stables and through the streets of the Citadel, back toward the barracks. Now he had to deal with the mage. Luckily, Haydar had sent a message via carrier pigeon the night prior assuring Damir that he would get private time with Coxani. While he wasn't sure how Haydar would arrange this, he'd begun to trust the durai—there was no question the man loved Tikran like a son.

He walked up to the door of Nasch's house and rang the bell. A servant girl opened the door. "Greetings, child. I am Doctor Damir. Is your mistress home?" She nodded and opened the door wider, letting him in. Damir looked around the home, which was very much what he imagined a soldier's home would look like—simple, uncluttered, austere. The girl led him to the inner courtyard, the entrance to which was guarded by a eunuch.

"My name is Alp," the eunuch said. "I have been tasked by Lady Saltanat with keeping an eye on the mistress."

"I see," Damir said. "And where is the lady at the moment?"

"She was called to the palace unexpectedly," Alp replied.

Damir nodded once. Now he had to figure out how to be rid of the eunuch so he could speak with Coxani alone. "I am here to examine madam Nasch—" The eunuch had been listening politely when he scratched his left hand and touched his right ear. *One of Haydar's agents.* "...so that I may prescribe the appropriate medicine for her recent condition. It will help prevent a relapse of the illness."

"Of course," Alp said. "Let me take you to her."

Coxani sat on a bench beside a rosebush, her ankles crossed, reading a book. She was dressed as the mistress of the house, in a blue kaftan over loose breeches. Her hair was down, glossy brown curls flowing down her back and framing her face. She would have been the portrait of a beautiful young wife, if not for the sadness that creased her face. She looked up and, upon seeing Damir, stood abruptly, the book tossed to the ground, her eyes wide with joy. Damir smiled. "Madam Coxani, I wanted to visit you before my journey back to Dilovar..."

"I will bring out rosewater and oranges," Alp said. "The oranges are especially sweet this time of year." With the phrase, Alp confirmed his capacity as Haydar's agent. The eunuch walked out of the courtyard and Coxani rushed to Damir, clasping his hands in hers.

"Damir! You're a beautiful sight," Coxani said, breathless. "How are they?"

Damir squeezed her fingers. "They are well—physically, at least. Naturally, their backs will be badly scarred, but the wounds are healing cleanly. Emotionally, they are both devastated over what's happened to you."

She shook her head. "Tell them not to waste their energy worrying about me. I'm perfectly fine!"

Damir tilted his head. "Are you?"

He saw her lip tremble just a little. "Come," she said. They sat on the bench side by side, and she exhaled as though she'd been holding her breath for days. "Will you promise not to tell the boys what I'm about to tell you?"

The boys. Damir would have smiled if he hadn't been anxious over what she was about to say. "Of course."

"He doesn't hurt me physically," she said. "The torture he inflicts on me is entirely mental."

Damir looked forward. "I'm assuming he's forcing himself on you."

"Yes," she replied, tightening her lips. "But... the worst part is that he's gentle and tries to please me. And I hate him more than anything because he succeeds."

Damir placed his hand on hers. "Our bodies don't always obey our minds, Coxani. It's not your fault. He's a manipulative monster who will do whatever it takes to get what he wants."

"I know," she said. "It still messes with my head, though."

Unexpectedly, he struggled with a gush of rage. He glanced at the chains sitting on the table. "Don't tell me he keeps you chained all the time."

"When he's here, he unchains me when I eat, bathe, or need to answer the call of nature," she said. "When he's not around, which is often, Alp unchains me until he returns. Alp used to watch over me when I was a child. I trust him."

"Then I'm glad he's here with you." Damir quickly pulled a small, double-edged blade from his jacket and placed it in her hands. "Its presence may be enough to give you the strength to get through this, and hopefully you won't ever need to use it. But just in case..."

Her eyes lit up as she turned the knife over in her hands. "Thank you, Damir."

Damir took a deep breath, redirecting his thoughts. "I have messages from... the boys."

She looked up, her green eyes bright. "Yes?"

Damir smiled. "Naran says he loves you madly. Forever."

She laughed through the tears that suddenly rushed down her cheeks. "Oh, Naran," she said, covering her face.

"He also says to be strong, that this is temporary," Damir added.

She nodded, sniffling and wiping her face. "Yes. Yes. It has to be." She looked at him. "And Tikran?"

Damir looked away, his smile fading. "He says that as long as he's alive, his mission will be to make you a widow."

Her smile disappeared as well. "Oh, my poor Tikran."

"Tikran is in a dark place. But I promise you he will come out of it, if I have anything to do with it." Damir met her eyes. "I promise you that I will protect him in every way I can."

Her brow cleared and her eyes scanned his face before she said softly, "Damir... are you in love with him?"

Shit. Was it that obvious? His face grew warm. He said, "This conversation is entirely between you and me, correct?"

She laughed uneasily. "I certainly hope so."

He sighed, leaning his elbows on his knees and rubbing his face. "I think I am. No. I *know* I am. It's completely ridiculous."

A small, curious smile hovered on her lips. "Does he know?"

"Don't worry. I think I snuffed out any inkling he might have had." He raised his eyes to hers. "I don't want to insert myself where I don't belong."

She frowned. "What? Is that what's worrying you? Tikran doesn't belong to me, Damir. You can't upset me by loving him."

"Still, it feels futile. I'd rather he never know."

Her eyebrows drew together. "But why? Are you afraid he doesn't return your feelings?"

"I think whatever feelings he *thinks* he has for me are

simply a product of my doctoring him. It happens to doctors all the time. It happened to me this morning, in fact."

Coxani placed her hand on his shoulder. "Damir, Tikran absolutely hates being reliant on others in any way. Plus, he is not prone to bouts of passing fancy—at all. He is utterly practical and probably the least romantic person I know."

This made Damir chuckle. "I get that feeling, yes." He sat up. "I've brought two remedies for you." He pulled two bottles from his bag. "The blue bottle will prevent any unfortunate accidents," he said, his voice heavy with meaning. "It will prevent your courses from coming, but don't be alarmed. Take a drop on the tongue once a day. The green bottle is that vile stuff I gave you before... just in case. Take only a spoonful, and only if you suspect... the worst. Any more than that could be fatal. Do you understand?"

"Yes," she said, taking the bottles from him. Then she tilted her head at him, her eyes full of emotion. "Why are you so good to me?"

Damir looked away. "Tikran loves you. That's enough for me." He hesitated before adding, "I was the product of an unwanted pregnancy that killed my mother. I'm not necessarily saying I wish I had never been born, but I certainly wish she had been given the opportunity to live." He stood. "I must go before that mage returns."

She stood, too. "Yes, of course." She smiled. "Damir, thank you. I don't know what I would do—"

Damir held up his hand. "You would figure it out, Coxani. I don't doubt it." He lifted his bag. "You Manzakars always do."

Autumn had arrived on the Continent and Tikran could feel a brisk coolness in the air. Gohar smelled distinct as the parched earth expelled the summer heat and brief, sporadic rain showers wet the grassy plains. When he was a child, autumn had meant cups of warm spiced wine and stories around campfires. It was when livestock was slaughtered and either eaten or salted to last the winter. He remembered loving the season, if only because he and his family tended to eat better. Full stomachs meant more cheer all around.

The Manzakar squadron that accompanied Tikran and Damir to Areg belonged to Commander Ramil. The plan was that once in Areg, Tikran would remain and Ramil's squadron would go on to Dilovar with the doctor. Tikran would then take part of Oter's Manzakar squadron at Areg to find the Sachin clan that had brought about the deaths of two Manzakars.

Bruneta's clan. *His* clan.

He doubted he would live long enough to even begin the mission—Ramil was fast friends with Nasch and of the same ilk. Both often campaigned in Gohar to keep the nomads "in line," and both had palpable contempt for Tikran. *It won't be long now.* It almost made Tikran smile. If they thought he'd go down without a fight, they had another thing coming. He was going to kill as many of them as he possibly could.

"It's actually fairly nice in Gohar this time of year," the doctor said, pulling his horse up next to Tikran's.

Tikran briefly closed his eyes. They had been traveling for little over a week, and Damir had hovered around him the entire time. Tikran didn't want to worry about the doctor's safety, nor did he want to be continually reminded of the pain Damir caused him. He couldn't wait until they reached Areg and sent Damir on his way back to Dilovar. "It is," he said, more for show than because he wanted conversation.

"Tikran. Look at me." Damir hissed.

Annoyed, Tikran glanced over. "Yes?"

Damir sounded almost desperate, his usual cool indifference gone. "People need you," he said as softly as he could. "This isn't nearly the end."

Tikran smiled sardonically. "I think everyone would be better off if I were dead."

Damir's expression grew fierce. "No. People need you. Coxani. Naran." Through his teeth, he said, "*I* need you."

"Doctor, has anyone ever told you that you have a problem?"

"Problem?"

"Yes," Tikran said without emotion. "You like your patients' attention. You like seeing them adore you long enough for you to reject them. Then you savor their heartbreak but continue to drop tiny morsels of affection to keep them hooked on you."

"Is that what you think?"

"It is."

"You're wrong, Tikran."

"What's the issue over here?" Commander Ramil rode back toward them, a scowl on his face.

"I'm telling my patient not to touch his bandages until I've given him explicit permission," Damir answered coolly. "He's stubborn."

Tikran smiled at Ramil. "Stubborn and treacherous. Terrible combination, wouldn't you say, Commander?"

Ramil smiled back. "Watch yourself, Caged Kingfisher. Much holds in the balance for you."

"Do you feel that?" Damir said as the wind picked up out of nowhere. The long grass rolled in greenish-gold waves. Dust and sand rose and swirled, clouding the air.

"Windstorm," muttered Ramil, returning to the front of the line and barking orders, Tikran forgotten.

For twenty minutes, gusts of powerful wind swept across

the steppe as the party struggled to continue moving, the tails of their turbans wrapped around their faces. By the time the winds died down, the party was exhausted from battling it and decided to stop for the night. They built campfires and pitched tents, tying them down doubly in case the winds picked up again. Tikran volunteered to hunt down some food before night fell, and Ramil consented—it would save his men having to do the work.

"May I accompany you?" Damir asked as Tikran sheathed his bow, loaded up his quiver, grabbed his shield, and attached no fewer than three daggers of various blade lengths to his person. He wore only a lightweight archer's cuirass and leather bracers on his arms.

Tikran let out a laugh. "No."

"Please."

"Why?" Tikran spun on him. "You can't hunt." Was the man getting some sick satisfaction out of torturing him? For some strange reason, Tikran didn't think that was it. He scanned Damir's face suspiciously. There was something in the doctor's eyes that he had never seen before: Fear. But what was he afraid of? Could it be Damir was worried about him? And if he was, why did he think hovering around uselessly would help? It was possible that the doctor knew Ramil and his troops would be far less likely to try and kill Tikran if he was there. Killing—or even injuring—Bilguun's royal doctor would no doubt usher in a second war with Dilovar. Tikran scratched his neck. It was then that the idea struck him. He asked, "Can you keep quiet? And I mean both out in the field and in regard to Ramil? I don't think he'd approve of you hunting with me."

"Yes, of course."

"Fine." Tikran grabbed a second cuirass and shield, then handed them to Damir. "You'll need these."

Damir's eyebrows rose. "What exactly are we hunting?"

Tikran lowered his voice and said, "It's not about what we're hunting. It's about what's hunting us. Or more specifically, me."

As they wandered out into the steppe, Tikran told Damir, "Small game is most active at dawn and dusk."

"What constitutes small game?" Damir asked.

"Antelope. Rodents."

"Rodents?"

Tikran glared. "Yes, Damir. Starving people eat rodents." He stopped, looked around, and crouched in the field, waving for Damir to do the same. The doctor obliged, his eyes darting about. Tikran couldn't help but smile. "Don't be scared."

"You really think I'm scared, Manzakar?" Damir said with a scornful shake of the head.

Tikran held a finger to his lips. He slowly pulled out his bow and a couple arrows, his eyes scanning the line between sky and grass. *Moment of truth.* He suddenly lifted himself to his haunches and shot his arrow at something rushing through the undergrowth—probably a marmot. When Damir's head was turned in the direction of his arrow, Tikran swiveled and shot an arrow in the opposite direction, grunting and yelling, "I've been hit!"

A hiss sounded, then an enormous rush of air was sucked from the atmosphere around them. Tikran covered his nose and mouth but kept his eyes open as the fire raced across the long grass instantly, just as the air whooshed back. A line of fire separated them from whatever Damir thought was attacking them. Tikran sat, knees bent, watching the fire as though it was a spectacular firework display, unable to hide his smile. He sensed Damir look at him and, nearly as instantly as the fire started, a fine mist of rain descended that quickly progressed into a brief downpour.

The rain stopped. The grass sizzled, charred and wet.

Damir was crouched beside him, breathing hard, looking for all the world like a drowned cat. An *angry* drowned cat. His eyes were like ice. "What the *fuck*, Manzakar," he managed to say from between his teeth.

"You have a lot of nerve, asking me that," Tikran said as he shook his head vigorously, spraying water in every direction, and wiped the rain from his face. He leaned further back, looking up as the clouds cleared. The sky behind was a pinkish purple, sharply colored in the dry air. "Would you care to tell me who you are, once and for all... Doctor?"

Damir fell back, rubbing his face. "You clever asshole." He shoved his wet hair from his eyes and let out his breath. "I am, in fact, King Bilguun's royal physician." He leveled a look at Tikran. "I'm also his head mage."

Tikran matched Damir's unflinching gaze. "Are you a spy?"

"When Delger requested I go back to Anzor with him to treat the prince, Bilguun realized he could benefit from the situation in more ways than one. So while I wasn't sent to gather specific information, he knew I would come back with enough. For instance, the strength of the Essence in Anzor."

"You know more than that," Tikran said. "You know the layout of the palace and the Citadel, intimate details about the king's daily routine, the strength of the military—"

"I'm a mage," Damir interrupted, "not a military strategist. Besides, I'm not as faithless as you seem to think."

Tikran searched Damir's face. "The unexplained fire, the rain... It was you all along. I knew it had to be."

"Yes. Listen, there are certain things you need to know before we lose our opportunity to talk privately. Haydar knows about me. He's recruited me, so to speak, to protect you on the way to Areg." The doctor lowered his voice. "He's master-minded an entire coup, Tikran. It's been in the works for decades. He plans to overthrow Delger."

Holy shit. Tikran was dumbfounded. Was it possible? A feeling like no other struck him, as though liquid lightning raced through his veins, making him short of breath and dizzy.

"There's more. He's recruited Naran and Coxani—in fact, he had them arrested to keep Delger satisfied and negotiate your punishment."

Naran and Coxani. His head spun. "How long have they known all of this?"

"Not long at all."

"And you?"

"As long as they have. Two weeks, at most," Damir said. "There's even more, Tikran. You are the key player in all of this. Haydar—who goes by Enlil the Weaver—simply hasn't had the opportunity to tell you without risking everything."

"Me?" Tikran swallowed. "How?"

Damir placed his hand on Tikran's shoulder. "He wants you to lead the rebellion."

Coxani stared listlessly as honeybees danced from flower to flower in the courtyard, wishing she were one of them. The air had turned crisp, and she tightened the silk wrap about her shoulders. She hadn't heard from Haydar in nearly two weeks, and her restless energy had devolved into crippling anxiety. Tikran and Damir must have been more than halfway to Areg, and Naran had to be quickly approaching Otebek as well. She had no way of knowing how they were and it was making her crazy. Why couldn't she have been banished to an outpost too? Anything was better than rotting away in this house, a prisoner in every sense. And as time crept on, she'd begun to fully grasp what Haydar had meant when he'd said that this phase would be difficult—she wasn't sure how she was going to get through it. For all she knew, it could last months, maybe even years. The thought made her want to scream in despair.

She refused to do any household management, so Nasch left the work in Alp's capable hands. The eunuch who had once chased her around the women's quarters as she'd grown up was now her only friend. She was grateful to Haydar for sending an agent to live with her—he was her only link to the outside world. Despite her pleading, Nasch would not even consider letting her leave the house or, Cenk forbid, ride a horse or do anything that would have given her some renewed strength. He was slowly draining her of vitality, and she sensed it was very deliberate.

He was out at dawn and gone most of the day, either training with his squadron in the hippodrome or tending to their horses and equipment in the royal stables. During the day, Coxani kept herself busy by reading the five books Nasch owned—all about military strategy. If she ever actually made it into battle, she would be prepared, if nothing else. Nasch would return home at dusk and wash before the evening supper, when he would expect Coxani to join him. After the meal, he would retire to his chambers and, every night without fail, summon Coxani. When the eunuch was gone and the door closed, he would lock her wrists above her head and have his way with her. He continued to be gentle with her, sensing that it was the way to bring her physical pleasure—unwelcome, unwanted pleasure that destroyed her, bit by bit.

Coxani would be forever indebted to Damir for bringing her the elixir that prevented her life from spiraling into a true tragedy. Without it, she was certain it would only be a matter of time before she found herself pregnant again. And this time, the father would be a monster. The mere thought made her shudder.

She was also grateful to Damir for the small, steel blade she kept hidden in her sleeve. She had taught herself how to slide it into her hand and wield it while her wrists were bound, careful not to cut herself on the extremely sharp edges. She hoped she could resist the urge to use it, since ending up in prison for murdering her husband would complicate things quite a bit. *I can endure this. For Tikran. For Naran. For Gohar.*

"Mistress, Master Nasch awaits your presence for supper," Alp said with a short bow, appearing from behind a lattice of dense, flowering clematis vines.

She stood and followed Alp into the house, where the meal had been laid out on the table. Nasch reclined on a cushion in his kaftan, sipping xew. She'd recently learned that his heraldic symbol—the silver chalice topped by a flame—was because Nasch drank the liquor before every competition, every campaign, and even before training, claiming it sharpened his abilities. He was never drunk, which meant he must have an incredibly high tolerance to be consuming xew pretty much all day. He smiled at her as she sat beside him, his eyes flitting over her greedily. "You look lovely tonight," he said, touching her hair. Compliments usually meant he was eager to get her into the bedroom and would likely rush supper. His hand gently caressed her arm and she flinched at his touch. He said, "By Cenk, you're looking at me like I'm the most monstrous thing you've ever seen."

She couldn't stop herself. "You are monstrous. You murdered those Gohari children. Tikran told me all about it." *You also murdered Tikran's mother and attempted to murder Tikran himself.*

"Tikran." A lock of deep contempt crossed his face, then he seemed to consider for a moment. "Imagine, for a second, that instead of being sold to a kindly slave trader, who in turn sold you to a lord who treated you like his own child, you were sold by your drunkard father to a sadistic slaver so he could have money to buy a steady supply of alcohol. Imagine that for almost a year, at the age of ten, you were beaten and raped almost daily. Then you were sold to the king through one of his commanders who treated you like scum, but it was so much better than anything you'd ever known that you believed you'd finally been saved. Eventually, your life was transformed. You were fed, sheltered, and when you performed well, you were praised and elevated. The price? To serve the king, no matter what."

Coxani struggled to keep the look of horror from her face.

Nasch looked at her, his jaw flexing. "Don't tell me you wouldn't do everything in your power to make sure that nothing destroyed you again."

Coxani pursed her lips. With such a brutal childhood, it was likely he only knew brutality as a means to an end. She could see now that he understood only one thing: Survival at all costs. Trying to reason with him about the value of human life would yield no results. So she kept silent and turned her head away. She couldn't afford to feel sorry for him.

He poured some xew into her glass and held it out to her. "Let's toast to the future. Does that sound benign enough for you?" She said nothing. They clinked glasses and drank, the alcohol burning a bitter trail down her throat. *To the future... one without you in it.*

"Master Nasch, forgive the interruption," Alp said, shuffling quickly over from the entrance, looking embarrassed and contrite. "One of the king's lords is at the door, asking to see you."

Nasch frowned. "Lord? That's strange. Which lord?"

"Lord Revaz, Master."

Coxani gasped audibly and Nasch spun his head to look at her. "You know him?"

"Not well, no," she said, her heart pumping loudly in her

ears. "I had tea with him at my first and only choosing party nearly five years ago."

His smile was gone. He stood. "Wait here," he directed her, then followed Alp to the door. She heard them speak and Nasch say, "Why don't you join me and my wife for supper, my lord? It would be an honor. Alp, make a third setting at the table."

She stood, unable to make anything of the brief look Alp gave her as he added a third plate and glass to the table. Nasch returned with Revaz at his side. "I understand you already know Coxani," he said by way of introduction, his mouth twisted in barely concealed displeasure.

Revaz smiled, his eyes as bright and blue as ever. "Yes, we met several years ago," he said, and gave her a short bow. "Good evening, Madam Nasch. I apologize for interrupting your meal."

The title grated on her. She bowed politely. "Good evening, my lord, what a pleasant surprise." *Feel free to interrupt anytime.*

They sat and Nasch poured xew into Revaz's glass. "What brings you to my doorstep, my lord?"

Revaz took a swallow of xew, looking at Coxani over his glass. "Your wife, Commander," he answered smoothly. "I have decided to take her as my mistress."

CHAPTER 22

Her hands braced on her knees, Coxani threw up in the bushes immediately after running into the courtyard. *No, no, no.* This couldn't be happening. She'd spent her life fighting this, and yet, here she was—wife to a man she despised and about to become an Anzori nobleman's mistress. Suddenly Alp was at her side with a handkerchief and cup of water. Her hands shook as she wiped her mouth and took a drink. "Thank you, Alp." She tried to hear what the men were saying but couldn't make out words. Nasch's tone, however, was one of clear exasperation. She took a deep breath and went back inside.

"Are you all right?" Revaz asked, frowning. "I'm so sorry that my proposition had that effect on you."

Nasch stood with his arms crossed. She could tell he was enraged by the way his jaw flexed and he cracked his knuckles. "Then perhaps you should reconsider. It would be unfortunate if Coxani expelled the contents of her stomach every time she had to be around you."

Revaz shrugged and looked at her. "My proposition is that I

would have you brought to me twice a week in the mornings to stay the day and night, then returned the following mid-morning. I am flexible with the schedule, of course."

She swallowed. "And... what would we do all day? Play backgammon?"

He smiled. "If that's what you wished."

Nasch snorted and glared at her. "You know very well that's not what you'd be doing." Unfortunately for him, there wasn't much Nasch could do—an Anzori lord's wishes superseded all but the king's. "My lord, I implore you to find someone else. Surely there is a bevy of beautiful girls at the palace waiting to be chosen. That you would choose a woman who is already married is highly unusual and, quite frankly, insulting."

Revaz seemed utterly unfazed by Nasch's mounting anger. "Insulting? Quite the contrary, Commander. It's a great compliment and a testament to your good taste." He bowed. "I apologize for ruining your meal. I will come and get Coxani in the morning, if it's all the same to you." With that, he turned to have Alp show him out the door.

When he was gone, Nasch growled, "I've lost my appetite." He stalked to his chambers and emerged a few minutes later wearing his Manzakar uniform. "I need to slash and stab at something," he said, slamming the door as he left.

So long as it's not me. Coxani let out her breath slowly and sat back down at the table. She poured herself more xew and tossed it back with a gulp. Revaz had actually offered her a temporary escape from this prison, unbeknownst to him. As her protector, he'd also ensure that Nasch couldn't beat her— unless he gave his approval. She exhaled, feeling a tiny bit relieved. The exception, of course, was marital rape. A husband had the right to do that regardless of a protector's objection.

Still, she was happy to be able to leave this place and have some pretense of freedom for a—

Wait. Perhaps Revaz *had* known what he was granting her. Perhaps that was the exact reason he did it. Her heart leaped. *Calm down.* She couldn't get hopeful. It was possible that he'd simply decided five years after the fact to force her to become his mistress. Who knew what his reasons were?

She went to bed at her usual time, thrilled that Nasch had not returned yet and praying that, when he did finally come home, he wouldn't summon her to his bed—or climb into hers. He did not, and she awoke feeling better than she had since Tikran's trial. Alp confirmed that Nasch had not come home, and she assumed he'd visited the mage. All the better. As she readied herself for the day with Revaz, she asked Alp, "What do you know about the lord?"

He shook his head. "Nothing, mistress." He paused. "Actually, I do know something. He is known to be very kind to his slaves. Even the eunuchs."

Coxani flashed Alp a sad smile, realizing that she had ignored the way people treated the eunuchs throughout her childhood only because the bald slaves tended to be so strict and forbidding all the time. She put her hand on his. "Alp, can you forgive me for making your life so miserable for so many years?"

He smiled. "Oh, yes, Coxani. Even though you were definitely difficult, I envied your spirit." He sighed. "Lord Haydar granted me the opportunity to have some of my own."

She squeezed his hand. "When this is over, you will have your freedom, Alp."

Alp squeezed her hand back. "So will you."

When Lord Revaz arrived, she took a deep breath and walked out the door to find an entire retinue awaiting her.

Revaz offered her his hand. "Madam, may I help you onto your horse?"

My horse. She wanted to scream with joy. She looked at Revaz incredulously, her brow furrowed. "Help me? Are you kidding?" She leaped onto the horse's back with ease, then laughed with mirth. Suddenly self-conscious, she looked at Revaz to find him laughing as well. Alp, standing at the door of Nasch's house, grinned at her. She closed her eyes and leaned down into the horse's mane, her arms around its neck. *Oh how I've missed this.*

Revaz said, "Are you ready to go?" His eyes twinkled with good humor.

"Yes, please," she replied, feeling weightless.

It wasn't until they left the Citadel that it occurred to Coxani to ask, "Where are we going?"

"My country estate," Revaz answered.

"Oh." She sat up, perplexed.

Revaz said, "Don't worry, Coxani. I promise you'll like it there."

She forced a small smile. *But will I be safe from you?*

It took three hours to reach Revaz's estate, and it was a glorious three hours to Coxani. The foliage had begun to change color, from bright shades of green to yellow, red, and brown. As they rode through the gates of the Citadel she stood in her stirrups, inhaling deeply, her eyes soaking in the city, bustling with life, and the quiet countryside beyond it, dotted with livestock and lined with fields of crops. She sat back down, grinning widely, and became acutely aware of Revaz's eyes on her. Her smile disappeared and she lowered her eyes.

"Coxani."

She looked over at him tentatively. "Yes?"

His face was lined with alarm as he lowered his voice. "Holy Cenk. What did that man do to you?"

She stiffened. "What do you mean?" She looked away, not wanting to see pity on his face and afraid her reaction to being away from Nasch had been a bit too exuberant. Luckily, Revaz let the subject rest for the time being, allowing her to enjoy the leisurely ride to their destination.

And what a destination it was. Haydar's estate had seemed expansive and opulent to her, but it was not like this. Haydar's manor had been downright rural by comparison, with its timber and gray stone. Revaz's mansion was a brilliant Anzori white, with elaborate patterns of drops and flames on the multitude of arches that adorned its exterior. It had red shingle roofs and an impressive wrought iron gate around its perimeter, enclosing fountains and manicured gardens. Coxani was rendered speechless as they rode to the entrance, where several grooms waited to take their horses to the stables. She dismounted and gaped at Revaz. "This is amazing."

Revaz seemed pleased with her reaction. "I'm glad you like it. Come in and let me show you around." He gave her a quick tour, showing her the vast inner courtyard with full-grown trees, the large windows of colored glass, and the enormous rooms with wooden ceilings that were inlaid with gold leaf and painted with red flowers. He took her into the gardens and she was overwhelmed by the potent fragrance of jasmine and rose. They sat under a pergola and were instantly served an assortment of fruits, cheeses, and juices.

Coxani took a careful sip of orange juice and said, "Why on earth would you ever leave this paradise?"

Revaz chuckled. "It is nice, isn't it? Unfortunately, I work in the Citadel. It's far more convenient to stay at my home there than to travel to and from here daily." He drummed his fingers on the table, preoccupied with something. Finally, he said, "Before we continue this conversation any further, I need you to know that I have absolutely zero expectations of you."

She looked at him curiously. "My lord?"

He shifted uncomfortably in his chair. "My intentions are honorable, I promise. I didn't do this to... get you in my bed."

"Oh?" She was interested now. "Then why did you?"

He sat back, his eyes scanning her face thoughtfully. "I was at the Caged Kingfisher's trial. I heard and saw everything that happened with my own ears and eyes."

She straightened. "And?"

"You were protecting your friend," he said. "You were unjustly punished for it. It was obvious, at least to me, that the king was punishing Tikran through you and the other Manzakar." She kept quiet, listening. He continued, "To strip you of your military rank was harsh enough. But to force marriage on you? And to that..."

She raised her eyebrows. "Yes?"

He hesitated before saying, "Commander Nasch has a reputation for being cruel, Coxani. Delger seems to love him for it, claims that Nasch is the only man who can keep Gohar tame. And, quite frankly, I don't like it. I can't imagine what a man like that would do to... a woman. Particularly one with as much spirit and defiance as you."

Her fists clenched convulsively. *I absolutely cannot cry right now. Get a grip.* She blinked repeatedly.

Revaz leaned forward, gazing at her imploringly. "Please tell me. Are you all right?"

"Are you saying," she said steadily, "that you made me your courtesan because you were worried about me?"

He shrugged. "Yes. And before you accuse me of rescuing you, let me honestly say that you had no chance. The odds are stacked against you, have been stacked against you from the start. They let you play the game thinking you can win, then they pull the rug out from under you. I've seen it done time and time again. I just couldn't let it pass... this time."

She nodded and looked down. She closed her eyes and took several breaths. Then she said, "You didn't rescue me, my lord. I had it under control. Truly. Still, I'm incredibly lucky that you—"

"Please don't," he said, frustration plain on his face. "You designed your fate. I'm just the semi-intelligent idiot who realized what was happening and decided to step in."

The possibility that Revaz was with Haydar occurred to her suddenly. Could it be? She felt jittery with anticipation. She looked out at the garden and said, "The juice is delicious. The oranges are especially sweet this time of year."

"Hmm?" He looked in the same direction distractedly. "Oh, I don't know. Are they? Aren't oranges always in season?"

She sucked in her breath. *No.* How was it possible? What was the best way to handle this? *Think!* She said, "Lord Revaz, I'm touched that you decided to help me. But if anyone heard you, they could accuse you, too, of treason."

He let out an earnest laugh. "I'm sure they could. But honestly, I don't really care at this point. Delger has been wearing on several of the Anzori lords of late. His taxes are much too high and his restrictions on trade with Dilovar and the northern kingdoms are utterly stifling." He looked at her, his eyes softening. "Enough about Delger. Has Nasch hurt you?"

She said, "Not with his fists, no. He's smarter than that." She hurriedly added, "Nothing I won't bounce back from, though."

It was too late. Lord Revaz's eyes were lit with anger. "Listen," he said. "I can't keep him from you. As your husband, he has rights that supersede my authority. But I will do my utmost to prevent as much as I can." She nodded, looking away. He took a deep breath then said, "Come. I have something else to show you. I think you'll like it."

She followed him out of the garden and through the gates that led to the fields beyond the mansion. A groom awaited them with two fresh horses. "Where are we going?" she asked.

"Not far," he said. "Mount up."

They rode to a field just half a mile away and Coxani gasped. Gourds had been hung from poles across an open field. She looked at Revaz to find him holding a bow and quiver of arrows. He smiled bashfully. "I thought you might want to shoot a bit. I can't imagine Commander Nasch has been allowing you to practice what you're best at."

Coxani grinned. "Lord Revaz, you are a gem. I could cry, I'm so happy."

"Well, don't do that." He handed her the bow. "Instead, take your pent-up frustrations out on those poor dangling vegetables out there."

And that's exactly what she did. After two hours of shooting she felt alive again, her resolve to help see Haydar's plan through renewed. She dismounted and sat beneath a tree next to Revaz, drinking deeply from a flask. Then she said, "My lord, as the king's advisor on law enforcement, do you oversee the command of the city soldiers?"

"Yes. Why?"

Because you could be a valuable asset to the cause, she thought. Out loud, she asked, "How well do you know Lord Haydar?"

"Not extremely well," he said. "He advises Delger on foreign affairs while I focus on domestic issues, so we aren't usually in the same councils with the king. That said, I do like the man. I think he's intelligent and principled, from what I know about him. Why? Come now, what's with this line of questioning?"

She tore at her bottom lip with her teeth for several seconds before asking, "Would you be willing to meet a friend of mine? He goes by Enlil the Weaver."

IN THE TIME it took to finally reach Areg, Tikran rode quietly, deep in thought. Part of him was ecstatic and ready to do what it took to see Delger dethroned. A different part of him, however, thought Haydar had lost his mind. What made the durai think the Manzakars would follow Tikran against the King of Anzor—the most powerful person on the Continent? As far as he knew, the only people who would follow him were lovesick Anzori women and teenage boys who worshipped the Caged Kingfisher for all the wrong reasons. And yet, both Coxani and Naran believed in him. They *believed* he could lead a rebellion.

How was it possible?

Oter was none too happy to see Tikran return. Tikran himself was happy that he'd arrived at all, considering he'd expected to die on his way there. Having Damir steadfastly at his side must have worked as a deterrent for any would-be murder attempts. The doctor-slash-mage had not left him alone for more than thirty minutes at a time, and Tikran hated it. It gnawed at him nonstop, making him resent Haydar for recruiting the Dilovari. How could Haydar trust Damir—Bilgun's spy and head mage, for Cenk's sake—with something as big as this?

"So, Caged Kingfisher," Oter said, his face set in a fierce scowl. "You will set out in the next couple days to find the Sachin clan that brought such sorrow upon Anzor's name."

Damir spoke up. "My patient is hardly healed enough to venture into Gohar and annihilate anyone yet." He smiled dispassionately. "Commander."

Tikran said, "I am ready, regardless of what the doctor says. And I will set out in the next couple days, Commander." He set his jaw firmly. "Doctor Damir is ready to head back to Dilovar whenever Ramil is."

Oter nodded, satisfied. Damir flashed Tikran an irked look.

"I'm going to rest for a bit," Tikran said, ignoring Damir and walking away. As a junior commander, Tikran had been granted a room in the fort separate from the other soldiers. It was small, dank, and dark, but at least he had a modicum of privacy. He sat on his bed with a puff of exhaustion, rolling the muscles in his back beneath the bandages. As if on cue, a knock on the door announced Damir's arrival to change his dressing and Tikran rolled his eyes. Holy Cenk, he couldn't wait until he was injury-free and didn't have to deal with Damir's constant attention, constant orders, constant touch...

The look in Damir's eyes was very different from what Tikran had grown used to—gone was the cool indifference, the insolent amusement, the self-righteousness. Instead of ice, at that very moment, Damir was fire. He'd changed out of his long robe and wore a simple tunic over breeches. Warily, Tikran said, "You haven't come to change my dressing, have you?"

"Let me make something very clear, Manzakar," he said, approaching slowly. "I am not leaving until you are healed. So stop trying to get rid of me."

"Your duty to Haydar is done," Tikran said. "We are in Areg. And I'm tired of being manhandled by you. I refuse any further treatment. You are free to go back to Dilovar."

"I will leave when I'm ready." Damir's entire body was tensed, and this time he moved far more like a leopard seeking a meal than one that had already eaten. "I'm not ready."

Instinctively, Tikran stood. "Easy, Doctor," he muttered. "What's gotten into you?"

In a single move, Damir swept his leg behind Tikran's ankles and, with one hard shove to the shoulders, laid Tikran flat on his back, on the bed. Pain shot through him and he grunted. Damir pounced on him, trying to straddle him, but Tikran immediately folded his legs around Damir's waist, grabbed his arm, and twisted it along with the weight of his entire body, flipping them off the bed and landing on top of Damir with a painful thud. Damir grabbed and pulled one of Tikran's arms while pushing on the other, then thrust his hips upward and wrapped a leg around Tikran's neck, locking Tikran's head and arm between his thighs.

Tikran snarled, saying, "Damir, let me go before I break your legs."

"Oh, you think you can break them? Submit, or I break your arm," Damir replied between breaths.

"I submit," Tikran said, "but only because I think I may have reopened every wound in my back."

Damir relaxed and lowered his legs, freeing Tikran from the grip of his thighs. "I win, Manzakar. Now get off me." He moved his hips in an attempt to sit up and his crotch rubbed against Tikran's thigh. Tikran sucked in his breath as he realized Damir was impossibly hard. Damir held up his hands, palms open. "As much as I enjoyed that, I didn't mean to do it. And I'd like to point out that you are still on top of me, even after I asked you to get off."

Tikran's breathing accelerated and he grabbed the front of Damir's tunic, tugging aggressively. "You say you don't want me, but your body tells a very different story. Why are you doing this to me?" he said.

Damir's eyes were like quicksilver as he propped himself up on his elbows. "I can't help how my body responds to you. Despite my best efforts... Curse you, Manzakar." He swallowed, a pained expression on his face. "I love you, Tikran."

What? Tikran was stunned. "If you love me, then why—"

"I was afraid," Damir answered firmly. "I'm still afraid. I

lied to you about who I was. And I worry that you only *think* you want me because I've been treating you."

The truth of Damir's words shone in his face. Tikran released Damir's tunic slowly and said, "What's changed, then?"

"Everything and nothing." Damir seemed to debate something for a moment, then reached out tentatively and traced Tikran's lower lip with his thumb. "The realization that, despite my skills as a doctor or even despite my Essence, I can't protect you at all times has finally sunk in. And if something ever happened to you, I'd be lost."

Tikran closed the gap between them, kissing the doctor gently, savoring the taste of his lips. "It feels like you've enjoyed tormenting me with your love, Damir," he muttered as his anger melted away, leaving a rush of joy and an animal exigency in its wake. He deepened his kisses as his fingers ran along the length of Damir's erection through his breeches.

Damir broke the kiss with a groan. "Manzakar, as much as I want you, now isn't really the time."

"I suppose not," Tikran grumbled reluctantly, the vision of Oter hovering about his door suspiciously making his skin crawl. With a deep sigh, he stood and pulled Damir up with him.

After readjusting his clothes and dusting himself off, Damir lowered his voice and said, "Tikran, please stop trying to send me back to Dilovar. I'm a part of this, whether you like it or not."

Tikran looked away. "Don't you have to go back eventually?"

"Eventually, yes. But not yet. Not until we've seen this through."

"You could die. We could all die." He looked at Damir then,

his expression grave. "Are you willing to die for a cause that isn't your own?"

"This is my cause too, Manzakar," Damir insisted. "In case you haven't realized it, I am half Gohari. Like you, I was taught that the Gohari were lesser, were savage, were dangerous. Like you, I grew up wondering if that savagery was inside me, threatening to come out. The difference between us is that, in my case, I very much believed I was dangerous and in need of containment on account of my Essence."

"Once and for all," Tikran said, "can you explain to me what the Essence does?"

Damir nodded. "Yes. But not here. Perhaps when we go out looking for your clan."

"You're not going."

"I absolutely am."

They faced each other, both resolved, unflinching. Finally, Tikran said, "I can't lose anyone else, Damir. It'll kill me."

"You can't control that, Caged Kingfisher," Damir said. "Me, Coxani, Naran, Haydar, your clan... We will fight and we may die. You may think it's because of you, but you're merely the inciting element. None of this is within your control."

Tikran scooped the loose strands of hair away from his face. "I need to think. Let's get out of here and take a look around the town."

"What about Oter?"

"He can wait."

They left the fort and walked through the town's sad little square. Tikran thought of Mago and his heart hurt. What had happened to Mago's wagon? To his body, for that matter? It was possible that the clan had taken care of the body, assuming they'd had time. The Gohari, he knew, believed in cremating the dead quickly, so that their spirits could escape back into nature. He looked at Damir. "How much do you know about the Gohari? Did you know your mother?"

"I did not know her. She died giving birth to me." Damir glanced at a woman as she walked past, a sleeping baby strapped to her chest in a sling and a hollow-eyed child holding her hand. She looked haggard and much older than her probable age. He lowered his voice. "My father was a physician, treating soldiers at an outpost on the river. There had been in influx of illegal Gohari refugees who'd managed to get across the Damla, and my father somehow convinced the soldiers not to shoot them on sight and return them the following day, after he'd had a chance to make sure none were deathly ill. My father was nothing if not a devoted doctor. My mother was wily... and beautiful, I was told." Damir chuckled. "Meeting Coxani when I first arrived in Anzor made me smile. I imagine my mother must have been a lot like her in spirit."

Tikran looked over, an eyebrow raised. "How did you meet Coxani?"

Damir seemed to hesitate. "We met after you were burned during the Fire Festival. She refused to leave you and threatened me if I tried to make her."

Tikran smiled then suddenly remembered Delger's sentence. "Oh, Cenk, Coxani... Of all of us, she's probably dealing with the worst fate of all."

"She is," Damir said. "But she has it under her control. And, she has some tools at her disposal to help her."

"What tools?" Tikran stopped walking and turned to Damir.

"I'm a doctor. I gave her something to prevent pregnancy and to... terminate it, if necessary."

Tikran felt bile rise in his throat. "But she still has to let him..." He squeezed his eyes shut. "I will tear him to pieces someday, limb by limb. Mark my word." He took several deep breaths and continued walking. "You were telling me about your mother."

"Ah, yes." Damir cleared his throat. "Let's just say that my mother was too clever for her own good. She seduced my father and he fell in love with her. He tried to hide her. But she got pregnant and died. He hid me then and was successful until I was around six months old. I would have died too, except I had the Essence."

"Bilguun must have been thrilled."

"He was, for a bit." Damir looked down. "Until he realized I was more powerful than anyone thought. Then he was afraid. Everyone was afraid. Even my own father. I was put under constant supervision. My life was not my own. Until, of course, I learned how afraid everyone was of me, and how to use that to get what I wanted."

Tikran stopped walking. "How powerful *are* you, Damir?"

Damir took a deep breath and looked around. "Is that a tavern? This town has a tavern?"

Tikran looked over. "Where there are soldiers, there's bound to be a tavern," he said.

"I could use a drink." Damir grinned. "Let's go in."

For a tavern, it was a quiet place. The innkeeper was an old Gohari with a braided black beard and heavy bags under his eyes. The patrons were all soldiers, some of them Manzakars. A bard, also Gohari, sat in the corner, strumming a lute and warbling an old Anzori folk song. Tikran was acutely aware of the eyes on them as they ordered two ales and sat at a corner table. He didn't like it here. He wanted to know how powerful Damir was. He wanted to murder Nasch. He wanted to find Bruneta. He wanted to return to Anzor and face Delger, once and for all...

"Caged Kingfisher."

Tikran looked up. No fewer than ten Manzakars stood at

their table, their faces grim. *Oh, shit.* Tikran's fingers immediately crept to the hilt of his saber. His mind raced, trying to determine how close Damir was to the nearest Manzakar and how quickly he could cross that distance with his sword if necessary. "Yes?" he heard himself say.

"I don't know if you remember me," the big fellow with red hair and dark brown skin in the forefront said. "My name is Tural. We trained as cadets together. We met again when you and the doctor came looking for the shrub to cure Prince Vazha."

"Yes, I remember," Tikran said, keeping his hand at his saber.

Tural seemed to be mustering courage, finally saying, "We stand with you, Tikran. We were tasked with ensuring you didn't deviate from the king's orders. We were told to——" The Manzakar tightened his lips. "We saw what happened with that clan. Many of us were there, ordered to kill the nomads even if they showed no aggression. We were to make an example of them. We were ordered to kill everyone save the doctor—including you. Especially you." He shifted, frowning. "Many of us saw what you did. We know why you did it. And we stand by you."

Behind Tural, the Manzakars nodded and murmured their assent. Tural met Tikran's eyes. "Say the word, Caged Kingfisher, and we fight at your side."

THE CHIRPING BIRDS AWOKE NARAN. *Screaming birds, more like it.* They sounded like they were perched on his head, they were so loud. He groaned, cracking open his eyelids and immediately regretting it. It was cold and mostly overcast, but the morning light still hurt his eyes. He sat up slowly, his head throbbing.

His mouth felt sealed shut, it was so parched. He needed water. He looked toward the bedside to find an expanse of smooth, golden skin and curly dark hair lying beside him.

Oh.

He looked around urgently. He was not at the fort, that was certain. A gauzy purple curtain hung in a narrow doorway and a woman's clothes were scattered about, hanging from every piece of furniture within sight. A small table with a polished metal mirror sat in a corner, laden with small pots, bottles, and combs. He heard other women's voices and saw their shadows as they passed by the flimsy curtain that served as a door to the room.

The Siren Song. He remembered now. It was his second— or third?—visit to the brothel. He'd only been in the cold, remote Otebek two weeks, but he'd ended up at the place quickly after finding the local inn. He scrubbed his face with his hands. Oh, Cenk. Who was the girl this time? At least once now, he'd ended up here after getting stupid drunk and imagining the woman looked exactly like Coxani. He looked at his bedmate now, afraid of what he'd find when he saw her face. The first woman had, not surprisingly, looked nothing like his Dolphin.

I really need to stop drinking myself into a stupor.

His feet landed on the cold stone floor and he stood, swaying a bit as he did so. Staggering to the curtain and sweeping it aside, he blinked, trying to force his eyes to focus so that he could find some water. A woman squealed, making him jump. It was followed by a cascade of delighted female laughter. Cool fingers danced down his chest and stomach.

"Why, good morning, Manzakar," a mirthful voice said. The woman must have been the madam—yes, he was certain she was the madam. Older, still attractive, but with a hint of tawdriness. She eyed him with appreciation, looking him up and down. Mostly down. "Did Karine not fully satisfy you? Do I need to wake the lazy slattern up?"

"Huh?" Naran looked down at himself. "No, don't bother... Karine. I have a more pressing problem, actually. I'm dying of thirst."

The madam spun around, glaring at the younger women who stared wide-eyed at him, half-smiles on their faces. "Get the soldier some water, by Cenk!" She clapped her hands. "Now!"

"Thank you," Naran muttered, finally realizing that he was completely naked and very hard, standing amidst women as they rushed past him, many of them barely taller than chest-level with his cock. He spun around and nearly fell back through the curtains, wanting nothing more than to climb back into the bed and go to sleep. Unfortunately, Karine was awake now and staring directly at his erection. *No, not Coxani.* She smiled. He held up his hands. "No, no. I just—"

"Water for the Manzakar." The madam brought two jugs of water and set them on the bedside table. She shot Karine a menacing look as she swept out of the room. Naran grabbed a jug and guzzled it thirstily, then moved on to the second one. He was sated and nearly done emptying the second jug when he felt a mouth on him. He considered for a moment, setting the jug down and looking at the young woman's face, then... "No. I'm sorry, Karine. I have to go. How much—?"

It wasn't that she was unattractive—far from it. She was lovely. The Naran of merely six months ago would have been thrilled to have a pretty girl like Karine gratifying his body. But the Naran of right now only wanted one woman, and he apparently only took a tumble in bed with someone else when he'd drunk enough to *imagine* the woman was she...

Karine's smile fell. Her eyes kept darting to the curtain

anxiously. "But sir... Are you sure? Madam will surely be disappointed with me if you leave now."

Well, shit. Naran rubbed his face. Why did he keep ending up in these situations? He needed to stop drinking so much. He swallowed and nodded at Karine, then clamped his eyes shut and thought of Coxani.

It took *far* too long. By the time he left The Siren Song, he was raw and chafed and ready to start drinking again, if only to forget the ordeal with Karine. He squinted up the road toward the fort, wondering how angry Commander Harut would be with him for missing his watch. Not that Naran gave a shit. Truth be told, he cared about nothing except the fact that Coxani was now married to that pile of human refuse, Nasch. It was slowly consuming Naran from the inside out. He couldn't stop imagining the things Nasch must be doing to her. And it wasn't just the fact that Nasch was raping her. That would be bad enough. It was that he would likely get her pregnant, and that she, being Coxani, would likely try to find a way to end it...

He dragged his feet, exhaling, his breath clouding in the cold air. If something happened to Coxani, he would lose his mind. Haydar's plans meant nothing to him if something happened to Coxani. He would go down and take as many men as he could with him—

"Naran, you asshole."

He should have felt for his sword. Instead, he looked over his shoulder in utter disinterest at the Manzakar rushing to catch up to him. "What do you want?" Naran grunted, continuing to walk.

"Are you just going to keep pissing off the commander, getting flogged, getting drunk, then getting laid until you die?" The Manzakar slowed, walking behind Naran. His voice indicated he was very young.

Naran chuckled without humor. "Yeah, that sounds about right."

"Naran, you're a pile of shit."

That made Naran stop and turn, his annoyance transformed into anger. "What's your name, kid?"

The young soldier stopped as well, standing several feet away, warily. "Moti."

"Moti." Naran scowled. "I used to be an Aslan Manzakar. And if you think, for even a second, that you can talk shit at me and get away with it, you've got something else coming."

Moti grinned. "Yeah, asshole. I think I can. Come at me."

Naran's nostrils flared. "Listen, you little fuck. I'm devastated, exhausted, hungover, humiliated, and my cock is rubbed raw. You do *not* want to mess with me."

The young Manzakar laughed gleefully then gyrated his hips in Naran's direction. "Oh, yeah? Boo-hoo, Stalking Lion!"

Naran would have drawn his sword but the weapon was obviously absent. Instead, he decided to use his brute strength and rushed the younger man, who crouched, prepared for the attack, looking both thrilled and terrified. Unfortunately, Naran was moving far too slowly. Moti managed to knee Naran in the gut then slam his elbow into the side of Naran's face. As the former Aslan fell to his knees, blood dripping from his nose, Moti leaned down, bringing his face close, and said, "Naran. Do the oranges taste especially fucking sweet this time of year, or is it just me?"

Naran's eyes opened. Wide. Oh. *Oh.* Through the haze, he looked up, finally understanding. The young soldier exhaled slowly, as though he'd been trying the same tactic for days. Naran groaned. *Right.* "Okay. Holy Cenk. I hear you."

Moti slumped with exhaustion. "Do you have any idea how long I've been trying to get your attention? It's been impossible. You're either brawling, being punished, too drunk to focus, or at the brothel."

"I'm sorry. Fuck! Have you heard anything?" Naran shook his mane and swiped the blood from his face with the back of his hand.

"Ha! You think I'm going to tell you now?"

Naran saw red. He grabbed Moti by the front of his cuirass and lifted his fist. "I will smash your face into a thousand pieces if you don't—"

"I haven't heard anything. Yet."

Naran kept his fist raised. "Are you lying to me?"

"Why would I lie to you?"

"Hmph." Naran let Moti go. "I need to send word to... Enlil. I need to find out how Coxani is."

"We can arrange that."

A feeling of intense relief made Naran weak at the knees. He really was a moron. If only he'd paid a modicum of attention instead of causing trouble and getting piss-drunk, he'd have realized Moti was an agent two weeks ago and gotten a message back to Haydar that much sooner. But he'd been too busy wallowing in self-pity. As they walked back to the fort, Moti explained that all "business" took place at the Firekeeper Inn, where those involved—approximately one hundred Manzakars and a little less than half of those stationed in Otebek—met twice a week.

Naran glanced at Moti's baby face. "You seem awfully young for a Manzakar. What year did you graduate?"

"216," Moti said.

Naran stopped. "That's not possible. That's the same year I graduated. I would remember you." He looked at Moti's insignia—a quill dipped in ink—and his eyes widened. "Zarina?"

Moti shrugged. "Yeah. I go by Moti now. Hardly anyone remembers Zarina anymore."

"Don't tell me you were sent to this Cenk forsaken place because you chose to become Moti?"

The young Manzakar let out a laugh. "I didn't *choose* to become anything. I've always been Moti." He sighed. "They threw me in prison for a while because I tried running away the night before I was to be married to some poor bastard who was cornered into choosing me. Thank Cenk for Haydar. He convinced them to let me be Moti with the caveat that I'd always be tucked away in this pisshole with the rest of the Manzakar misfits."

"That Haydar," Naran said, shaking his head. "He's something else."

They approached the fort and Moti said, "Sorry about your face, Naran. You'll likely be in deep shit when Harut gets ahold of you, but if you can get away from whatever punishment he has planned, we're gathering at the inn tonight. We can get your message sent."

Naran smiled bitterly. "Oh, I'll be there. Nothing can stop me."

CHAPTER 23

The rolling slopes of hills appeared on the horizon as Tikran led a squadron of one hundred and twenty Manzakars further east into the steppe. Tural nodded. "There. That's where our Gohari informant said they were hiding for now. They've only been there a couple days, but they don't stay in one place long."

"How many clans have banded together at this point?" Tikran asked.

"Last we heard, there were three clans, including Donaba's."

Damir, who had somehow managed to convince Oter that his participation in the mission was critical to its success, rode alongside Tikran wearing a lamellar cuirass and carrying a shield on his back. He said, "Assuming there are approximately twenty-five people in each clan, that's a total of seventy-five nomads." He shook his head. "Sending this many Manzakars after them seems a bit much."

Tikran said nothing. Of course, he agreed. And of the Manzakars in his squadron, he knew only fifty-three of them were loyal to him—Tural had given him a list of names of those men who had begun to meet regularly in the cellar beneath the tavern. He stopped and turned to face his men, mostly heavy cavalrymen whose primary weapon was the lance, with a smaller portion of them serving as cavalry archers. "From this point on, it's likely the nomads will spot us and begin preparing for our arrival," he said to the formation of Manzakars before him, their armor and weapons blindingly bright under the autumn sun. "I expect them to send their archers around to attack us from behind. Remember! We are *not* to attack. I want every one of them brought to me alive."

He turned as the men readied their shields before them. He knew the chances of all the Manzakars obeying his order were slim, particularly if the nomads began shooting first, which they would most likely do. But his goal was to have zero casualties as a result of this campaign. He looked at Damir. "Helmet on, Doctor," he muttered. "And get that shield in front of you." He'd given Damir a brief tutorial on how to defend with a shield. He wished they'd had more time—getting accustomed to wielding the heavy shield for long periods of time was the biggest challenge. But they had no time. He was hopeful Damir would adjust quickly—the doctor was definitely no weakling.

As they approached the hills, Tikran began to suspect that the nomads had decided not to use yarms in order to hide themselves better. He also sensed that his squadron was surrounded. His plan was fairly straightforward: The nomads would attack in their usual manner, by riding up from all directions, loosing arrows, then retreating. They would continue to do this until they ran out of arrows. Tikran had left a good number of cavalry archers behind, in anticipation of a flank attack. The Manzakars would then aim for their mounts with the intent of unhorsing the archers. Once unhorsed, the nomads would be easy to capture.

He took a deep breath. After they captured most of the nomad warriors, the *real* battle would begin.

It didn't take long for the volleys of arrows to begin. Finding the archers was the hardest part—many of them knew how to shoot from great distances. They had a limited number of arrows, however, and after about three hours of volleys, they stopped. Tikran signaled to his men. "Find them, now. Remember, I want them alive!"

While the warriors were harder to catch—several lost their horses and were injured—the clan families sat huddled together under the cover of larger shrubs, shaking with fear. Tikran's heart hurt as the women and children sobbed. *They think we're going to slaughter them.* He had his men gather them up and bring in the young nomad warriors, who were bound and furious. He dismounted, walking among the captured rebels. He immediately found Bruneta. Her wrists were tied behind her back and she was gagged. He walked toward her, hoping to reveal himself, when a scream pierced the air.

He turned to find one of the nomad youths crumpled to the ground, his blood staining the earth around him. A lance protruded from his gut as he struggled to breathe. Two women wailed luridly, rushing to the boy's side. A Manzakar—a fellow named Shalva, from Tikran's graduating class—stood over the boy, smattered with the boy's blood. *Why, Shalva?* Tikran had hoped he wouldn't have to do this. Without hesitation, he drew his saber and drove it into Shalva's armpit, one of the few places left exposed by the cuirass, then quickly yanked it out. The Manzakar stumbled back a bit, a look of surprise on his face, then sank to the ground slowly as blood streamed down the side of his cuirass. Damir had shown Tikran where on the human body to stab in order to avoid vital organs or major vessels. According to Damir, if he avoided the axillary artery, which ran through the shoulder and into the arm, he reduced the chances that the wound would be fatal. Perhaps Shalva would live.

Forcibly shutting out Shalva's gasps, Tikran turned to face the other Manzakars, who either stood bewildered or moved restlessly in confusion. He heard Damir, who had been tending to the injured nomad, turn to the injured Manzakar as well. Tikran nodded to Tural subtly, and the Manzakars of the Caged Kingfisher (much to Tikran's annoyance, it was what they insisted on calling themselves) suddenly formed a protective wall around the captured nomads. They drew their swords and shields, waiting for Tikran's signal.

"I *commanded* you not to attack!" Tikran yelled at his squadron. "Who else disobeyed me? Who would follow orders other than my own?" His wording was very deliberate. As he looked out at the Manzakars before him, his faith faltered. *Haydar's gone crazy, to think these men would follow me...* To his astonishment, the soldiers began to dismount and take a knee before him. Shalva's blood dripped from his sword onto his boots as nearly all one hundred and twenty Manzakars kneeled before him, their heads bowed in obeisance.

For several moments, Tikran felt, once again in the span of a few weeks, as though he was outside his own body. He heard himself speak the words he and Damir had composed the night before at the tavern, over some bitter ale. "We will take these nomads back to Areg and feed them. We will take the fort from Delger, the king who has perpetuated the suffering in Gohar and the strife with Dilovar. Then, we will march on Anzor City with our brothers. Don't forget, Manzakars, it was Delger who starved our families and bought us as child slaves to become Anzor's soldiers. Our time has come. Now, we will be Anzor's masters."

Manzakars never cheered. Rather, they slammed the butts of their lances into the earth, making no other sound. It was eerie, the echo of a hundred and twenty-ish lances pounding into the grass, almost like a heartbeat. Tikran signaled to them to rise. He turned to Bruneta, who had been ungagged and untied.

"Tikran..." She swallowed. "When I first realized you led this squadron, I was determined to kill you."

He nodded. "I would have wanted to kill me too."

She tilted her head. "Are you okay?"

"Mostly." He glanced at the bloody tip of his saber. "We need to get back to Areg. I have one more thing to do before you and your clan can be safe from Oter's squadron." He looked back at Damir, who was attending the injured diligently, and motioned to him. Damir approached Tikran and Bruneta, his hands stained with blood. "Damir, I'm leaving you and twenty Manzakars with most of the clans here. We'll come back and get you when we've taken the fort. If you don't hear back by sunset, Tural has orders to get everyone away from here, and quickly. I have a faction of Manzakars at Eter who are loyal to me and will protect the clans."

"No." Damir frowned. "You may need my help in Areg."

"Damir, trust that I can do this without your... assistance," Tikran said, avoiding the word "Essence" in front of Bruneta and Tural. He hadn't decided how to handle that particular issue yet—he didn't want to put Damir in danger. "I plan on using deceit. Bruneta and her gang will come with me and most of the squadron as prisoners. Once we're inside the fort, the nomad warriors will help us. Things will happen quickly and, if we're lucky, with as few casualties as possible."

Damir was still frowning, his brow deeply furrowed. "That's assuming Oter doesn't suspect anything."

Bruneta put a hand on Damir's shoulder. "The injured need you, doctor."

Tikran could see the frustration in the doctor's eyes. Damir finally said, "Fine. But if you haven't returned by sunset, I'm not going to Eter with the clans—I'm coming to find you."

Although Tikran hated that idea, he didn't have time to argue. "It's settled then." He turned and mounted his horse, sliding his saber back into its scabbard at his hip. His eyes moved briefly to the injured soldier and boy on pallets behind Damir. "Will they live?"

Damir looked over his shoulder. "Shalva will. You were precise. The nomad boy's situation is more precarious. I will do all I can."

Tikran pulled his helmet over his head. "I know you will."

"Manzakar." Damir looked up at Tikran, his expression fierce. "Do everything and anything you have to do to ensure you come back in one piece."

Tikran smiled slightly. "Hopefully it won't come to that."

As he, the rest of his squadron, and the ostensibly bound nomad warriors rode back to Areg, his mind raced. Current situation aside, he and the other renegade Manzakars had quite the challenge before them. What would happen when deceit and the element of surprise were not options? What would happen on the battlefield? They weren't fighting an enemy with different armies and strategies. They were fighting *themselves*. This was far more difficult, and any plan Tikran could devise would be quickly deciphered by his fellow Manzakars. Moreover, he had no idea how many Manzakars in total would support the Caged Kingfisher, let alone the overthrow of the king. They were badly outnumbered.

They arrived at Areg and Tikran ordered his Manzakars to wait outside the fort with the prisoners. He went into the fort to find Oter waiting for him in the chancery. Oter looked out over the captured nomads from his window. "Where are the rest of them? I understood there to be three clans hiding together."

"I was tasked with bringing only one of those clans to justice," Tikran said. "We will execute the captives promptly." Before Oter could move away from the window, Tikran stepped behind him and held a dagger to his back.

Oter went rigid. "What is the meaning of this, Tikran?"

Tikran signaled to Tural from the window. The Manzakars and nomads drew their weapons and entered the fort. "Summon your men and have them turn all of their weapons over to mine," he said. He pressed the tip of the dagger firmly against Oter's jacket. "Now."

Oter turned his head, his eyes wide. "*Your* men?"

Tikran said, "Yes. We can do this civilly, with no bloodshed, or you can die. Your choice." The dagger's handle was slick in his hand. His voice was too loud, even over the steady pulse of his blood as it rushed through his veins. He sensed every slight movement Oter made in his core, saw every thread of silver in the man's hair as he marched Oter out of the chancery. "Call to the junior commanders. Have them order their men to hand over their weapons."

After several stuttered breaths, Oter obeyed. The Manzakars of Areg slowly set aside their weapons, confusion and suspicion in their eyes. Tikran passed Oter to Tural and shouted for attention. "Manzakars! This is your chance at true freedom. Join me and my faction in ending Gohari enslavement, both in Anzor and Gohar. If you choose not to, you will become our prisoners. If you become violent, not only will Commander Oter pay the price, but so will you—I have two hundred men approaching from Eter this very second." Tikran was bluffing, of course. But they were outnumbered and he needed Oter's men to believe they had no chance.

To his utter relief, the Manzakars did not put up a fight. Moreover, another hundred of them joined his faction. Once the prisoners—including Ramil—had been secured, Tikran mounted his horse and said to Tural, "I'm going back to get the men and nomads we left behind. Send a message as quickly as possible to Enlil the Weaver." He let out his breath. His hands shook ever so slightly. "Tell him Areg has fallen to the Caged Kingfisher."

Tural smiled. "Right away, Commander."

"Oh, and Tural," Tikran added, his face grim. "Tell him to hide Coxani immediately. I'm afraid Delger might come after her."

HAYDAR STOOD in the great hall, his legs apart and arms folded across his chest, watching Delger pace among his advisors, his stride and posture making him look for all the world like an angry bear. The word had reached the king's ear a mere half day after Haydar had received Tikran's message by pigeon.

Areg has fallen to the Caged Kingfisher.

Of course, half a day had been just enough time for Haydar to act on the second part of Tikran's message: *Hide Coxani immediately.*

"I should have had him publicly executed," Delger said, his voice rough with rage.

"He has no chance, King Delger," Haydar said.

At that moment, Nasch entered the hall. "You summoned me, Your Highness?" he said, kneeling and bowing his head.

"Stand, Commander," Delger said, approaching him. "Prepare to head into Gohar within the next couple hours. You will lead as many men as needed into battle."

A very subtle twitch of his mouth revealed Nasch's bemusement. "Immediately, Your Highness. And the enemy is...?"

"The *fucking* Caged Kingfisher," Delger spat with

contempt. "He has somehow taken Areg with a faction of two hundred and fifty men and a handful of nomads. I want him—and every single person who supports him—annihilated. And I want Tikran's head on a pike and displayed for the Gohari to see."

The bloodlust was clear in Nasch's eyes. "Yes, my king. I will cut him down and enjoy doing it."

Haydar had perfected the art of showing no emotion. He'd learned to remain impassive, particularly when Delger's savagery emerged, which had happened often throughout Haydar's life as the king's childhood friend, Aslan Manzakar, and trusted advisor. On the outside, Haydar was calm. On the inside, he wanted nothing more than to swing his saber and neatly lop off the heads of both men before him. Haydar spoke, pushing his true feelings aside as he'd done hundreds of times before and taking a step forward. "Unfortunately, Commander, one of the conditions of Tikran's sentence was that if he went rogue, he forfeited Coxani's life. As such, we will have to arrest your wife immediately and prepare her for execution."

A flash of dismay passed quickly over Nasch's face. "It's regrettable, but I understand, of course. I live to serve my king."

Delger appeared satisfied. "You will be honored on your return, Commander, as well as rewarded. But you must prepare your troops and leave now. Take two mages with you, they can provide extra assurance that none of the insurgents survive. Not Saltanat—I need her here with me. I want this little mutiny squashed before it goes any further." Nasch bowed deeply and turned, striding from the great hall with purpose. Delger looked at Haydar. "The woman..."

"Taken care of, Your Highness," Haydar answered. "Soldiers are on their way to Nasch's house as we speak."

Delger grunted. "I would have her executed on the spot if I could."

"I completely understand, Your Highness," Lord Bagrat said. He was one of the advisors and Haydar's ally. "But you must consider public opinion, Highness. Have her killed outside prison walls and you risk your reputation as a magnanimous leader. Not to mention, bolster the reputation of the Caged Kingfisher."

A murmur of agreement rose from several of the other advisors. Of the fifteen advisors, six of them were Haydar's conspirators. Five of the six were durais and former Manzakars themselves. The sixth, Lord Revaz, was the only Anzori and not currently in attendance. Haydar hoped Delger wouldn't notice.

"I absolutely disagree, my lords." Lord Gennadius, one of the Anzori advisors, pounded his fist in the palm of his other hand. "My king, the people of Anzor do not need or want a monarch so benevolent that they cease fearing him. This situation with the Caged Kingfisher is an opportunity to show your people that you will not tolerate insubordination, and doing so has dire consequences!"

Delger nodded gravely. "I will have her executed as soon as she arrives. Hopefully that will send a clear message—to both Anzor and the insurgents."

At that moment, the Manzakars sent to arrest Coxani returned. "Your Highness, when we arrived, she wasn't there. The eunuch there seemed startled as well and said she must have snuck out."

"Well, she couldn't have gone far!" Haydar said. "Find her and—"

"Your Highness," Gennadius said, "she must be with Lord Revaz."

The king looked around. "Where is Revaz? And why would she be with him?"

"It is said that he very recently became her protector."

Lord Haydar turned to the Manzakars. "Find Lord Revaz and Coxani immediately."

COXANI CLUNG to Revaz as they rode swiftly through Anzor City, weaving between the carts in the marketplace, past the shops with brightly colored awnings, and down the narrow streets of one of the residential quarters. He'd appeared at Nasch's door unexpectedly, breathless and clearly in a hurry. He didn't have time to explain, he said, nor to prepare a horse for her. She just had to trust him.

And she did.

Now, the anticipation was gnawing at her, her heart pounding. They stopped at a small, unassuming middle-class townhouse nestled amidst others that were nearly identical. They hopped off the horse and Revaz knocked quickly. A small, wizened old Anzori man opened the door; his face lit up upon seeing Revaz. He ushered them in hastily and closed the door.

The room was covered in half-sewn clothing, scraps of fabric, and spools of wool. Revaz said, "As you might have guessed, Anvar is my tailor. He is also someone I trust implicitly."

The old man nodded at Coxani. "Any friend of my lord's is a friend of mine."

"Thank you," Coxani said, then turned to Revaz. "What in Cenk's name is going on?"

"Tikran has taken Areg," he said.

Coxani reached out to the nearest piece of furniture to steady herself. "Holy shit!"

"The news reached Enlil just a bit before the king got word. Delger intends to execute you, since your survival depended on

Tikran's compliance with the terms of his sentence." Revaz took a deep breath. "Enlil asked me to hide you. You can't stay with me, since it's only a matter of time before they come looking for me. The rumor that I'm your protector is currently making the rounds at court. You'll be safe with Anvar. No one would look for you here."

"Are you in danger, my lord?" Coxani said. "If they think you've hidden me..."

"I'm an Anzori nobleman. I'll be fine. Delger would be loath to punish one of his own at this point, particularly as he knows nothing of the cause." He stepped closer to her. "Nasch is already preparing to leave for Gohar with two thousand Manzakars and two mages. They are headed to confront Tikran and his men."

All the blood rushed from her head at once. "They'll crush him," she said. "I can't stay here. I have to help—"

"Coxani." Revaz took her shoulders between his hands. "Listen to me. I have two hundred Manzakars in my household that I maintain for the king. Lord Bagrat has two hundred more. They have all committed to the cause. Go with them and help Tikran."

Coxani could have kissed him. She swallowed the lump in her throat and said, "Yes. Yes. When?"

"I will send for you as soon as the king's men aren't poking around my estate. I promise it will be soon." Revaz smiled. "Also, I have something for you, direct from the weaver himself."

He nodded at Anvar, who brought out her bow with a full quiver of arrows, saber, Manzakar uniform, and armor. She gasped in delight and took the bow, cradling it lovingly.

He headed for the door and turned one last time. With a grin, he said, "Wait for my message and stay safe, Manzakar."

THE BOISTEROUS NOISE of the inn was driving Naran crazy.

He sat in a dark corner with a mug between his hands, pensively staring into its golden, bubbly contents. He'd been drinking far, far less since Moti had smacked some sense into him. He'd been a model soldier for one whole week—attending his duties (while sober), refusing to let antagonizing comments work him up, and not even glancing in the direction of the brothel. Truth was, the brothel held little interest for him when he wasn't drinking himself into a coma.

Moti had been his confidante and support for that week. The smooth-faced Manzakar had patiently listened to him as he'd ranted, raved, and sobbed over Coxani. And Tikran. And the whole bloody situation. And rather than nodding and appeasing, Moti had cursed at him, punched him, and told him multiple times that he was a huge piece of shit. It had helped immensely. He felt like he owed Moti some sort of doctor's fee.

Regardless, he *needed* to hear from Haydar. He needed to know how Tikran and Coxani were faring. He felt like he was on the brink of a rampage. Truth be told, he'd likely be on the brink of a rampage either way. Ultimately, he needed something to happen.

Soon.

"Naran." Moti stood over him, panting, grinning, holding a small scrap of parchment between his fingers. "It's from Enlil."

Naran wanted to stand and scream. Instead, he said calmly, "What does it say?"

Moti read, "'Tikran has taken Areg. Nasch and Manzakars headed to confront him.'"

Naran wanted to pound the table with his fists. *Yes!* "Any word on Coxani?"

"Nothing about Coxani, but there's more," Moti said, setting his hand on Naran's shoulder.

Naran looked up. "Well?"

Moti struggled to keep his expression calm. "'Take Otebek.'" As soon as he'd spoken the written words out loud, Moti held the scrap over the candle's open flame. Both men watched it wither, blacken, and turn to ash.

Naran stood. He felt lit from within. *Finally.* He looked at Moti. "Let's do this."

"Wait." Moti looked like an excited child. "Follow me outside. To the stables. For just a second."

Puzzled, Naran stood and followed. Moti led him to a back stall and began digging through the hay. Naran's Manzakar suit, saber, and armor emerged from the straw, clean, polished, and waiting for him. Moti beamed at him. "Welcome back, Lion."

Naran suddenly felt like sobbing. "Shut your fucking mouth." He strode over and grabbed his equipment. "I'll hug you afterwards, soldier," he said to Moti.

"Please don't," Moti begged, grinning. "I *will* make you bleed again."

As they trudged back to the inn, the wind blowing bitterly, Naran said, "There's no way these Manzakars will follow a disgraced Aslan into rebellion and probable death."

Moti shook his head. "You underestimate the power of the Caged Kingfisher, Naran. He's inspired every one of us Gohari slaves who was too malcontent, too ill-suited for Anzor, and discarded because of it." He gave Naran a meaningful look. "And there are a whole lot of us."

Back at the inn, he, Moti, and a few rebel Manzakars laid out their plan. Moti, Naran had realized, was the leader of the Otebek renegades, of which there were a little over forty men out of a hundred. As he leaned over a table in the corner of the dimly lit lodge, his face stern as he explained the details of their strategy, it was clear that Moti had been planning this moment for years.

"Tonight, during the second night patrol, each of us will take up watch at key points around the fort—the gate, the commander's suite, the armory, three at the barracks, and the stables. We'll use our signal to let the others within know that the plan is in motion. That should divide us evenly around the garrison. Naran and I will give the commander a surprise visit around midnight. You'll know we've disarmed Harut when we lower the Anzori flag." Moti looked at the eager faces around him. "Be armed and ready. At that point, disarming the rest of the Manzakars should be easy and free of any bloodshed."

His blood humming with nervous energy, Naran couldn't have slept even if he'd wanted to. Instead, he took both the first and second night patrols—the first at the front gate and the second at the commander's chambers, with Moti. He wasn't wearing his Manzakar uniform and armor, but had taken his saber back and now wore it on his hip. As the sky grew dark and darker still, Naran stroked the pommel of his sword, deep in thought. Why hadn't Haydar said anything about Coxani? Surely she was in danger now that Tikran had put the wheels in motion. At least Nasch would be away from her for the time being, too busy going after Tikran. He wanted to trust Haydar to ensure her safety, but not knowing how she fared gnawed at him relentlessly.

Shortly before midnight, Naran passed his watch to a Manzakar ally with a knowing look and made his way to the commander's suite, where Moti already stood guard. They exchanged nothing more than curt nods before falling silent on either side of the heavy oak door. They waited ten excruciating minutes before Moti knocked on the door. "Commander Harut, it's Moti. It's urgent."

After several seconds, the door creaked open. Harut was in a state of semi-dress, a scowl on his face. "Well? This better be worth it."

Moti pointed into the room. "There are soldiers approaching from the north, Commander. They aren't Anzori. You can see them from your window, if you look."

"Holy Cenk," Harut gasped. "Dilovar!" He rushed to the window, whereupon Moti and Naran shut the door and followed. Harut squinted into the darkness outside. "Where? I see noth—"

Both Manzakars had drawn their sabers. Moti smiled. "Order the men at the front to lower the flag, Commander."

He blanched. "What? You can't be serious."

Moti and Naran exchanged looks. Naran said, "I think the fact that we're pointing our sabers directly at your guts conveys just how serious we are."

Harut turned and called down to the guards, ordering them to lower the flag. For twenty minutes, the pair kept their swords on Harut, listening intently to the eerie quiet in and outside the fort. Suddenly, several rebel Manzakars burst into the room. One of them said, "Moti! Naran! It's done. Otebek is ours!"

To Naran's astonishment, nearly all the Otebek Manzakars joined the insurgency that night—even Harut himself. Naran turned to Moti. "Take as many men as you can and head toward Areg to fight with Tikran. I'll join you as soon as I'm able."

"What are you going to do?" Moti asked, frowning.

Naran slid his saber back in its scabbard. "I'm going to get Coxani."

CHAPTER 24

Nasch, *two mages, and 2,000 Manzakars headed your way.*

Tikran and Damir leaned over the watch tower battlements of Areg's fort. Tikran alternated between watching the men train within the walls and looking out over the steppe beyond the town, the bitter winter wind lashing at them. He still held Haydar's message in his hand. *How are we going to win this?* He tore at his lower lip with his teeth. Even with Eter's Manzakar faction, he had a grand total of 350 soldiers. Bruneta had rallied some of the nomad warriors from other clans and tribes to fight with him, which added another two hundred, but still not nearly enough. He was confident Naran would bring whatever troops he was able to assemble after taking Otebek, but that would likely yield less than a hundred men.

He began to pace before Damir. "I'm not sure what to do. I would say we could rely on you to incinerate them with your fires, but they're bringing two mages, who will likely create their own fires."

Damir winced. "Between myself and the mages, I have a

feeling this will be a very soggy battle." He raised an eyebrow at Tikran. "I hope you've trained during heavy downpours."

"Two thousand Manzakars and two mages." Tikran dragged his fingers through his hair. "They're going to slaughter us. On top of that, we're quickly running out of food. Without supplies coming from Anzor..."

Damir nodded. "Tikran, it's time I showed you everything the Essence does. Can we go for a short ride?"

Finally! "I'm glad you've decided that things have gotten dire enough for you to tell me," Tikran said, his tone thick with sarcasm. "Let's go."

They rode a few miles away from Areg and stopped in an area of low shrubs and tussocks of long grass. Damir dismounted and squatted to the ground in a small clearing of barren earth, rubbing the sandy dirt between his fingers. Tikran lowered himself beside Damir. The doctor said, "That fateful night when you became a wanted man, we hid in the hills and I removed the arrow from your leg. Do you remember what else we did?"

Tikran peered at Damir sidelong in mild disbelief. "Is that a serious question?"

Damir rolled his eyes and stifled a smile. "Besides that, Manzakar."

Tikran looked down at the ground. "We found water."

"Yes." Damir set both his hands on the ground, burying his fingers in clumps of dirt. The earth began to darken with moisture, slowly expanding outward. Tikran touched the now-wet ground, watching as water bubbled forth, slowly creating a puddle at their feet.

"Holy Cenk," Tikran muttered. "How are you doing that?"

"The groundwater must exist below the surface—I'm not creating it," Damir explained. "I am merely calling it. If the groundwater is very deep, I'm not certain I would be able to. I've never had to try."

"What about creating fire?" Tikran asked.

"It's similar," Damir said. "The heat comes from my hands, but there must be air and kindling to create it. Gohar's dry grass is perfect tinder. A powder cartridge is even better. Wet clothes? Not so much. It's the same with rain. If there is no moisture in the air, no clouds, I can't make it rain." As the earth reabsorbed the water Damir had summoned, the air around them warmed and the wind died down. He buried his hands further in the now-moist soil. Tikran held his breath as green buds emerged, rising, thickening, unfurling leaves and sprouting buds. Across the patch of moist earth, flowers bloomed and berries ripened—wild grapes, buckwheat, strawberries, onions, cabbage thistle, prickly wild rose... "I can only summon plants native to the soil," Damir explained. "So asking me to grow an apple tree in Gohar would be futile."

Tikran plucked a strawberry and popped it into his mouth. *Delicious.* He gaped at Damir. "Are you saying that this is why the Essence has been kept from Gohar? So the nomads have no choice but to rely on Anzor?"

"That's the gist of it."

"Can Saltanat do everything you can do?"

Damir tilted his head. "Everything you've seen me do, she and the other mages can do—with the help of Archil's spells. I have more Essence than they do, so I don't need to write a set of specific runes in the air for it to take effect. I've never needed them. I just... summon it from within me. It's a very conscious act."

Archil's spells. "I thought this was Cenk's magic?"

Damir smiled. "So we've been told. And yet, Archil wrote the spells for his followers, so that even those with weak Essence could use it."

"Does your power weaken if you use a lot at once?"

"Yes," Damir said. "Just as swinging a sword would eventually wear you out, continuously using my Essence wears me out eventually, and the strength of it weakens. All things being equal, however, I can maintain it longer than most mages, just because I have more of it."

Tikran was quiet before asking, "Are there any mages in the southern kingdoms as powerful as you?"

"No. Of course, that doesn't rule out that there's someone with the Essence who is as powerful as me in the southern kingdoms. With the ability to mask it, who would know?"

The air was cold again, the wind biting at them. Tikran said, "What else can you do that the other mages can't?"

Damir turned away for a few seconds, his long black hair waving in the wind. Finally he looked back, storm clouds in his eyes, his lips twisted in anguish. "Terrible things."

A knot of dread formed in Tikran's chest. "Tell me."

In response, Damir slipped his fingers in the earth again and the moisture vanished. Suddenly the flowers withered, the berries rotted, and what was green became brown and crumbled back to the cracked, bone-dry earth. He met Tikran's gaze. "I can summon life, but I can also destroy it. And this ability, because it is based in water, extends beyond just shriveling plants. All living things are made of water." He swallowed convulsively. "Obviously, I've never deliberately tested this on an animal or human. But when I was a young boy, I had a dog that was attacked by a wolf and was badly injured, losing a lot of blood quickly. I thought I could stop the bleeding, since so much of blood is water. I didn't understand what I was doing. What happened then was one of the most horrific things I've ever seen. That incident is why I followed in my father's footsteps and became a doctor. I had to convince myself that I wasn't a monster."

"I understand." Tikran's heart hurt at the mental image of a young Damir trying to save his dog and inadvertently killing it in a most grisly way.

"The Essence, if powerful enough, is incredibly dangerous," Damir said. "All mages know this. We learn about the mages who came before us, and while they were few and far between, there have been those as powerful and perhaps even more powerful than myself, and there no doubt will be more. The kings know this too. It's the main reason the Essence is so strictly regulated, why they seek out children who have it. If a child with powerful Essence is found before the child learns how to mask it, then that child could become a weapon. Luckily, using the Essence to kill physically hurts. Killing those plants and drying the earth made my hands ache. When I accidentally killed the dog, it felt as though there was liquid fire in my veins."

"Does Bilguun know the extent of your power?"

"No. No one does." He smiled bleakly. "Not even me, if I'm being honest. I haven't had the courage or opportunity to explore it." Damir finally pulled his hands from the dirt and dusted them off, standing. "Tikran, I have reason to believe that my powers can cause quite a bit of destruction."

Tikran put an arm around Damir's neck, desperate to show the mage some affection, but unsure of how to do it. When it came to his relationships with men, Tikran only knew how to show affection through sex. Without the physical act, however, he felt frozen, awkward. The truth was, he wasn't convinced he knew how to show love to anyone, man or woman. "Well, I'm certainly glad you're on my side."

"And I'm glad you're on mine, Manzakar," Damir said warmly, hooking his arm around Tikran's waist in return.

As they walked back to their horses, Tikran said, "We're going to have to reveal to everyone at the fort that you're a mage before we start growing gardens in the middle of Areg."

Damir snorted. "That would probably be wise."

HAYDAR WALKED at a good clip to the palace. His city house was close enough that a horse wasn't needed. He kept his expression placid as he walked, even as his mind ran in a hundred different directions. He was heading to an emergency audience with the king—in the middle of the night.

He knows.

Haydar had no way of knowing how the information was leaked or who leaked it, but with the number of ally Manzakars rising, it was bound to happen at any moment. Truth be told, he felt relieved it hadn't happened sooner. But now he had to be even more careful with his movements.

Oh, he didn't think Delger suspected him—if he had, Haydar would not be walking casually to the palace right then. He knew Delger well enough to trust that, had Delger known Haydar was involved, he'd be dead already. He'd known Delger since childhood, and the man was nothing if not petulant and impulsive. Not to mention entitled, self-absorbed, delusional, and utterly cruel when he felt threatened. But that was neither here nor there.

I just needed a little more time.

He tightened his jaw. No matter. Time was up.

The king was in his suite, fully dressed and waiting for Haydar, with Saltanat sitting behind him and his Aslans forming a semi-circle around them. His eyes were icy blue, his hands balled into fists. "Lord Haydar," he said, his voice low. "How has this happened?"

Haydar frowned. "My king, I made a mistake with Tikran.

And Coxani, for that matter. When they first arrived here, I saw such spirit in their little faces that—"

"Haydar," Delger said, "you dimwit! That's not what I'm talking about. I'm talking about the fact that there is an entire resistance movement plotting a coup against me, right here in Anzor City!" He stood, overturning a table laden with plates of food and snarling. "Who is this Enlil the Weaver?"

Haydar blinked. "Who, Your Highness?"

"Haydar, I swear to Cenk, sometimes I think you're the smartest man in Anzor, and other times I think you're the biggest idiot Anzor has ever given the privilege of enslaving." He was pacing, his favorite pastime. "Who can I trust? Who among my lords is betraying me?" He spun on his heels and glared at the Manzakars in the room. "Who among my very own Aslans is betraying me, for that matter?"

"Your Highness," Haydar said, "Before you begin accusing the very people who have dedicated their lives to your service and sworn to die protecting you, let's discuss this rationally. Based on the fact that I knew nothing of this, I can promise you it is likely a small faction of malcontents that we can eliminate with ease. Now, tell me what you know, and we'll decide what our course of action will be."

Delger looked behind him. "Ayaz, come forth and tell Lord Haydar what you have told me."

The commander of the Aslans stepped forward, only the spastic sliding of his throat revealing his apprehension. "My lord, I was in the royal stable and overheard several Manzakars speak in low voices about the Caged Kingfisher's capture of Areg. One of them said to the other, 'If you would join his cause, then come with us to the Loom tonight. We anticipate a message from Enlil the Weaver.'"

"Ah," Haydar said. "So it's something that must have cropped up recently because of Tikran. In that case, Your Highness, this little uprising will still be in its infancy and easily crushed."

Delger tugged at his beard anxiously. "I certainly hope you're right. Ayaz, do you know the identity of the Manzakar who spoke?"

"I don't. But I got a look at his face and I'm certain I could recognize him if I saw him again," Ayaz said.

Haydar smiled. "Perfect. Ayaz will be our spy. Ayaz, find the young man in question and quietly tell him you want to join Tikran's cause. He will tell you the location of this Loom and we will have found the nest."

"I want the identity of this Enlil the Weaver. I want him dealt with quickly." Delger glowered at Haydar. "I am willing to bet that Coxani knows who he is. I would have Revaz questioned again if he hadn't just sent his Manzakars to fight with Nasch in my name. Revaz is a blue-blood Anzori and my cousin. He's the last person on the Continent who would betray me."

"If we can find the Loom, Your Highness, we will likely find Coxani as well," Haydar said, fully aware that Coxani was with Revaz's squadron and preparing to head out of Anzor as they spoke.

Delger's mouth lifted in a cruel, cynical smile. "Indeed. I look forward to making an example of all of them."

CHAPTER 25

Naran had no trouble getting into Anzor or through the gates to Anzor City. The soldiers saw his Manzakar uniform and gave him immediate entry. *What's going on?* Even after the uprisings in Areg and Otebek, Delger was letting Manzakars into the city freely? Haydar must have had a hand in it.

Naran had covered his distinct hair and wore another Manzakar's heraldic emblem on his arm as he headed directly to the Crooked Street Inn. There, he'd be able to speak to an ally about what had happened since he'd left and get better information on how Coxani was doing and where she was. Hiding in an alley down the street from the inn, he removed his Manzakar armor and uniform and shoved them in his sack, then shrouded himself in a long, hooded cloak. Shouldering his sack, he turned out of the alleyway and started toward the inn.

"Naran? Is that you?"

He turned, his hand on his saber, his heart hammering. If the king's men got their hands on him, he was done for. He blinked. "Jan? What are you—?"

The Manzakar shook his head almost imperceptibly, widening his eyes. He jerked his head to the side, indicating Naran should follow him. Naran kept his hand on his sword as he followed. Last he knew, Jan was a king's man, and therefore technically a danger to him. However, what Jan was doing outside the Citadel—and directly in front of the Crooked Street Inn—was a mystery to him. Jan led him through several twists and turns back into a dark, abandoned alley, then stopped and turned.

"What the fuck are you doing here?" Jan's voice was low but severe. "Everyone knows about Otebek. You should be almost to Areg by now!"

"I needed to stop by—" Naran hesitated. Could he trust Jan? "Where's Coxani?"

Jan was shaking his head. "I don't know. Information has been sparse since... Listen, you need to get out of Anzor. Thank Cenk I stopped you before you wandered into the inn. An informant tipped off the king. The inn was raided and at least fifty rebels were caught. I'm one of the Manzakars tasked with guarding the place." He looked over Naran's shoulder. "I have to return to my post, and you need to leave immediately."

As he brushed past, Naran said, "Wait! Jan, how do you feel about the oranges this time of year?"

Jan briefly looked over his shoulder and smiled. "Sweet as fuck." Then he hurried away, his armor clinking.

Naran stood idly, trying to think what to do next. Where was Coxani? There was only one place left for him to look, and it would lead him directly into the Citadel. *So be it.* He waited until the sky grew dark, then returned to his Manzakar's uniform. He expected it would allow him entrance into the Citadel, unless someone recognized him. Not for the first time in his life, he cursed his size and distinct yellow dreadlocks. He could hide the hair but was stuck with his towering frame. He would have to join a caravan and hope he didn't stand out.

He waited until a caravan crossed the moat to the gate and followed. The men who guarded the gates to the Citadel were not Manzakars and the chances of being recognized by city soldiers were slim. As he'd predicted, the guards were busy checking the wagons in the caravan and he passed through without issue. He would have exhaled with relief, but the hardest part was yet to come—he had to pass by the barracks to reach Nasch's house.

It was the only place she could be. If she were anywhere else, *someone* would surely have mentioned her whereabouts to him. The only other place he could think to look was Haydar's manor, which was next on his list. He strode through the Citadel, careful not to draw too much attention to himself as he passed the barracks. Luckily, none of the Manzakars paid him any mind. After what felt like far too long, he reached Nasch's house. His heart rate kicked up as he rang the bell. The door swung open and Naran found himself looking into a pair of startled lavender eyes. *What the...?*

A broad smile crept across Saltanat's face. "Lion! What an unexpected surprise!"

Naran began to draw his sword when three Manzakars tackled him, managing to take his weapons and restrain him as he struggled against them.

Saltanat giggled almost compulsively, as though she could hardly contain her mirth. She pressed herself against him and said, "King Delger will be so pleased to see you, Stalking Lion. In fact, you're one of three people he's simply *dying* to see."

TIKRAN BUCKLED his lamellar cuirass over his shoulders, then fastened his plated shoulder armor under his arms. He pulled on his helmet with the mail aventail in the back and strapped on his sword belt, from which all his weapons hung. Finally, he mounted his horse and rode calmly from the stables. Nasch and his Manzakars were but hours away, and the Manzakars of the Caged Kingfisher were as ready as they would ever be. Bruneta and her nomads had been given the imprisoned soldiers' armor and weapons, and all of the rebels' helmets and cuirasses had been adorned with strips of black leather to distinguish them from the king's men.

As Tikran rode from the stables toward the fort, he saw them wait for him: A small sea of black striped Manzakars and nomads, standing under a bright but cloudy sky, their gaze on their leader. His eyes swept briefly to Damir, who himself sat amongst the soldiers, armed and armored.

Tikran stopped and drew an unsteady breath. He was keenly aware of his tunic's rough texture against his skin, the weight of the weapons around his waist. In the distance, a crested lark chirped and trilled as though today was just another day. When he finally spoke, the words sprang from his heart, unscripted. "I can't, in good conscience, ask you to fight with me today. We're badly outnumbered, and this may very well be our last day in the realm of the living. And yet, even if I'm the only man fighting on that battlefield, my blood is hot and my mind is completely free of doubt. Manzakars, our people have been suffering by our hands. Our mothers and fathers and sisters and brothers—whether we remember them or not—have been dying in droves by order of King Delger. Our families sold us because they were coerced—they had no real choice. They were told that they were doing the right thing for us. What they didn't know is that Anzor has kept the Essence from Gohar for the very purpose of stealing their children to feed their armies and to amass the power of the magic for themselves. This is no act of an angry god. This is the act of self-seeking men." He was shouting now, his words thick with passion. "I was once a proud Manzakar. There was nothing I wanted more than to serve the king. I dreamed of becoming a Manzakar, then an Aslan, then a durai, each one a crumb that led to an illusion of freedom. I'm done with illusions. I'm done living a lie. I will not live for a cruel king, and I will not live as a slave. And if that means I die today, then I die for Gohar, a free man."

The sound of hundreds of lances pounding the earth broke through the silence like rolling thunder. He drew his saber and held it aloft, signaling the start of what could be a very brief, very brutal battle.

Bruneta rode to him, smiling. "Inspirational speech, brother."

He shrugged. "It's how I really feel."

"Yes. Which is what makes it so effective." She reached over and squeezed his hand. "We're off, then." Bruneta would lead the flight archers toward Nasch's troops and do what the nomads did best—tormenting their attackers by riding up, loosing a hailstorm of arrows, and retreating quickly.

"Bruneta," Tikran said, "be careful. They'll be prepared for you with their own flight archers playing the same game."

She grinned from underneath her helmet. "Their archers don't know Gohar like we do." With that, she wheeled away, shouting for her small squadron of lightly armored archers. Tikran thought of Coxani. *She and Bruneta would get along.*

"Manzakar." Damir approached, his eyes limpid. "I will say this once again: You need me on the front lines. I can—"

"Absolutely not." Tikran sliced his hand through the air. "You will stay at the fort where—"

"Tikran! Listen to me," Damir snapped. "I can do more damage to their numbers if I'm on the ground. You know this."

Tikran clenched his jaw. "No. You will wait at the fort until the time is right, then Tural will escort you to me."

"Are you hearing yourself?" Damir said. "You have no qualms about sending your own sister to skirmish against the enemy but you won't let me stay on the ground and fight with you?"

"My sister is a warrior," Tikran said.

Through clenched teeth, Damir said, "I am a mage. And in case you've already forgotten, a *very* powerful one. You need to stop thinking of yourself, Commander. Without me, your soldiers are done for."

Tikran met Damir's furious gaze. He was afraid the doctor was right. *But if something happens to him...* "Fine. Try and stay with me if you can."

Damir's eyes softened. "I will."

Tikran's eyes focused on the still-quiet horizon. Nasch's heavy cavalry would be positioned behind the infantry, with the cavalry archers in the wings. The cavalry would be in line formation, waiting for the infantry line to open up and allow them to charge through and strike Tikran's army in the flank. They would make limited attacks and withdrawals, alternating units to prevent any one from growing too fatigued. Tikran's men would use a different tactic, since their smaller numbers put them at a major disadvantage. His mounted archers would pack together closely in various units and shoot en masse at high speeds. The standard bearer would be among them, holding a solid black banner aloft. They had a decent supply of arrows that would be run out to the cavalry by swift nomads. Two units of flight archers, bearing their own standards, would attack the flanks while a third would shoot from a distance, standing along the battlements of the fort. The men at the fort would also catapult firepots—small, round clay pots filled with flammable oils—at the enemy as they approached, and Damir would ensure any fires inflicted on Tikran's men would be promptly extinguished. While Damir had the ability to put out a normal fire by withdrawing oxygen, which was something the other mages were unable to do, a larger or mage-controlled fire would have to be quenched with rain, however briefly. If there was enough rain, the grounds would become muddy and fighting difficult.

And mud was the main reason Damir wanted to be on the ground.

Damir's plan, incidentally, was the primary reason Tikran wasn't going to predominantly defend from the fort. Besides, allowing Nasch's men to lay siege on Areg's pitiful fort would do nothing but expedite the rebels' defeat.

Tikran chewed on the inside of his cheek. He hadn't seen Damir work the earth on a large scale, but he believed the doctor that it was possible. As unreal as Damir's idea sounded, if successful, it could be what saved them all. Tikran's problem was his practicality—magic was all good and well, but it wasn't what Manzakars learned. He didn't trust what he didn't know.

The flight archers suddenly appeared in the distance, galloping toward Tikran, Bruneta's saber raised. He nodded then turned and signaled to Tural, who watched from the fort. A great battle-cry went up, and Tikran's rebel Manzakars began to move across the grassy plain. With Damir at his side, Tikran rode in the rear, his eyes razor-focused on the hazy horizon. The arrows rained down on them several times before they saw Nasch's men—which Tikran had expected. No doubt Bruneta was showering his troops in return. When the king's Manzakars finally emerged from clouds of dust, lamellar armor glinting, horse hooves pounding, it seemed like their lines stretched through all of Gohar. Tikran shouted orders and encouragement to his men, but meanwhile his chest was tight with fear. He had to stop thinking defeated thoughts—it was doing no one, least of all his men, any good. *I will go down fighting with these courageous Manzakars proudly.* He pulled his bow from his hip and held it behind his shield along with six arrows.

The shouts of men, along with the jangle of armor and harness, marked the start of the battle. The air reverberated with the sounds of arrows whistling and bows twanging, and eventually, maces and lances crashing. The king's cavalry archers rode up from the sides and Tikran fired steadily at them, moving from right to left. Every time his tightly knit bowmen created a break in the enemy's cavalry lines, more would flood in, filling the gap. Behind him, a catapult was released and earthen fire pots soared into the enemy's midst. *We're not even putting a dent in them.* Shouts became screams as men fell around him, even as he continued to loose his arrows in all directions, one after the other. Unnatural fires began to catch among the rebels and Damir called the rain, torrential and blinding. The fighting paused as men and horses stumbled beneath the weight of the water, struggling for purchase on the soggy ground. Then the rain stopped abruptly and the clashing of weapons resumed.

Nock... Draw... Anchor... Aim... Release...

Tikran's arrow joined the volley from his archers. The arrows soared, crossing paths with the enemy's volley mid-air. "Shields!" Tikran yelled, and as the rebel Manzakars covered themselves, the arrows pelted against iron, steel, and wood in a rapid staccato. One of his men let out a lurid scream as an arrow lodged in his eye, knocking him from his horse. A lump formed in Tikran's throat as he forced himself forward, swearing he would learn the names of every man who died today if he survived. In the distance, the rebels' arrows landed with a chorus of screams. A horse's knee shattered as it fell, taking its rider with it. Both were trampled by oncoming horsemen who were likewise battered by rebel arrows.

"Lances!" Tikran yelled, as the enemy cavalry charged. Tikran and his men leaped into action, their horses soon at full gallop. A man Tikran recognized from his youth led the king's men. *What was his name? Elnur.* They'd been fencing partners as cadets. Now, they lowered their lances at each other, anticipating the inevitable collision. A firepot launched from the fort landed between them in that moment, setting Elnur on fire. He cried out, boiling in his armor as the rain surged down on them. Tikran's horse reared back as lances shattered around them, sending splinters through the air like assassins' knives.

"Commander!" Tural rode up to Tikran swiftly, lance in hand, dirt and sweat trickling down his face. "More Manzakars coming from the west, hundreds of them."

Oh, shit. "The king's men?"

"I don't know. Red ribbons are streaming from their helmets and they bear red banners. Does it mean something?"

Tikran shook his head. "It could mean nothing—or everything. Tell Bruneta not to shoot at them yet. Watch them and report back as soon as you know."

He nodded and rushed away, kicking his mount into a full gallop.

A young nomad replenished Tikran's quiver with arrows scavenged from the battlefield and quickly rode back to the fort. The only reason an army of Manzakars would try to distinguish themselves with ribbons was if they were fighting with the rebels. *Naran?* He didn't want to get hopeful. Another fire caught directly in front of him, and three horsemen screamed in terror. Immediately, water gushed from the sky, knocking the men and their horses to the ground with force.

Tikran spun in a circle, blinking rain from his eyelashes, looking for Damir. Where was he? Tikran clenched his jaw. He had to hope the doctor wasn't doing anything reckless.

He rode back, scanning the melee before him, and his heart sank. The king's Manzakars were closing around them, line after endless line of horsemen. The rebels' black standard still flapped in the wind, but Tikran imagined it wouldn't for much longer. He drew his saber to encourage his men forward when Damir was suddenly beside him again.

"Tikran, have your men retreat quickly several meters," he said between breaths. "I need a gap between them and the enemy."

"All right, but I'm escorting you to the front," Tikran said. He wasn't sure what Damir was about to do, but they were desperate. He had Tural sound a horn, signaling the horsemen on the front lines to continue shooting while falling back. Then he and Damir rode to the front while Tikran shot his arrows and both men blocked the rapid fire of enemy arrows with their shields. Behind Tikran, Damir slipped from his horse, holding his shield aloft, and crouched to the wet earth. Tikran drew his sword as the king's cavalry charged toward them, maces swinging and lances poised.

Tikran shouted, "Whatever you're going to do, Damir, do it now!"

His horse suddenly spooked, jumping to the side, as the ground beneath its hooves rumbled and shifted. Like an ocean's wave, the ground surged upward thunderously between him and the oncoming horsemen. For several minutes, Tikran couldn't see past the rolling wall of muddy earth and grass that rose as tall as five men and extended to the left and right as far as he could see. Beyond the roar of the moving ground, desperate, terrified screams arose. Behind him somewhere a fire ignited, and almost immediately the rain fell in sheets. The wall was fully mud now, and it began its undulating descent forward. As the earth leveled out before him, he saw the men and horses drowned or suffocating in the mud, arms flailing and grasping desperately, lances and helmets half-buried. Tikran sucked in his breath in horror. Hundreds of men were down, and the enemy stood at the other end of the sea of devastation at least two hundred yards away. They began to advance again, their blue, mud-splattered Anzori banner still fluttering in the air.

Damir mounted his horse. The doctor was pale, his eyes stormy. Tikran said, "Go! I'm behind you." Shooting his arrows to the rear, Tikran followed Damir back to the waiting troops and ordered them back into ranks. Damir's trick had done some serious damage to the king's Manzakars, but he worried that, even if they weren't outnumbered anymore, they were in dire need of more arrows—most of which were now buried in mud. They would likely have to retreat to the fort.

As his horsemen met the enemy once again, Tikran couldn't help but notice that the king's cavalry was struggling to keep formation and falling into disarray. He sought the reason for it, squinting into the distance, and finally caught sight of the Manzakars with the red banners on the flanks of the enemy, waves of them, firing their arrows into the enemy's midst. *Oh, thank Cenk!* He drew his sword and let out a battle-cry, urging his troops on. *For Gohar!* His front lines were holding, breaking through the enemy and engaging in hand-to-hand combat, while the red rebel Manzakars were crippling the flanks. He was beginning to see an end to this that wasn't total defeat and his heart surged with hope.

It was then that he spotted Nasch on the fringe of the melee, watching him. Even from a distance, Tikran could see the murder in his eyes. Tikran turned and signaled to Tural, who quickly approached. "Take command. I need to take care of something."

He reined his horse back around to face Nasch, who was still watching him. Tikran approached slowly, nodded at him, and drew his sword. *Come and get me.*

It was time to finish this.

CHAINED by his wrists from the ceiling in the middle of a dark prison cell and stripped to his breeches, Naran was forced to stand. *I really walked right into that, didn't I?* He sighed deeply, frustrated that he'd spent so much of his time in Otebek being a pathetic excuse of a human being, frustrated that he still didn't know where Coxani was. He was quickly realizing how completely the mischievous, green-eyed Manzakar had consumed him. She was, besides Tikran, pretty much all he cared about. In fact, she was what he cared about above all else. He should have been on the battlefield with Tikran. Instead, he'd walked right into the lion's den looking for her.

He glanced up, jerked at the chains. His back wasn't entirely healed, and another flogging would be... rough, to say the least. He heard a clang and voices. *Here goes.* The iron door to his cell opened and in swept Delger, Saltanat, Haydar, and a large cleric. Naran kept his eyes on Delger's face, deliberately not looking at Haydar. The king stood before him, his hands behind his back, his lips downturned, his gaze fixed on the ground. He said, "We caught around fifty of the Caged Kingfisher's rebels at the Crooked Street Inn several days ago. They've been thoroughly interrogated. It's clear they don't know the identity of Enlil the Weaver." He looked up at Naran and stepped closer. "But I'm willing to bet *you* do, Stalking Lion."

Naran met the king's gaze steadily. "I have no idea what you're talking about, Your Highness."

Delger laughed. "How easily devotion rots, eh Haydar?"

"Indeed, Your Highness," Haydar answered. Naran's eyes darted quickly to the durai's face to see a hint of fear. *Haydar? Afraid?* Naran swallowed. *Delger must be close to figuring it all out.* Naran wished he could reassure the old Manzakar: there was no way the king was getting Enlil's identity out of him.

Delger bared his teeth at Naran. "Unless you tell me the identity of this Enlil the Weaver, I will have you flogged to within an inch of your life, Naran. But rest assured, I will not kill you. No, you will dangle between life and death until you tell me what you know. Do you understand?" Naran made no answer but kept his eyes even with the king's in defiance. Delger nodded, then turned to the whip-bearing cleric. "Just don't kill him. Yet."

Naran clenched his jaw as the flogging began, the lashes biting through his half-healed flesh, over and over again. *Five... six...* The knotted tails tore through him, alive with fire, as he grew dizzier, retching and twisting helplessly. *Thirteen... fourteen...* His vision blurred before everything faded to black.

When he opened his eyes again, his back was an inferno and his arms ached. He forced his legs to bear his weight in order to take the pressure off his arms. He teetered, groaning in pain. He opened his eyes and the room whirled before him, shapes and colors slowly forming faces and bodies. The cleric stood before him and nodded, readying his whip and walking around him. *Oh, fuck, no.* This would surely kill him. The cleric administered just two full lashes when waves of pain consumed him, rendering him unconscious.

He had no idea how long it took to regain his senses this time around, but it was long enough that he found himself bound to a chair, his shredded back pressed against slats of wood. He didn't even have the strength to cry out in agony. Everything was sticky with his blood, which dripped from his body to his bound hands. Somewhere in the back of his consciousness, he heard the door to his cell clang open and shut. At this point, he hoped it was the cleric coming to finish him off. He opened his eyes and saw a flash of red flutter as his vision swam back into focus. The nauseatingly sweet scent of perfume wafted at him through the metallic smell of his blood.

"Stalking Lion," Saltanat said softly. "Let me help you. Will you let me help you?"

Naran blinked the haze from his eyes and tried to focus on the mage. He licked his dry lips. "What do you want?" His voice sounded foreign to him.

Saltanat kneeled before him and placed a hand on his thigh, her face a mask of concern. "Tell me the identity of this weaver, and I will have Delger release you," she said softly.

Despite everything, Naran tried to grin. "Oh, yeah? I have no idea who this weaver is. Tell your king..."

The mage's lavender eyes went cold and her lips lifted in cruel delight. "Well, then." She stood and pulled a dagger from her robe. She ran her forefinger along its blade as she said, "Coxani and I had several heart-to-heart conversations, you know. Between women." Naran tried his best not to show any interest in her words. She continued. "After all, she and I have much in common, not least of which are the men we've been intimate with." Naran felt bile rising from his gut. Saltanat continued. "I told her about our passionate nights together in Gohar, which upset her quite a bit..."

Naran found the strength to growl at her. "That never happened."

The mage giggled. "I know. But she certainly believed it did. I told her how spectacular you were in bed."

He sucked in his breath and closed his eyes. Holy Cenk,

why wouldn't they just finish him already? As if in response, he felt a flash of pain across the front of his left shoulder. His eyes sprang open to see blood bloom from a line of cut flesh and drip from her blade. She smiled at him as she carefully swiped a drop of his blood from the tip of the dagger and licked it from her finger.

"You're seriously sick," Naran muttered, turning his head away.

She laughed. "You know, Nasch and I have been lovers for quite a while. So when he married Coxani, he asked me to help her prepare for her wedding night."

Against his better judgment, Naran began to struggle against his constraints. *No. I can't hear this.* She must have seen the panic in him, because her face lit with pleasure. She kneeled again, her hand kneading his thigh. "I watched, Naran. I watched Nasch take her. He brought her to pleasure again and again..."

She's lying. She's trying to torture you. Despite his internal pep talk, Naran heard himself cry out in anguish as he fought against the chains, feeling the metal slice into his wrists, seeing nothing but the red of his rage. Saltanat laughed and he felt her blade slash across the front of his right shoulder in a streak of pain. He saw and tasted his blood, then sank back into that sea of darkness where he felt nothing.

No words were exchanged—no words were needed. They rode a small distance away from the melee and turned to face each other across a stretch of dry grass. A strange calm settled over Tikran as he looked at Nasch, his eyes resting on the flaming chalice briefly. He mentally skimmed through every offense Nasch had committed. Delger's favorite commander would continue to commit them if Tikran didn't stop him. The sounds around Tikran faded to a muffle—the clash of metal, the stomping of horses, the shouts of the soldiers. His vision crystallized and the rhythm of his heart slowed. Every sensation was briefly heightened, from the roughness of his saber's grip, slightly moist against his palm, to the pinch of his armor's strap under one arm. Then it all fell away as Nasch held out his sword, curled his lip over his teeth, and kicked his horse into action with a roar. Tikran moved quickly, looping around to pick up momentum as Nasch approached, nearly at a gallop. Nasch dipped the tip of his sword behind his back and sliced at Tikran diagonally as they closed on each other. Tikran countered with a thrust, and the steel of their blades clashed with such force it made his teeth ache. They circled around and came at each other again, and this time Nasch swung with a cut from above. Tikran parried the blow, but Nasch wrenched his sword around and, as he passed, swung again and hit Tikran in the upper calf.

Pain shot through Tikran's leg and erupted behind his eyes for a brief instant. Still, he didn't stop preparing for his next move, riding back around, knowing that now, while pain consumed him, would be when Nasch would try and end it. As he'd predicted, Nasch came in hacking, trying once again for Tikran's leg, but this time Tikran parried. The pain receded into the background, along with everything else, save for Nasch, who swung up and chopped down. The tip of his saber bounced off Tikran's helmet and chimed like a bell, making Tikran's ears ring. For a brief moment, everything felt surreal, as if in a dream, and he couldn't feel the wound in his calf. Nasch slashed down on him again and Tikran blocked it, jolted back into reality. Their blades locked, the steel rattling as both men trembled with effort. Their faces were inches away from each other, and the men's eyes met.

There was no humanity in Nasch's pools of black, only hatred. Tikran clenched his teeth, his muscles quaking. Sweat streamed from Nasch's hairline down across his eyebrow.

Nasch suddenly flinched and grunted. An arrow buried itself in the back of Nasch's left arm, giving Tikran the opportunity to shove Nasch's saber away and loop around. He made a wide circle, giving himself the chance to once again gain momentum as Nasch readied himself, ignoring the arrow in his arm. Tikran charged then, anticipating Nasch's cut from above. He caught Nasch's saber with his own and immediately thrust, letting the impetus of his moving horse do the work. *This is it.* With a hissing exhale through his teeth, Tikran twisted the tip of his sword as he drove it into Nasch's throat.

For Coxani.

For every Gohari you've starved and killed.

For my mother.

Blood sprayed Tikran as he rode past. He dropped the hilt of his saber, gasping. He heard Nasch fall from his horse with a thud, his armor clanging. Tikran dismounted, his leg throbbing, his entire body shaking, and yanked off his helmet. He was covered in Nasch's fresh, dark blood, wet from the rain, spattered with mud. He limped over to his opponent, who was unconscious and dying; blood gushed and gurgled from his open throat. Tikran leaned down and picked up his saber, dragging his eyes away, feeling dizzy, nauseous, and short of breath. He felt no remorse, and yet...

"Tikran! Tikran!"

A flight archer ripped off her red-ribboned helmet and leaped from her horse, her green eyes on him. *Coxani.* He began to lower himself to his knees as she grabbed him, crying, going down with him. Her hair tickled his nose. He managed to say, "Was that your arrow?"

She looked at him with watery eyes. "Of course. I couldn't just watch—"

"He won't hurt you anymore. He won't hurt anyone anymore," he muttered hoarsely, wiping the blood from his mouth with the back of his hand and burying his face in her curls.

"Holy Cenk." Damir stood over them, helmet off, even paler than before, looking at Nasch's body. Then he kneeled in front of Tikran, a faint smile on his lips. "It's over, Tikran. It's done."

Tikran tried to stand. "I have to... Tural is waiting for—"

"Commander," Tural said, "it's over. We've won. Whatever was left of them—and there weren't many—retreated. Can you stand?"

Tikran stood a bit too abruptly in response, then limped forward, his eyes scanning the distance. Manzakar bodies littered the field, which now had a ridge of earth running across it. Smoke rose from extinguished fires and the air was filled with a devastating silence. He asked Tural, "How many did we lose?"

"We're missing two hundred of them, Commander," Tural answered gravely.

"We have to look for survivors." Tikran stumbled forward.

"Commander," Tural said, "I have men looking now. Go tend to your wound."

"Two hundred, Tural," Tikran said, his voice breaking. "I was looking at their trusting, brave faces just a few hours ago, about to lead them to their deaths." He would have started sobbing right then if a shout didn't suddenly ring out.

"Victory for the Caged Kingfisher!"

It was followed by the haunting sound of hundreds of lances beating the ground. Tikran turned to face what was left of his army and saw their exhausted, bloody, dirty faces lit with awe as they gazed on him. Bruneta was among them, her eyes bright with hope. He held up his hand and the drumming stopped. They probably expected some valiant words on strength and honor, on how they'd won against all odds, on how Cenk must favor them. Instead, in a voice that hardly sounded like his own, he said, "We did it." The drumming resumed in earnest. He licked his dry lips and tasted blood— likely not his own. He turned to Coxani and Damir. "I need a bath."

Damir glanced down at Tikran's leg. "You also need a doctor... again."

"Where's Naran?" Coxani asked, her brow furrowed with sudden concern. "He should be here."

Tikran turned to Tural. "Where are the Manzakars from Otebek?"

Tural shook his head. "I don't know. I don't think they ever made it."

Tikran's heart dropped, but he immediately turned to Coxani and said, "They're probably just running late. I'm certain their trip was a bit more treacherous than they'd anticipated."

Coxani was not pacified. "Tikran, what if something happened to him?"

"Coxani, Naran isn't helpless. And he's with other Manzakars. Plus, they're coming from the north and it *is* winter, after all."

She nodded. "Maybe you're right. But I suddenly have this urgent need to get back to Anzor."

He nodded and sighed deeply. "So do I. Hopefully when we get there, we're greeted with more friends than foes. Another battle like this one and we're done for."

That night, Areg's fort was filled to the rafters with Manzakars. Many spilled out into the inn or stayed in tents. Tikran was happy that, at the very least, they had enough food to go around, thanks to Damir's Essence. After scrubbing himself in a tub of hot water and letting Damir dress his new wound, Tikran sat in a hall crowded with soldiers, eating vegetable stew, drinking ale, and listening as they processed the events of the day, whether through contemplative discussion, prideful boasts, or intoxicated grieving.

"What are you thinking about?" Damir asked, nudging Tikran with his elbow. Coxani looked over as well, as if interested to hear his answer.

Tikran frowned, rubbing his temples. "So that was it. That was battle. It's... more horrific than I ever imagined." He gazed at the flames that danced in the fireplace. "I don't know what I expected, exactly. I knew there would be gruesome death. But the death of a theoretical enemy, or one I've imagined is pure evil, is one thing. The gruesome death of someone you know nothing about, who mirrors your fear, your humanity..." He swallowed. "My entire life has led up to this. They train us to believe it leads to glory and honor, that it's righteous and just." He stopped and smiled sadly. "And yet, as I watched the battle today, I could only think about all these people ready to kill each other because a few men want more than their fair share." He felt Coxani's warm hand on his.

"Tikran," she said, smiling wistfully, "you would be—"

"Commander," Tural interrupted as he strode briskly towards them from the front of the hall. "The Otebek Manza-kars are here."

Coxani stood up so suddenly her chair screeched and fell back. Tikran followed her outside into the cold night, his eyes seeking Naran. The commander of the squadron, a young fellow named Moti, explained, "It took much longer than we'd anticipated. The weather in the north is getting worse, I swear. I can't believe we missed everything!"

"Be glad you did," Tikran muttered.

"Where's Naran?" Coxani asked, the panic in her voice apparent.

Moti looked at her and his eyes widened. "Are you Coxani?"

She nodded.

"Fuck." Moti swallowed. "Naran went back to Anzor City to find you."

CHAPTER 26

For the first time in his life, Haydar was terrified.

The news of Tikran's triumph over the king's army of two thousand Manzakars had spread more quickly than a mage's fire, and Anzor City was in a state of dangerous agitation. The small seed of discontent that was planted those decades ago when he was just a boy had grown and was ready to bear fruit. If he was being honest with himself, he hadn't believed he'd see it happen in his lifetime. But from the moment Tikran had stepped foot in Gohar, things had progressed very quickly.

Almost too quickly.

And now, Naran's life hung by a thread, and Delger hovered around that thread with shears, aching to snip away. Tikran, Coxani, and Damir were, according to Tural's last message, racing back to Anzor as swiftly as possible, but if Haydar didn't act, they would arrive too late.

He sat with the king and all his advisors, mages, durais, and Manzakar commanders in a council of war. With the help of Lord Revaz and Tikran's stunning victory, they had swayed another Anzori lord to join them. But they were still outnumbered, and the most powerful lords—particularly Lords Gennadius and Prem—still stood with the king—some firmly and openly, others a little more ambivalently. Without the majority on his side, the coup would fail, and all those brave Manzakars, noblemen, and nomads would pay with their lives.

"...isn't that right, Lord Haydar?"

"Hmm?" Haydar blinked, finding all eyes on him.

"Forgive Lord Haydar," Delger said, a sardonic hint in his voice. "He is heartbroken by the betrayal of some of his favorite Manzakars, one of which will die a grisly death in my prison unless he tells me the identity of the Caged Kingfisher's right-hand man."

Haydar touched the dagger at his hip beneath the table. He glanced quickly at Jan and Kazbek, the two Aslans who flanked the king. Then he said, "Your Highness, I know the identity of Enlil the Weaver."

Delger stared. When he finally spoke, his voice was quiet, threatening. "Do you?"

Haydar smiled. "Indeed." He leaned back in his chair. "*I* am Enlil the Weaver."

At first, the king laughed out loud. His laughter echoed throughout the otherwise quiet hall, tinny and hollow. Haydar remained still, his expression unchanged, meeting the king's gaze. *Yes, Delger. I am your greatest enemy. I always have been, always will be.* A fraction of a moment's silence was all it took. Something shifted, as though someone had thrown a window open and let the cold winter air into the hall. A few men around the table shuffled, muttered, gasped. Some even began to slowly stand. The Aslans moved immediately, surrounding the king in their protective wall.

"Let me warn everyone here that a single whistle from me will summon hundreds of Manzakar rebels waiting outside this hall," Haydar continued, still sitting back comfortably. "I don't think any of us want to see blood spilled, so gentlemen, please resume your seats."

Reluctantly, the men obeyed, their hands on the hilts of their daggers. Delger's red-rimmed eyes were fixed on Haydar, who could see the horror, rage, indignation, and hurt in the king's face. And yet, Haydar felt nothing but contempt.

In a dangerous voice, the king said, "You seem to have forgotten that you are a *slave*. Without me, you are nothing but a savage, mere shit on the heel of my shoe."

Yes. Haydar had counted on this side of Delger emerging. He glanced around the table at the darker-skinned faces. "I believe that would apply to several of us here, then, wouldn't it?" His confidence growing, Haydar continued, "Delger, several of us have long believed you are unfit to rule Anzor, and your recent mismanagement of Gohar and the Caged King-fisher has compelled us to act." He looked at the men around him. "To those of you who would see Delger peacefully deposed, raise your hand."

Three hands went up immediately. Then a forth and a fifth, and a sixth...

Delger stood abruptly and his Aslans moved in closer, facing outward, their sabers drawn. His eyes fixed on Haydar, Delger's chest rose and fell rapidly beneath his red suede tunic as he slowly removed his turban and set it carefully on the table before him. "You still don't have a majority, Haydar. I will see you hanged yet."

His voice slithered into Haydar's mind as it had innumerable times in their youth when Delger was feeling cruel, particularly when he'd intended to use Haydar as a scapegoat for some perceived offense. It still had the power to inspire dread in Haydar, even after all these years. "Give me time, Orwen," Haydar replied calmly, calling Delger by his given name—

something he had done only a handful of times their entire relationship, and only after accepting that there would be repercussions for doing so.

And there was no doubt Delger intended repercussions now.

Delger laughed. It was a genuine laugh, Haydar knew. *He thinks he's won.* Haydar himself would have believed it, too, if he didn't have one or two tricks up his sleeve... tricks he desperately hoped would come through.

"Haydar," Delger said, that condescending gleam in his eye, his mouth twisted with promises of pain, "surely you see you're doomed."

As Haydar's mind raced, desperate for ways to stall, a clamor at the door of the great hall caused the council to rise, hands at their daggers. Lord Revaz burst in, accompanied by Lord Gennadius. "Has the council commenced?" Revaz asked, pretending to sound unconcerned.

Oh, thank fucking Cenk. Haydar nearly blacked out with relief.

"It has." Baring his teeth in smile that was more of a grimace, Delger hissed, "And Haydar has confessed to being Enlil the Weaver."

"Indeed," Revaz said, his cheeks flushed, his chest puffed. "Because we are here in support of him."

Haydar looked at Delger steadily even though he felt anything but steady. His hand touched the hilt of his saber. They still needed one more vote.

"Revaz," Delger uttered with a mortified wheeze. "My own kin. I can't believe it." His eyes darted about frantically. "You still don't have a majority, Haydar. All of you will hang."

"Not so fast, Your Highness," Lord Prem, another prominent Anzori nobleman said, raising his palm. "I suspect my reasons for wanting you deposed differ from those of most of the others here, but I am with Haydar."

Haydar stood. "Delger, we are placing you under house arrest with your own Aslans to guard you. And rest assured that the ones in your company are entirely loyal to the Caged Kingfisher." He looked at Revaz. "I must tend to something urgent. Please continue to hold council until I return."

"Of course, Haydar," Revaz said and motioned for the other lords and advisors to take their seats.

Then Haydar turned to Jan and Kazbek. "Kazbek, find a doctor immediately. Jan, help me get Naran out of that cell."

The smell of blood assaulted Haydar as he hurried into the prison and approached Naran's cell. He stiffened as he saw Naran, bound to a chair, his head lolled back, smeared entirely in his own blood from head to toe. "Naran," he said as he entered the cell and kneeled before the chair, thrilled to feel a pulse in the Manzakar's neck. Naran croaked, his eyes opening just a sliver as Jan unlocked the chains around his wrists and ankles. "Naran, can you hear me?"

From between cracked, stained lips, Naran whispered, "Did we win?"

A wall of emotion slammed into Haydar then, and tears filled his eyes. He took Naran's blood-encrusted hand in his. "Yes, lad. We won."

WHEN THE GREAT walls of Anzor City finally appeared in the distance, Coxani's heart began to palpitate wildly. She, Tikran, and Damir had managed to get from Areg to Anzor in nine days by stopping infrequently and for as little time as possible. Damir's ability to summon water, food, and warmth during the Gohari winter had helped immensely, but the doctor was bone-weary from both travel and the repeated use of his Essence. They were *all* bone-weary.

Conversation was sparse among them as they dwelled on what awaited them in Anzor. Coxani hardly ate or slept as her mind inevitably returned to Naran. Delger had certainly gotten his hands on the Stalking Lion. And that meant Naran had likely been imprisoned and flogged. *The king may have killed him.* The thought made her want to double over in pain. She wanted to believe Haydar would stop it from happening if he could, despite the risk to himself or the cause, but... what if he hadn't been able to?

She knew Tikran's thoughts mirrored hers from just glancing at his face. When she tried to talk about it, Tikran refused to discuss it, shutting both her and Damir out as he rode, ate, and rested in silence, lines of worry carved around his mouth and between his eyebrows.

Hope sprang into her heart when they reached the Gohar-Anzor border and the soldiers there greeted them with reverence and smiles, letting them pass quickly. "What's happened in Anzor City?" Tikran asked one of them.

"We're not certain, Commander," the soldier answered. "Things have been quiet since the news of your victory."

Now, as they approached the gates of Anzor City, Coxani said to Tikran, "Do you think it's a trap?"

Tikran shrugged. "It might be. Although I'm not sure what that would solve for Delger. At least half of Anzor's armies are on our side. This is much bigger than us, and it will continue even if we're dead."

"Hmph," Damir uttered. "Hopefully Delger is more prudent than I think he is. He strikes me as the type of man who acts out of ego regardless of the consequences."

"That's what I'm afraid of," Coxani mumbled, her palms growing clammy against the reins.

The Citadel loomed beyond the gates; its golden turrets dull in the gray sky. When the soldiers in the guardhouses recognized Tikran, they began to shout excitedly. Tikran immediately reached for his saber, nodding briskly to Coxani and Damir. "Shields at the ready. I have no idea what to expect."

Coxani pulled her bow from its sheath and readied five arrows behind her shield, her heart still hammering away. The voices were indistinct until they came closer, then Coxani heard, "The Caged Kingfisher has returned! Victory for the Caged Kingfisher!" Several soldiers ran to greet them, cheering.

Tikran said, "What's happening in the Citadel?"

"We aren't entirely sure, Commander," one of them said, "but rumor has it that the king has been forced to step down. Our orders came directly from the palace, and they were to keep watch for you and usher you in immediately."

"Oh, holy Cenk," Coxani said breathlessly, "let it be true!"

People had begun to line the main road into the city, cheering and gawking in awe. Tikran turned to the soldier. "Keep the crowd under control. We have to get to the palace quickly."

The soldiers at the Citadel greeted them likewise with cheers, and within its walls, Manzakars filled the streets that led to the palace, all dressed in uniform and armor, standing at attention and quietly waiting. As Tikran rode in, the sound of wooden spear shafts striking stone echoed in the air like a steady drumbeat. They rode to the royal stables, gave the grooms their horses, then hurried to the palace, accompanied by a large group of Manzakars. They were led into the palace and to the great hall, where they found Haydar seated among the king's royal advisors, durais, mages, and Anzori lords, including Lord Revaz.

Haydar's eyes were lit in a way Coxani had never seen

before. Everyone stood as Tikran walked in, but he barely seemed to notice. He strode up to Haydar and said, "Naran."

"He's alive," Haydar confirmed.

Coxani heard a sob escape her mouth as her knees shook. Tikran said, "Take us to him."

Installed in a luxurious suite, Naran lay in bed, on his side, turned away from them. His back was covered thickly in dressing that was stained through with blood. Coxani covered her mouth, willing herself not to start crying uncontrollably. They walked around to see his face and her will faltered. He'd been cut repeatedly across the front of his shoulders and chest, and even his face bore thin welts, across his nose and down his cheeks. Coxani fell to her knees beside him. "Naran, Naran, Naran..."

He opened his golden eyes and, as they focused on her, the deep dimple in his cheek appeared. "Coxani," he said. "Have I died? I thought I'd never see you again."

She stroked his face gently. "Who did this to you?"

"Oh, you know," he said. "One of Cenk's thugs with a whip and a deranged mage with a dagger." His eyes moved to Tikran. "Brother. You did it. You fucking did it."

"*We* did it," Tikran said, his voice rough with emotion.

"I can't believe I missed all the action," Naran muttered. "Haydar told me about Nasch. What I wouldn't have given to see that."

Tikran flinched. "Be glad you didn't. It was... ugly."

Damir touched Naran's dressing with feather-light fingers. "Who's the idiot doctor tending to you? Tell him he's dismissed. I'm taking over."

Naran continued to smile. "Yes, Doctor."

"Tikran," Haydar said, "you're needed in the great hall now. You can return to Naran afterward. Damir, stay and tend to Naran for the moment. Coxani, it's up to you if you'd care to join us."

Coxani stood, dropping a kiss on Naran's mouth tenderly. "I'll be back."

Naran's fingers gripped hers. "I just got you back. Don't leave," he protested.

"I promise to be quick," she said, pressing his knuckles against her cheek. "I have some unfinished business with a certain mage."

WITH THE STRESS of Naran's fate lifted from his shoulders, Tikran wanted nothing more than to crumple to the floor and sleep for days. Instead, he followed Haydar back to the great hall. He felt as though he'd aged decades in just a month. No, not aged so much as transformed into someone he didn't know. He didn't recognize the man who inhabited his body. He wasn't even sure how to define his qualities or his flaws, his hopes or dreams.

Once again, everyone in the hall stood as he entered. It made him uncomfortable, seeing Anzori lords and powerful durais rise in deference to him, when he'd spent his whole life rising in deference to *them*. Haydar indicated a seat next to his at the table, and only after Tikran sat did everyone else follow suit. Delger was surrounded by Manzakars, his eyes bloodshot but gleaming angrily.

"I know I speak on behalf of everyone here when I express my utter awe in the feat you were able to accomplish in Areg," Haydar said.

"I had a lot of help. Many of your lordships sent your Manzakars to my aid," Tikran said, looking meaningfully at Revaz. "And the nomads rallied two hundred of their own for the cause as well." He paused, debating on his next words for a split second. "Finally, Doctor Damir provided Essential assistance, without which we surely would have been defeated."

"You mean *Master* Damir," Lord Gennadius interjected, scowling. "Nasty trickery from Bilguun, sending a mage to spy on Anzor."

"We can discuss the issue of Bilguun's intentions at a later time," Haydar said. "For the moment, suffice it to say that Damir was critical to the victory of the Caged Kingfisher, and for that we owe him our thanks." Haydar turned to look at Tikran. "The king's council has deemed Delger unfit as king following his egregious actions against all people of Gohari blood, within and without Anzor that, as a result, endangered the welfare of the kingdom. We believe that only a man who has been trained to protect and defend, who has seen battle firsthand and can lead his kingdom into glory, is fit for the crown. As such, the council has chosen you, Tikran of the Caged Kingfisher, as the new King of Anzor."

Tikran stared. He swore he heard Coxani choke from somewhere in the back of the hall. *What in the actual fuck?* Was this a joke? He scanned the earnest faces of the men around him, all waiting to hear him speak. *Say something.* "I'm a Manzakar," he heard himself say. "I'm no statesman."

"Exactly," Gennadius said. "We are all statesmen here to advise the king. We don't need more politicians, least of all as king. We are finished with blue-blood Anzori kings who had privileged, pampered upbringings and who don't know the first thing about leading men to battle. What we need is a warrior who inspires awe in his people and fear in his enemies."

"You are exactly what Anzor needs," Lord Bagrat concurred.

A murmur of agreement filled the hall as Tikran continued to stare, unable to believe his ears. What was he supposed to say? "Then... I suppose I'm honored." *Genius, Tikran. Good grief.*

As if he had spoken a magic spell, the hall exploded in applause. What followed was mostly a blur—questions and opinions put to him about Delger's fate (Death by execution? Forced suicide? Or perhaps just exile?), schedules for the coronation (the day after tomorrow being ideal for the council), housekeeping issues (What were his favorite foods? Did he prefer coffee or tea? How many pillows did he sleep with?)—and he had no idea what words came out of his mouth.

The hall abruptly grew quiet as shouts erupted from outside. "Your Highness, *King* Tikran," Delger scoffed from behind, his voice like gravel and tinged with glee. "You and Lord Haydar assume all the Manzakars stand with you. And that it is a serious mistake."

Tikran was on his feet and drawing his saber before the deposed king had finished speaking. The enormous double doors shuddered with the pounding of fists and weapons, and all the lords, mages, and attendants leaped from their seats in panic. The Manzakars rushed to the doors while everyone else drew what weapons they carried and scrambled back in terror.

While all eyes were fixed on the entrance, Tikran spun to face the former king—and just in the nick of time. Ayaz's saber cleaved through the air at him from the side and struck Tikran's blade hard enough that Tikran stumbled back. He quickly steadied himself as he parried a flurry of spinning horizontal strokes, keenly aware of the rage in Ayaz's face. *The man has never liked me.* Still, the need to seriously injure—if not kill—the commander of the Aslans distressed him.

"Ayaz," Tikran managed to say, moving back and away quickly to buy himself time, "is this how it ends?"

The commander hissed, "I die for my king!" He rushed

Tikran with purpose, thrusting his sword as he lunged forward. Tikran stopped Ayaz's blade and counterattacked, plunging a foot of steel into the Aslan's torso. Ayaz's eyes widened and his mouth opened, even as he continued to swing. Tikran knocked the commander's sword from his hand, grabbed the front of his jacket, and yanked his saber free of the man's body.

"I'm sorry," Tikran murmured, feeling a sharp stab of sadness in his own chest before turning and facing the pandemonium in the great hall.

The rebel Manzakars within the hall had managed to keep the king's men from bursting in while combatting the ones already there. Coxani stood on a trestle table, bowstring drawn, firing her arrows into the former king's Manzakars as they hazarded into her line of vision. Haydar turned toward Tikran, bloodied saber in hand, a Manzakar writhing in agony at his feet. The durai began to stride in Tikran's direction when Delger emerged from behind a column, dagger brandished, a mere few feet away from Haydar.

Tikran heard himself yell as he sprang forward, plowing past Haydar. He tackled Delger just as the former king's dagger slashed across Haydar's back. A chair shattered beneath the two men as they crashed to the floor. Tikran wrested the dagger from Delger and, grabbing Delger's scalp, pressed the blade to his throat, hard enough that a line of crimson sprouted against the blade's edge. Though rage flowed thickly through his veins, blinding him, Tikran saw and smelled Delger's fear and it made him pause. "You're too fucking pathetic to kill," Tikran snarled.

He eased the dagger from Delger's throat and stood, suddenly aware that the room watched him. Several rebel Manzakars swooped down on Delger, restraining him. Kazbek grabbed Tikran's shoulder. "Delger's men have been subdued outside the hall. It's over, Tikran."

How many times would he hear those words before it was true? Tikran turned to where Coxani, Jan, and several others helped Haydar into a chair. The durai's jacket was sliced open diagonally across his shoulder blades and soaked with blood. He looked at Tikran, sweat streaming down his face, and said, "It's just a flesh wound. I'll live, unfortunately for Delger."

"Get Damir in here," Tikran said to Jan. "Get all the doctors in here."

As faces and words whirled around him, a flash of red caught his eye, and he saw Saltanat quietly trying to make her way out of the hall. He waved to the Manzakars along the wall. "Stop her!"

Saltanat began to run as a fire ignited on the rug at Tikran's feet, flames licking high and forcing him back. He heard Coxani growl as she ran after the mage, "Not so fast, bitch." She leaped through the fire, arrow nocked and four more in her bow hand. Just as Saltanat reached the door, five arrows struck her in the neck and back, one after the other in lightning-fast succession. Saltanat turned, a look of confusion on her face, before blood began spilling from her lips and she sank to the floor.

Coxani turned, hair wild around a face that was flushed and fierce, looking every bit a vengeful Gohari huntress.

BATHED and dressed only in a pair of clean breeches, Tikran rubbed his face and ran his hands through his wet hair in utter exhaustion. Haydar hadn't sustained any organ or bone damage from his wound—Tikran's interference had prevented it—and Damir was confident the durai would recover completely. Delger was locked up in a prison cell along with any remaining Manzakars who still sided with him.

The fight was officially over... for now.

He slumped, staring at the enormous bed before him. There were too many pillows. Did none of these people realize that he was a *soldier*? He'd spent months sleeping on cold bedrolls, in his armor, using his jacket as a pillow. In the barracks, his mattress was paper-thin and barely wide enough for his body. He'd likely sleep better standing and propped against a stone wall than drowning in this bog of softness.

How did this happen? Where am I?

He felt lost. He'd seen too much blood and death in the last few days and was desperate for something familiar, something soothing. He considered heading to Naran's room to sleep, but Coxani was likely there, and while Naran may have been badly injured, the man could get it up in the most unlikely circumstances, so it was probably best he not venture that way. He could head to Coxani's chamber in the improbable chance she was there, but Cenk forbid he get too "needy" with her and end up as Naran's—or Coxani's—target practice. *No, thank you.* While neither of them had explicitly told him about their relationship, he knew them both well enough to understand what must have transpired between them since he gave Naran permission to pursue Coxani. *I'm happy for them. Really.* Still, he needed company at the moment and he sensed the only company either of them wanted was each other.

His thoughts wandered to Damir and he stopped himself. *Shit!* These people were determined to make him king. Would they tolerate a king who liked men as much as he liked women in his bed? On the *very* remote chance that they did, would they additionally tolerate a king who liked men in his bed who also happened to be head mage to the kingdom's long-time enemy? *I'm going with "no" on that one.*

Tikran had resigned himself to a lonely night in a terrifyingly soft bed when someone knocked at his door. He looked down at himself in alarm. He was wearing breeches, after all. Surely no attendant would be scandalized by a shirtless soldier in breeches, even if that soldier was supposedly a future king. He winced as he caught a glance of himself in the full-length silver mirror that hung on the wall, at the stripe of discolored, textured skin that ran from his wrist to his neck and the livid ridges slashed across his back. He walked over and opened the door to find Damir standing there, his hands behind his back and his eyes lit with mischief.

"Your *Highness*," he drawled, bowing low.

"Stop it." Tikran tried to stifle a smile unsuccessfully. He grabbed Damir's arm and pulled him into the room quickly, hoping no one saw.

Damir cleared his throat. "Tikran, I'm not here to get you in trouble. I'm merely here to see how you're doing. You seemed... overwhelmed after everything."

Tikran sighed. "Overwhelmed is an understatement. And if you're not here to get me in trouble, then leave, because I'm exhausted—*Master* Damir."

They gazed at each other for less than two seconds before coming together, their hands and bodies and mouths seeking each other's skin and warmth. Both finally naked, they tumbled into the ridiculously soft bed, giddy and terrified and delirious, determined to find solace and pleasure in each other. Tikran rolled onto Damir, pressing him into the bed and looking into his eyes. There were words he wanted to say but they all clogged in his throat. *I want you. I need you. I love you* Instead of speaking, he lowered his head and slowly dragged his lips along the curve of Damir's throat, pressing their bodies together. "I love the way you smell," Tikran finally managed to whisper.

In response, Damir reached between them and took them together in his fist. Lost in Damir's gentle, skilled strokes and the feeling of Damir's arousal against him, Tikran soon found himself consumed by molten heat and blinded by a burst of white-hot sparks behind his eyes. He heard Damir utter his name and he slumped, his head against Damir's shoulder, breathing heavily, the aftershocks of his climax rolling through his body.

Tikran fell to the side and into the bed, his eyes on the doctor's face. Damir turned his head, panting, smiling, saying something in that deep, beautiful voice of his, when Tikran's eyelids drooped and he slipped into the depths of unconscious sleep.

He awoke at dawn to find Damir sitting on the edge of the bed, half-dressed, looking every bit like a work of sculpted art in the dim light. The doctor smiled at him. "Good morning, my liege."

Tikran groaned and buried his face in the enormous pillows around his head. "I told you to stop that," he said, his voice muffled.

Chuckling, Damir said, "You're to be King of Anzor. You need to get used to it."

"It's complete insanity," Tikran said, lifting his head.

"I happen to think you are the perfect choice," Damir said. "I don't think the council grasps how perfect you are for the role. They see a young warrior that the people respect. If they saw what I see, they might reconsider."

Tikran frowned. "What does that mean?"

"It's a compliment, Manzakar." He reached over and stroked the jagged, raised scars along Tikran's mostly healed back with his fingers, a pensive look in his eyes. "I must return to Dilovar in a few days. My absence has become a concern to Bilguun. Initially, he was thrilled that I had become involved in

Anzor's politics. But a new king has been chosen, and my time is up."

Tikran moved away from Damir's hand and sat up. "You've been communicating with him this whole time."

Damir hesitated. "Infrequently. But yes."

Realization crashed over Tikran like an avalanche. "What does he know, Damir?"

"He has a high-level understanding of what's happened." Damir gazed steadily into Tikran's eyes. "Surely you trust me enough to know that I would never divulge sensitive information."

Tikran was very still. "You know *everything*."

A desolate look came over Damir's face. "You don't trust me. Even after all we've been through together."

Tikran buried his splayed fingers in his hair, against his scalp, and spoke through his teeth. "It's not about trust. It's about the fact that I am going to be crowned King of Anzor, and I've been fucking Anzor's greatest enemy!"

Hurt flashed in the doctor's eyes. He stood and threw on the rest of his clothes. "I will ensure Naran and Haydar are properly healing and in the hands of a competent doctor before I leave."

"Wait." Tikran leaped out of the bed. "Damir. I'm sorry. This is all so..."

Damir appeared cool and composed. "I understand, Manzakar."

"No, you don't," Tikran said. "Stay. Become *my* head mage."

Damir smiled wistfully. "That would not go over well with Bilguun. You would have a much larger problem on your hands."

Tikran swallowed. "Maybe he can be negotiated with."

"Maybe." Damir looked down. "But for now, I must return to him. If not for Bilguun's sake, then for your kingdom's." He turned and put his hand on the door's latch. "Perhaps you should put some clothes on, Your Highness."

Tikran didn't bother to cover his nakedness as Damir left, the door shutting firmly behind him. He felt gutted. He did trust Damir. He *loved* Damir. He just didn't know what he was doing. And he was terrified.

As he dressed, a servant knocked and informed him that Haydar awaited him in the palace gardens for breakfast. In his Manzakar uniform, he wandered through the palace and through the central courtyard to the lush palace gardens. It was divided in four sections by channels of rushing water. The water streamed into limpid pools that reflected a brilliant array of colors around them. It was early spring, and the air was rich with fragrance that ebbed and flowed, emanating from jasmine, roses, narcissi, violets, and lilies. Fruit trees lined the pathways, including pomegranate and fig trees, both exotic and delicious. He finally found Haydar seated in the shade of an orange tree, looking utterly in his element. The bandage that wrapped his torso and peeked out from the collar of his tunic was the only sign that he had been injured at all.

He grinned at Tikran. "Ah! The future king arises on a new dawn."

Tikran groaned and flopped down in one of the dainty chairs next to the durai. "Lord Haydar, this whole thing is ridiculous. With your wisdom and experience, *you* should be the successor."

Haydar shook his head. "I have never seen battle, let alone commanded. In fact, no Manzakar has seen battle for a century —until now."

Tikran huffed. "What's the big deal about seeing battle? It's the most ghastly, traumatic thing I've ever experienced."

"Exactly." Haydar smiled. "A king who is also a warrior will be far more reluctant to begin endless, senseless wars if he knows firsthand what it's like."

"I nearly killed Delger," Tikran said darkly, his voice low. "I probably should have."

"No, lad." Haydar sighed. "You did the right thing. It bolsters the argument that you are the right choice for king, no question. Now, Delger will pay for his crimes by his own hand, as a true villain." He squinted into the trees. "You know, Tikran, I hand-picked you and Coxani that day Mago brought you to the Citadel. In fact, Mago sent me a message shortly after your purchase informing me that he had found the 'perfect child.'"

Tikran gaped. "Mago... was a part of this?"

"Oh, yes," Haydar said. "When Mago asked your father about your history, your father shared that your mother had recently been killed by Manzakars for having the Essence and he worried that you may have witnessed it. I often wondered if you had any memory of it, and if that memory would shape who you became."

Tikran's mouth was still open in shock. "It did."

"While I hoped it would, I didn't rely on it," Haydar said. "What I relied on was who you were as a human being— honest, hard-working, empathetic, and absolutely unable to sit by and watch injustice done." He looked at Tikran. "Mago knew what he was doing that day he stole the food for you to take to the nomads. He'd often done it before. The difference this time was that you had begun a cascade of events, and the stealing of food would actually *mean* something on a grand scale."

Tikran exhaled. "I still don't see how I'm going to do this. I don't know the first thing about being king. Holy Cenk! Lord Haydar, there are so many issues to deal with... We simply can't keep importing slaves from Gohar for any purpose. It's barbaric. We need to allow the Essence back into Gohar and allow it to become independent again. And the Gohari in Anzor must be freed and given all the same rights and privileges of Anzori citizens. But I'm not sure any of that will go over well with many of the Anzori, which is a whole other problem— and a big one. And enough with the forced marriages and procreation between the Gohari! If a Gohari woman chooses not to marry, she should be able to support herself. It's ludicrous that..."

He trailed off as Haydar's face cracked into the biggest grin he'd ever seen on the man. Haydar's eyes shimmered. "What were you saying, about not knowing the first thing about being king?" He leaned forward, wrapped a hand around the back of Tikran's neck, and pressed their foreheads together. "I will be here to help you. We have some good men on the council. They will help you."

Tikran felt the most delicious warmth blossom in his chest as he sat brow to brow with his hero. He said, "I want Naran to help me command the entire Manzakar force. And Coxani... I need Coxani to advise me on everything."

Haydar stood. "Sounds like we need to get you crowned already."

They strolled back to the palace and Haydar said, "I think we need to change your name. You are no longer the Caged Kingfisher."

Tikran smiled. "Who am I, then?"

The sunlight dotted Haydar's dark eyes with flecks of auburn. "Tikran of the Freed Kingfisher."

The name sat well with this new man inhabiting Tikran's body.

Freed Kingfisher, don't let me down.

CHAPTER 27

Anzor
Seven months later
Year 222 of the Dark Age

Tikran shaded his eyes against the setting sun, watching the figure silhouetted in the distance loose her arrows at an elevation so high they plunged down perfectly vertically, whistling into their target at lightning speed. He shouted, "Excellent form, Captain Coxani! Keep that forefinger pressure on the arrows!"

She turned toward him and began to run. He hopped off his horse, prepared for the tackle. She hit him with enough force that he thought they might topple over. "Oof!" Tikran laughed as they teetered then steadied. "Somehow, I'm never completely prepared for your attacks."

Coxani laughed, breathless. "Hopefully the enemy never catches on to my winning strategy."

"That would doom Anzor for sure." He smiled widely at

her. "What are you doing here without me? These training grounds belong to *us*."

She rolled her eyes. "Yes, and with all your extra time, you should be out here playing soldier with me when you have a kingdom to run."

He looked down, shrugging. "I suppose you're right. But hopefully you haven't let anyone else sit under *our* tree with you."

Coxani's smile faltered and she hesitated. "Just Naran."

"Oh, well, Naran is fine, of course," he said, feeling a strange, unexpected ache in his chest. "Can we sit there now for a moment?"

"Of course." They walked over to the large oak tree and sat in its shade. With her arms wrapped around her knees, Coxani looked at him curiously. "Are you okay, Tikran?"

Tikran leaned back on his arms, his legs extended and crossed in front of him, looking up into the branches of the tree. "I guess so. It's... a lot."

She looked down. "I know. But you've already done so much, Tikran. You abolished slavery! That in itself is enough to call your reign a success."

"I suppose. But the effects of abolishing it... it's impacted so many things that I have to deal with now... Many noblemen are displeased with my first act as king, and I worry about losing their support. Especially since I'm now trying to convince the council to provide the ex-slaves with some sort of compensation and education so that they can support themselves. It's been an administrative and financial nightmare."

"With the help of Lord Haydar and the council, I have no doubt that you can handle it," Coxani said. "What else are you grappling with? Perhaps I can offer some guidance or reassurance."

He sighed. "Several members of the council seem unhappy

with my decision to have Vazha exiled to eastern Gohar rather than executed. They think he might try to avenge his father and, because of his claim to the royal bloodline, become a serious threat to me." He pressed his lips together. "They're likely right. Though he's dead, Delger still has many supporters, and now they will probably support Vazha. But while I can understand and justify the execution of a king as cruel as Delger, I can't justify killing his innocent son simply out of fear of what he might do in the future." He looked at Coxani. "So he lives. My conscience won't let me choose otherwise."

She rested her hand on his. "I think you made the right decision, for what it's worth. You can't kill an innocent man out of fear, even if his father was a monster. Stand by it, Tikran. What else?"

He flexed his jaw. "I have to find a new head mage. But I honestly don't know how to go about that without doing something that feels *wrong*. Until Gohar becomes somewhat self-sufficient, looking for those with the Essence and bringing them back doesn't feel right."

"Even if you give them the choice?"

"Coxani, at this point, a choice still isn't really a choice," he said. "Under the truce, Delger granted Dilovar six months to go into Gohar to find those with the Essence. I had to honor it. But I can't, in good conscience, do the same on Anzor's behalf. Until things are... normal in Gohar, the nomads will likely say yes to anything Anzor asks of them."

Coxani crossed her arms. "The Gohari see you as the second coming of Archil. Of course they'll say yes. They'd likely say yes even if Gohar was a bloody utopia. What's wrong with that?" When Tikran said nothing, she leaned forward. "Tikran, what's really bothering you?"

"That *is* really bothering me," he said, his eyes firm. "But also..." He took a deep breath. "I know who my head mage should be. *He* should be my head mage. But I feel like he betrayed me."

Coxani frowned. "How did Damir betray you?"

By leaving. By not coming back. As the thoughts occurred to him, Tikran realized how stupid they sounded. He said, "He knows everything. How do I know what he has or hasn't told Bilguun?"

She stared at him. "Are you saying you don't trust him?"

"Why should I?" Tikran snapped.

"Holy Cenk, Tikran," Coxani said. "Are you listening to yourself? Damir saved your life at least twice. He saved mine— at least twice. He risked his own life a multitude of times, on Gohar and Anzor's behalf."

Tikran met her gaze. "I'm King of Anzor. I can't rely on gut instincts anymore, Coxani. Two entire kingdoms depend on me making the right choices." She was silent and he said, "I should go."

"Tikran," she said, "are you lonely?"

To his embarrassment, his answer tumbled out as if he had been waiting for her to ask. "Yes. Desperately."

"Oh, Tikran. There are so many men and women who would—"

"I don't want them," he said, his voice coming out strangled. "There are only two people I want. One of them is you. And one of them is the enemy."

She looked startled, her face flushing slightly, then shook her head. "You need to stop seeing Damir as the enemy. It isn't like you to think so... indiscriminately." She scooted toward him, taking his face in her hands. "I will come to you tonight and hold you. Not because you're king, but because you're Tikran and my first love."

"That's not a good idea," he said, sounding wrecked. "I need... more of you, Coxani. It would just be torture."

They were quiet for a long time, listening to the tree rustle in the cool breeze. Finally, Tikran stood and offered Coxani his hand. "I guess I should get back to the palace and do whatever kings are expected to do."

She took his hand and looked into his face as she rose. "Tikran, I..."

"Autumn is coming," Tikran said, not meeting her eyes. "Gohar's favorite season. Let's create an official holiday, yeah? Hot spiced wine and salted beef and stories around campfires."

Misty-eyed, Coxani smiled and wrapped her arms around him, pressing her face to his chest. "That sounds amazing, King Tikran."

ALSO BY R. LAHAM

The Slave-Soldier Series

Manzakar

ABOUT THE AUTHOR

I've done everything under the sun—I have a BA in archaeology from the University of Pennsylvania, a law degree from the University from Houston, and have worked as a graphic artist, romance editor, writer, UX designer, frontend developer... the list actually goes on. Yet through all these endeavors, I've always known my true calling was storytelling. I'm a huge nerd and draw my inspiration from actual history and RPGs, particularly video games (Dragon Age, Mass Effect, Horizon, Dark Souls...). I write "approachable" fantasy that is meant to be an escape from all of our real-world trials and tribulations while subtly (and not-so-subtly) challenging the status quo.

www.ingramcontent.com/pod-product-compliance
Lightning Source LLC
Chambersburg PA
CBHW020522110726
47899CB00004B/1208